PARTS UNKNOWN

PARTS UNKNOWN

LONG JENN SILVA SERIES: BOOK 2

SCOTT QUINN

Copyright © 2022 by Gainer Press LLC

All rights reserved. No part of this publication may be reproduced, distributed, or transmitted in any form or by any means, including photocopying, recording, or other electronic or mechanical methods, without the prior written permission of the publisher, except in the case of brief quotations embodied in critical reviews and certain other noncommercial uses permitted by copyright law.

This is a work of fiction. Any characters, names, or likenesses are purely fictional. Resemblances of any of the items listed above are merely coincidental.

For permission requests, please contact the author, via e-mail, with the subject "Permissions Request," at the e-mail address below:

scottquinnbooks@gmail.com

ISBN
Paperback: 978-1-7368397-2-0

COVER DESIGN by Moonpress
www.moonpress.co

INTERIOR ARTWORK by Audrey Lindsay
audreylindsay2018@gmail.com

www.gainerpress.com
www.scottquinnbooks.com

To my three sons...

*Always remember to keep your
eyes and ears open,
your nose in a book,
and your mind free
to dream of new adventures!*

AUTHOR'S NOTE ABOUT TIME

TIME plays an important role in this book/series.

The Author utilizes flashbacks.

Various "Alien" species travel through space, occasionally steering their space crafts through wormholes (folds in the time/space continuum).

The "PRESENT DAY" action in this series begins on JANUARY 1, 202_ (an unspecified year in the mid- to late-2020s).

Time may pass at different rates at different points in the universe. The DATE (as presented throughout the novel) is the date it is (or would be) perceived to be by those that were on Earth when the PRESENT DAY action in this series began.

Throughout the book, JANUARY 1, 202_ will be referred to as "YEAR 0 + 1 DAY/JANUARY 1st."

JULY 19th from the same year would be referred to as "YEAR 0 + 200 DAYS/JULY 19th."

JULY 19th from the next year would be "YEAR 1 + 200 DAYS/JULY 19th."

JULY 19th from twenty years earlier would be "YEAR -20 + 200 DAYS/JULY 19th."

The action in this book begins exactly one year after the action at the beginning of the series. That date is depicted as YEAR 1 + 1 (JANUARY 1st).

AUTHOR'S NOTES RE: VARIOUS ALIENS

Several alien species are introduced in this series.

The Author is honored to include the artwork of Audrey Lindsay within the pages of PARTS UNKNOWN. At age 18, Audrey has done an outstanding job illustrating her view of the Nawerssians, Hamurkans, Davi-Loga, and cyborgs described in this book.

You can see those illustrations beginning on page 384.

Jennysis Quevedo & Brady Emerson
Home Planet: Earth

1: THE BLADE

**YEAR 2 + 238 DAYS (AUGUST 26th)
A YEAR & A HALF AFTER <u>OUTSIDE INTERFERENCE</u>**

"Welcome to The Middle of Nowhere. Our humble establishment has exactly what you seek."

These words rang out of a translator robot positioned at the door of the extraterrestrial tavern that served as both a watering hole and a brothel. Such "service bots" could perform few other functions. But with the recent influx of additional alien species that arrived on Oquezzi, the devices had become an essential part of transacting business at this crossroads for space travelers.

Peering through goggles, Ray Yandee appeared to be a typical Valtayan. He stood at a height of about four feet, six inches. Despite the outrageously hot temperatures on Oquezzi, the tiny alien wore a hooded coat lined with fur. A thick blue cloth covered his mouth and nose, leaving almost none of his ghostly grey skin exposed to the elements. He belched out a series of words in his native language. *The indecipherable syllables sounded like "Robba fobba bobba robba" to Jenn's untrained ear.*

After a brief pause, the bot provided the once highly popular women's wrestling champion with an interpretation. "Long Jenn Silva. Let me guess, are you here for a drink and a dance? Or are you finally going to take me up on my offer to come work for my crew?"

"Don't hold your breath, Yandee." Not waiting for the bot to spit out a translation, she stepped through the door and into The Middle of Nowhere.

Inside, Jenn immediately became engulfed by the sounds of thumping music. "Oquezzi Disco" featured a synthetic beat. The instruments sounded like a collection of electric guitars and steel drums. The vocals resembled the squawks of a teenage boy randomly attempting to rap words off the page of an algebra textbook. One of her fellow Earthlings once observed, "The music on this moon all sounds the same. It reminds me of the worst cover of 'We Didn't Start the Fire' you could possibly imagine."

The brothel was not well lit. That suited Jenn just fine. It obstructed her view of the shameless debauchery taking place all around her. Adventurers and mercenaries from at least a half dozen solar systems frequented The Middle of Nowhere. Though most were in search of inebriating substances, others came to sample the wares of the establishment's android entertainers. The soulless robots were extremely lifelike, and able to satisfy even the most extreme perversions.

Do they have to do it out in the open?

Patrons seated at the bar were downing shots of Villetra. The green liquor glowed florescent and was served warm. To Jenn, it tasted like someone had dumped grain alcohol into pea soup. Despite its off-putting texture, the potent beverage did the trick for those hoping to forget the past and drown their sorrows.

As far as she could tell, the luchadora somehow made it to the back of the establishment without being spotted by any of Nixx-O-Fee's henchmen. Jenn eyed the door, sucking in a deep breath and saying a silent prayer before she stepped into the gangster's office.

He came from Hamurka, a planet whose natives regularly eclipsed seven feet in height. The males from his home world seldom donned any clothing above the waist. They preferred to show off their chiseled torsos and brick red skin. Hamurkan men customarily shaved their faces, but never cut their hair. Instead, their snowy white locks were woven into a single thick braid and often thrown over the front shoulder.

As expected, Nixx was not alone. He was enjoying the company of two beautiful cyborgs, female in form. Considerably different from the "pleasure bots" that had been entertaining various scoundrels within the brothel, these machines were born human. They were from Na-Werss, like the ones Jagger and Armstrong had battled decades earlier. Deadly levels of pollution in the southern hemisphere of the planet necessitated a series of surgeries in which the brains, hearts, and other key organs of healthy adults were transplanted into synthetic shells. The belief was that survival depended on undergoing drastic transformations into bodies that were less susceptible to the toxins that blanketed their local environment. It was worth the high cost, if doing so would add decades to their lives.

The first cyborg sat across the table from the Hamurkan. Her jacket was already on the floor. Slowly and seductively, she worked her way out of a gold, glittery dress. Before long, she would move on to removing the unnecessary undergarments that covered her mechanical frame.

The second was positioned behind Nixx. This cyborg remained fully clothed. She had been assigned the task of massaging the muscles covering the vast landscape that was the gangster's upper back and shoulders.

Nixx spoke to Jenn in English. "I want to apologize for what transpired a few days ago... I understand you and he were extremely close."

Though he spoke the words, there wasn't a hint of an apology in his voice. The heartless bastard was rubbing it in. He was celebrating his triumph with no regard to who may have been impacted by his latest kill.

A bitter taste filled the pirate's mouth. She found herself wishing she had worn her wrestling mask. That might help obscure her facial expression. Instead, she was forced to rely on what she had learned during her days inside the squared circle. She did her best to utilize her talent for selling a particular angle. With a shrug, Jenn responded, "I'm not happy, but I get it. Business is business."

Nixx-O-Fee let out a low groan, signifying his pleasure. Smiling, he glanced upwards towards the beauty that had been massaging his pronounced shoulder muscles. He brushed his thick braid to one side, then repositioned the cyborg's soft—but mechanical—hands so they rested at the base of his neck. "Right here, princess... That's it. Rub right there."

Jenn began to seethe. "Are we done?"

"Sadly, no," Nixx replied without making eye contact. He looked across the table, gesturing for the stripping cyborg to speed up her act. Only then did he make an effort to look towards the luchadora. "You said it yourself: 'Business is business.' From my perspective, you and your comrades are loose ends. Unless we can figure something out, each one of you is going to meet the same fate as that chump you called a friend."

"That's why I'm standing here. I didn't come to get some phony apology. I came to tell you that the rest of my gang and I are going to join Ray Yandee. We'll be making some repairs to his ship. After that, we plan to stay aboard until it's time for The Slingshot. Oquezzi will be a distant memory. And we'll be outta your hair for good. That's not just a promise."

Nixx stroked the braided rope attached to his scalp. His smile grew even wider. "Good. That's what I like to hear... You should know, Hamurkans have a tradition. When a man and woman enter into an agreement, they seal the deal with a kiss."

Long Jenn Silva had no intention of kissing that slimeball. Not to memorialize an agreement. Not to maintain an illusion. Instead, she peeled away the glove that had been covering her left hand.

Nixx's eyes widened when his adversary quickly extracted the dagger she had sheathed along her hip. He settled back into his chair when Jenn said, "Back on Earth, pirates seal a covenant in blood."

She glided the edge across the top of her exposed hand, causing crimson to flow to the surface. Revealing the murky liquid that ran along her brown skin, she instructed the gangster, "Now we blade *your* hand. We smear our blood together... Then our covenant cannot be broken."

Nixx gestured for the stripping cyborg to step aside to allow his uninvited guest to move closer. *Finally.* Then he placed his palm atop the table. Looking at Jenn, he said, "I like the way you conduct business."

The pirate's frown vanished. A smirk appeared a split second before she drove the dagger through the back of Nixx's meaty hand. The steel point lodged deep into the table, anchoring the

Hamurkan's palm to the spot in which he had confidently planted it a moment earlier. Turning to the nearly naked cyborg, Jenn spoke over the scream of her foe. "Get dressed."

The screaming stopped. It was replaced by the sound of crunching bones. The cyborg Nixx had called "Princess" now clamped her soft, mechanical hands around his throat like a vice. She would continue tightening her grip until she had squeezed the life out of him.

The post-apocalyptic pirate pulled out a second dagger and used it to saw off the monster's ponytail. "A trophy. A reminder to everyone on Oquezzi... You don't cross Long Jenn Silva."

Carrying the rope of Nixx-O-Fee's hair over her shoulder, Jenn confidently led her cyborg accomplices across the tavern and out the door. Once she had made her exit from The Middle of Nowhere, she looked back and spoke to Ray Yandee. "Grab your bot and come with us... if you still want to join *my crew*."

☠ ☠ ☠

TWENTY-ONE MONTHS EARLIER
YEAR 0 + 358 DAYS (DECEMBER 24th)

Jenn occupied the fourth of five seats positioned one behind the other in a small shuttle. The craft resembled a bobsled or a silver bullet, depending on the perspective of the observer. It made very little noise as it tore through the air with lightning-fast velocity. It was designed to transport aliens (known as Nawerssians), their abductees, and a minimal amount of cargo from Earth to their large spaceship hovering tens of thousands of miles away from the surface of the planet.

Jenn's friend, Brady Emerson, occupied the seat in front of her. Like the former women's wrestling champion, Brady had been abducted by the Nawerssians several months earlier. A freak accident led to their unexpected release from the virtual reality tanks in which they were being observed. In the days that followed, Jenn and Brady took part in a heated battle between two factions of the aliens who possessed drastically different opinions on how those from Earth should be treated.

Seated in front of Brady was Armstrong, the senior statesman among the visitors from afar. He was humanoid. Like all who had been born and raised on the distant planet of Na-Werss, he had grown to a height considerably taller than typical residents of Earth. Hair no longer appeared atop the bulbous heads or along the thin bodies of his people. Their noses grew wider and flattened to the point to where there was almost no bridge at all.

Most notably, though, exposure to high levels of silver caused fair, tan, and brown skin tones to change gradually into various shades of blue. Pigmentation varied little. Whether the skin was cornflower, cerulean, robin's egg, or even turquoise, it all looked blue through the weak, red eyes of the people of Na-Werss.

A Nawerssian female named Monroe occupied the pilot's seat in the front of the shuttle. She was considerably younger than Armstrong. Long strawberry blonde hair was woven into two shoulder-length braids that protruded from her scalp. In addition to her hair implants, she had opted to undergo procedures to give some height and depth to her once flat nose and a bit of volume to whisper-thin lips. It was all designed to make her appear more like the humans that lived on Earth. *"The more I resemble them, the easier it will be to abduct specific specimens for observation and study,"* she had once said as a justification for modifying her features.

Monroe was born in space. Her biological parents originally came from Na-Werss. It was a distant planet in which the people were being choked out of their home world by deadly levels of silver in the water and atmosphere. The Nawerssians descended from Earth more than two thousand years earlier (or just a few years from the present day, depending on what side of the wormhole you were on).

Her parents had been scientists assigned to Project *Vilnagrom*. Translated literally, the name meant "return home." The blue-skinned aliens believed that Earth's doomsday was imminent, and that they could relocate there and rebuild the planet once its original inhabitants were gone.

"Traveling from Earth into space can be physically demanding," she said as a warning to the novice space adventurers seated in the back of the shuttle. "It could be particularly difficult on the two of you if you are not sedated like you were the first time. We could knock you out again if you prefer."

"Heck no! Not a chance! This is a once in a lifetime experience. I want to be one hundred percent awake, aware, and alert for this." Brady said, replying for both himself and Jenn.

Those on the outside would have heard something that sounded like the cracking of a whip, followed by a noise that resembled a tennis racket striking nothing but air. That was it. No other sounds would follow. Their ascent into space had no accompanying roar or rumble. They disappeared like a quickly forgotten breeze.

Inside the transport, the passengers shook violently as the silver bullet bounced against pockets of air and fought against the mighty pull of gravity. Soon, the sky around them was black instead of blue, and the turbulence was non-existent.

The sounds disappeared, too. They were replaced by dead silence.

Brady turned around in his seat. He looked over his shoulder at the radiant sight of the Earth as it appeared smaller and smaller. Through his headset, he told Jenn, "You're missing it!"

Hearing this jolted any melancholy thoughts out of her mind, and she joined Brady in gawking at the amazing sight.

A loud humming sound interrupted the silence. "This next part might be difficult for a moment, but you will adjust," Monroe announced. The Nawerssian's voice had a metallic ring to it because of rapid changes of pressure on the eardrums of the passengers. Now free of the planet's gravitational pull, the transport spiraled as it propelled itself through space.

Neither Jenn nor Brady said much for the next several hours. They were busy admiring the view... and desperately fighting the urge to vomit.

Monroe had made the trip dozens of times in her relatively young life. Her focus was on the spacecraft they were approaching. "What happened to our ship?" she asked. "It looks like it got pelted by a meteor shower."

Her adoptive father, Armstrong, sat in silence. Beginning as an Explorer aboard the original *Vilnagrom* ship, he had accumulated almost forty years of life in the shadow of Earth's moon. Even so, what he was observing took his breath away.

Monroe repeated her question. "What happened to our ship?" This caused Jenn and Brady to refocus their collective attention to the massive spacecraft ahead of them. Both had been feeling a nervous excitement about living aboard the *Vilnagrom-II*. The questions posed by the blue-skinned alien concerned them.

"What happened to our ship?" Monroe asked for a third time, now with much more urgency in her voice.

Armstrong became gravely serious. "Abort the approach. Now! Abort the approach! That is NOT our ship."

"What do you mean 'not our ship?'"

"I have no explanation," the Explorer responded while Monroe mashed controls to allow the bobsled transport to drift. They were floating in the weightlessness of space.

A voice came over the radio. It was one that neither Jenn nor Brady had ever heard before. The old Explorer, however, recognized it immediately.

"Armstrong, is that you, ol' buddy?" The voice was far more gruff and gravelly than that of any Nawerssian that Jenn had ever heard. It was almost as if he was imitating a character from *Pirates of the Caribbean*.

Armstrong was enraged. It was the voice of his enemy. It was the voice of a man who should have been executed twenty Earth Years earlier. Someone must have betrayed Armstrong and the cause of the people of Na-werss.

Frozen by fear, Monroe understood they were in an extremely vulnerable position. The tiny transport would provide virtually no protection against an attack. If the being on the other end of the transmission opened fire from the massive spacecraft, it would take no more than one shot for them to be absolutely obliterated. Making matters worse was the fact that they had no options. There was nowhere else they could go.

With Armstrong silent, Monroe connected the dots for the passengers. "That's the *Vilnagrom-I*."

"With Jagger at the helm," Armstrong interjected. He sounded defeated.

"Avis and the *V-II* had ta make an unexpected departure. Good thing fer you, yer ol' mate Jagger drifted into the harbor at just the right time."

Panic fell over Jenn. Both her best friend and her husband had been aboard that ship. "If the *V-II's* gone, then where is Cocoa? Where is Lazz?"

Jagger continued taunting his rival. "I understand ya might have some pirates along wit' ya... Now why don't y'all come on aboard? We've got lotsa things to discuss... We'll call it a parley if that'll put ya at ease."

☠ ☠ ☠

"I understand ya might have some pirates along wit' ya." There was little doubt who he was talking about.

She was born "Jennysis Quevedo." At the age of sixteen, she moved from Florida to Puerto Rico. There she trained under a legend in the business of professional wrestling. Once she was deemed ready, Jenn donned a mask and began fighting under the name "Lady Pirata." She utilized a popular gimmick in which she portrayed a leather-clad, post-apocalyptic pirate. That, paired with her natural athletic ability and an endorsement from an icon in the industry, made her wildly successful.

After a couple of years, she decided to relocate to Mexico. She quickly became a shining star in the world of Lucha Libre. With her popularity soaring, she dreamed of bigger and brighter things. Eventually she returned to the United States and took on the persona of "Long Jenn Silva."

She had been the All-World Wrestling Association's Women's Champion at the time the Nawerssians first snatched her off a commuter train in downtown St. Louis. The aliens studied Jenn and her friends for weeks before an accident led to their abrupt removal from a virtual reality tank. Jenn and Brady participated in a battle between competing factions aboard the *Vilnagrom-II*.

Because their side came out the victors, their alien abductors agreed to return them to their homes on Earth. Things changed while they were away. Jenn ultimately decided that joining Armstrong, Monroe, and the others in space was the next bigger and brighter thing for her to pursue.

Now, just a few hours into the adventure, Long Jenn Silva was beginning to have doubts about her decision to return to a life away from the comforts of Planet Earth.

☠ ☠ ☠

ONE HOUR LATER

Jagger's idea of a parlay meant intimidating and interrogating each person in isolation. Jenn was not sure how much time had passed since she was sequestered. *An hour? Two? Maybe even three?* However long it was, it was more than enough time to spin the hot-tempered wrestler into a rage.

Jenn scanned the room in which she had been "asked" to wait. *Destroying the monitors on the walls might not do any good, but it sure would bring momentary satisfaction.* Her fiery temper was about to get the best of her when the door disappeared into the wall.

Jagger propelled himself by swinging a bulky, metallic leg in front of him. Then he dragged himself forward and repeated the process. The Nawerssian war hero came from a world and a time in which much more highly sophisticated prosthetics were readily available. He rejected the opportunity to be fitted with such technology. He was far too stubborn to allow himself to take on an appendage that would bring him any bit closer to the cyborg devils that warred against his people.

"Please accept me apologies..." he began. "I didn't want to keep ye so long, but most of yer friends didn't have much to say."

Jenn snarled, "If they didn't have much to say, then why the hell did it take so long?"

The blue-skinned tyrant took another step towards her, completely closing any gap between them.

The former women's wrestling champion braced for the alien to strike her.

The left end of his mouth curled upwards in a half-smile. He had deep pockmarks on display across his face. The deep, unnerving scar over his right eye was so long his dark glasses couldn't obscure it. It cut into his face enough to make Jenn wonder if the man was capable of a full smile.

Instead of hitting his captive, Jagger reached forward and grabbed the bottom of her T-shirt. He tugged on the shirt, pulling it flat so he could study the image printed atop the fabric. After removing his glasses and squinting his left eye to read what was scrawled in black letters across a red background, he said, "Be glad ye got two good eyes. It be a pain in the arse to always hafta twist and contort me neck to look out me one good one..." He took another look at the shirt before releasing his grip and taking a step back. "Long Jenn Silva. 'Tis a good name... A name be important. I never much liked the sound of 'the *Vilnagrom-I.*' Don't exactly roll off the tongue whether ye be speakin' English or Traditional Nawerssian... Once me lot in life improved from 'imprisoned General' to 'Captain of me own ship,' I renamed her somethin' more pleasin' to the ear. Long Jenn Silva, welcome aboard the *Valentine's Kiss.*"

"Some welcome. Taking me prisoner wasn't enough. You separate me from my friends and leave me locked in this room for God knows how long!"

"Fifty-eight minutes. It woulda been a wee bit quicker, but I found this while goin' through yer belongings." He pulled out the dagger that Jenn had brought along. It was the weapon she'd used to finish off her rival in their gruesome brawl a few months earlier.

"You have no right to take that!"

"Oh, but I do," Jagger replied with a confidence that bordered on mocking the luchadora.

He paused and paced around the room. It seemed clear that this was a tactic he employed quite often. The sound of the metal of his prosthetic leg clanging against the hard floor sent chills up Jenn's spine.

The alien made it no secret that he, like Long Jenn Silva, embraced a pirate persona. He wore a tricorn hat and a black, knee-length frock coat over his sun-faded Nawerssian flight suit. It was a clash of styles. The fashions of 1720 mixed with those worn in 3720. It somehow worked... especially when paired with the fact that the man wearing the clothes talked with a voice that sounded like a shovel being dragged down a rocky road.

"I dare say this dagger came into me possession before ye were even born, young lass. Just takin' back what be rightfully mine."

Jenn felt no reason to back down. "Armstrong told me the story of that dagger. He said you used it to murder a young Nawerssian named Adam. I'll have you know, you're not the only one that's used that blade to kill."

"Methinks ye like ta pretend yer tough."

Long Jenn Silva was intent on winning this verbal bout. "We're not so different. Like you, I used to *play* at being a pirate. I did so in front of thousands of people every night. Sometimes they loved me, sometimes they hated me. It was always the response I was aiming for... Like me, you've picked up more than your share of bumps and bruises along the way. We're fighters. We're survivors. Am I right?" Jenn shifted, eyeing the blade in Jagger's hand and momentarily considering if she should attempt to snatch it away from him. "Then something happened. I was abducted... abducted by your kind. Playtime was over. I went aboard the *V-II* and got pulled into a fight where those on the other side were not in on the act. Life and death were the stakes. Look around, *Captain*. They're gone now. I'm still here. That knife is one reason why. I faced an enemy who was driven to kill me. She wanted to make it hurt. I used that knife to slash her throat. Her blood covered the floor, and then she died. I walked away. But I didn't walk away the same."

Jagger nodded his head. Then he spun the dagger in his hand so that he held the razor-sharp metal in his palm. He pointed the handle towards Jenn. "Well said, friend. I'll give ye this blade fer safe keepin'. So long as ye promise to never stick it in me back."

Jenn took the dagger. Looking directly at Jagger, she nodded.

Then Captain Jagger placed his hand on her shoulder and offered an additional welcome. "I'd be honored if ye would be so kind as ta join me crew, Long Jenn Silva."

2: GOING OVER

> *"Ten years of driving five hundred miles to wrestle in front of thirty people... Eating cold cut sandwiches and sleeping in seedy motel rooms... Rope burns, pulled muscles, and broken bones... Winning this championship makes it worth all the struggles and sacrifices that came along with it."*
>
> *-LONG JENN SILVA promo given after winning the AWWA Women's Championship. The fans responded with chants of "You deserve it... You deserve it!"*

ONE WEEK LATER - PHILADELPHIA
YEAR 1 + 1 DAY (JANUARY 1st)

"Let me get this straight. You're asking me to put a girl with a clown gimmick at the top of the women's division? And you wanna do this at the same time we've got a magician as the men's champ? Son, are you booking a wrestling promotion or a birthday party for some spoiled eight-year-old?"

Fireball Freeman conducted business the way he saw fit. The legend earned that right. He was a pioneer and one of the most successful black wrestlers in history. The man scratched and clawed his way to the top. He did so even though his best years came in an era in which most African-Americans struggled to get through the door of many of the regional promotions.

Now in his sixties, Fireball still strapped on the boots from time to time. He liked to show the world that he wasn't ready to be put out to pasture. *(At least not yet.)* Plus, it helped generate buzz for the All-World Wrestling Association (aka the AWWA). He was the principal owner and the face of the promotion. That meant that the AWWA was his baby. And he'd make damn sure his booker didn't run things into the ground... even if that booker was his son.

"Pops! Ailani's making the jump to the IWO before our next pay-per-view. If she's going to drop the title, it's gotta be tonight."

Fireball's son KaPhonso (aka "The Great Kayzo") was gradually taking the reins as the AWWA's top booker. He was training to be the head of the creative branch of the promotion. The job required him to set up the matches, develop angles and storylines, and decide who would and wouldn't wear the championship belts.

Kayzo was easing into the role. His older sister, Cocoa, previously held the position. Unfortunately, she went missing almost six months ago. As great as she was at running the ins and outs of the AWWA, and as much as Fireball longed to see his daughter return, he knew that the show must go on.

The longtime veteran removed his straw fedora, carefully placing his signature piece of attire in the center of the desk. Next, he leaned back in his chair. With the fingers of each hand interlocked, Fireball took a deep breath and rubbed the top of his head. The friction helped him get into his "thinking position."

"Correct me if I'm wrong. The plan has been to have her drop the title to Killer Bee. Killer Bee is a beautiful woman. Solid in the ring. Why not put the strap on her? If you wanna give it to your girl Kelly, you've gotta convince me... Convince me."

Kayzo scooted forward in his chair. He intended to make the most of his pitch. "Killer Bee *is* a pretty woman. And it's true, she's solid in the ring. But that describes Ailani to a T. Has she been what we hoped for as the face of our women's division?"

Fireball interrupted, "We've had a lot of unexpected issues we've had to deal with lately. I shouldn't have to tell you this hasn't exactly been an ideal time."

Saying that the times had not been "ideal" was an understatement. His daughter's disappearance wasn't the only unexpected departure that occurred in the previous summer.

Long Jenn Silva was the AWWA's wildly popular woman's champion. The spitfire with a pirate gimmick vanished at the same time as Cocoa, only to reemerge a few months later. However, she provided no details about where they had been or what had happened to Cocoa. *Zero. Nothing. Nada.* That lack of an explanation added to the mystery surrounding the situation. It caused the media to buzz with rumors and speculation that Jenn had been the culprit of some sort of foul play against her friend. It didn't take long for the controversy to mar the reputation of the promotion and those who ran it.

"We're not out of the woods," the son told his father. "That's why we should deviate from our original plan. Go with Kelly because she's not just 'solid' in the ring. She's dynamite. Every single match, she lays it all on the line. The fans can see that." Kayzo paused a moment to let his first point sink in. "And you know as well as I do that she's gold on the microphone. Every promo she cuts walks that fine line between hilarious and deadly serious. The fans see that too. That's why she always has half the crowd cheering for her, even when she's supposed to be the heel."

The legend pushed down on the top of the desk, using the object to assist his weather-beaten knees as he stood. Once up, he turned, took a deep breath, and faced the wall. (This was all part of his "deep in thought" routine.)

"Answer this one question for me..." he said before getting interrupted.

A man in a dark suit pressed his way into the room. The arena's head of security followed closely behind.

"I'm sorry, Mr. Freeman," the lanky security guard said. "I told him you were in a meeting, but..."

Fireball whipped his body around. He instantly recognized Yaron Harazi, the over-caffeinated scientist who was quick to flash his credentials from the Department of Defense. "Dr. Harazi, I'm in a meeting right now."

"I can see that. Mr. Freeman, this cannot wait. I'm here on urgent business."

Kayzo arose from his chair. He didn't like this interruption. It jeopardized his chances of convincing his father to agree to the last-minute booking change. "Doctor, I know we've only met once or twice, but my pops and I have always been cooperative and respectful to you. You come in here usin' the phrase 'urgent business' like we were just sittin' in here playin' a game of tiddlywinks. We're conducting business in here, and it too is urgent. Before we go any further, tell me if you've found my sister."

"Well, no…"

"Thank you," Kayzo responded without letting the pushy government agent say anything else. After glancing at the security guard's name tag, he continued. "We've got a show tonight. The opening bell will ring in a little over an hour. Please go with Mr. Abernathy here. He'll get you a ticket. Watch the matches on us. Then my pops and I will be happy to meet with you after the show."

Harazi stood motionless. He was accustomed to his D.O.D. badge getting him and his associates what they wanted *when* they wanted it. After a moment, he yielded. "That's fair. Thank you. I apologize for barging in the way I did. I will see you after tonight's show." Then he exited the room.

Fireball gazed at his son with a sense of pride. A massive grin spread across his face as he told Kayzo, "You need to get movin'. Go tell those girls there's been a change in plans. Make sure Killer Bee knows we've still got big things in mind for her, but for the time being, Kelly Ka-Pow's gonna be our new women's champ."

☠ ☠ ☠

ONE HOUR LATER

In wrestling lingo, the term "over" refers to when a performer gets a specific reaction from the audience. It's a good thing if a villain (or "heel") gets booed. That's called "generating heat." On the other hand, it's bad news if a good guy (or "babyface") gets jeered. They aren't achieving the desired result. That's a disappointment, because they aren't *over* with the fans who shelled out good money to watch the match.

A chorus of boos serenaded Ailani Diamond on her way to the ring. Though the curvy Hawaiian played the role of a babyface, most AWWA diehards had turned on her. They'd heard the rumors; and they were unhappy about her decision to leave the promotion. The women's titleholder was perceived as a turncoat. They didn't like it that she was jumping ship at the first opportunity to grab the big paycheck that Griffin Conrad and the mighty International Wrestling Organization (IWO) had to offer.

Killer Bee was the next combatant to stroll down the aisle. Her entrance featured pyrotechnics and a dazzling light show. Still, the crowd seemed underwhelmed by the sculpted beauty with a golden skin tone and platinum blond hair.

A creepy organ version of "Entrance of the Gladiators" began playing over the loudspeakers. The same audience that booed Ailani and greeted Killer Bee with a lukewarm reception shot to their feet and roared with approval as soon as the classic circus music could be heard.

The ring announcer introduced the third participant in the Triple Threat Match. "And their opponent… from Anaheim, California… she is the 'Laughing Lunatic,' the 'Felonious Fool…' Kelly Ka-Pow!!!"

If Kelly's theme music and kitschy nicknames weren't enough of a clue, her clothing and makeup certainly made it clear that she was utilizing a clown gimmick. Her bright leggings expanded into polka dotted bellbottoms just below the knee. Those tights were held up by blinding yellow suspenders that she frequently used to choke her opponents. Above the waist, her rainbow-striped bikini top matched an afro wig of many colors. Not surprisingly, her face was painted white, with her lips made fire engine red, while royal blue triangles were plastered over her eyes.

The painted prankster pulled the audience in as she paraded towards the ring. She stopped long enough to plant a kiss on the top of a bald man's head. The smooch left a massive lipstick stamp atop the fan's shiny dome. She paused a couple more times, once to spray one of Killer Bee's fans with a bottle of seltzer water, then again to snatch and tear up the homemade sign being held by one of Aulani's few remaining supporters.

Kelly concluded her entrance by stepping through the ropes and rolling into a somersault. The crowd roared with approval when she posed like an Olympic gymnast who had just stuck the landing. The fans loved her. She was as "over" as any woman who had ever wrestled for the AWWA.

Kayzo and Fireball were watching on a backstage monitor. The father was smiling from ear to ear. He wrapped his arm around his son, pulling him into a half hug. Though the match had not yet begun, he was ready to announce his verdict. "I'd say you made the right call, son. Good job."

☠ ☠ ☠

TWENTY-FIVE MINUTES LATER

The new title holder was seated on a table in the women's locker room. A trainer was helping her remove the tape from around her ankles.

Kayzo peeked his head through the door. "Knock knock?"

Kelly poked the trainer on the shoulder. Speaking like a wise-cracking actress from a 1940s movie, she said "Beat it, bucko... My man's here, and I need to teach him a lesson. I'm going to start by smackin' him around with these deadly lips. If that doesn't do the trick, we'll see where things go from there."

The magician couldn't take his eyes off his girlfriend. She was sweaty. Her makeup had smeared during her match. That didn't change the fact that he found her irresistible.

He removed his white gloves, then his top hat. He dropped the gloves into the hat before removing his red-lined black cape with a flourish.

"I'm not sure if I'm supposed to applaud or stuff a couple singles in your g-string?" the clown quipped.

Kayzo laughed but said nothing. His girlfriend frequently snapped off one-liners that left him unable to respond.

"Anybody ever tell you that you look like a Chippendales dancer?" Kelly asked, commenting on both Kayzo's chiseled torso and the fact that he was wearing tight, black slacks with nothing but a bow tie above the waist.

He advanced, quickly closing the gap between himself and the object of his affections. The shirtless Kayzo wrapped his arms around her and pulled her towards him. He pressed his mouth into Kelly's, aggressively kissing the new champion.

Only a few seconds passed before Kayzo had yanked Kelly's suspenders down and reached around to unfasten her top. Things came to an abrupt stop, however, when Fireball interrupted the celebration.

He cleared his throat. Stepping towards them, the wrestling legend reminded his son, "Let's not forget that you still have a match tonight. You might want to save your energy for when you lock horns with Bubba Brunocelli."

Somewhat embarrassed, Kayzo pulled away from the horny harlequin. Clown makeup had smeared onto his face.

"Here... Let me get that for ya, fella," she said. She pulled out a handkerchief that had been tucked inside her bra. She licked at the piece of cloth, then moved it towards his face.

"Eww! No! I can do it myself!"

She feigned indignance. "What? You don't mind swappin' spit with me? But suddenly you're too good for a tiny bit of that same saliva when it comes to wiping off your messy face?"

Fireball shrugged. "The girl's got a point, son."

Though the paint that remained on her face said otherwise, Kelly's smile disappeared a second later.

Two massive figures stepped through the door of the locker room. Each stood well over seven feet tall and weighed upwards of 350 pounds of solid muscle. Their exposed skin resembled crushed bricks. Atop their heads were mighty braids of snow-white hair. They appeared human but looked like no human being Kelly had ever seen.

A cyborg followed the red beasts through the door. It stood just under six feet in height. Taking the form of a beautiful woman, she certainly could have been confused for an Earthly human under conditions in which the light was dim. Her face appeared grey, a thin layer of a rubbery material covering metal. Red eyes served as a stark contrast to the greyness all around them. Perhaps because of the beautifully sculpted face that surrounded them, the orbs did not appear menacing or evil.

Four black cables protruded from the top of her mechanical skull. They somewhat resembled dreadlocks as they traveled to a small compartment on her back. These devices were the cyborg's lifeline. The compartment sucked in air and pushed water vapor out, while the cables delivered hydration and oxygen to the organic brain, eyes, and heart within her mechanical shell. (A separate internal compartment held and filtered the blood that ran through those organs.)

Though it was doubtful that any clothing was necessary to cover her manufactured body, the cyborg wore dark garments woven from a synthetic material. Curiously, from the waist up, the attire was styled in such a manner that it greatly resembled formalwear—specifically a sleek, black tuxedo vest with a goldenrod dress shirt underneath. It was a look that would have been popular a hundred years earlier on Earth.

Kelly's gasp alerted Kayzo and Fireball to turn around. They did so just in time to see their attackers.

Fireball managed to let out a deafening yelp before one of the aliens bashed him over the head.

Kayzo met a fate similar to that of his father.

Still seated on the trainer's table, Kelly managed to blast the cyborg by thrusting both feet into its metal chest. This sent the third attacker sprawling backwards.

Reinforcements arrived. Three of the All-World Wrestling Association's top heavyweights had come running at the sound of Fireball's cry for help.

Santa Saws was a monolithic figure with a mosaic of biker tattoos that were partially obscured by a tattered Kris Kringle costume. He was the first to attempt a rescue. He grabbed the cyborg by its arm. She defended herself by shocking the wrestler with an electric pulse. He held tight, though. With a mighty tug, he managed to rip the alien's metallic arm completely away from her body.

The next two heroes to make it through the door were Bubba Brunocelli and Wee Willie Winningham. They instinctively double-teamed the first red giant. With the beefy Bruno momentarily holding his foe in place, the acrobatic Winningham executed a back handspring that ended with his boots crashing into the giant's jaw with violent force.

An explosion brought an end to the fight.

☠ ☠ ☠

FIVE MINUTES LATER

Kayzo was the first to awaken. He saw several others spread across the floor. Santa Saws, Brunocelli, and Winningham had been knocked out either by the blast or the noxious gas that had been discharged.

Where was his father? Where was his girlfriend? "Pops? Kelly? Kelly! POPS!!!"

Additional figures came through the door. Harazi barged his way to the front of the group. He lifted his arm to cover his face. Though he was trying to avoid sucking in any toxins that still lingered in the air, he asked, "What just happened in here?"

☠ ☠ ☠

Harazi's first move was to contact the Department of Defense. They needed to act immediately. There wasn't a moment to lose if they were going to scramble fighters from the nearest Air Force Base in an effort to locate the aliens' ship. "Under no circumstances should they open fire!"

His next order of business was to demand a lockdown of the facility. He told the grossly underpaid head of security, "No one is getting in or out of here without running it by me first! You hear me, Abernathy? I'm going to conduct my preliminary investigation. *Then* we'll discuss how we can dismiss the audience in an orderly fashion, and in a way that my office knows how to contact each and every person here if follow up becomes necessary."

Harazi's partner arrived within minutes. Together, the two agents from the Department of Defense's Unidentified Aerial Phenomena Task Force devised a plan to interview anyone who might have observed anything.

"From what I've been able to gather thus far, Mr. Freeman and several of the wrestlers in his employ had direct, physical contact with at least three alien beings. The subjects were attempting to physically..."

The UFO hunter stopped midsentence. A flash from light bouncing off metal appeared in his periphery. He walked towards a bench positioned in front of a collection of lockers. Resting underneath was the detached arm of the cyborg attacker.

His boss would want to know about this! *The President would want to know about this!*

The shock the doctor was experiencing caused his words to sound much less enthusiastic than intended. What he was looking at was a life-changing discovery. "Call Preston Ivy… Better yet, get Director Singleton on the phone. We'll need every available agent from the Task Force working on this."

Dr. Harazi walked over to Kayzo and the collection of heroes that saved him. "My partner and I will be interviewing each of you in great detail. I suspect it goes without saying that what you have witnessed could have a profound effect on national security… even *global* security…"

After finishing her phone call to the Pentagon, Harazi's newly assigned partner returned. She looked at the men the wrestling universe knew as The Great Kayzo, Santa Saws, Bubba Brunocelli, and Wee Willie Winningham. Cutting Harazi off midsentence, the intelligence officer reported, "D.O.D. says we are to put these four in protective custody."

Despite protests from some of the wrestlers, all but Winningham being considerably larger than him, Harazi explained, "It is for your safety as well as for the safety of your friends, loved ones… and everyone else in the country, for that matter. A worldwide frenzy could result if word of this occurrence gets out. The information must not be leaked to the media or even shared with your friends and family."

Kayzo momentarily considered the fact that his sister had vanished the previous summer. Now his father and his girlfriend were gone, too. He had a pretty good idea where all of them had gone. Unable to look up to make eye contact with the government agents, he sadly muttered, "What family?"

☠   ☠   ☠

**THREE WEEKS LATER
TOP SECRET GOVERNMENT FACILITY, NEVADA
YEAR 1 + 22 DAYS (JANUARY 22nd)**

After studying the people of Earth for one year, the crew members of each *Vilnagrom* ship followed a custom of choosing a new "Earth name." They felt it helped them identify with the specimens they were observing. Most often, the blue-skinned aliens who called themselves "Nawerssians" selected monikers that served as a tribute to cultural icons or historical figures from Earth.

"Hazel" was the name chosen by a female pilot on the *V-II* crew. She picked it to honor Hazel Ying Lee, one of many unsung heroes of World War II. Though the U.S. Military would not allow women to fly combat missions, Lee and the "WASPs" (or Women Airforce Service Pilots) played an integral role in delivering newly manufactured planes to the European and Pacific fronts. Like her namesake decades earlier, the Nawerssian pilot was involved in a mid-air collision. The other-worldly being's reconnaissance mission was cut short. Her time in the cockpit ended with a crash landing on a golf course not far from Baltimore, Maryland.

"Dr. Harazi, what brings you to Area 51?"

She was not angry about her imprisonment in the Top Secret military prison which may or may not have been located in the heavily guarded area known for nuclear weapons tests and long-rumored to be a hotbed of extraterrestrial study. As far as Hazel knew, she was the facility's only resident. The military officials treated her with dignity. They allowed her two hours a day outside of the glass cage that housed her. Perhaps best of all, she was fed a variety of foods that were far preferable to the tasteless, synthetic protein she had grown accustomed to consuming aboard the Nawerssian spacecraft that she once called home.

Noting that the alien expert carried a case under his arm, Hazel asked, "Did you bring me a present? The anniversary of my crash and capture is not for several months."

Over the last six years, Harazi had made numerous trips to Nevada to dialogue with this particular alien. He found her candor refreshing, her wit engaging, and her devotion to the people of her native planet unwavering. She gladly shared information about her life spent on a planet whose people were choking to death due to pollution. She didn't hesitate to discuss her travels across the galaxy and the idiosyncrasies that came with spending most of her adult life aboard a massive spacecraft. The flow of information abruptly stopped at any point in which she worried she might somehow endanger her brothers and sisters still living and conducting their mission aboard the *Vilnagrom-II.*

"Not exactly a present. More like a game of Show and Tell. I'll show you an object, and I want you to tell me anything and everything you can about it."

He placed the box on the table in front of her. The Yemeni-born scientist struggled to tear through the packing tape. As he grew frustrated with the task, he complained, "They wouldn't let me in here with a knife."

"I am sure they are fearful that I would take it away, use it to gut you, escape this lovely facility, and then take over the planet."

He shrugged. "You never know." Finally able to remove some of the tape, Harazi tugged the robotic arm through the opening. He handed it to the alien and asked, "Ever seen anything like this before?"

Hazel instantly recognized it. She did her best to mask her concern and maintain her sense of humor. "What? No lunch first? You know I am much more talkative when you bring General Tso's in from the outside."

"It's coming. I couldn't carry that bulky package, along with our food *and* our drinks. Not enough hands... The guards said to buzz them when we're ready to eat and they'll bring the food in to us. Do me this favor... tell me about the arm first."

"Nawerssian Cyborgs... Much more machine than organic. The dark-souled monsters hail from the southern hemisphere of my home planet." She rotated the mechanical appendage, carefully studying the advanced technology used by her sworn enemies. "Was this found on Earth? If so, that could be a bad omen for both your people and mine."

3: FIRST RULE OF IMPROV

"What's the old cliché? It's not the size of the dog in the fight, but the size of the fight in the dog... Based on what I just saw, ladies and gentlemen, that better be one ferocious chihuahua."

-Ad-libbed comment by KELLY KA-POW moments after her in-ring promo was interrupted by a male streaker.

FOUR WEEKS EARLIER
ABOARD THE VALENTINE'S KISS
YEAR 0 + 358 DAYS (DECEMBER 24th)

Monroe eased the shuttle into the landing bay. Before she cut the engines, the craft was surrounded by a collection of aliens.

Two massive, red-skinned humanoids moved towards the front of the pack. Each wielded a Nawerssian Stun Blaster. It was doubtful that the high-powered weaponry was necessary. The alien giants stood over seven feet in height. They were shirtless, openly declaring to the galaxy that they possessed the physical strength necessary to rip the limbs off the scrawny Earthlings and their Nawerssian friends with little difficulty.

Behind them stood a tall, slender being. Feathers covered this extraterrestrial figure. They were mostly green in color, with some yellow ones thrown in to add some flair to her outer layer. The feathers grew darker atop her head, across her back, and over her winged arms. With the distinct curvature of two breasts, the being appeared to be feminine. Unlike a human, she lacked defined shoulders or a neck that was separate from her torso. Instead, she looked like a mighty bird standing upright on a pair of muscular legs.

There was no beak on the face of the "birdwoman." The feathers grew smooth with vibrant yellows and greens around her eyes. The plumage stopped below the eyes and across her forehead to reveal that she possessed smooth, olive skin beneath. Her black irises filled far more space than the tiny whites of her eyes. Her long, slender nose reached down towards lips that were plump, black, and perhaps inviting. Whether her appearance was because of centuries of evolution, a curious mutation, or carefully crafted genetic manipulation, the result was a mesmerizing and potentially seductive appearance.

She may have been just as dangerous as the mighty, red-skinned beasts that stood in front of her. She carried a five-foot, metallic staff. The lustrous weapon was sharpened to a deadly point. It appeared capable of tearing through clothing, skin, bone, and even light armor.

"Friends of yours?" Jenn asked.

Armstrong spoke in the same hollow tone he had used upon realizing that Jagger and the *V-I* had returned. "I have never seen creatures like any of these."

"Do you think they, too, could have descended from those who fled Original Earth?" Monroe wondered.

"I suspect we will discover the answer to that question soon enough."

The bobsled shuttle's overhead panel slid open. An instant later, a blaster was pointed in the face of each passenger.

"Easy, crew," Jagger said as he maneuvered his broken-down body towards the newly docked ship.

The Captain was flanked by humanoid cyborgs. All three appeared to have adopted a feminine form. Regardless of their selected gender, the man-machines dressed androgynously in attire that closely resembled black tuxedo vests that might have been designed and crafted on Earth. The outfits were sleeveless and snugly-fitted to provide little space between the garments and the silver-tinted mechanical shells they covered.

Armstrong balled his fists and readied himself for an attack. Though he did not recognize the red or green aliens, there was no mistaking the cyborgs. Their origins were from the southern hemisphere of Na-Werss. He *(and Jagger)* had spent most of their pre-*Vilnagrom* lives warring with such cyborgs on their home planet.

Continuing to direct his crew to stand down, Jagger reassured them, "This be a parley. If I know one thing about me ol' buddy Armstrong, 'tis that he considers himself ta be a lad of utmost integrity. He wouldn't dare employ any monkey business under a flag o' truce."

It was theater. Upon hearing their cue, each of the alien enforcers took at least one step back. The well-rehearsed action was designed to hammer home the notion that Jagger was calling the shots.

The leader swung his metal leg around and dragged himself to the front of the shuttle. He held his hand out to help the female Nawerssian exit the vehicle. "Can it be…? Monroe? I haven't laid eyes on ye since ye were wee little..." The gravelly-voiced Captain pushed on the young woman's chin to get a better look at both sides of her face. He smiled with approval as he observed her hair implants and surgically enhanced nose. "I must say, developed into a beautiful specimen, have ye. Methinks others from our home world should be considerin' the modifications ye have made to yer appearance."

Though her red eyes were concealed by dark glasses, the creases in her face betrayed her expression. Monroe was not flattered by Jagger's purported compliments. As far as she knew, the last time he had spoken her name, the scumbag suggested that Armstrong send her out the ship's launch tubes. The air lock was his proposed alternative to the burdensome task of raising an orphaned infant on the spacecraft.

She climbed out of the shuttle without any assistance.

Undaunted, Jagger shifted his attention to his former rival. He held his arms open wide, as if inviting him in for a hug. "Armstrong, me boy!"

Jenn and Brady were greeted by the members of the crew. The red giants and the tall, green-feathered woman moved in close to inspect the duo.

The female spoke flawless English in a melodic tone. "Please excuse my companions. None of us have ever seen any who hail from Original Earth. Unfortunately, courtesy seems to be non-existent among the Hamurkans." She placed her hand on her midsection and offered a slight bow. "My name is Sareena. My sisters and I are known as the Davi-Loga. We come from the Ocean Planet of Davi 4."

Jenn mirrored the woman's bow. "I'm not sure what all of that means, but it's a pleasure to meet you. I am Jenn Silva. And this is Brady Emerson."

"Is he your mate?" she asked. Then she turned her head. It whipped rapidly from one point of focus to another. Looking at Monroe, she asked, "Or is he hers?"

"Neither..." Jenn also looked at Monroe. An awkward tension hung in the air. It was enough to cause the pirate to question her previous response. "Neither, as far as I know."

Brady was at a loss for words. Like the red giants from Hamurka, he was fascinated by the sight of new species from far off solar systems. *And Sareena!* She possessed a radiance that caused him to wonder if the uneasiness he was feeling was left over from a turbulent space flight. Or was he experiencing love at first sight?

Jagger wanted to stick to his agenda. "We'll all have plenty o' time for how-do-ya-do's later... Right now I want ye to listen up. I wanna say a few things to the lot of ye, then we'll see where things go from there."

This was the cue the aliens and cold, quiet cyborgs were waiting on. They raised their weapons once more, forcing Jenn and her friends up against a wall.

☠ ☠ ☠

NINE YEARS EARLIER
AGUADILLA, PUERTO RICO
YEAR -9 + 291 DAYS (OCTOBER 18th)

Just a few weeks shy of her seventeenth birthday, Jenn was preparing to make her debut in single's competition. Her coach, wrestling legend Manuel Vargas, spent the previous six months giving her a crash course in the ins and outs of the business. It began in Florida. There he taught her the basic locks, holds, and rolls. Any down time was spent analyzing matches, listening to promos, and learning wrestling lingo. He gradually worked in opportunities to allow her to spar with established grapplers. Now her training was about to shift to participating in matches in front of rabid Puerto Rican audiences. As Manny explained, "If you want to learn to swim, there's no substitute to diving in headfirst to see what happens."

He walked her down a long hallway beneath the arena in Aguadilla. The venue was designed for basketball or volleyball. It seated about 2,500 for those events. Thanks to the additional folding steel chairs placed on the floor, it could accommodate almost 3,000 spectators for live wrestling shows. "It'll be a big crowd tonight… but I know you can handle it."

Once they reached the door in front of the women's dressing area, Manny handed a package to his prized pupil. "You should wear this for your first match."

Jenn instinctively went to tear open the gift. Manny held up his hand, stopping her. "Don't open it here..." Then he whispered, "I have a reputation to uphold. I can't have these people here seeing Manuel Vargas with tears in his eyes."

He pulled her in for a hug. *Without a doubt, it was the tightest he'd ever given her.* After a quick peck on the cheek, he told her, "Go now. I'll see you before the match begins." Then he turned and walked away before he started to cry.

☠ ☠ ☠

The fluorescent lights flickered. The mirror was cracked from top to bottom, with a fist-sized impression near the edge. This dark and dirty dressing room wasn't the most glamourous of settings to prepare for her big debut. None of that bothered Jenn.

"Tonight: Lady Pirata is born!"

They were the words Manny had written on a note tucked inside the package. Jenn repeated the declaration again and again, while staring into the cracked mirror and admiring her new ring attire.

Her mask was black with red outlining the holes around the eyes and mouth. A large, white skull 'n crossbones covered the forehead. Her outfit also included a simple, amateur-wrestling singlet. It was all red, except for the Puerto Rican flag embossed across the chest. Though she was born and raised in Florida, her association with the great Manuel Vargas meant that she would be billed as hailing from the proud Caribbean island.

The door swung open with a bang. A woman carrying a large, canvas duffle bag backed through the doorway. She swung around, revealing that her face was covered with clown makeup.

"Oh good! You look like you're almost ready. You can tape my ankles while we talk about tonight's match."

Jenn didn't respond. Confused, she stood there waiting for additional information from this loudmouth who was interrupting her special, *private* moment.

Her opposition for the night held out her hand. "Oh! I'm sorry. I'm Kelly Powers. Known as Kelly Ka-Pow to at least ten or twelve of my adoring fans..." When Jenn offered no response, Kelly decided to connect the dots for her by imitating a ring announcer. "You know... 'the Body-Slamming Bozo... the Joking Jabroni... Kelly Ka-Pow!' You and I are fighting tonight."

Jenn wrapped her hand around Kelly's. Then she recoiled. "What the hell was that?"

Kelly let out a deranged laugh. "Oh this!" She showed the classic hand buzzer that was tucked into her palm. The childish contraption had given the pirate a surprising jolt. "Tell Manny he owes me a *cerveza*. He said you'd never fall for the shocking shake gag."

Seconds later and without warning, the crazy clown stripped down to her underwear. Without missing a beat, she tossed a role of athletic tape to her opponent before taking a seat atop a wooden table.

"You're gonna love it here. The fans are nuts... in a good way. They like bruising hits and bloody finishes, which totally plays into my style," Kelly spoke rapidly as she discussed wrestling in Puerto Rico. "I refuse to be tied down to one promotion. That gives me the freedom to fly down here a couple times a year. I get my ass kicked three or four times over a two-week period. But it's worth it because I get a chance to work on my tan and get a fat paycheck before flying back to home sweet home. If I'm *really* lucky, I hook up with some random, sexy guy. It's my idea of a perfect vay-cay!"

Jenn stared at Kelly. Her skin tone was so light that she'd almost certainly burn after any substantial amount of time outside. "I believe everything but the part about the tan."

"You're right. I turn into one huge freckle after twenty minutes in the Caribbean sun. That's why I sleep until way past noon. Then I spend the rest of the day guzzling fruity cocktails in a spot that's got plenty of shade… You're a quick study. Good."

Jenn knelt and began to wrap the tape around this odd woman's ankle. "Like this?"

Kelly nodded. "So, Lady Pirata, you got a real name you go by? Or are you one of those kayfabe devotees who never shares that type of information?"

Kayfabe. It was the dying art of protecting the secrets of the wrestling industry. Staged events were treated as if they were genuine. Those who were serious about kayfabe wanted the world to believe that each ring warrior desperately wanted to send his (or her) opponent to an early grave! They refused to expose the special details that made the partially scripted performances and predetermined outcomes look authentic. They would *never* let on that the show wasn't one hundred percent real. Pulling back the curtain carried the potential of undoing all the hard work, spilled blood, and broken bones sacrificed to create their illusions.

During their training, Manny had hammered home the importance of maintaining kayfabe. Jenn intended to keep her identity a closely held secret. "'Lady Pirata' is good."

"Well, *Lady Pirata*, you and I have four matches scheduled over the next two weeks. The way these programs work is the heel typically wins the first match. The babyface gets their revenge at Saturday night's show. The celebration is short lived. After the match is when I attack and really do a number on you. That'll have the fans clamoring to see our feud through to the finish. You follow me so far?"

The fast-talking clown paused to spit out her gum. She launched the chewy pink wad out of her mouth. It soared through the air, landing with a thud at the bottom of a metal trashcan several feet away. "Bullseye!" Then she continued, "Next week we have a double-DQ on Thursday. A blood bath where we really show the fans how much we hate each other. Then we cap it off with a kickass, banger of a match where we pull out all the stops in front of Saturday's sellout crowd." Reaching down towards her ankle, she gave Jenn instruction on the tape job. "A little tighter."

With the teenager offering little resistance to her counterpart's rapid-fire directions, Kelly continued. "As far as tonight's match goes, here's what I was thinking... I like to pay a fan ten bucks ahead of time so I can spray him in the face with seltzer water on my way down to the ring. Classic clown gag. You see, messin' with the fans is part of my schtick... I figure our match could end with me busting that bottle over your head and then getting a quick pinfall. My tainted victory will set the stage for our little rivalry and it'll really get a rise out of the crowd!"

The suggestion got a rise out of Jenn. "You want to break a bottle over my head? You've gotta be kidding me! Wait... are you kidding?"

It wasn't the response the ring veteran was expecting. "No joke. Wrestling is improv, kid."

"*'Kid?'* How old are you? Twenty? Twenty-one? You're only a couple years older than me."

"You're sixteen. I'm twenty-three. Seven years difference…"

"I turn seventeen in November. November fourteenth."

"Whether the difference is seven years or six, in the wrestling biz, that spread might as well be twenty or twenty-five years. Capiche? Now stop interrupting... Where was I?"

"'Wrestling is improv.'"

"Exactly... Do you know the first rule of improv?"

"I'm not even sure I know what 'improv' *is*."

"Improvisational theater. Unscripted acting. Improv..." the chatterbox explained. "The first rule of improv is to always agree. Never deny."

"That sounds like two rules."

"Well, it's one... and it's the most important," the clown assured her. Pointing her finger like a gun, she went on, "If I say 'this is a gun' and you say 'no it isn't,' you just killed the scene. In wrestling, if I slam you to the mat and you bounce back up right away, it's called a 'no-sell.' Now everyone in the audience thinks I can't hurt you. Don't make a habit of that or you'll tick off the wrong person and you'll get your young ass run right out of the business."

Jenn argued her point. "I know what a 'no-sell' is. A body slam is one thing. You're talking about smashing a glass bottle over my head!"

"We aren't here to play Pin the Tail on the Donkey. It's a fight, right? Some of the things we do are gonna hurt a little bit. I've been doin' this for long enough to know that the bottle isn't going to cut you. In fact, as long as you're wearing that mask, your pretty little face isn't going to take on any major damage."

"Isn't there some other way you can beat me?"

The jester hopped off the table. "There are a million other ways I can beat you. That's not the point. If you wanna get over with the crowds here, you need a certain degree of gore. That's what wrestling fans come to see in Puerto Rico. That's why Manny has all those grody scars on his forehead, and all over the rest of his body, for that matter. Violence is what they expect. Blood, weapons, *fire*. It's what they pay their hard-earned money to see... Trust me. Manny does. That's why he hand-picked me to pop your cherry on your maiden voyage. Let me beat you this way tonight, and we'll see where it takes us for the rest of our program together."

Jenn sucked in a deep breath. The exuberance the teenage wrestler felt earlier had disappeared. Now it was replaced with doubt, fear, and uncertainty.

"Trust me. First rule of improv. Always agree. Never deny. There are two artists dancing across the wrestling canvas. Give me a chance to create and see where it takes us."

☠   ☠   ☠

ONE HOUR LATER

It was ten or fifteen minutes after her debut match. Jenn still couldn't wipe the smile from her face. The roar of the crowd was intoxicating. Even though she'd taken the loss in tonight's bout, she was eager to return to the ring and do it all over again.

She and Kelly sat in folding chairs near the lockers. They were going over their contest, blow by blow. The young veteran in clown makeup kindly offered suggestions to the rookie about what they could improve on for next time.

Rising from her seat, Kelly said, "I need to hit the showers and scrub this paint off my face. If I keep it on too long, it clogs my pores. Then it's Zit City. Trust me, it's not at all pleasant."

Jenn wasn't ready for the experience to end. "I'm gonna sit here a little bit longer... Go over the match in my head, you know?"

A few moments later, Manny marched into the women's dressing room. The wrestling coach triumphantly held a six-pack over his head. "Where's my pirate princess?"

Jenn smiled and waved.

"I know I told your mother that I wouldn't let you come down here and party, but I figured tonight we have a good reason to make an exception." He handed her an ice-cold bottle of Puerto Rican beer.

The teenager and a couple of her cousins drank a few Rum 'n Cokes at a family wedding the previous summer. This, however, was the first mouthful of beer she'd ever consumed in her young life. She managed to choke it down.

Manny guzzled half of his *cerveza* in one gulp. "When Kelly hit you with that bottle... Oh man, I wasn't expecting that! What a great way to end the match! It made the fans sympathetic towards you. Plus, it brought some major heat on Kelly. You two have set up the rest of your program really well!"

"Did I hear someone say my name?" the unmasked clown stepped out from behind the row of lockers. A dingy towel was wrapped around her. "One of those brewskis is mine. Your protégé fell for the hand zapper gag."

Manny shook his head. "Put some clothes on. Then you can have all the beer you want."

Kelly playfully lifted her hands into the air in surrender. This motion allowed the towel to drop to the floor. She gave Manny a moment to gawk before saying, "Wipe that frown off your face. It's nothin' you haven't seen before, Big Guy." Then the clown turned and disappeared behind the lockers.

Jenn's mouth dropped open. She made eye contact with her coach. Her facial expression asked her question without the need to utter a word.

Manny said to Jenn, "What happens in P.R. stays in P.R. Got it? Now shut up and drink your beer."

Kelly returned a moment later... dressed in a vintage *Charlie's Angels* T-shirt and a tight pair of khaki shorts.

Manny popped off the cap, then handed Kelly the beer she was owed. "While I've got you both together, let's talk about Saturday night's match."

☠ ☠ ☠

NINE YEARS LATER
ABOARD THE VALENTINE'S KISS
YEAR 0 + 358 DAYS (DECEMBER 24th)

Jagger spun the dagger in his hand so that he held the razor-sharp metal in his palm, pointing the handle towards Jenn. "I'll give ye this blade fer safe keepin'. So long as ye promise to never stick it in me back... I'd be honored if ye would be so kind as ta join me crew, Long Jenn Silva."

She took the weapon without hesitation. Then she eased backwards until she reached a metal bench near the wall.

The Captain took a moment to assess the mood of his newest "crew member," then asked to sit next to her on the cold, hard slab that protruded from the wall. "Mind if ol' Jagger joins ye?"

The luchadora held her hand out, communicating that he was welcome to do so.

"Yer friends haven't been too cooperative. Very disappointing. I was beginnin' ta fear it might be a quick trip out the launch tubes for the lot o' ya." He shifted in his seat. His body had been ravaged from years of wear and tear fighting wars on his home planet. "But now that ye and I have met, I'm able ta hold out some hope."

"Hope for what?"

"A joint endeavor. Your crew and mine, workin' together to save your beautiful little home planet."

"What makes you think it's *my* crew?"

Jagger stood as he responded, putting great emphasis on the woman's name. "Humor me, *Long Jenn Silva*. I've already talked to yer pal Brady, the lovely Monroe, and me ol' buddy Armstrong. Ye may not be the Cap'n of the crew at the moment, but somethin' tells me they go where you go. And ye have pirate blood in ye. Do ye not? So how 'bout it? Can ye convince yer mates that a partnership might benefit us both?"

Jenn studied the fidgety space veteran. Armstrong had told her a little about his rivalry with the top military man on the *V-I*. Even so, there were many details that she was missing. *Where had Jagger been for the last twenty years? How many aliens made up his crew? Could he be trusted? Perhaps most importantly, could partnering with him lead to her being reunited with Lazz and Cocoa?*

Execution via the launch tubes didn't exactly sound like a pleasurable end to Jenn's space adventure. Since she seemed short on options, she harkened back to the advice Kelly Ka-Pow gave her when she was making her wrestling debut. *Always agree. Never deny.*

"Don't worry. I can convince them that a partnership could benefit everyone involved," answered the post-apocalyptic pirate.

Jagger let out a victorious laugh. "I may be pressin' my luck, but I gotta ask… Ye fight for a livin', do ye not? Though Poff and

Mach be mighty hunks o' red meat, our crew could use a bit more muscle. Do ye know of any possible recruits we might be able to grab?"

Jenn suggested Lazz, Cocoa, and the crew of the *V-II*.

That idea was quickly vetoed. Jagger explained, "Like I said before, those aboard that ship have their own marchin' orders. They face a daunting task if we don't join 'em in time. But I have confidence in 'em... Actually, I was thinkin' of makin' a quick trip down to Earth and grabbin' a couple more soldiers for the journey. As a token of good faith, I figured I'd let you suggest one or two of yer wrestlin' buddies."

4: ESCAPE ARTIST

"One... two... Kayzo kicks out again! Unbelievable! Vesuvius has hit him with slam after slam, powerbomb after powerbomb... but the explosive mountain of a man cannot keep The Great Kayzo down!"

   - ROOSEVELT HILL'S on-air commentary from when THE GREAT KAYZO "refused to be pinned" no matter how many times VESUVIUS slammed him.

TWO WEEKS LATER
YEAR 1 + 14 DAYS (JANUARY 6th)
ABOARD THE VALENTINE'S KISS

Brady walked into the galley of the *Valentine's Kiss*. After entering the sequence of letters and numbers as he had been instructed, he waited patiently for his breakfast. In less than a minute, he was holding a bowl full of lukewarm synthetic protein. The food had a consistency of instant oatmeal that had been left in the microwave for too long. It was mushy on bottom, with a tough film towards the top.

The athletic Earthling looked across the room. His gaze fixed on Sareena as he tried to determine whether the birdwoman from Davi 4 was looking for company.

She had her own serving of partially eaten food. Like her sharp, metallic staff that leaned against the table, her bowl had been set to one side. A portable reading device now occupying her attention.

"Would you mind if I joined you?"

Sareena smiled. "Please do. It will give me an opportunity to practice my English." She spoke with a tone and cadence that was so melodic that it almost sounded like she was singing.

"It sounds perfect to me already. English isn't the language you speak on your home world?"

"Oh no," the birdwoman laughed. "Though it is an ancient language, it is the newest tongue that has come to Oquezzi. I believe Jagger brought it when he arrived a few years ago."

Brady didn't know who or what Oquezzi was. Opting to forego questions that would take them away from the current topic of conversation, he remained silent.

"My sisters and I are quite adept at learning other languages. Still, it is different to hear it spoken by someone who is conversing in their native tongue. It is a much more natural sound than the electronic ones that come from translator bots... or the ones we imitate in our efforts to learn the language."

"You use robots to translate? Interesting. When my parents took me on a trip to South America, we used an app on my phone."

There was a look of confusion on Sareena's face. She shut her eyes and pursed her lips together, as if these actions helped her search her memories. With a slight shake of her head, she apologized, "I'm sorry. I do not know what 'app' means? Is that what they call translators on Original Earth?"

"Nah. It's silly. Not important. Don't worry about it," Brady replied. "Tell me about your home. Please. I've noticed you mention your sisters quite a bit. How many sisters do you have? Do you have any brothers?"

"Thousands of sisters. No brothers."

"Thousands? That's going to require a little more explanation," he said with a smile.

Sareena smiled back. Before long, however, her upward turned lips seemed to sink into a frown. It was clear that she liked Brady but continued to have some reservations. She hesitated for a few awkward moments before continuing the conversation.

"Centuries ago, those that lived in our cluster of planets looked much like you." She briefly placed her cold hand atop his. "Soft, warm skin..." She reached up and briefly dragged sharp talons through Brady's blond curls. "Long, flowing hair... These outer coverings were not ideal for living on the ocean planet of Davi 4. We needed to be able to glide through the air rather than walk on the ground. We needed to be able to live in tall trees when the high waters washed over our islands. Our scientists manipulated our genetic code. At first, the changes were gradual. Strong claws allowed us to climb trees and survive while living in the branches for weeks at a time. Feathers kept us warm and helped as we soared from tree to tree. Hundreds of years passed. Now we look like this."

Brady hung on every word. When the alien storyteller paused, he jumped in with a question. "You said, 'Thousands of sisters. No brothers.' Is that because of the scientists, too?"

The green-feathered alien grinned as she wagged a talon towards Brady. "Your people are highly intelligent, Brady Emerson. There are others that assume those from Original Earth were little more than barbarians. They are wrong. That is obvious. I can tell by the questions you ask that you are very intelligent."

He appreciated the compliment, but still wanted an answer to his question. He didn't want to make his new friend—assuming they *were* friends—feel like she was being interrogated. But it was starting to feel like she was trying to evade this particular inquiry. "So...?"

Sareena finally answered, revealing a fact about her home world that caused her hesitation. "Centuries ago, it was determined that the males of our species were disruptors of peace, purveyors of violence. The geneticists manipulated our eggs so that only a few males were born each year throughout Davi-Loga. To this day, my people keep the males of our species in isolation. They live in a space station that orbits Davi 2. In our cluster of planets, only females live on the surface."

This revelation caused Brady to shift nervously in his seat. He didn't run away, though. He didn't even try to steer the conversation in a different direction. Instead, he glanced at the alien's staff, then looked directly at Sareena. "Did it work? Is the ocean planet of Davi 4 free of violence?"

"Oh, no. There is plenty. You must understand, the universe is filled with sin, violence, and war. That goes for my planet, too." She snarled, then hissed her words to make her point. "The Davi-Loga are mighty warriors. It would be unwise to trifle with us. We are as well-versed in violence and war as any in the Milky Way... The only distinction is that we have different motivations for when we wage war."

"Whoa!" Brady said as he held his hands in the air to show that he intended to take a non-threatening posture. "I'm sorry if I offended you. I wasn't trying to be pushy or judgmental."

Sareena laughed. Her melodic voice returned. "I took no offense. However, you should take note that we Davi-Loga can turn from pleasant to vicious in an instant."

☠ ☠ ☠

APPROXIMATELY FORTY-TWO YEARS AGO
NA-WERSS
YEAR -42 + 76 DAYS (MARCH 17th)

Gar-Vizza Rey'otia stood at the bottom of the steps that led up to the Nawerssian Capitol. The cyborg devils from the southern hemisphere were on the brink of winning the biggest battle in the latest of countless wars between the two peoples who had colonized the planet.

A fleet of "cyborg chariots" buzzed through the capital city. The war machines surgically picked off top officers from the Nawerssian military forces. The result was chaos and confusion.

Gar-Vizza—who would begin calling himself "Jagger" just a few years from this point—was a skilled mercenary, known for his ability to walk away from seemingly hopeless situations. He'd been conscripted back into service after several years away from the military.

"Follow me! We have a mission to complete!" he shouted to those who remained from his battalion.

Many of those who complied soon regretted doing so. Their opposition had them surrounded. They were trapped in a "Cyborg Storm," a highly effective military formation in which their mostly mechanical foes encircled them and sprayed rapid fire laser blasts into the group. Stray blasts of "friendly fire" took down many cyborgs when they employed this tactic. They knew their mechanical shells could be repaired as long as the fleshy hearts and brains inside were not damaged.

It would not take long until no one was left standing in the middle of the circle.

Gar-Vizza watched as the bodies of his fellow soldiers piled up around him. Their mission had been to plant explosives on or near key targets. Had all gone as planned, the pilots flying above would have swooped in and ignited those bombs. It seemed like the perfect plan for knocking out cyborg communications with the small, remote-operated killing machines that were inflicting so much damage.

Outnumbered and significantly under-armored, the remaining Nawerssians were in danger of witnessing the fall of their Capitol. Desperate action was needed.

"I can think of another use for these explosives!" His shouts went unheard over the sounds of blasters firing all around him.

With no other survivors around to object, Gar-Vizza entered a sequence of numbers into a keypad that was embedded into the side of a warhead. Then he strained to listen for the sounds of whistling air above him.

Everything went dark. Gar-Vizza never heard the rocket-powered fighters diving towards him. He failed to catch even a momentary glimpse of bright pink laser fire rapidly barreling in his direction. And he wasn't conscious when the bomb planted near him detonated.

☠ ☠ ☠

125 DAYS LATER
YEAR -42 + 201 DAYS (JULY 20th)

The skirmish known as "The Silver and Black War" had come to an end. The blue-skinned people of the northern hemisphere were considered the "victors" over the menaces from the south. When factoring in the tremendous destruction of property and the considerable number of fatalities they had suffered, it was difficult to decipher what they had gained from their victory. Nevertheless, they were happy to gather in celebration of their latest armistice.

Deputy Magistrate Mua-Quana Eesafoa had pinned dozens of metals on Nawerssian heroes to commemorate the victory. None brought the popular politician more joy than the opportunity to honor his friend, Gar-Vizza Rey'otia. "He stood on the steps of our Capitol and ordered that our pilots rain fire from above. He must have known that doing so meant certain death, yet he was willing to sacrifice himself for the good of the Nawerssian people. Somehow, he survived the barrage of laser fire and the explosions that followed. Every other member of his battalion and over three hundred cyborgs perished on the Capitol Steps. Miraculously, Gar-Vizza survived… a national hero. He tells me he cannot wait for the day that he no longer pulls shrapnel and tiny pieces of cyborg out of his wounds. As for me, I cannot wait for the day he is once again able to serve the good people of Na-Werss. More importantly, I am pleased to have been given the opportunity to announce that, should he choose to return to the Nawerssian military, he will do so at the rank of General. Friends, neighbors, and good people of Na-Werss... It is my privilege to introduce *General* Gar-Vizza Rey'otia."

☠ ☠ ☠

TWENTY-THREE YEARS LATER
ABOARD THE VILNAGROM-I
YEAR -19 + 31 DAYS (JANUARY 31st)

Now known as Jagger, the former Nawerssian hero sat alone in the brig tucked away at the end of a long, empty corridor of the *Vilnagrom-I*. On most occasions, his imprisonment took the form of solitary confinement. His food was delivered through the network of pneumatic tubes that ran within the walls of the ship. When he finished eating, he was to dispose of his bowls and utensils through the same soulless tubes.

A series of tones rang out. They served as a signal that his evening sustenance was about to be delivered. But no food came through the tubes. Instead, Armstrong stepped into sight. He was there to bring the prisoner a plate that included a grilled chicken breast and steamed carrots.

Years had passed since Jagger had been offered anything but rations of the synthetic, algae-like protein that was cultivated in large tanks contained within the bell of the *V-I*. The opportunity to eat savory foods from Earth was not just a pleasant surprise. It came as a shock. He desperately wanted to take the chicken breast and devour it before it was snatched away. He knew, however, that the special meal came at a price. At the very least, he was going to have to engage his greatest enemy in conversation.

"What be the occasion, *Cap'n?*" *(Every time Jagger addressed Armstrong as "Captain," he did so with obvious disdain.)*

"This is your last meal in the brig," the *V-I's* Senior Explorer announced. As he glared at Jagger, Armstrong did not try to hide the fact that he had not forgiven him for the insurgence the once-proud General had led. It was a rash move that led to the deaths of multiple crew members, including a teenage male named Adam.

"If I be receivin' a pardon, then lemme out. As much as I'd appreciate eatin' some tasty vittles, I'd much prefer ta move around and stretch me one good leg."

Armstrong was in no mood for playful banter. "There is no pardon. I trust you know that. The *V-II* will dock with our ship within a few hours. We will be moving to the next phase of your imprisonment. You will be placed in the life suspension tanks until…" His voice tapered off. Even after five years, the ship's de facto leader was uncomfortable discussing the terms of the sentence he had pronounced.

"Until *forever*. Say it, ya yellow-bellied coward… Until ye strip down this ship and set it on a collision course with a far-off star. Seven or eight years in VR, then I'm gone… consumed by a mighty ball o' gas and fire… I'm not sure how ye live with yerself."

Though his voice remained steady and cold, the wrinkles atop his bald forehead bunched together as a sign of his anger. "I live every day remembering the violence that you brought to this ship. I live every day confident I made the right decision. You were drunk with power. You gave orders that would materialize only in the mind of a madman. Your decisions led to several needless deaths.

That makes you a murderer. And the sentence I pronounced is justice."

"Then cancel the mission, *Cap'n*! What be the point of *Vilnagrom*? Just fly down ta that beautiful green planet below and tell the Earthlings that their God is here… His name be Armstrong, and he be sendin' the devil away ta where he can ne'er hurt 'em again."

☠   ☠   ☠

EIGHT MONTHS LATER
ABOARD THE VILNAGROM-I
YEAR -19 + 267 DAYS (SEPTEMBER 24th)

Magellan's time aboard the *V-I* had been filled with tragedy. As the Skipper of the ship, he was tasked with piloting the spacecraft through the Eye of Jupiter Wormhole. His partner, Tey-Rixia, died as the result of a childbirth made tumultuous by their voyage through that interstellar passageway in which time and space did not adhere to the Laws of Physics.

Years later, their son, Adam, died during an insurrection aboard the ship. Jagger's hand was on the other end of the blade that ended his life. That fact made the choice even more difficult for the frequently indecisive Skipper.

He stood and stared at the large tank of murky, purple liquid. His feet had been planted there for hours. His eyes locked on Jagger. The murderer was floating inside, condemned to remain in the realm of virtual reality until the ship crashed and he died.

Magellan possessed the power to grant the pardon that Armstrong had been unwilling to offer. *It should be my decision. It was my son that he killed.*

With the others having moved on to the *V-II* and continuing the mission as part of a new crew, Magellan was the only conscious being left aboard the ship. He had told Armstrong, "I cannot rely on autopilot. The only way to be certain that Jagger meets his just result is for me to steer this ship into the star myself." In actuality, he was buying time to consider further his very difficult choice.

"I choose…" he said aloud, though he was the only conscious being aboard the entire ship. "I choose forgiveness."

He pressed a sequence of buttons. A mechanical arm lifted Jagger out of the life-suspending purple goo. From there, the two of them would travel through a second wormhole that Magellan had discovered… Hidden beneath the rings of Saturn was a one-way passage out of the Earth's solar system.

☠ ☠ ☠

YEAR 1 + 146 DAYS (MAY 26th)
ABOARD THE VALENTINE'S KISS

While the *Valentine's Kiss* was traveling through deep space, the bridge served as the center of the spacecraft's nervous system. It housed a bank of computers at stations that monitored the communications, navigation, flight, and integrity of the ship.

The Communications Grid kept track of those within the ship, and previously served as a lifeline for those flying observation, collection, or abduction excursions down to the surface of the Earth. Now, however, outside transmissions—most notably, communications with those aboard the *Vilnagrom-II*—were highly discouraged because of fears of being detected by those manning radio telescopes on Earth.

Positioned nearby was the Navigation Grid. Precise readings from the maps and star charts were imperative for interstellar travel.

The Integrity Grid quite possibly was the most important station on the bridge. It was used to ensure that the *Valentine's Kiss* remained structurally sound. If there was significant damage to the outside of the vessel, the entire thing could be ripped apart in minutes. Additionally, the water collection and filtration, air scrubbing and circulation, and artificial gravity systems were monitored at that area of the control center.

Gunner stations were positioned on the port and starboard sides. From there, a crew member could fire stunning electronic pulses that could momentarily disable a fighter or small spacecraft. For larger ships or situations in which fatal blasts were preferred, the gunner could employ the laser cannons. In extreme situations, nuclear missiles were available. Four of those indiscriminating killers were loaded into the *Valentine's Kiss*.

Jagger stepped towards his Captain's Chair. It was elevated and positioned at the front and center of the top level of the flight deck. Rather than sitting in the chair, the Nawerssian war hero preferred to stand next to it. His prosthetic leg made climbing in and out an arduous task. Still, from this vantage point, he could look down and observe his three cyborg crew members dutifully manning the ship's controls.

Nawerssian Cyborgs were meticulous beings. They required little sleep and few breaks for sustenance. Over the years, Jagger had come to admit that his once sworn enemies proved to be much more useful on an interstellar spacecraft than their blue-skinned foes from the northern hemisphere of Na-Werss.

Several months had passed since the moment Fireball Freeman and Kelly Ka-Pow had been abducted and been made the most recent additions to the crew. In that time, the *Valentine's Kiss* raced away from Earth and towards the Eye of Jupiter. If all went according to plan, they would rendezvous with those aboard the *V-II* in less than a day.

For the first time in months, the rugged old Captain had asked everyone aboard the ship to join him on the bridge. He was excited to tell his crew that they were about to be reunited with their friends and loved ones who resided on their sister spacecraft.

"With any luck, we'll catch up with the others before the next *Vilnagrom* ship comes squirtin' outta that wormhole," Jagger announced to all who had joined him. "We'll get the jump on 'em. We'll attack before they e'er know what hit 'em."

"Traitor! Why would you do that?" Armstrong demanded.

Jagger was not rattled. "Mind yer tone, old man. While ye were busy watchin' Original Earth from yer perch in the shadow of the moon, I had me ear to the ground and me eye on the sky… keepin' tabs on as much o' the Milky Way as any man who e'er lived. I'm tellin' ya, those aboard the *V-III* are no friends of ours. They be tyrants, conquerors lookin' ta wipe out those on O.E., and anyone who gets in their way."

"Why should I believe *you*?"

"Ah, Armstrong… Ye've been waitin' a long time fer this confrontation, haven't ye? Well, it not be the time nor the place. I don't give a damn if ye believe me or not. Stand back and lemme do my job. If ye need any assistance, ol' Poff and Mach will be happy to keep ye anchored in one spot."

The pair of mighty Hamurkan bodyguards moved towards Armstrong. They motioned for him to step against the wall. Then they positioned themselves on opposite sides of the old Explorer.

Without saying a word, Sareena signaled that she, too, was willing and able to enforce Jagger's order. The green feathers on the back of her neck stood straight up as she tightened her grip on her staff. The birdwoman from Davi-Loga appeared poised and ready to impale anyone who made an aggressive move towards the man in charge.

The tense moment was interrupted by an alert from the cyborg seated at the Navigator's Station. "Captain Jagger, you need to see this."

☠   ☠   ☠

Jagger looked down at Som Obostoo. Seated at the Navigator's Station, the female cyborg had a panoramic view of the open space in front of the *Valentine's Kiss*. A look at the monitor in front of her gave her the ability to zoom in on whatever was in the ship's direct path.

"What is it we be lookin' at? With me one good eye, it looks like Jupiter… thousands o' miles away, just like we expected. Although I do hafta ask… what be that flickerin' and flashin'?"

"Captain, we have run multiple analyses," Som Obostoo reported. "It is a virtual certainty that those flashing lights are laser cannon blasts. The *Vilnagrom-II* is engaged in battle at this very moment."

This revelation shocked the others who occupied the bridge. "A battle!"

With the flip of a switch, the Navigator raised the blast shield several feet. This gave the others a less-obstructed view of the space that separated them from the *V-II* and its unknown attacker. Even with the better view, it remained quite difficult to see what was transpiring tens of thousands of miles in the distance.

"Can ye enhance the image on yer monitor?"

Som Obostoo responded with some highly technical mumbo jumbo that basically meant that it would take some time for the ship's flight cameras to refocus on a point so far into the distance. "At first, the images will be quite blurry. We will have to run them through a computer program to make them acceptable for viewing. Because this process takes time, there will be a short delay from when we receive an image to when we can display it for all to see."

"Get to it!" the Captain demanded.

Most of those on the deck of the *Valentine's Kiss* were unwilling to wait for the cameras to refocus and the cyborgs to run those images through a computer program to get a better picture. And, for the time being, they chose to ignore the breathtaking view of Jupiter in the background. They collectively squinted and strained, trying anything they could think of to improve their focus on the ships that waged war against one another… and their friends and loved ones whose lives were in danger.

Jagger barked out orders. "Transfer all available power to the propulsion units! Close the gap between us and those ships!"

"Sir," Som Obostoo protested, "Even with all power redirected to Propulsion, we will not arrive until the battle is over. We are, at the very least, ten to twelve hours away."

"Go!" he demanded. *Even if the V-II gets destroyed, we may still be able to rescue some of those aboard the ship.*

Though he continued to be guarded by the duo of Hamurkans, Armstrong wanted more information. "Who is attacking the *V-II*?"

Jagger pivoted, shook his head, and shrugged. "'Tis a mystery. Could it be someone from the Space Force on O.E.?"

America's newest branch of the military was still in its infancy. "That's not possible!" said Brady, boldly speaking up. "There isn't a country on Earth with the technology to get a ship that large so deep into space…"

"Especially one with that much firepower," Monroe agreed.

"Even if they combined forces with every other country in the world..." Brady continued before coming to his ultimate conclusion. "They couldn't possibly be from Earth."

Jagger barked an order to the cyborg seated at the Communications Grid. "Viv Mystova... Break radio silence. Get the *V-II* on the horn and find out who be their attackers."

Armstrong objected, "Unencrypted radio communication from that distance? Need I remind you of the radio telescopes on Earth? The astronomers will spot us... *Without a doubt!* The entire *Vilnagrom* mission will be compromised!"

"Look at that firefight! A battle with Jupiter in the background, no less? It be damn near certain that they've been spotted already. There be no time ta worry 'bout that now. We need ta move quickly if we're gonna help our friends!"

As Jagger and Armstrong continued to argue, Sareena moved towards the front of the top level for a better view of the distant firefight. The feathered Davi-Loga clutched her staff as her breathing grew more rapid.

The cyborgs ignored the squabble between Jagger and Armstrong, as well as the birdwoman's movement towards their station. They had been spending the time conducting their own analysis of the distant battle.

A select few known extraterrestrial civilizations were capable of travel through deep space. Each of these peoples utilized uniquely designed ships. Enhanced images revealed that the spacecraft that was waging war with the *V-II* had a distinct boomerang shape to its body. Accordingly, Som Obostoo's announcement was confident, but polite. "Though there remains a degree of uncertainty, it is likely that the attack is coming from a Davi-Loga warship."

Upon hearing this, Sareena whipped her head from side to side. It spun almost 360 degrees as she quickly measured the reactions of everyone standing on the bridge. Her people were attacking the *V-II*.

With no further delay, she let out a high-pitched shriek and spread her wings wide. These actions served as a warning to stay away. Following a short running start, Sareena sprang into the air with her deadly staff pointed directly at Jagger. While advancing directly towards the Captain of the *Valentine's Kiss*, she shouted in her native language, "Utta foxturna Davi Loga!"

Sareena failed to reach her target. Instead, she crashed to the floor with another blood-curdling shriek. She let out an additional cry as she reached up to grab the dagger embedded deep into her right shoulder.

Long Jenn Silva had thrown the blade from a considerable distance. It lodged into bone and muscle. Some assistance would be needed to pry it out.

With the Davi-Loga injured and her assassination attempt momentarily thwarted, Jenn stepped forward to take on the feathered alien. "I'm still new to this," she announced as she readied for a fight, "But I know that attacking our Captain is mutiny."

☠ ☠ ☠

The others backed against the wall to give Jenn and Sareena all the room they'd need for their confrontation. The luchadora and the wounded birdwoman circled the upper level of the bridge. Neither took their eyes off the other for a split second.

Gone was Sareena's sweet, melodic voice. Now the sounds she made were frequent low growls and occasional hideous shrieks. Both were designed to intimidate her opposition. As she continued to pad around the room in a counterclockwise fashion, she stretched out her winged arms to reveal that razor sharp talons had torn through the tips of each finger. What had looked like small, but menacing, claws just a few moments earlier now looked like treacherous blades that could inflict a tremendous level of damage. "I am going to rip you to pieces!" she said with a demonic hiss.

Sareena's threat triggered a response from Brady. He stepped forward, ready to join Jenn in her efforts to take down this feathered monster. The young man's progress was impeded, however, when Poff grabbed him by his bicep.

"No. Is fair fight," the big red alien said in broken English.

Likewise, Mach held Monroe back. He announced to anyone else who might be thinking of joining the fray, "One on one. Way it should be."

☠   ☠   ☠

Long Jenn Silva eyed the claws protruding from Sareena's hands. *If I move in close, she'll sink those things in deep and this will be one short fight. I've got to stay away. Use speed and surprise. In quick, out quick. Speed and surprise.*

As she assessed her foe, the luchadora took a moment to wonder if her wrestling attire would help or hinder her in this brawl. She purchased black leather boots from an online company that sold upscale Halloween costumes. She preferred to wrestle in men's boots over those made for women. Ridiculous heels might draw the attention of those with a stiletto fetish, but Jenn valued function over fashion when she locked up against a formidable opponent. The expense was worth the extra money, even after she paid to have the soles replaced with those that would not damage the wrestling canvas.

She wore custom made spandex tights. The right pant leg was black with red and silver markings. It was long and tucked into her boot. The left pant leg, however, was chopped off and frayed along the upper thigh. Complimented by the hinged knee brace she began wearing years earlier to support the narrative of a kayfabe injury, she imagined that fans would buy into the story that she was a battle-worn pirate who was lucky to not be walking on a peg leg. *But what will Sareena think? If she perceives the brace as a sign of a weakness, Jenn could work that to her advantage.*

Above the waist, Jenn opted for black fingerless gloves and a crimson halter top. It featured a lattice detail that gave the appearance of two strips of material being held together by twine. The glimpse of cleavage that could be viewed behind the strings that held her top together made this the piece of the wardrobe that amped the level of sexiness up to eleven. *The va-va-voom factor doesn't matter much right now... unless it causes Sareena to underestimate me.*

With no ropes to bounce off to gain momentum, Long Jenn Silva ran towards the Captain's chair. Sareena lunged but missed as she made her pass. Then the luchadora sprang into the air, grabbing the top of the chair and riding its swivel around until it flung her back towards the unbalanced Davi-Loga assassin. Her boot caught the surprised birdwoman across the jaw.

Jenn rolled out of the way. She found herself wishing that she was wearing her mask. That would partially obscure her look of surprise. *A knife in the back and a kick to the jaw... and this alien is still on her feet!*

The most recent blow dazed Sareena. She took a couple of staggered steps before regaining her composure.

Having experienced success with a high-flying maneuver, Jenn hopped onto a handrail. She didn't remain atop her perch for long. Instead, she leapt into the air, intending to floor her opposition with a cross-body attack.

Sareena responded by squatting down, folding her wings in, and hiding as much of her body as possible behind her winged shield. The defense mechanism worked, and Jenn bounced off, having taken more damage than she administered.

With Jenn on the floor, Sareena sprang to her feet and stepped over her. She swiped her talons. Two caught Jenn's shoulder, slicing through the material of her wrestling gear and opening painful gashes along the skin. The birdwoman continued to the side of the room and retrieved her long and deadly staff.

Each spectator instinctively took an additional step back. Now even closer to the wall that surrounded the upper level of the bridge, they seemingly gasped in unison. Sareena was armed and ready to kill.

"So much for a fair fight," Jenn snarled as the assassin stepped towards her.

Sareena unleashed a wild swing of her weapon. Jenn ducked under the staff and somersault out of the way.

She looked up, expecting to see the birdwoman directly above her. When she did not, the former women's wrestling champ realized that killing her was never her foe's primary objective. "Jagger! Look out!"

Sareena's head twisted almost 180 degrees. Her body coiled, and she raised her staff to launch it like a javelin.

If Brady had not acted quickly, Jagger would have been impaled by the long, metallic missile. The spear dug deep into the wall. It grazed against the young man's loose-fitting baseball jersey as he dove to push the Captain out of the path of the deadly projectile.

With Sareena turned away from her, Long Jenn Silva hopped on her back. In one fluid movement, the pirate clutched the knife that remained lodged in the alien's back and wrapped her legs around her waist. Then she wrapped her left arm around the throat of her feathered foe. When Sareena reached up to break the stranglehold, Jenn used her free hand to grab her wrist. She yanked upward on the assassin's winged arm.

Sareena let out a blood-curdling shriek as she dropped to the ground. Long Jenn Silva had used the birdwoman's own taloned hands against her. She pulled Sareena's deadly claws into her face.

Now on her knees, the Davi-Loga yanked her hand downward. The talons snapped off and remained embedded deep in her face. She snarled as she tried to rise to her feet. Though blood gushed out and collected on the floor, Sareena was hellbent on continuing the fight.

Jagger had calmly meandered over to retrieve the Davi-Loga's staff. He tugged and pulled until he liberated it from its place deep within the wall. The Captain carefully tossed the weapon to Jenn. Then he nodded his head, as if he was giving the pirate permission to slaughter the mutineer on his bridge.

Long Jenn Silva grasped the staff with two hands. She glanced back at Jagger once more. When he offered a second nod of his head, the luchadora thrust the weapon forward until it pierced the alien's feathered chest. Jenn had defeated the assassin and saved the Captain.

5: GORILLA POSITION

> *"From the top of the card to the Main Event, I watch every one of our matches from the Gorilla Position. I wanna know everything that goes down in that ring. And I wanna see it firsthand... not have it filtered by someone else's slanted perspective. Understand?"*
>
> *- Excerpt from FIREBALL FREEMAN shoot interview on the "Chatting with Champions" podcast.*

SEVENTEEN MONTHS EARLIER
SAN DIEGO, CALIFORNIA
YEAR 0 + 1 DAY (JANUARY 1st)

Named after former wrestling legend and promoter Gorilla Monsoon, the "Gorilla Position" is the backstage area just behind the curtain through which wrestlers come to the ring. During a live show, it is an area routinely occupied by bookers, promoters, and members of the production crew. Over the years, many wrestling organizations have attempted to name the area after a titan within their own promotion. Inevitably, most in the business end up referring to the area as the "Gorilla Position" (or sometimes simply "Gorilla").

With his favorite straw fedora resting atop his head, Fireball Freeman occupied his regular spot in the Gorilla Position. He stood entirely too close to the large television monitor, studying every move from every match. He was there to make sure that the "New Year's Nightmare" was the best—and most profitable—pay-per-view extravaganza in the history of his All-World Wrestling Association. And if he just happened to be munching on a plate full of sliders as he performed these duties, then so be it.

KaPhonso Freeman (aka "The Great Kayzo") joined his father. Fresh off a Triple Threat Match victory in which he bested both the ring technician Henri Arceneaux and the musclebound Braxton Gore, Kayzo grinned before remarking, "You sure you should be standing so close to the TV? I'm no doctor, but I know that can't be good for your old eyes."

Fireball glared at his son. He didn't like being called "old." Though he tried to maintain a good sense of humor, it infuriated him to receive constant reminders that his battered and beaten body wasn't as reliable as it had been in his youth. "You may be the magician, but I've got a few tricks up my sleeve myself. I could whip your sorry tail. Hell, I might even be able to make you disappear. Do we need to book a 'Father Versus Son Match' to remind you and the world that I've still got it?"

"Na, Pops. You know I was kiddin'."

"Where's your sister?"

Before Kayzo could answer, Cocoa turned a corner. The tall, slender knockout was dressed in her signature wrestling attire: shiny, pink and black leopard print tights with a matching halter top. "I'm coming. I'm coming!" she called as she briefly broke into a jog before slowing to a walk.

"Your girl's been doin' a number on Savannah," Fireball said, summarizing the first few minutes of the championship bout he had been observing. "The crowd's eatin' it up. Looks like you made the right call. Booking her to take the title tonight will make Long Jenn Silva a household name. More importantly, I suspect it's going to bring in more viewers and make *us* a lot of cold, hard cash."

The sound of skin smacking against skin and a collective "oooh" from the crowd interrupted their conversation. The champion had nailed Jenn with a blistering chop across her chest.

"Speaking of cold and hard, that looked like it hurt!" Kayzo declared. "That's gonna leave a mark."

Fireball agreed, adding, "Damn right it is!" Then he threw in some additional analysis. "Savannah was never known for her gentle touch. If she's ticked off about dropping the strap, there might be a little extra whack in those smacks."

Cocoa suppressed a growl. Once she collected herself, she offered, "If she's into receipts, I think I've got one or two of my own that I can dish out when I go out there."

☠ ☠ ☠

Long Jenn Silva gave up at least a hundred pounds to the reigning champion, Savannah Lyons. But momentum was on the side of the challenger. The electricity within the arena grew with every drop kick and every forearm smash the post-apocalyptic pirate landed.

Though she was athletic for her size, Lyons needed a breather. She rolled out of the ring to buy some time and suck in some air.

Jenn refused to let up. She went for a suicide dive. The high-flying maneuver was accomplished by leaping over the top rope and crashing down on her unsuspecting opponent as she stood on the floor. Lyons was completely blindsided. The fantastic move ended with a collision that left the champion splattered across an unforgiving surface on the outside of the ring. It was at this point in the match in which the audience began to suspect that the Goliath was about to be slain.

Lyons was staggering upon her return to the ring. It appeared the AWWA Women's Championship was about to change hands.

One little girl lucky enough to be seated in a ringside seat yelled out with a bit of encouragement. "You got this, Long Jenn Silva! You can do it!"

Jenn took a moment to glance at the audience and smile. The roar of the crowd made it clear that her fans were ready to see her choose a finisher that would put Savannah away for good.

Unfortunately, the wily Lyons eluded Jenn, ducking out of the way of a running clothesline. The luchadora's momentum forced her into a collision with the referee.

While Jenn checked on the downed official, Lyons rolled out of the ring long enough to retrieve a foreign object that could be used to sway the tide back in her favor. SMACK! Without hesitation, the champ drilled the fan favorite with a steel chair!

☠ ☠ ☠

Upon hearing the champion pelt Long Jenn Silva with a punishing blow across her back, Fireball Freeman turned to his daughter. "That's your cue. You're on, Cocoa. Give 'em hell!"

As the wrestling pioneer watched his daughter sprint down to the ring, there was no hiding his smile. It stretched across his face from ear to ear. The radiant expression was an occurrence that came much more frequently as he watched his children grow and mature into talented performers with solid minds for business.

Kayzo asked, "What are you grinnin' at, Pops?"

"Son, I've been in the business for parts of five decades. I've seen plenty of wrestlers whose stars shined bright when they were in the spotlight, only to fizzle out any time they found themselves in a supporting role. Your sister has a talent. You have it too. You don't have to be main eventing a show to be one of the biggest stars of the night. That's not a skill you can teach. It either develops naturally or it never comes at all."

☠ ☠ ☠

SEVENTEEN MONTHS LATER
ABOARD THE VALENTINE'S KISS
YEAR 1 + 146 DAYS (MAY 26th)

"We have finished enhancing the footage of the battle," announced Som Obostoo. After pecking a couple of keys on the control panel, the video was displayed for everyone on the bridge to see:

The *Vilnagrom-II* was being hit by laser cannon blasts from the Davi-Loga warship. The "bell" at the front of the ship was effectively absorbing and even repelling many of those shots. However, more than a dozen Davi-Loga fighters zipped through space, quickly disabling out the few small armed shuttles that the *V-II* had launched to defend the ship.

Monroe gasped. "Avis?" Fearing that one of her adoptive fathers may have been shot down, she clutched Armstrong's hand. With his long, blue fingers intertwined with Monroe's, Armstrong tried to comfort his daughter. "Those did not look like kill shots." Despite this observation, the Nawerssian remained extremely concerned about his partner as well.

The Davi-Loga fighters swarmed around the *V-II*. They fired blast after blast into the arms of the Nawerssian ship. Pieces of the gigantic space vessel tore away indiscriminately.

"We must hope that our friends had sought shelter within the bell."

The *V-II* turned in the sky.

"Are they trying to run?" Monroe asked.

With almost no emotion in his voice, Armstrong answered hollowly, "They are preparing to launch a nuclear warhead."

"What about our pilots that are still out there?"

The Davi-Loga fighter pilots recognized the maneuver. They darted away, trying to put as much distance as possible between their relatively tiny vehicles and the massive explosion that would come if a nuke struck the warship.

Those in the cockpits of the disabled Nawerssian fighters did not have the luxury of fleeing. If a nuke was detonated, those aboard the drifting vessels would almost certainly perish as collateral damage to the nearby explosion.

A blinding flash followed. For several seconds, the "enhanced display" showed nothing. When a clear image finally appeared, the *V-II* was significantly farther away from the warship than it had been a moment earlier. The hijacked Nawerssian spacecraft drifted towards Jupiter's Red Spot, while the Davi-Loga warship spun uncontrollably in the opposite direction.

"What's happening?" Monroe asked with a raised voice that invited anyone with any knowledge of deep space warfare to enlighten her.

"Recoil," the cyborg Navigator explained. "Rearward thrust that comes from launching the missiles. After impact, the blast waves appear to have blown the ships farther apart."

☠ ☠ ☠

**SEVENTEEN MONTHS EARLIER
SAN DIEGO, CALIFORNIA
YEAR 0 + 1 DAY (JANUARY 1st)**

The masses in the crowd jeered Savannah Lyons as she stood over Long Jenn Silva. Some overzealous spectators even launched balled up hot dog wrappers and crushed soda cups towards the villainous champion. The debris didn't bother the titleholder. She merely batted it away with the chair she continued to wield.

The boos turned to excited cheers once those in the audience spotted Cocoa. She and Savannah had engaged in a red-hot feud over the last several months. Cocoa was there to settle a score… and the fans couldn't wait to see this unscheduled clash.

Cocoa got in a few good shots, but the reigning champ regained the momentum after deliberately poking her bitter rival in the eye.

"Thumb to the eye gets 'em every time!" she called out, mocking the crowd. Ignoring the protests from the fans seated at ringside, Savannah lifted Cocoa high into the sky before powerslamming her onto the canvas below.

They were telling a story: Savannah didn't like the boss's daughter. And she certainly didn't appreciate Cocoa's attempt to intervene in a championship match. The attention of the massive heel had completely shifted away from her fight with Long Jenn Silva. Now she was focused on punishing Cocoa.

The pirate looked to work the distraction into an advantage. While Savannah was powerslamming Cocoa for a third time, Jenn hurried up the turnbuckle pads and perched herself atop the ropes.

It was clear Savannah wanted to inflict even more punishment on her motionless foe. As she lifted the steel chair over her head, Jenn leapt from her skyward position. The airborne luchadora drove her feet onto the top of the chair, forcing the foreign object downward at a violent rate of speed. It all stopped following the chair's thunderous impact against the champ's skull.

The crowd erupted. Savannah Lyons fell to the mat. She was out cold. The pirate was on top of her in a flash. The revived referee could have counted to thirty, but a three-count was all that was needed to make Long Jenn Silva the All-World Wrestling Association's new Women's Champion!

☠ ☠ ☠

SEVENTEEN MONTHS LATER
ABOARD THE VALENTINE'S KISS
YEAR 1 + 146 DAYS (MAY 26th)

As they continued to watch the battle from afar, the bridge of the *Valentine's Kiss* starting shaking. "Feels like an earthquake," California-native Kelly Ka-Pow calmly observed.

The unexpected vibrations rattled Jagger. He'd spent more than two decades traveling through space. Never in that time had he felt so vulnerable aboard his own ship. "Som Obostoo! What be the cause of this rumble?"

The cyborg went to work on an analysis. Before she could reach a conclusion, the answer presented itself on the monitors that broadcast the battle.

"Look!"

As the *V-II* drifted towards Jupiter, a third massive spacecraft entered the picture. The *Vilnagrom-III* came rocketing out of the Eye of Jupiter. With the Skipper of the *V-III* having very little control of the ship as it shot out of the wormhole, there was nothing that could be done to avoid the destructive collision. A second blinding explosion left the observers without a video feed for a few moments.

Screams and gasps filled the bridge of the *Valentine's Kiss*.

Brady ignored the rattling of his own ship. Instead, he paused to whisper a prayer for those who had been aboard the others. "God, have mercy on their souls."

When the picture returned to the *VK*'s monitors, they saw that both Nawerssian ships were ripped apart and briefly engulfed in flames that soon were snuffed out due to the lack of oxygen in space. Massive remnants from the *V-III* bounded back towards the mouth of the wormhole from which it had just been expelled.

Jagger scrambled to take his position in the Captain's Chair that he rarely occupied. Once seated, he stared at the distant carnage for a moment longer. Then he barked out his orders. "Strap yerselves in, Crew… Navigators, chart a course and get us outta here! Get us as far away from that wreckage as possible! Now!"

Many of the crew members on the bridge had just witnessed the likely loss of loved ones. From the looks of things, Armstrong and Monroe had lost Avis. Jenn's husband was gone. Fireball

Freeman lost his daughter... This time, it looked like it was for good. Collectively, they protested Jagger's orders to evacuate. "Shouldn't we try to help them?"
"Shut up and hold on! We be in grave danger ourselves!"

☠ ☠ ☠

THE EYE OF JUPITER

The *Vilnagrom-III* shook violently as it approached the end of the fold in space that would take its crew into another solar system... and more than two thousand years into the past. The Skipper and her co-Pilot did the best to observe, record, and address the alerts from the onboard computer. That was an impossible task. It took one hundred percent of their physical strength to steady the spacecraft as it approached the mouth of the wormhole.

Once they were beyond the threshold, the *V-III* shot out of the one-way celestial portal like a speeding bullet. There was nothing either of them could do to avoid colliding with the ship that was hovering near that same opening.

Dozens of separate, simultaneous explosions seemed as one. The *V-III* and its sister ship, the *V-II* had been diminished to scores of pieces of adrift space debris. The rubbery "bells" of each spacecraft had been designed to repel rocks, debris, and other objects that drifted into their path during space travel. Though these safety features were not enough to save either ship, the bell-to-bell impact resulted in an end of the *V-III's* rapid advance.

The collision of the two Nawerssian ships also led to the detonation of one of the nuclear warheads aboard the *V-III*. The recoil pushed the ship back in the direction from which it had come. Hurtling end over end, the largest remaining pieces of the *V-*

III spun out of control... and directly into the mouth of the Eye of Jupiter.

The exit of the wormhole had been penetrated from the wrong direction. The result was a breach in the mystical fold in space, time, and reality. A titanic eruption followed. Massive waves of gravity pulled at everything within thousands and thousands of miles. The *V-III*, the *V-II*, the Davi-Loga Warship, and all the smaller fighters vanished from view. They were sucked into the Eye within a matter of seconds. The gravity bomb pulled in millions of tons of nearby rock, ice, and debris, as well.

A small black hole had ripped its way into the solar system. It had devoured three massive spacecrafts... and it shook the *Valentine's Kiss*, threatening to drag it into its perpetual darkness even though the spacecraft was tens of thousands of miles away.

☠ ☠ ☠

SEVENTEEN MONTHS EARLIER
SAN DIEGO, CALIFORNIA
YEAR 0 + 1 DAY (JANUARY 1st)

Long Jenn Silva bounced to each of the four corners of the ring. She triumphantly held her new championship belt over her head while the crowd celebrated her victory.

One by one, the other occupants of the ring rolled out and made their way up the ramp towards the backstage area. Savannah Lyons was the first to step through the curtain. The referee was not far behind her.

Cocoa, however, continued to lie in the ring.

"Pops! She's not movin'!" Kayzo declared.

Fireball had noticed. He signaled for the on-site paramedics to join him before racing towards his downed daughter.

The veteran wrestler and promoter traveled the length of the aisle in near-record time. Without breaking stride, he rolled under the bottom rope and grasped Cocoa's hand.

"Pops, I can't move... my back..." She bit down hard on her bottom lip to keep from crying. Reaching her arm around to identify exactly where it hurt, she said, "I can wiggle my toes and move my legs, but it feels like a gigantic vice is gripping my back. I need to get to a doctor."

It was every bit as hard for Fireball to hold back the tears. He wasn't accustomed to feeling helpless. And he hated not being able to come to the rescue when his only daughter most needed him. "Don't worry, Sweetheart. I'm right here. We're gonna get you to a hospital right away."

☠ ☠ ☠

SEVENTEEN MONTHS LATER
ABOARD THE VALENTINE'S KISS
YEAR 1 + 146 DAYS (MAY 26th)

Fireball Freeman stood motionless on the flight deck. He stared down into the straw fedora he had removed from his head. The old man knew he should twist his neck to stare out the window. Another look would bring on too much heartache. He couldn't stand the thought of taking one more desperate glimpse at the black spot in space that had swallowed his daughter.

I said goodbye once. Then it looked like I was gonna get my girl back. This time, though... This time it feels final. And I can't muster up the strength to look.

Fireball was not alone in his sorrow.

Jagger and his crew had friends aboard the *V-II*. Armstrong and Monroe mourned the loss of Avis: Armstrong's longtime partner, Monroe's adoptive father.

Of course, there was Jenn. "Cocoa didn't have to be on that ship," she muttered to no one in particular. "I should have done more to convince her to leave with me and Brady. I should've knocked her out and dragged her kicking and screaming back to Earth. If I'd done that, we'd all be back home right now... clueless about this craziness happening worlds away."

Then it hit her. It wasn't just Cocoa that she had lost. The shock had momentarily prevented her from realizing that she'd never see her husband again. "It's bad enough that I'm forced to think about moving forward without him... But I'm always going to know... Lazz was on that ship because of me. If these blue bastards hadn't come to recruit me to join them on their stupid space adventure, they would've never abducted him. Lazz is gone... Lazz is gone, and it's my fault."

Fireball stepped towards Jenn. They had not said a single word to one another the entire time they had been in space. The last time they spoke, the wrestling legend insinuated that the woman with a pirate gimmick was responsible for his daughter's disappearance.

Now they shared a feeling of unquenchable grief. He stepped towards his daughter's friend. The grudge he'd held for several months melted away in a flash. Reaching around her side, he wrapped his arm around her shoulders and pulled her in for a hug.

Jenn had no words. She ignored the fresh cuts across her shoulders. She leaned her head into the taller man's chest. Only once she sank into his embrace did she finally let go... the luchadora allowed herself to weep.

☠ ☠ ☠

EARTH
TWELVE HOURS LATER

The White House Staff scrambled to arrange an emergency video conference. There could be no delay in addressing the unprecedented event that had occurred near Jupiter. Many opinions would be given regarding how the nation should respond to what had transpired some 390 million miles from Earth.

A sea of faces blanketed the monitors that lined the walls of the Situation Room. Yaron Harazi and Preston Ivy appeared on behalf of the UAPTF: Unidentified Aerial Phenomena Task Force. The President had specifically requested that the alien experts be included. Unbeknownst to Ivy, however, she had contacted Harazi directly and asked him not to speak. His take was just about the only one that could sway her opinion. Even so, the newly elected Commander-in-Chief wasn't ready to reveal to those who served under her that she put so much faith in a doctor that many had characterized as a "goofball in a tinfoil hat."

"We can't tell them that alien motherships are blasting each other to bits in our solar system!" The emphatic declaration came from one of several four-star generals on the call. "It would send the country into mass hysteria!"

The top-ranking representative from the Space Force took umbrage with that position. "Let me see if I understand your position… You don't deny that there are aliens within a stone's throw of Earth? You don't deny that they may possess enough firepower to blow us to Kingdom Come? You simply think the American people are incapable of handling the truth?"

"Like Jack Nicholson said… they 'can't handle the truth.'"

The questions, opinions, and the sounds of fear grew to a cacophonous roar. Throughout the call, military officials and political bigshots blurted out their opinions without waiting their turn. The President was looking for answers. No one was helping.

"What about the aliens? Are we simply going to ignore them?"

"We certainly can't tell the public about that…"

"But we also can't ignore them…"

"Aliens have been sniffing around here for decades…"

"Should we be more concerned about a few aliens up there or the reaction of the billions of people here on Earth?"

"We can manage the reaction here on Earth. There's nothing we can do about bloodthirsty aliens!"

"We need to be working on a plan to defend our country…"

"We need to be working on a plan to defend *the entire planet!*"

"I say we nuke 'em!"

"Nuke the little green men!"

"'Little green men!' Are you even taking this seriously?"

"Enough!" The President had absorbed all the bickering and political posturing she cared to hear. Having been dragged away from the tennis court, she wore her graying hair in a ponytail. She even had a tiny glob of suntan lotion that remained on her nose. Despite her informal attire, she was all business when it came to running this meeting. "I will not have this video conference devolving into name calling and hysterics! We're going to take a five-minute break. No one go anywhere. I suggest you use the time to collect yourselves."

With the press of a button on her computer, President Caroline Hogue muted all participants. With another keystroke, she moved into a private conference with Dr. Harazi.

She introduced him to those in her inner circle who remained with her in the Situation Room. "We have Dr. Yaron Harazi from the UAPTF on the call. Please, Dr. Harazi, I want to hear from *you*. What can you tell us about the aliens and the space battle that transpired near Jupiter? Who are they? Where did they come from? Are our concerns warranted? What's their next move? Are we next? Please tell me there's something we can do... I'm hoping to God the human race doesn't end on my watch."

It took a moment for Harazi to successfully unmute his microphone. He nervously cleared his throat and took a large gulp of soda before addressing the most powerful woman on the planet.

"Though my expertise is in the field of extraterrestrial communications, I would suggest to you that both the 'aliens' and the collective response of those on Earth are equal causes for concern. I believe I heard one official on the call say, 'Aliens have been...' How did he put it? 'Sniffing around here for years.' While that is true, these are the first war-waging extraterrestrial beings we've ever seen in our solar system. They appear to possess incredible firepower."

"Who are these aliens, doctor? Where do they come from? And should we be bracing for an invasion?"

"I don't exactly know the answer to any of those questions. No one does... What we must do is hope for the best but prepare for the worst."

Echoing her earlier remark, the President reminded him, "Things don't sound much worse than 'end of the human race.'"

Harazi tried to put her mind at ease. "It doesn't have to be the end. In fact, the solution is one that I briefly mentioned when we met in the Oval Office back in January... If we believe humanity and our way of life is worth preserving, we must spend all of our efforts devising a plan to establish colonies far, far away from here. We need to respond by launching rockets deep into space... deep enough to colonize planets in solar systems millions of miles away from whatever extraterrestrial beings have the sort of firepower that we've seen today."

"How long would that take?"

"Quite a bit of time if we want to do it correctly. Researching the destinations, building the rockets, recruiting the astronauts... all of that will take time. That is why we need to begin working on the project immediately... before the aliens with the firepower are the ones that are sniffing around Planet Earth."

6: STAR-CROSSED LOVERS

> *"Jenn is an amazing woman... I'm not gonna lie. Life on the road is tough when you're in one promotion and your girlfriend is in another. Even though we may be apart for a couple weeks straight, we make the most of our time together when our paths cross... That's just one of the many reasons I love her."*
>
> - Excerpt from LASZLO BARBA shoot interview on the "Repeat the Heat" podcast.

ABOARD THE VALENTINE'S KISS
YEAR 1 + 146 DAYS (MAY 26th)

Jenn sought solitude in one of the gunner's stations. The turrets provided a spectacular, unobstructed, 360-degree view of space. From there she could take the time to soak in the magnitude of what she'd seen and done over the last few hours.

Been a hell of a day!

She'd watched helplessly from thousands of miles away as the *V-II* was annihilated in an open space battle. There were several people she cared about that had been aboard that ship. Her husband, Lazz… Her best friend, Cocoa… It even caused her heart to ache to know that she would never again see Avis and several other Nawerssians that she'd once called "friends."

I stood alongside those guys in a fight for life-and-death… aboard that same spacecraft that's now in a million pieces.

Of course, Jenn also nursed two deep gashes across her shoulder. They were beginning to sting even more now that she was coming down from the adrenaline rush she'd experienced while fighting Sareena. If the luchadora hadn't thwarted feathered alien's efforts to assassinate Jagger, the Davi-Loga might have led those on the *Valentine's Kiss* to the same fate as those who had been aboard the *V-II*.

I can't help but feel a little guilty. Jenn placed her hand against the glass and squinted to view the area where she had last seen the *V-II* intact. She looked at the quickly vanishing haze that hovered around the Eye of Jupiter. *Doesn't seem fair that I'm here, and you're gone. They only abducted you because they wanted to speak to me without any interruptions.*

With no more tears left to cry, Jenn began pounding the glass with her fist. She drove them into the glass at least a dozen times.

The punches didn't stop until blood was smeared across the window and her knuckles throbbed. She was convinced she'd broken a bone or two.

The image of one of the Nawerssian cyborgs—Som Obostoo—appeared on a small video screen in the gunner's station. "I apologize for the interruption... Miss Silva, I humbly request that you take great caution while you occupy the gunner's turret. There is delicate equipment at that station. While we are traveling through space, we have limited resources to repair any damages."

Jenn pressed random buttons near the monitor. Ignoring her cyborg lecturer, she asked no one in particular, "How do I shut off this stupid thing?"

"Perhaps more importantly," Som Obostoo continued without acknowledging Jenn's attempts to mute her, "corrupting the computer panel in the gunner's station could lead to an unintentional launch of the ship's nuclear weapons."

That got Jenn's attention.

"Perhaps you should join the others in the galley."

"Don't you get it? Or do you have some wires crossed in that robot brain of yours? I want some privacy. I want to be left alone..." Jenn insisted. She held her hands up in the air, adding, "I promise I'll stop hitting things."

Jagger's face replaced the cyborg's on the display screen. His long, blue fingers were wrapped around a bottle. He moved his hand around to reveal that he had been holding a popular brand of spiced rum. "Ye should be commiseratin' with others right now. If it'll help, ye can take me bottle o' rum. It has a way of makin' yer memories all the happier."

Jenn turned her head away. She refused to succumb to the temptation of hard liquor. She pouted and stewed for what seemed like several minutes. After taking one final glance in the direction of Jupiter, she turned to face the monitor. "Where did you get that?"

"Grabbed it on me last trip down ta Earth's surface. A bottle like this would sell for a pretty penny where we be goin'."

The women's wrestling champ sucked in a deep breath. Next, she climbed the ladder that would take her from the gunner's station to the main level of the control center. When she made it to the top, she asked, "Got any tequila?"

"Ah, lass, ye will find I possess a whole lotta things that others want. On Oquezzi, that be one o' the keys to survival."

"Well, if you've got tequila, I'd prefer that to rum. I'm not looking for a happy trip down Memory Lane. I'm in the mood to drink so much that I don't remember a thing."

"How 'bout this…? Stay outta that turret and let Zek Evrazda tend to yer wounds. Before she be done, I'll return with some of the finest nectar of the blue agave ye ever drank."

"Huh?"

"I'll come back with a bottle of tequila."

☠ ☠ ☠

TWENTY MINUTES LATER
YEAR 1 + 146 DAYS (MAY 26th)

Fireball, Kelly, and Brady were seated around a small table in the galley. Brady and Kelly had just begun working on their second mugs of beer. Fireball was halfway through his third.

Armstrong and Monroe positioned themselves at the next table over. Both stared into their steaming mugs of Meezuh, a fermented tea traditionally reserved for celebrations on their home planet of

Na-Werss. Neither looked up. They'd already spoken their condolences to one another. There was nothing left to say.

"Ye should be wit' yer people at a time like this," Jagger told Jenn as the peg-legged Captain escorted her into the room. Then he looked in the direction of his fellow Nawerssians. He offered them a quick tip of his tricorn hat before making his exit.

Jenn stepped towards Brady and asked, "Mind if I join you?"

"Please do," he replied. "Is that a bottle of tequila you've got there? Have you been holding out on us?"

"Why, Church Boy… I didn't know you were that much of a drinker!"

"Please don't call me that." He glanced away for a moment before looking back at Jenn. "I drink from time to time. I generally try not to get wasted, but I figure we've all got a pretty good excuse today."

"That we do." The pirate set her bottle and a saltshaker in the center of the table. As she settled into her seat, she said, "Sorry I'm a little late to the party. Jagger insisted that the cyborgs patch up the wounds on my shoulder before… Before I came here. They put some sort of smelly ointment on my cuts. The one with the black arm—I think she's called Som Obostoo—said it won't even leave much of a scar. All in all, I guess I'm not doing so bad."

"That's great news, Warrior Princess," Kelly replied, "But how's your face?"

Fireball instantly recognized that Kelly was about to launch into one of her clown gags. He scowled and gestured for her to stop right away. "Too soon, honey. Too soon."

Kelly nodded her head in agreement. She sheepishly confessed, "After you said your face was 'fine,' I was gonna shoot back with something like, 'It sure is killin' me.' But I suppose Fireball's probably right. Too soon."

The wrestling pioneer tried to apologize for Kelly while explaining her quirky behavior. "Trust me. This girl never fully turns off the clown gimmick. I'm always checkin' for whoopie cushions before I sit down next to her."

Kelly shook her head. "No need to worry about any gags like that. Not while we're up here. I didn't exactly have time to pack my things before the spacemen grabbed me and brought me on this fantastic voyage. That means no bag of tricks and no extra undies for yours truly."

Now it was Brady who tried to get the conversation back on track. "Anyway…!" Pointing to Jenn's bottle, he asked, "Got any shot glasses? I think we could all use a shot."

The emptyhanded pirate shrugged. Apparently, Jagger thought she was going to chug the entire bottle herself. "Tell you what… Go ahead and lick the back of your hand," she said while removing her glove and demonstrating the action herself.

Long Jenn Silva spread a thin layer of salt atop the freshly moistened spot on her hand. Next, she took a swig directly from the bottle. She never broke her gaze into Brady's eyes as she stuck out her tongue and licked away the salt. "That's to kill the burn from the tequila," she explained. "You don't really need it if you're fortunate enough to be drinkin' the good stuff. But beggars can't be choosers when you're thousands of miles from Earth."

Brady followed suit. He downed the liquor, then licked the salt off his hand.

Without being conscious of what he was doing, he placed his hand on top of Jenn's. "That was good. But that shot is going to hit me like a freight train in ten or fifteen minutes."

From their nearby table, Monroe spoke up. "We studied a great many humans as part of Project *Vilnagrom*. I am unaware of any that responded to tragedy and the loss of loved ones quite like you."

"Oh really?" the luchadora said while turning her body towards the Nawerssians. "I see you're drinking, so that's not the issue. Tell us... what would you have us do?"

Monroe glanced to the table next to her. Brady's hand still lingered atop Jenn's. *Jenn... the new widow.* "Why don't you tell us a story about your husband. His name was Laszlo, right? Where did you and Laszlo go on your honeymoon?"

The pirate slid her hand away from Brady's. Then she paused. A bitter taste filled her mouth as she considered Monroe's request.

Kelly tried to break the awkward silence. She shut up as soon as Long Jenn Silva raised her hand.

Still considering the request for a story about her husband, Jenn raised the bottle to her mouth and downed a healthy gulp of the tequila. She no longer required a salty chaser. "I'm not sure I'm ready to talk about my honeymoon. At least not here and now... with the two of you at the next table. Monroe, you and Armstrong are my friends, but you're also the only reasons Lazz was on the *V-II* to begin with. Swooping down to Earth and taking someone against their will is no way to operate. It doesn't matter how pleasant you are when we're face-to-face. It doesn't matter that you think you have honorable intentions. You're kidnappers. You plucked Lazz away from the life he knew on Earth. Without asking. And now he's gone for good. So please excuse me if I'm not in the mood to reminisce about the good time with my husband if I'm doing the reminiscing with the ones that... that a responsible for the fact that there will be no more good times between me and him."

Armstrong drove his palm down onto the table. "I lost more than a partner. Monroe lost more than a father... The Eye of

Jupiter closed! Our people may never find another passage into this solar system. Our people may never make it back to Earth, the planet of our ancestors. Everything we worked for… *Vilnagrom*. In our language, that means 'coming home.'" Gesturing towards his daughter, Armstrong emphasized his point, "Because of what happened today, there are the only Nawerssians that Monroe will ever see throughout the remainder of her life? Me and that piece of filth, Captain Jagger! A devil who quite quickly has become your friend! I am truly sorry for your loss, but our losses dwarf yours, *Long Jenn Silva*."

Jenn's head dropped. "You're right. That was a stupid thing for me to say… Or, at the very least, it was a stupid time to say it. I'll just shut up and drink."

Monroe removed her dark glasses so she could give Jenn and unobstructed view of her orangish-red eyes. "You need not be quiet. We want to hear you tell a story about your husband… And I, for one, would like to sample whatever you have in that bottle."

☠   ☠   ☠

TWO YEARS EARLIER
PRINDLE LAKE, ALABAMA
YEAR -1 + 146 DAYS (MAY 26th)

Jenn couldn't take her eyes off her new wedding ring. She had selected a band with braided gold and rose gold strips woven across the middle. It wasn't the big, gawdy diamond that many girls dream of when they're younger. That didn't matter. In the eyes of the luchadora, the ring was perfect. Because it lay flat on her finger, she could wrap tape around it. She wouldn't have to remove it when wrestling. "This way I can wear my ring all the time," she told Lazz after he tried to convince her to select the biggest, shiniest rock in the jewelry store. "Besides, I'm a pirate. And pirates love *gold*. Remember?"

Lazz approached his new wife. He tilted his head and made it no secret that he was admiring the outfit she had chosen for their honeymoon at the lake. "If I had a body like yours, I'd never wear anything but *that* bikini and *those* jean shorts. You look absolutely amazing, Mrs. Barba."

Jenn happily accepted an aggressive kiss from her groom.

"That one was sloppy… just like I like 'em," she said with a twinkle in her eyes.

She chose not to remind him that, although her legal name might be Jennysis Quevedo Barba, most of the world would continue to know her as Long Jenn Silva.

The newlyweds were forced to break their embrace and step to the side. Their guides were backing a 24-foot, four-seat catfish boat into the water.

Lazz placed two fingers under Jenn's chin and gently guided her head upwards so she would be forced to look at him eye to eye. "You're absolutely sure this is how you want to spend our honeymoon? It's not too late to cancel this little fishing trip. If you'd rather, we could take a few days off, hop on an airplane and stay at a luxury resort in the Caribbean or maybe Cancun."

Jenn shook her head from side to side. "Did you forget that I wrestled in Puerto Rico for two years? Then Mexico for five or six more? Our busy schedules eased up just long enough for us to meet up in Birmingham. Right now, there's no place on Earth that I'd rather be. Hillbilly handfishing right here in Alabama is how I want to spend my honeymoon. I wouldn't have it any other way."

The young couple who would serve as their guides had finished prepping the day's trip out on the lake. Dana Coolidge stood near the edge of the boat. "Y'all ready to go? Gibby's geared up and roarin' to get us to the first honey hole."

☠ ☠ ☠

ONE HOUR LATER

Though the first two "honey holes" had been empty, the fishing guides had used the opportunity to explain the "science" behind hillbilly handfishing (or, as they preferred to call it, "noodling for catfish").

The basic concept was to use gloved hands to catch spawning catfish in shallow waters. During the spawn, catfish enter a hole (or submerged box, if one is placed there by enterprising fishermen). The female lays her eggs, leaving the male to guard them. The noodler places his or her arm inside the hole, and the fish instinctively latches onto the intruding hand. "Then ya grab guts or gills or whatever y'all can get yer hands around," Dana Coolidge explained. "With any luck, ya just snagged a beautiful flathead."

"How big?"

"Thirty-five, forty pounds. Heck, I've caught a couple as big as sixty."

"I gotta good feelin' about this spot," Gibby announced as he hopped into the water. He squatted down and poked the hole with a stick. "Yep... Jenn, put that sleeve back on yer arm and come here. I'll be your spotter. Just like last time. Only this time you're gonna come up with the biggest catfish you ever saw in yer life."

The adventurous newlywed reached down. She sank beneath the water for thirty seconds.

Still positioned inside the boat, Lazz began to show concern. "Is she okay?"

Seconds later, Jenn reemerged with an ear-to-ear grin spread across her face. "That thing bites hard!" She stood upright, showing her new husband the forty-four pounder latched onto her arm. "But I bite harder!"

Lazz shook his head and laughed. "I guess you couldn't have done that in Cancun."

☠ ☠ ☠

TWO YEARS LATER
ABOARD THE VALENTINE'S KISS
YEAR 1 + 146 DAYS (MAY 26th)

Poff-O-Lan and his brother, Mach, sat at a table in the corner. The Hamurkan brothers were pounding shots of a thick, grainy liquid that glowed fluorescent green. Mach had been downing the concoction at a much greater rate. After a couple of hours of steady drinking, he was barely able to lift his head off the table.

Poff raised his glass and called out, his voice deep and tongue thickened by the liquor, "Long Jenn Silva... Come... Join us!"

The luchadora excused herself from her spot at the table with Armstrong and Monroe. She wrapped her hand around the neck of the bottle of tequila and marched across the galley.

She stared at the massive, red-skinned aliens. Gesturing towards Mach, she asked, "What's his deal?"

"We're mourning loss of our friend," said Poff. "There was Hamurkan aboard *Vilnagrom* ship, too."

"Oh?"

"Her name was Bail. Bail-E-Xor. Perhaps best gunner I've ever known... Mach and Bail were romantically linked... for a time."

Poff stopped to gesture towards the open seat. "Please join us."

After a quick swig from her bottle, Jenn folded her arms and shook her head. "I'm still not sure how I feel about the two of you. You stopped my friends from helping me in my fight with Sareena. What gives?"

"What gives?" Poff laughed, having never heard that expression. Again directing her attention towards the available chair, he reiterated his prior request. "Please join us. I will explain by telling you story of ancient Hamurkan legend called 'Roam-E-Ohh and Jewl-E-Yet'"

Jenn laughed aloud. She was drunk. She hadn't been this drunk in a long time. Now she was desperate to hear the "ancient Humurkan legend" with a title strangely similar to Shakespeare's most famous work.

She swiveled the open chair until its back rested against the table. Then she plopped down and straddled the base. Feeling like someone holding the handlebars while dropping onto a motorcycle seat, she revved an imaginary engine. "Vroom, vroom."

"Roam-E-Ohh and Jewl-E-Yet were romantically linked..."

Mach's head shot up long enough for him to interrupt his brother's telling of the story. "...For a time." Once these words were uttered, he crumbled back onto the tabletop.

"For a time... One night there is party, and Jewl's brother fought with Roam's closest comrade. Roam is in love with Jewl. What does he do? He tries to break up fight. Because he gets in way, Roam's comrade is left exposed. He is killed. Out of anger, Roam then kills Jewl's brother. Terrible tragedy," Poff explained.

Mach sat upright again. "That is why Hamurkans believe so strongly in fair fights. One-on-one. Two-on-two. Never unbalanced."

Poff took over. "You and Sareena were fighting one-on-one. Fair fight. The gods would not have looked favorably if your friends intervened."

"Sareena was a serious threat. Next time my friends want to jump in and help out, let them. I'll gladly swing the odds in my favor. Afterwards, I'll take my chances with your unseen Hamurkan gods."

Poff's white braid swung back and forth as he shook his head. "Don't let them hear you say that on Oquezzi."

☠ ☠ ☠

Jagger returned to the galley to fill the rest of the crew in on their next move.

"Though we be in unknown territory here, our cyborg navigators have made some preliminary calculations," he began. "Fact is, the wormhole has the potential to turn into a black hole. After what we saw today, I'd be shocked if the Eye of Jupiter don't collapse upon itself and become a full-fledged planet eater. We don't wanna be anywhere close to that giant, heartless beast in the sky if that happens. If that were ta happen, we'd be devoured by darkness and ripped apart by gravity. There'd be no safe place in this solar system. Earth would be a distant memory."

The room filled with expressions of surprise.

"Say what now?" blurted Kelly Ka-Pow.

"That cannot be!" Monroe declared.

Whether he was emboldened by the liquor coursing through his veins or he simply didn't give a damn anymore, Fireball

Freeman arose from his seat and took a few steps across the galley. "Alright, *Captain*..." (His mocking tone didn't match the respect that usually came with that title.) "They say you're the only one who knows where we can go. So how 'bout it? You care to fill the rest of us in on where we're headed?"

"Aye," Jagger replied, keeping his cool. "There be no place safe in *this* solar system. And even if immediate doom don't be the fate of this collection of planets, astronomers on Earth surely be aware that somethin' be amiss. We'd be fools to return to that orbit, lest the militaries of the world unite to blast us into oblivion."

Fireball was done with Jagger's propensity to monologue. "Alright, I'll ask again... Where are we headed, *Captain*?"

"Safe haven... There be another wormhole a considerable distance from here. Leads to a tiny moon in another solar system. 'Oquezzi.' Hotter than hell and filled with some of the nastiest animals ye ever laid eyes on... And also rats. Some really nasty rats."

VALENTINE'S KISS

MANIFEST

NAME	PLANET OF ORIGIN
JAGGER	NA-WERSS
SOM OBOSTOO	NA-WERSS (CYBORG)
VIV MYSTOVA	NA-WERSS (CYBORG)
ZEK EVRAZDA	NA-WERSS (CYBORG)
SAREENA (deceased)	*DAVI-LOGA (DAVI 4)*
POFF-O-LAN	HAMURKA
MACH-O-LAN	HAMURKA
ARMSTRONG	NA-WERSS
MONROE	NA-WERSS*
BRADY EMERSON	EARTH
FIREBALL FREEMAN	EARTH
KELLY POWERS	EARTH
LONG JENN SILVA	EARTH

7: NUMBER 12...

> "I've got movie star good looks and the chiseled physique to match. I wear this magnificent AWWA Championship Belt around my waist. It all adds up to this... The ladies love me. When I step into the room, they can't help themselves. Not that I'm complaining, but the ladies don't act entirely ladylike when they get around me!"
>
> -BRICK VANDERWAL promo given prior to his Steel Cage Match against SANTA SAWS at "Battle of the Barbarians II."

FOUR YEARS EARLIER
SOUTHERN INDIANA
YEAR -3 + 122 DAYS (MAY 2nd)

It was finals week at Burroughs College in Southern Indiana. That meant that only the most rabid fans of the BC Burros occupied the grandstands at the nearly empty stadium. Many of those seated in the bleachers sat with textbooks in their laps, cramming Biology or Sociology or English Lit until the sounds of the ballyard signaled that they should look towards the diamond.

The public address announcer alerted those in attendance that the top of the seventh inning was beginning. "Your attention please... Now pinch hitting for Central Illinois... Number 12... Brady Emerson."

Neither applause nor boos followed the introduction. That didn't particularly bother the Freshman walk-on who was getting his eighth at bat of the season.

It had been a difficult stretch for Brady. He was experiencing a personal void that had been created from the loss of both parents within the last few months. His fun-loving father dropped dead of a massive heart attack at a co-worker's wedding reception. His strict mother overdosed on her husband's muscle relaxers a few days after the funeral. The back-to-back tragedies left the young athlete wondering how many priceless moments he had missed out on while he chased fly balls over grassy outfields. Suddenly all those extra ballgames seemed like a lot of wasted time traveling across parts of Illinois, Missouri, Kentucky, and Indiana. All that made it hard to focus on the pastime he once loved.

"Come on, Number 12!" his manager called out from the third base coach's box. "Put the bat on the ball. Make something happen."

Unfortunately, the lefty on the mound made quick work of the Freshman. He swung through two inside fastballs. On the third pitch, Brady froze. He helplessly watched a breaking ball glide over the outside corner of the plate.

"STRIKE THREE!"

☠ ☠ ☠

TWO HOURS LATER

Brady sifted through his notes. He thought his scribbles made sense when they were jotted down during the mind-numbing Econ 101 lectures. Now that he'd reached the end of the semester, he wasn't so sure.

A pile of hand-crafted notecards spilled onto the floor of the bus. Brady did his best to hold his tongue and fight the temptation to unleash a barrage of F-bombs. *I hate this guns and butter nonsense.* Reducing the production of a fictitious economy to nothing but two goods was designed to illustrate the basic concepts. To Brady, however, the graphs and charts seemed repetitive. The oversimplification made things potentially confusing. *Why can't they give us real world examples?*

Most of his friends and classmates believed he was going to ace the upcoming final exam on his way to an easy A. Brady, on the other hand, feared he was about to bomb it. Making matters worse, he wasn't entirely sure he cared. He was ready for a break from school, from baseball, from just about everything.

His study session was interrupted by CIU's head coach. Former major league infielder Chip Torrez walked towards the back of the bus. "Mind if I sit?" the coach asked.

Brady shoved his overpriced textbook and notes into his backpack. "Sit."

"I've been watching you play ball for a few years now," Torrez told his scrappy outfielder. *It was true. He aggressively recruited Brady's high school teammate—a power hitting catcher named D'Angelo Jenkins. Even though Jenkins chose to sign a letter of intent to suit up for Vanderbilt, it allowed Brady to catch the eye of the coach and walk on to the hometown CIU Eagles squad.*

After a long silence, the coach continued. "You're 1-for-8 this year. That's not terrible for a kid getting his first taste of Division I pitching. That at bat today, though..." He shook his head. "I look and I don't see a spark. You struck out on three pitches, but you seemed ready to go back to the dugout before they even announced your name."

Though he felt some shame in admitting he'd lost his passion, Brady nodded in agreement. "You're right. Coach, I have to be honest. Losing my dad and then my mom just a couple weeks later... It's taken the wind out of my sails. When I was little, I'd rather play baseball than eat. Sometimes my mom had to drag me to the supper table. When I got to high school, if given the choice, I'd sit through a double-header in hundred degree heat over taking my girlfriend to the movies. But now... Now I look back and I worry about all the things I missed. How much of life did I waste standing in centerfield playing a meaningless game."

"Are you saying what I think you're saying?"

"Yeah, coach... I can't shake the feeling that I'm missing out on too much of the world around me because I've been so focused on baseball. I'm hanging up my cleats and putting away my glove until I have kids of my own."

☠ ☠ ☠

FOUR YEARS LATER
ABOARD THE VALENTINE'S KISS
YEAR 1 + 148 DAYS (MAY 28th)

If all went according to plan, the voyage would take approximately two years. The cyborgs would pilot the *Valentine's Kiss* into a wormhole whose point of entry was hidden along the Rings of Saturn. This passageway would take the ship out of Earth's solar system, thanks to the wonders of that fold in space and time. The ship would be propelled far into the cosmic distance and into a system that housed the hot and tiny moon known as "Oquezzi."

Most of the crew would be placed in hibernation for the duration of the inter-dimensional journey. Those who spent the passage in such a state would be contained in the life suspension tanks. While inside, the aging process would slow significantly. Each person, however, would remain alert and conscious of the virtual reality setting around them. As Jagger explained, "Time in the tanks not only keeps ye young… it be like an extended vacation to the paradise of yer choosin'."

At the first opportunity that arose, Armstrong pulled Monroe, Jenn, and Brady into a huddle for a private conversation. "We cannot trust Nawerssian Cyborgs. Especially ones who are working for Jagger." His concerns were not surprising. Talk of allying with the sworn enemy of his people was unsettling to the old explorer. He and the residents of the northern hemisphere of Na-Werss had warred against the cyborgs from the south for decades. "How can we be sure they will pull us out of hibernation at the appropriate time? Who is to say that they will not keep us imprisoned in those tanks for as long as they see fit? What would stop them from reprogramming the settings so that our 'extended vacation to paradise' became a never-ending nightmare?"

"What are you saying?" Jenn asked.

"I am saying that at least one of us cannot go into the life suspension tanks. Someone must stay conscious to watch the cyborgs. I am willing to do it, but given my advanced age…"

Monroe cut her adoptive father off midsentence. "No. You must not waste two years of your remaining lifespan traveling through space. It should be one of us."

There was a pause. Each member of the group contemplated the concerns Armstrong had raised and the ramifications of "wasting" two years of their life flying to the distant moon.

Brady looked at Jenn. She wasn't herself following the recent loss of her husband. *She can't do it.* Similarly, Monroe had just witnessed the death of Avis. *She needs to spend this time with Armstrong.* "I'll do it," he said, breaking the silence.

"You? No!" Monroe protested.

"Why not? I make the most sense. I'm the youngest." *It was true. Jenn recently turned 27. Brady wouldn't celebrate his 24th birthday for several more months. Monroe, too, was born before him… though her past stints in life suspension made determining an actual age somewhat difficult.* "A couple of years won't be that big of a deal for me. I'll use the time to learn Spanish. I'll teach the cyborgs everything I know about baseball. It'll be like I'm an exchange student. Trust me. I can do this…" He tapped against the glass of the life suspension tanks. Staring at the murky purple liquid contained within, he added, "Besides, I've spent a good deal of time in those tanks. I prefer real life to any fantasy world that can be created on a computer."

☠ ☠ ☠

NINE MONTHS EARLIER
INSIDE THE LIFE SUSPENSION TANKS - VILNAGROM-II
YEAR 0 + 244 DAYS (SEPTEMBER 1st)

Armstrong, Monroe, and the other Nawerssians aboard the *Vilnagrom-II* abducted Jenn, Brady, Cocoa Freeman, and two others in early-August. Thanks to an intricately detailed virtual world that had been mapped out by a Cartographer named Polo, the aliens were able to place their new specimens into VR without them realizing that any abduction had taken place. Instead, they went almost two full months believing that a catastrophic event had occurred. They were duped into thinking they were the only survivors left in the entire St. Louis Metropolitan area.

The "survivors" spent several hours of each day convinced they were walking southbound along the deserted Interstate 55. Their plan was to trek from St. Louis to Cocoa's hometown of Memphis. If they didn't find rescue (or additional survivors) along the way, they would reassess their situation from there.

Intent on keeping an eye out for others using the highway, they always opted to camp near the main road rather than venture down the exit ramps to stay in vacant homes or hotels.

While Jenn and Cocoa went into a nearby town to scourge for food, Brady and Tavia Patton were tasked with gathering wood and building the night's fire.

"Blytheville, Arkansas. Ever hear of it?"

Brady shook his head "no," barely looking up at the attractive young woman who posed the question.

Tavia wasn't often ignored. She was accustomed to commanding the attention of others, particularly heterosexual men! She fulfilled most of the characteristics required to be the star of the typical midwestern college guy's fantasy. Her straight, shoulder-length hair was so blond it almost looked white when contrasted with her year-round golden suntan. (*Thank God for tanning beds!*) Things only got better from there! Blue eyes? Beautiful smile? A flat stomach that complimented bouncy breasts? Check, check, check *and check*!

Tavia tossed a few more twigs into the fire and remarked, "I hope Jenn and Cocoa bring back some fresh fruit. Apples, bananas, something... I'm getting tired of eating stale potato chips and the tasteless powdered donuts that they take from convenient stores."

"That would be nice," Brady said. The young man's words indicated that he agreed with the breathtaking co-ed, but his tone revealed that he was nowhere close to giving her his undivided attention. Instead, he craned his neck and struggled to see if he could catch a glimpse of Jenn in the distance.

"Hey, Brady, do me a favor."

"Huh?"

"If you ever play poker, let me know. I want to get in on that game so I can take your money. I'm guessin' you'd be the worst poker player on this planet or any other."

"What? Why?" Brady asked, somewhat hurt by this attack that seemed to be coming from out of nowhere.

"Well, for one thing, you've done a miserable job hiding the fact that you've got it bad for Jenn. And it's not just a little crush. We're talking total infatuation."

He tried interrupting, "Wait a minute..."

"What makes it worse is you either can't read the signs or refuse to accept reality. The senorita's a married woman. Her number one priority is being reunited with one Laszlo Barba. And from what I've heard her say about him, it sounds like her hubby could tear your head clean off your shoulders… I bet he wouldn't even break a sweat."

Brady again tried to interrupt. "You're being unfair…"

Tavia continued to talk over him. "Look around you! It's the end of the world as we know it. You've got three attractive women to choose from, but you're dead set on focusing on the one who isn't interested and won't be interested as long as she thinks there's even a slight chance she'll be reunited with her Romanian Romeo."

There was a great deal of truth in the words she spoke. Brady took a deep breath, then refocused his attention on snapping twigs and feeding them to the fire. Though he'd twice tried to interrupt earlier, he now chose to say nothing.

It didn't take long for Brady's silence to annoy her. Tavia let out a half-laugh intended to signal her continued disbelief. "What is it you find so amazing about her anyway? Are you star struck because she's a wrestling champ? Would you even guess she's a wrestler if you just saw her on the street? Jenn can't weigh more than 120 pounds soaking wet. Hell, even knowing what she does for a living, I'd like my chances if she and I ever got into a fight."

Was that a threat? Brady tilted his head to one side and studied Tavia.

Perhaps worrying she had crossed a line, she sought to clarify her position (or at least do some damage control where her reputation was concerned). "Not that I've ever been in a real fight. Just little scraps with my brother, Charlie, when we were younger."

Her words were met with a rolling of his eyes. "Can we please talk about something else? Anything else would be fine."

Eventually their conversation gravitated to a discussion about the Kinesiology class Brady and Tavia had taken together at CIU.

He had been a Senior when she was a Freshman. Neither remembered ever speaking to the other until he and his two best friends sat at her table at The End Zone.

"That class was a joke. The professor was stuck in the dark ages," Tavia remarked. "Were you one of the students who walked out when he went off on that tangent about interracial dating?"

Brady nodded.

Tavia continued, "I don't know how that man keeps his job."

Once again, Brady twisted and contorted, stretching and straining to see if Jenn was on her way back. *It's getting dark.* Because he was preoccupied, he didn't contribute anything more than a nearly imperceptible shake of his head in response to Tavia's latest complaint.

"What a friggin' joke! Your drop-kicking dream girl may have you feeling all hot 'n bothered, but that's not going to keep the rest of us warm through the night. I'm going to go gather some more wood to add to the pile. Don't let this fire go out… if you know what's good for you. Got it, Loverboy?"

☠   ☠   ☠

NINE MONTHS LATER
ABOARD THE VALENTINE'S KISS
YEAR 1 + 149 DAYS (MAY 29th)

With two Hamurkans (Poff-O-Lan and his brother, Mach), three Nawerssians (Jagger, Armstrong, and Monroe), and three Earthlings (Long Jenn Silva, Kelly Ka-Pow, and Fireball Freeman) going into hibernation, they would need to utilize a pair of tanks from adjoining rooms. This would permit all eight to be joined together at the beginning of their extended sleep. It was important that they were linked so that they could journey together into their upcoming stints of virtual reality. From the starting point within the VR, the subjects could go to the "destination" of their choosing (provided the appropriate virtual maps had been created and uploaded into the mainframe).

Once the other four were submerged in the next room over, the cyborgs instructed Monroe and the three Earthlings to prepare to enter their allotted tank of purple goo. They stood in a line, stripped down to their undergarments that resembled boyshorts.

Fireball remained in excellent physical condition for a man in his mid-to-late sixties. Even he had to admit, however, that he had grown a little chunkier over time. "Not leavin' much to the imagination," the wrestling legend said as he tried to turn and contort his body away from curious gazes (even though there were none).

Jenn and Kelly opted for additional covering. Jenn donned a black sports bra that she had packed prior to departing her Florida condominium. Kelly wore the rainbow-striped bikini top that she'd been wearing when she was abducted.

The cyborgs seemed confused but unconcerned by the modesty of the Earthlings. Som Obostoo explained, "Once inside the virtual realm, your avatars will be outfitted in the clothing we have programmed... The two of you will be dressed in your wrestling ring attire. This extra covering you have selected serves no purpose."

"You mean I'll be dressed like a clown the entire time I'm in there?" Kelly asked. "What if I want to put on some overalls and weed my virtual garden? What if I want to change into some sexy lingerie and have a little fun with my virtual..."

Som Obostoo interrupted. "Miss Powers, please... We must place you in the tanks without delay! You will start each 24-hour cycle in the same outfit: the clothing selected for your avatar. In your virtual setting, you will be able to change into whatever clothing you like, as long as it has been programmed into the virtual realm."

"How do I know…"

Monroe shushed her. "It will be fine," the Nawerssian said to the Earthlings who understandably had many questions about what the experience of living in VR would be like. She then turned to Som Obostoo and repeated her previous sentiment. "It will be fine." This time the words were spoken in defense of her friends from Earth. Even though she had not seen the need for the extra covering, it would not negatively impact the experience for Jenn and Kelly to enter the tanks with a little more clothing than was customary.

The cyborgs affixed the last few wires, electrodes, and 40th Century medical devices to Fireball's body. They were preparing to place him into the tank when a bit of panic flashed across the face of the wrestling pioneer. "Silva… You've been in these tanks before. You're sure it's safe?"

"It's safe. If it wasn't, I wouldn't have agreed to go back in there."

Kelly had no less concern about the life suspension tanks than Fireball. She remained uncharacteristically quiet, however, as Zek Evrazda adhered electrodes and miniscule gadgets to her forehead, under her armpits, and across her chest. These preparations were interrupted when Viv Mystova buzzed from the Control Center.

"I require assistance on the flight deck."

Knowing that it would take some time to travel from the "arms" of the *Valentine's Kiss* to the flight deck within the ship's "bell," Som Obostoo pointed to her cyborg counterpart. "Go. Brady Emerson can help me with the others."

Som Obostoo pivoted and stepped towards Kelly. The cyborg turned her head, then gestured for Brady to step forward.

The cyborg's movements are so fluid!

The machine possessed a woman's soul, brain, and a few other key organs. Her instructions were simple and direct. "Step forward. You can assist me. I will go through the devices attached to Kelly Powers while you apply the same to Jenn Silva."

Brady complied. He closed most of the distance between himself and Jenn. Then he offered an awkward half-bow, not unlike one he might have been instructed to give little Suzie Baker back in seventh grade during Square Dancing Week in his Physical Education Class.

Jenn suppressed a laugh.

The exercise became even more uncomfortable when the cyborg directed Brady to adhere an instrument designed to monitor the luchadora's heart. The action required the young man to press the small, electronic gizmo into Jenn's chest.

Brady had known Jenn for about eight months. During that time, there were stretches in which the two were almost inseparable. She'd become one of his dearest friends. It was true that he once was infatuated with the women's wrestling champ. The two of them even shared one passionate kiss on the eve of a battle with a faction of the Nawerssians who abducted them. Still, Brady strived to maintain appropriate boundaries with her. *She was a married woman... at least until a few days ago. Now she's a widow, and the anguish she's feeling must be overwhelming.*

When all of this was taken together, it made any sort of romantic advances seem awkward, if not altogether inappropriate.

Brady eased his hand back slowly to avoid any more contact in the vicinity of her breasts than was necessary. "Sorry," he said apologetically.

Jenn tried to reassure him. "There's nothing to be sorry about."

Thank God one of us can keep it professional! She rubbed her fingers against the newly attached device. It was a little bit smaller than a credit card, and she worried that he hadn't pressed it against her skin securely.

"Do not touch that!" Som Obostoo demanded.

The interruption should not have been a surprise. Brady had been warned that the Nawerssian Cyborgs were rigid in their adherence to schedules, routines, and protocols. He glanced towards Som Obostoo and briefly considered whether he'd made a mistake in agreeing to live in the company of three cyborgs for the foreseeable future.

Brady continued to walk on eggshells as he was instructed to place additional wires and electrodes against Jenn's skin.

Though it may have felt like it took forever to prepare her for an extended trip into virtual reality, Jenn soon was ready to be placed into hibernation. Som Obostoo operated the controls to the mechanical arm that would lift the post-apocalyptic pirate into the life suspension tank.

As the mechanical arm wrapped around her, Jenn reached her hand out to clutch Brady's shoulder. "I'll miss you."

The sentiment caught him off guard. Following a brief delay, Brady was eventually able to spit out the words "I'll miss you, too."

He desperately searched for additional words to say. A parting shot before he would be separated from his dear friend for approximately two years. Instead, all he could do as watch as her eyelids sank.

The intravenous sedation kicked in and the body of Long Jenn Silva went limp.

A mechanical arm lifted her upwards, then lowered her into the enormous container of murky, purple liquid in which her body was scheduled to float for twenty-four long months.

Brady placed his hand against the glass and whispered a quick prayer.

Monroe stood to the side. The tall and slender Nawerssian with surgically implanted strawberry blond hair was the last of those scheduled for departure into the virtual realm. She brushed her braids back over her shoulder and looked to Brady to assure him. "Jenn will be fine. We *all* will be."

"Step away from the tank, Brady Emerson."

These cyborgs aren't going to be barking orders at me for two straight years, are they?

"Brady Emerson, please… step away from the tank. We must prepare Monroe for her hibernation."

☠ ☠ ☠

SEVEN AND A HALF MONTHS EARLIER
ABOARD THE VILNAGROM-II
YEAR 0 + 291 DAYS (OCTOBER 18th)

Alarms rang throughout the *V-II*. The human specimens had escaped the life suspension tanks, largely due to the assistance of a faction of Nawerssian crewmembers led by Armstrong and Avis.

Monroe and Brady had been dispatched to the Control Center. The duo was tasked with the pivotal assignment of maintaining control of the flight deck. From there, they could see and hear everything that was happening throughout the spacecraft. That position also gave them the ability to control the flow of traffic throughout the ship. By opening air locks for their allies or sealing them shut and making their foes take less convenient routes when moving from one part of the ship to another, they could gain major advantages that might lead them to victory in this high-stakes battle.

Making their role even more important was the fact that they were manning the Control Center while protecting two young Nawerssian children, Cleo and Ptolemy.

Monroe stood behind Brady, watching as he demonstrated that he had understood her quick tutorial on operating the key functions on the control panel.

"Flip this to switch cameras. Press this and this into the communication board to speak directly through a monitor in a particular compartment... I think I've got it."

"And the weapon?"

Brady showed her that he knew how to hold a Nawerssian Stun-Blaster, the aliens' firearm of choice. He demonstrated how a quick twist of his back wrist was needed to fire a shot, and how to switch the setting from Stun to Kill. "I'm good with guns, remember?"

Monroe inhaled and exhaled a deep breath. "Yes, I remember," she said with a smile. Then she leaned in and kissed him. Her thin, blue lips pressed against his. It was a long, deep, passionate kiss.

With the giggles of Nawerssian children permeating through the obnoxious blasts of the spacecraft's alarms, Monroe pulled away and admitted, "I never kissed anyone before."

Brady stood with his mouth agape. Though not unwanted, the kiss had caught him off guard. He didn't know what to say. (He'd later think of dozens of things he could have and should have said in this moment.)

Letting out another deep breath, Monroe nodded her head. "I have to help Avis." She turned to Cleo and Ptolemy, "Stay with Brady. He is a good person. You can trust him..." She looked into his eyes and smiled before finishing her thought. "I do."

☠   ☠   ☠

SEVEN AND A HALF MONTHS LATER
ABOARD THE VALENTINE'S KISS
YEAR 1 + 149 DAYS (MAY 29th)

Few words were spoken as Brady attached the collection of electrodes, wires, and tiny devices to Monroe's skin.

With the task almost complete, the tall and slender Nawerssian took off her glasses. Removal of the dark lenses revealed her red eyes, which were surrounded by an orangish sclera.

Unlike prior times in which seeing the red eyes caused him to flinch, this time Brady stood and smiled. "Should I hold onto these for safe keeping?"

She handed the glasses to Brady and asked, "Put them with my things?"

Brady often encountered difficulty finding the right words to say to members of the opposite sex. At this moment, he found himself struggling to reply with any more than a nod.

Monroe's lips turned upwards into a smile. "Shh. Do not say a word." She lifted her hand upwards. Her long fingers slithered down his cheek and momentarily danced through his stubbled whiskers. She leaned in and pressed her lips against his for a long kiss that seemed to tease she'd be ready for more once she was out of hibernation. Gesturing towards the tank, she explained, "That was so I can be sure you are thinking about me while you are out here and I am in there."

Brady started to reply, but Monroe reminded him that his instructions were to "not say a word." She placed a single finger atop his lips, then rested her head on his shoulder.

Som Obostoo looked to ensure that all involved remained on schedule. "It is important that we place each of you in life suspension in close proximity. Doing so will maximize the believability of the virtual setting."

As she lifted her bulbous head off his muscular shoulder, Monroe gave Brady's earlobe a playful nibble. Shortly after doing so, she whispered, "If you suspect the cyborgs intend to harm us—or you, for that matter—pull me out of the tanks. It is imperative that you keep a careful watch on those cyborgs. Our lives may depend on it."

8: ...LOOKS JUST LIKE YOU

> *"In a week, this black eye and this busted lip will be healed up. Then the ladies will be falling at my feet once again. Santa Saws? That's a different story. No matter how much time passes, people will scream and run away every time he comes near!"*
>
>   -BRICK VANDERWAL *promo following his bloody match against SANTA SAWS at "Battle of the Barbarians II."*

SEVEN AND A HALF MONTHS EARLIER
INSIDE LIFE SUSPENSION TANKS - VILNAGROM-II
YEAR 0 + 244 DAYS (SEPTEMBER 1st)

"Storytime, kiddos... Gather 'round." Long Jenn Silva and Cocoa Freeman had gone into town to scrape up some food. Brady Emerson and Tavia Patton were assigned the tasks of gathering wood and starting a fire. As they did so, the fifth member of the group took a nap. Corporal Arnie Grayson, a veteran law enforcement officer, always volunteered to take the first watch. He'd tend to the fire and scan the area for potential dangers (or long-awaited help) while the others slept. Before his guard duty began, he would provide some late-night entertainment. Most of the time he did so by retelling the plot of one of his television favorites.

"I can't believe none of you ever watched *The Twilight Zone, The Outer Limits, Alfred Hitchcock Presents...*" the pudgy, fortysomething cop mused while settling into his seat around the fire. His nostalgic list of black and white TV programs ended when he shoveled a handful of stale pretzels into his mouth.

Cocoa wasn't interested in hearing him ramble on concerning this oft-raised topic. "Grayson, do we really have to hear you preach about the glory days of television every night?"

He held up his hands in surrender. "Okay... okay... Geez, you're a tough crowd..."

"We're just in a hurry to hear tonight's bedtime story," Jenn said, playfully trying to diffuse any tension.

That bit of diplomacy satisfied Grayson. He scooped a few more pretzels past his gullet, let out a cough, then settled into his seat to tell his tale.

"Tonight's story... 'Number 12 Looks Just Like You,'" he began. As he did so, the boob tube lover held his hands out, creating a rectangular frame with his thumbs and index fingers.

Cocoa jumped in once again. "Why do you always do that with your hands?"

Grayson was getting frustrated by Cocoa's frequent interruptions. "I swear! You're Statler and Waldorf rolled into one!"

Cocoa didn't get the cop's reference to the pair of persnickety Muppets. "Who?"

Jenn placed her hand on her friend's knee. "Hush... Let the man talk."

Cocoa defiantly held her hand up, just a few inches from Jenn's face. "No no no... I'm serious as a heart attack here. I wanna know..." Turning towards Grayson, she demanded, "Who exactly are Stalin and Orndorff? And what did *I* do to *you* to get compared to them?"

The cop couldn't believe what he was hearing. "*Stalin* and Orndorff? Are you joking?"

"He didn't say 'Stalin,'" Brady said, trying to join Jenn in the role of peacemaker. "Stalin was Russia's leader during World War II. A real bad guy. I think Arnie's talking about the guys that sang *Countin' Flowers on the Wall.*"

Jenn smiled. "Aww, Brady! Sing it for us. I bet you've got a nice voice!"

"Na, I don't... Trust me."

Grayson held up his hands. Attempting to regain the attention of his audience, he declared, "I'm not talking about Joseph Stalin. I'm not talking about the Statler Brothers. And I'm not talking about 'Mr. Wonderful' Paul Orndoff..."

Cocoa talked over Grayson. "I've heard of *him*."

"...I'm talking about Statler and Waldorf, the old, cranky critics from *The Muppet Show*."

This set Cocoa off once again. She jumped to her feet and took a few steps towards Grayson. She balled up her fists and puffed her chest out as she demanded, "Just to clarify... When you were comparing me to them, did you mean I'm old? Cranky? Or maybe I'm nothin' but a puppet to you? How 'bout I shove my hand and arm halfway up your fat butt and we'll see who's old and cranky?"

It became clear that Grayson would never get the opportunity to tell his story. "Oh, forget it!"

☠ ☠ ☠

EIGHT MONTHS LATER
ABOARD THE VALENTINE'S KISS
YEAR 1 + 169 DAYS (JUNE 18th)

Viv Mystova reached into her leather glove to grip the rawhide-covered ball.

Brady had packed both items (as well as a second mitt) into the single carry-on suitcase he'd brought after Monroe recruited him for his latest space adventure. Now, three weeks after the rest of his friends had gone into hibernation in the life suspension tanks, he found himself teaching a pair of Nawerssian Cyborgs the ins and outs of America's Pastime.

"Impressive," Brady remarked after watching the orb travel sixty feet down the corridor.

Viv Mystova had flung the ball to Som Obostoo... exactly like Brady had shown her. Exactly the same form. Exactly the same throwing motion.

"Teaching cyborgs to play baseball is easy!"

Viv Mystova nodded in agreement. "It takes only a few observations for us to learn how you want us to move our bodies. Then we communicate with our synthetics, applying the precise force and motion we want to implement. Simple cyborg mechanics."

Som Obostoo's return throw was not nearly as picture perfect. Her form looked identical to that employed a moment earlier by her fellow cyborg. But her throw bounced several feet in front of the target and skipped down the long corridor.

Her rubbery lips stretched downward in a frown. She gestured towards her throwing arm. Unlike the rest of her silver body, the arm was black. It was a makeshift replacement thrown together and attached by the other two cyborgs aboard the *Valentine's Kiss*. The emergency procedure became necessary after Santa Saws had torn the original limb from Som Obostoo's body during the abductions of Fireball Freeman and Kelly Ka-Pow.

She explained, "Viv Mystova and Zek Evrazda did the best they could with the limited resources we have available on the ship. I need to see a Cyborg Surgeon to replace my arm with one that is equipped with the appropriate nerve simulators. It is no easy task programing and manipulating the fibers that are used to transfer the neuro signals from artificial nerves to my brain. Until that procedure occurs, this arm is virtually useless."

Brady smiled and shrugged. Som Obostoo's explanation quickly eclipsed his understanding of physiology. "Well, you could try throwing southpaw. Then again, you hurl a baseball pretty doggone good for someone with no feeling in her arm."

Som Obostoo answered the young man's smile with one of her own. "'Southpaw?' 'Pretty doggone good?' Those are expressions I have never heard before."

"Stick with me. I'll teach you plenty of baseball lingo and all of the Southern Illinois figure of speeches…" Brady paused to consider, then correct, the wording of his last phrase, "…figures of speech… you could ever want to learn."

☠ ☠ ☠

TWENTY-FIVE YEARS EARLIER
SOUTHERN HEMISPHERE OF NA-WERSS
YEAR -23 + 347 DAYS (DECEMBER 13th)

A female Nawerssian slept comfortably in a hospital bed. The tight, lavender colored skin across her forehead revealed at least two things. The lack of scars or wrinkles indicated that she was a healthy young woman. The light purple skin tone meant she likely came from the southern hemisphere of Na-Werss. It was a hue that differentiated her people from their blue-skinned rivals from the northern half of their world. Both shades were the result of mutations brought on by centuries of exposure to dangerous levels of silver (and other metals) in the water, air, and dirt that surrounded them.

A cyborg stood over the young patient. Her outward appearance offered no clue as to her age. She could have been outfitted with her machinery on the previous day or eighty years in the past. Only someone extremely well-versed in the subtle changes made to her model would be able to garner any sort of guess at the age of the heart, mind, and eyes tucked behind her flawless mechanical shell.

With a broad smile and rapidly blinking eyes, this cyborg exhibited an uncharacteristic amount of emotion. Her uncontrolled fluttering of mechanical eyelids was the equivalent of crying. The minor malfunction was the result of confused neuro signals being transmitted to tear ducts that had been surgically removed years ago.

The young woman awoke. She reached up with a mechanical arm to address an itch on the top of her bald head. It took a moment for her red eyes to adjust to the light. Once she could see clearly, she looked up at her smiling "mother."

"It appears I survived."

"Yes, you did, Som Obostoo. Yes, you did."

"And the infants?"

"Both the male and female are in perfect health. You did a fantastic job throughout the birthing process."

A single tear rolled down Som Obostoo's periwinkle cheek. (Her tear ducts remained intact… for the time being.) "Mother, may I ask… What names were they given?"

"You know I cannot tell you that," remarked the woman who raised Som Obostoo, along with nineteen others, at Girls Academy 1120. "You should be overjoyed! You have done your part to extend the people of the southern hemisphere for another generation… on your first attempt! You will be cleared to receive your cyborg body. No more pain. No more itching and aching. You will be able to enter university and chart your course for the next phase of your life."

Som Obostoo was unable to mask her sorrow. "I know, Mother. And I mean no offense. I simply wish I could hold the children one time before they were taken away and placed in Academy for someone else to raise."

"Mother" placed her mechanical hand across Som Obostoo's upper chest. The action was intended to signify love. "I understand, Som Obostoo… It is better this way. Trust me."

☠ ☠ ☠

FOUR DAYS LATER
YEAR -23 + 351 DAYS (DECEMBER 17th)

The cyborg Som Obostoo knew as "Mother" was dressed in garments commonly worn by inhabitants from the southern hemisphere. Above the waist, her outfit closely resembled a form-fitting tuxedo vest and accompanying dress shirt. Other than the fact that her shirt was sleeveless—a conscious omission made to keep mechanical elbow joints from snagging in the material—the clothing looked like it could have been manufactured on Original Earth approximately two thousand years earlier. Below the waist, most cyborgs who adopted a feminine form wore only a bikini-like covering, along with boots and a minimal amount of padding over the knees.

"Please focus! Look through these images," the older female said as she scrolled through a series of holographs depicting various cyborg designs. "Your final transplants are set for tomorrow. Your sore and itchy flesh will be replaced with a glorious shell. You need only select which model."

Som Obostoo sighed. *This procedure is necessary to preserve my life.*

She tried looking at the images. *I will still have my heart, my brain, and my eyes. I will still be Som Obostoo... My appearance and my long-term health prognosis will be the only differences.*

Perhaps detecting that the youthful woman needed some guidance and encouragement, "Mother" offered some unsolicited advice. "Have you seen the newest Model 14? They say the 14-D-1 could surpass the Model 12 in popularity. Of course, I have always been partial to Model 12-J-6. I am a 12-J-2, after all. The improvements the engineers made to the shoulders, arms, and waist! I am envious of those that select the new Model 12."

Som Obostoo peered into her red eyes and smiled. *Model 12-J-6 admittedly has an appealing structure. But do I really want to look like Mother?* After a little consideration, the young Nawerssian asked, "What about the 10-P-1?"

The Cyborg Surgeon had entered the room. He was a Model 5. His baritone voice was a booming contrast to Mother's sweet tones. "I would caution against selecting that particular variety. The neck has been known to stick. It leads to delays in turning the head from side to side. That becomes a frustrating defect if you are placed in a profession that requires mobility."

"Doctor, what design do you recommend?"

"I agree with Mother," he answered. "The 12-J-6 currently is our most popular model. The twelves are most years. I may be biased, however. Three of my last four romantic partners have been twelves."

It feels like even the choice of my appearance is being taken away. With tears streaming down her face, Som Obostoo announced her decision. "It is decided. The Model 12… as close to Mother as I can possibly get."

"Excellent choice," the surgeon declared. "Get plenty of rest tonight. Your transplants have been scheduled for first light."

☠ ☠ ☠

FOUR YEARS LATER
YEAR -19 + 266 DAYS (SEPTEMBER 23rd)

Centuries earlier, the cyborgs of the south established three neighboring campuses for their university system. Once young adult females had successfully given birth to at least two genetically engineered children, they were allowed to complete their transition to a fully-cyborg body. Those scoring highest at Academy were enrolled in one of the three Universities: Cyborg Science, Cyborg Military, or Cyborg Art.

Som Obostoo had hoped to enroll at Cyborg Art. She aspired to study law, become involved in the Cyborg Senate, and hopefully bring about change to the archaic system that mandated the separation of children from their birth parents so they could be raised by the Communal Academies. *Our ancestors wrote of love, trust, and loyalty. Now those concepts are completely foreign to most of my people.*

Unfortunately, her scores revealed that she was far more proficient in Mathematics and Geometry than Communication and Legal Principles. As a result, she was directed to enroll at Cyborg Military so she could study Navigation.

Homework for Som Obostoo involved standing within a three-dimensional holographic star chart. She was to calculate how much interplanetary travel time a Cyborg Star Cruiser could save by using the slingshot propulsion method around various asteroids, planets, and stars in nearby systems.

Repeated distractions came in the form of sounds of nearby children at play. She spoke the command "Hide Star Charts." Once the holographs disappeared, she stepped to look out the window of her dormitory room.

Som Obostoo saw a female. She was an older Model 12, not unlike the one she knew as "Mother." This Model 12 was hurrying a group of Academy girls across the Cyborg Military campus.

The eldest among the young students had received their first transplants. For the time being, their only mechanical parts were their arms and legs. It would not be long, however, before they would undergo an implantation procedure in which they received embryos that were crafted in a nearby lab.

Thank the Original Creator that I was directed to study Navigation. It would be terrible if I was forced to work in Reproductive Sciences!

A second look out her window revealed that there was a degree of panic surrounding the students as they crossed the campus. The Academy Mother had stopped to check on the stragglers lagging towards the end of the pack of young girls. She frantically waved her arms as she tried get the smallest of her charges to pick up the pace.

Though she wanted to, Som Obostoo could not look away. *That girl is the right age... For all I know, she could be one of the children I carried in my womb.*

A low whistle and the words "Viv Mystova" buzzed in Som Obostoo's ear. The radio transmission was designed to alert the cyborg that another was nearby. It also announced the identity of the individual that was approaching. This was a necessary feature in allowing the cyborgs to recognize and distinguish between various beings that shared the same design.

A split second later, the Model 10 burst through the door. "I have been trying to reach you. Why did you not answer? More importantly, why are you still here? Have you not heard the news?"

"What news?"

Following the twist of two digits on her mechanical hand, a plate covering Viv Mystova's left forearm rotated upwards. This created a dark background and a small platform for the display of a holographic media transmission.

The new arrival spoke the command "Play live broadcast: Cyborg Underground."

"Cyborg Underground?" Som Obostoo was alarmed. "We can receive serious disciplinary action for viewing an unauthorized broadcast. Cyborg Underground is…"

"Please! Be silent and watch!"

☠   ☠   ☠

THIRTY MINUTES EARLIER

The three Cyborg Universities converged at a site known as the Union. Dozens of students gathered at the Union Amphitheater to hear Roq Izcoogin issue his latest proclamation against the Cyborg Government.

The radical Roq Izcoogin wore a Model 1 shell. The Model 1 was by far the least selected variety of all eight male options. Though a few cyborgs viewed the original design as "classic," the vast majority detested it as a reminder of the hideous creatures from which they had evolved.

"Many of you look at my mechanical body, and your fleshy minds instantly jump to the conclusion that I am a barbarian. I ask you this… What do we really know of the barbarians of Original Earth?"

After a pause for effect, Roq Izcoogin continued. "Simply put, the only things we truly know of the O.E. barbarians are what those at the top of the Cyborg Government have permitted us to know. We have been told 'They were hairy beasts who spent all of their time filling their stomachs and feeding their primal sexual desires. They were ignorant monsters who obeyed only one law: Kill or be killed.'"

Roq Izcoogin threw in a lengthy pause. He looked down, as if considering whether he dared make his next point. "What if I told you of another group of ignorant monsters? Those that created hundreds of rules and regulations and decrees that eliminated choice, forcing innocent girls to carry fetuses crafted in a laboratory…"

This time the speaker's stop was unscripted. An Academy Mother dragged the oldest of her charges away from what quickly was becoming a public spectacle. She forced them to join the rest of the girls from the Academy as she led their hurried departure from the campus.

"I feel such anguish for those young ones. They trust their 'Mother.' They have been forced to follow this horrible system that is said to have been created in the name of preserving our people. They never think to ask if there are other sinister reasons that the Cyborg Government has for removing their choice, and later their autonomy! They never think to ask if we are a people who even deserve to live on for another generation!"

The crowd grew louder throughout the impassioned speech. A few dozen spectators soon became a couple hundred. Some on the periphery wore clothing that made it clear that they were members of the Cyborg Military.

"We now have soldiers and perhaps government officials in our midst. Perhaps we should give them an opportunity to speak. I would like for them to answer this… Why are we fighting those from the northern hemisphere? We expend virtually all our resources warring instead of trying to solve the problems of pollution, famine, and injustice. If we were to work *with* those from the north, could we not solve at least some of these issues that divide us and rip our planet apart? Go ahead… Ask them. Unfortunately, they will not answer because they *benefit* and they *profit* from this never-ending cycle of war and destruction."

The spectators roared with approval. Those wearing military regalia withdrew to a safe distance away from the masses.

"What they do not want you to know is that the solutions to our problems are not here, but on another planet. The answers may take us…"

POP!

Roq Izcoogin raised his mechanical hand to the back of his head. His life support cables were no longer connected. Air, water, and blood sprayed the area behind him. A second later, the speaker's knees buckled and he sank lifelessly to the ground.

The Cyborg Military had silenced another outspoken radical. They had done so by detonating an explosive that had been implanted at the base of his brain during the final surgeries to complete his transformation from mostly flesh to mostly machine.

☠   ☠   ☠

THIRTY MINUTES LATER

By the time Som Obostoo and Viv Mystova had finished watching the video, the view outside the window revealed a scene of total chaos. The radio receivers implanted within the cyborgs picked up an emergency transmission. "Effective immediately: The campuses of Cyborg Art, Cyborg Science, and Cyborg Military are being placed on lockdown. All faculty and students must return to their respective dormitories and await further instruction."

Viv Mystova had no intention of obeying the directive. She grabbed both of Som Obostoo's arms, turning her so that she could look directly into her friend's red eyes. "Som Obostoo, you frequently talk of 'trust.' After what we just witnessed, can you say there is anyone or anything worthy of trust on this poisoned planet? I know of a group that intends to hijack a military space craft and fly far, far away from this awful world. They need Navigators. Come with me… Now… Before this escalates any further… before the order is given to shoot anyone who is not confined to their room."

☠ ☠ ☠

TWENTY-ONE YEARS LATER
ABOARD THE VALENTINE'S KISS
YEAR 2 + 118 DAYS (APRIL 28th)

The *Valentine's Kiss* approached the wormhole tucked away beneath the rings of Saturn. Eleven months had passed since Long Jenn Silva, Monroe, and six other members of the crew had entered hibernation. The journey through space was long enough for Brady to grow a full beard, but nowhere close to the two full years that was expected!

The cyborgs had crunched the numbers. Som Obostoo explained, "Following the anomaly surrounding the Eye of Jupiter, the slingshot around the planet gave us far greater momentum, thus much more velocity, than originally expected. As a result, we are arriving at the precipice of our destination in a fraction of the time originally projected."

The only response Brady could provide was an expression that indicated he was confused by the barrage of scientific terminology.

Rewording her explanation, Som Obostoo said, "More gravity around Jupiter meant that sling-shotting around the planet provided a far greater rate of propulsion than expected."

"Gotcha." Brady stood just outside the life suspension tanks. "You're certain I have to be in there during the trip through the wormhole?"

"If you want to keep your teeth, you do." Som Obostoo offered a reassuring squeeze of his hand. "Take it from me. Keep as many of your original body parts as possible. Besides, you have nice teeth. Please… go into life suspension."

He smiled and nodded. His acquiescence came even though he was not a big fan of the purple goo or the fantasy worlds that existed inside the tanks.

The cyborg momentarily stopped affixing wires to the young man's chest. "You understand that things may be different when you see your friends again? Things between you and Jenn… Things between you and Monroe?"

"Why would they be different?"

"They will be, Brady Emerson. Time continues to move forward. Intelligent beings can attempt to thwart that with wormholes, time travel, and life suspension. Flesh can go back. Machines can go back. Our minds cannot… Our minds keep traveling forward with the passage of time. That's true whether we hail from Original Earth, Na-Werss, or anywhere in between."

Som Obostoo paused long enough to assess if her explanation was sinking in. "In your mind, in my mind, we are always going forward. Then we cross paths with others who also believe they are going forward. Our minds refuse to go back. Forward progress would be upset. Everything made by our Original Creator would be corrupted... Because we cannot go back, things *will* be different. The days and weeks and months continue to press on."

"That's some philosophy that's a little bit above my paygrade," Brady admitted, using another phrase that may have been unfamiliar to Som Obostoo. "I don't know what to say."

Though she—like all Nawerssian Cyborgs—typically would have taken great time to double and triple check each connection, Som Obostoo hurriedly finished preparing Brady for his foray into life suspension. She repeatedly turned her head away from him, hoping he would not see the rapid fluttering of her mechanical eyelids.

As her friend was being lifted into the tank, Som Obostoo finally responded. In a voice just above a whisper, she told him, "Do not say anything, Brady Emerson. Simply remember that you will always be able to trust me."

9: TRAINING MONTAGE

"In this business, if you're not moving forward, you're sliding back. That's why I train nonstop. That's why I work my butt off every single day. It's the reason I stay one step ahead and why I'll remain on top of the wrestling universe."

-LONG JENN SILVA *promo given prior to her AWWA Women's Championship defense against VOODOO DUBOIS."*

ELEVEN MONTHS EARLIER
INSIDE LIFE SUSPENSION TANKS – VALENTINE'S KISS
YEAR 1 + 150 DAYS (MAY 30th)

Jenn sat at the end of a wooden pier. She dangled her legs over the side, watching as the ocean waves occasionally climbed high enough to cover the tops of her feet. She smiled... then immediately felt guilty for doing so.

Armstrong took soft steps as he approached. He wasn't trying to sneak up on her. He simply didn't wish to disturb Jenn if she was deep in thought.

"Do you mind if I join you?"

The pirate gestured to a spot at her side. "It's a free country. Or maybe a depiction of a free country created especially for our virtual world. I'm not sure which."

Armstrong didn't know how to reply to her curious response.

"I'm sorry," Jenn explained. "I'm in an odd mood. Mourning my husband. Mourning Cocoa. Even mourning Avis, I suppose. Whatever I do these days, it's with the goal of trying to move on. But anything and everything trips me up... Like right now I just can't wrap my head around how strange it feels to dip my feet in water that I expect to be cold, but instead it's lukewarm."

"Ah... Do you wish to be alone?"

She shook her head "no." *Stop trying to be so polite. Say what you came to say.*

After a few moments of additional delay, Armstrong finally said, "I want to apologize for yelling at you."

"Really?"

"I admit it was rather rude of me to raise my voice. If I had the opportunity, I would take back the hurtful things I said, as well."

"Don't worry about it, cue ball... It's water under the bridge. We were all under a great deal of stress."

"That is quite magnanimous of you. Thank you, Jenn."

She nodded her head, then looked back into the water. "I wonder if there are fish in this virtual ocean?"

Her sudden move away from the topic of conversation rattled the Nawerssian. His people had no idea how to respond to non sequiturs. Jenn's musing about fish had the effect of taking the Explorer off script. Because of this, he opted to sit in silence... at least for a moment.

Armstrong had ventured down the pier for another reason. His apology was only one of the pieces of unfinished business he had with Jenn. He eventually got around to explaining, "I must confess, I have ongoing concerns. I have told you about my history with Jagger, and yet it seems that you are spending a lot of time with him. Please help me understand why that is."

Jenn exhaled. "You're not going to let us sit here quietly, are you?" She continued looking at the ocean waves as she searched for the best way to frame her answer. "The long and short of it is that I've got daddy issues. Don't quote me on that or I'll deny I ever said it. The truth? My father split the moment he found out my mom was pregnant with me. She was sixteen. He was twenty-four or twenty-five at the time. Not exactly legal in the State of Florida... I saw him two or three times that I remember. Once he bought me a pair of shoes and some dresses that were way too small. Last time I saw him I was ten, maybe eleven. He threw a big fit because my mom wouldn't let him take me to the mall for the day. He wanted us to see a movie, eat at the food court, and maybe buy some clothes that actually fit. My mom was worried he would try to kidnap me, so she threatened to call the cops."

Her voice trickled off. The luchadora refused to shed any tears... *Not for that man.*

"I am truly sorry for you."

"Don't be. I never asked for anybody's pity. My mom and I got along just fine when I was young. Then she fell in love—I guess—and married another guy. *Josh... Josh O'Malley.* They had a baby. After that, I was treated like an annoying reminder of the biggest mistake my mom ever made in her life."

Armstrong offered no response.

This time Jenn filled the void. "I don't think she was ready to deal with a teenager. She wasn't trying to be mean. For her it became easy to say, 'Fix yourself one of those hot sandwich things in the microwave. I've got to feed the baby and put her down for a nap.'" She looked down towards the virtual waters once again, then continued her longwinded story. "When she was talking to me, my mom always referred to her as 'the baby.' Never 'your sister.' Never 'Avery.' I honestly don't know why... but to a thirteen, fourteen-year-old girl, it felt like my mom didn't want to acknowledge that my sister and I were related in any way."

Armstrong nodded, continuing to sit in silence.

So much for peace and quiet. Now I can't shut up.

"Me and Jagger? I suppose he's the latest father figure in my life. Like I said, *'Daddy issues.'* I've always looked for advice from older men or even older women. As long as they're in positions of authority, I'm a sucker for listening to what they have to say. That's why I was so close to my first wrestling coach, Manny Vargas. Then there was Tigresa Roja, and Fireball Freeman... now there's Jagger. I promise I won't let him turn me into a monster. But he has been a good friend. He sees things in me that I never even saw in myself. Does that help you understand?"

☠ ☠ ☠

TEN YEARS EARLIER
KISSIMMEE, FLORIDA
YEAR -9 + 106 DAYS (APRIL 16th)

Eight o'clock on a Tuesday morning. Jenn normally would have been going to school at this hour. With her mother signing the appropriate paperwork to complete her withdrawal from the attendance roles, the sixteen-year-old was free to chase her new dream of becoming a professional wrestler.

The young woman rode her bicycle up to a rundown building. The cold structure once housed a garage that specialized in brakes and mufflers. There wasn't a sign on the wall (or even a laminated 8½ x 11 sheet of paper taped to the door) to announce that the facility now housed a gym.

After locking her bike to a pole, Jenn threw her backpack over her shoulder and headed towards the door. Now, instead of containing books, the pack held a change of clothes and brand new flat-soled wrestling shoes.

A pair of chubby Puerto Ricans were locked up in the ring. They were brothers, but not twins. Both appeared to be in their early twenties. Neither looked like the type of dastardly monster that immediately came to mind when Jenn thought of the typical professional wrestler.

Manny barked instructions from his vantagepoint on the outside of the ring. The heavier of the two brothers (Hector) slung the lighter one (Edgar) by his arm, forcing him against the ropes before bounding back towards him.

Manny shouted, "Down!"

Hector dropped face down, flat on his stomach. This action allowed Edgar to hop over him on his way to the opposite rope.

"Up!"

Hector struggled to return to a standing position. Momentum was working both for and against Edgar. He could not stop. He crashed into his brother, and they toppled onto the canvas beneath them into a sweaty heap.

"Alright, that's enough. Hit the showers!"

As the brothers were gathering their things, four other prospective wrestlers—three males and the meanest looking woman Jenn had ever laid eyes on—stepped through the door marked "Locker Room."

Though he was still sucking in air, Hector gestured towards Jenn and asked. "Hey, Manny... who's the kid?"

"*This*... is my new star protégé. I was thinking about calling her Sling Blade. I haven't made up my mind, though. She's much prettier than Billy Bob Thornton."

"You never game *me* a ring name."

Manny slapped Hector on the back. "That's because the main reason you're here is so you don't balloon up to 350 pounds. You might jerk the curtain for some fly by night Central Florida promotion, but not this young lady... Mark my words, she's gonna be world champion someday."

The woman amongst them scowled. "April Fool's Day was two weeks ago, Coach. She don't look that tough to me." The angry wrestling student marched past Jenn. As she did so, she slowed and tilted her head to make sure that the newcomer could read the words "Bad Bitch" tattooed across her throat. "Lookin' forward to sparring with you, rookie."

"That's enough, B.B.!" Manny interrupted. "Sling Blade, you got three minutes to get your shoes changed and your scrawny butt into this ring."

☠ ☠ ☠

THREE HOURS LATER

Manny walked into the tiny office just off the gym. The wall was lined with autographed pictures of wrestlers. Some were legends in the industry; others were lesser known to the masses, but still held a special place in his heart.

Jenn was planted in the seat across from Manny's cluttered desk. The rickety wooden chair was lined with cushions that were once an obnoxious shade of orange. After years of having sweaty, smelly wrestling wannabees resting in the seat, the fabric now looked more brown than orange.

The teenager paused the DVD when her new coach stepped into the room. A pair of masked grapplers were frozen on the television screen.

"Almost done with the video?" Manny asked. He followed the same script on the first day with each new protégé: Two hours of rigorous (and seemingly pointless) workouts, followed by an hour of viewing hand-selected wrestling clips. He could tell a lot about a new student based on their attitude at the end of the three hours.

"Yeah, I actually finished it a few minutes ago. This match was my favorite. I decided to go back to watch it again. I hope that's okay."

Manny smiled. "Estrella Bella and Tigresa Roja… In certain parts of Mexico, they are a couple of household names."

"I like their style… So much flash! Much more aggressive, much more exciting than some of the other matches you picked out."

"You like Lucha Libre?" He was still smiling when he caught a glimpse of Jenn's shoulder blades. Running the ropes had left her delicate skin bruised and bloodied. "How's your back?"

She turned her head, trying unsuccessfully to look over her own shoulder. Wincing, she groaned, "My back, my side, the palms of my hands... they all feel like raw hamburger."

"I told you to wear a sweatshirt."

"It's ninety degrees outside! Besides, the wrestlers on the video weren't wearing sweatshirts. Some weren't wearing very much at all!"

"You'll get used to it. Your skin will toughen up. Until it does, wearing a sweatshirt will provide a little more protection. You might want to think about gloves next time, too... There is going to be a next time, right?"

"Hell yeah. I'm ready to get back in the gym for my next lesson."

"Love the enthusiasm... ¡*Venga conmigo!*" he said, motioning for her to follow him.

Manny carried a single sheet of paper and a beach towel he'd picked up at the gift shop next door for three bucks. He led Jenn into the locker room. The coach dipped his hand into a deep metal trough. It was filled with water brought down to arctic temperatures after he'd dumped in several bags of ice. "Last lesson for the day... The ice bath. It's cold as hell, but it's an essential step in helping your muscles recover. Stay in as long as you can tolerate it. When you're done, you can dry off with this towel. Remember, there aren't separate locker rooms here for the guys and girls. Strip down as little or as much as you like, then hop in. Once you're done, you can take this grocery list and start following my suggestions for eating foods that are clean and high protein."

Jenn looked at the sheet of paper, opting to wait until Manny left the room before she removed her shorts and climbed into the tub.

The ice bath took her breath away. "Ho-lee...!"

"What's that?" Manny called from just outside the door. Suppressing a laugh, he asked, "Is everything okay in there?"

She wrapped her arms around her chest. She hoped this would warm her enough that her heart rate would return from a violent thump to a normal beat. Not wanting her new mentor to think she was weak, she called to him. "Everything's fine. I'm probably just gonna chill in the tub for about a half hour… if that's okay."

"Yeah, that's fine. I'll be in my office."

"Thanks for everything, Coach. I'll see you bright and early tomorrow morning."

☠ ☠ ☠

SIX AND A HALF YEARS LATER
EL PASO, TEXAS
YEAR -3 + 334 DAYS (DECEMBER 1st)

Tigresa Roja was the undisputed Queen of Mexican wrestling. She sought to expand her legacy—and pad her bank account—by exporting some of her country's top female talent to venues in Texas, New Mexico, Arizona, and Southern California. Though Lucha Libre wasn't a completely foreign concept in that part of America, Luchadora USA exploded by making it clear that the ladies possessed some impressive wrestling chops, as well!

Jenn was still being billed as "Lady Pirata" when she first signed with the upstart promotion. Since she was usually billed as a *rudo* (or heel), she often wore the black luchador's mask that Manny gave her at the beginning of her career. She was looking through the eyeholes of that mask when she told her new employer, "I'm thrilled to be wrestling with such a talented group of women. I'm excited about learning whatever I can from a legend like you."

Like Jenn, Tigresa Roja was serious about following kayfabe. She stroked the red and black faux fur affixed to the side of her own mask. Then she answered, "¡*Muy bien!* We still have some time before anyone else arrives. Let's get in the ring. You can show me what you've got."

The two women soon were standing face to face in the ring. Lady Pirata's hand rested atop Tigresa Roja's, while Tigresa Roja's rested inside Lady Pirata's. Jenn tried to choreograph their next move. "From here, I'd throw you off the ropes. I'd jump up and hit you with a huricanrana into the corner. When you come to your feet, you're leaning up against the turnbuckle pads…"

"No no no no no no." After uttering her series of "nos," Tigresa Roja stepped away and mumbled something to herself. The only word Jenn could decipher was *gringa.*

Jenn did her best to not become frustrated or take offense to the derogatory term. "Is there a problem?"

"No, no problem. Just a classic American mistake. I thought you'd been in Lucha Libre long enough to know better."

"Care to elaborate?"

"The hurricanrana… Do you know who Huracán Ramírez is?"

Jenn nodded. "I've never met him. But I've heard of him."

The seasoned veteran rolled her eyes. "Of course, you've never met him. He died when you were a child, perhaps even before you were born. Huracán Ramírez is one of the founding fathers of Lucha Libre. He was in movies. He is a Mexican hero. And… he is the inventor of the hurricanrana… Americans always think any leg scissors takedown is a 'hurricanrana.'"

"It's not?"

"No! A *'rana'* is a double-leg cradle pinning hold. The classic end to Huracán Ramírez's matches was a leg scissors takedown directly into a double leg cradle. When you want to flip me into the corner and call it a 'hurricanrana,' you are spitting in the face of Lucha Libre history."

Jenn signaled she understood by nodding her head. But she resented the suggestion that she was some kind of American ignoramus. *I wasn't trying to spit in anyone's face!* She waited a few seconds for Tigresa Roja to regain her composure, then diplomatically offered, "I guess you learn something new every day." She moved back into a wrestling posture and asked, "Ready to go?"

Tigresa Roja waved her off and exited the ring. "Not today," she said dismissively. "Go home. You need to brush up on your Lucha Libre history if we're going to bring our traditions to America. Go on the internet. Look up Huracán Ramírez. Watch clips from his matches. We'll talk tomorrow, Lady Pirata."

☠ ☠ ☠

ONE AND A HALF YEARS LATER
MEMPHIS, TENNESSEE
YEAR -1 + 188 DAYS (JULY 6th)

Fireball Freeman had asked Jenn and Voodoo Dubois to come in early so they could run through their match scheduled for later that night. The pioneer stood in the center of the ring. He was dressed in his black wrestling boots, gray sweatpants, a white tank top, and his trademark straw fedora.

Spotting his attire, Voodoo called out in her phony Haitian accent, "Firebowl, awe you wrestleen' to'nide? I did naw see yo name on dee cawd."

"Naw… I'm just here to coach up you ladies since Long Jenn Silva is a newcomer to All-World."

Jenn and Voodoo took a few minutes to run through a rough outline of their match as Cocoa had scripted it. Voodoo described the ending, "Den I spray her wid my Devil's Mist. I turn an' brag to dee crowd. Even doe she iz blind, Jenn sawprizes me wid a roll up and gits the one, two, tree."

Fireball rubbed his head and considered what he had just seen. "Not bad. That could work. Long Jenn Silva, tell me this… Do you have a submission finisher?"

She shrugged. Somewhat embarrassed, she said, "Not really. When I wrestled in Mexico, I'd occasionally use a sleeper or an ankle lock as a rest hold. But not as a finisher."

"Are you a quick learner?" he asked. "If so, I've got an idea on how to make your finish more believable… and just plain better."

☠   ☠   ☠

FIVE HOURS LATER

The crowd was enthralled by the back-and-forth match between Long Jenn Silva and Voodoo Dubois. Just when it seemed that Jenn was going to secure the pinfall victory, Voodoo found the strength to kick out.

A few moments later, the tables had turned and it was Jenn who was squirming to the edge of the ring. She grabbed the bottom

rope, which prompted the referee to instruct Voodoo to break her cloverleaf submission hold.
  The post-apocalyptic pirate looked ripe for the kill. Voodoo moved in to spit her blinding Devil's Mist into her eyes. Long Jenn Silva ducked out of the way, however, and the mysterious red spray covered the face of the ref.
  Voodoo was shocked to have temporarily blinded the official. Jenn took advantage of the momentary distraction. She leaped forward, wrapping her legs around the neck of her opponent in a perfect headscissors. Her weight and her momentum caused the witchdoctor to slump forward. While leaving her left leg wrapped over Voodoo's head, she dropped her right leg down, contorting her body and twisting her leg like a grapevine around her opponent's. This move—known as an "Octopus Hold" or sometimes a "Black Widow"—was designed to inflict pain across the neck, chest, and abdomen. Voodoo struggled to stay on her feet while supporting her own weight and all of the luchadora's, as well. Jenn seized the opportunity to grab her foe's right arm and yank back.
  With tremendous pressure being applied to her shoulder, Voodoo had no choice but to submit. Jenn didn't break the hold, though, because the blinded referee had not seen her opponent tap out.
  Unable to stand the pain one more second, Voodoo cried out, "I geeve up! I qweet!"
  The ref heard this and waved his arms as a signal for the timekeeper to ring the bell.
  The crowd roared with approval. The ring announcer declared, "Here is your winner, by submission, Long Jenn Silva!"

☠ ☠ ☠

TWO YEARS LATER
INSIDE LIFE SUSPENSION TANKS – VALENTINE'S KISS
YEAR 1 + 150 DAYS (MAY 30th)

Those occupying the life suspension tanks opted to pass the time in very different manners. While Jenn sought extended periods of solitude, Monroe chose to use it as an opportunity to learn a new skill.

"Today you're gonna learn the belly-to-back suplex. Kelly, step into the ring and we'll demonstrate how it's done," Fireball said with an enthusiasm for coaching that he hadn't felt in years.

"You sure you're up for it, Pops?" the clown asked.

"You better believe it! Remember, we're in virtual reality. In here I feel like I could wrestle till I'm eighty or maybe even ninety years old! Now get in here."

Kelly Ka-Pow stepped between the ropes and immediately charged towards Fireball. She took a wild swing at him. He easily ducked out of the way. The momentum of her "uncontrolled" attack caused her to turn her body so that her back now faced the veteran wrestler. This made it easy for him to wrap his right arm around her waist. With his left hand positioned against her hamstring, Fireball leaned backwards and lifted her off the mat. After holding her suspended in midair, he plunged backward. The move forced Kelly to land flat on her back, while Fireball twisted his body at the last second so that he landed on his side.

Kelly flopped around, writhing in fictitious pain.

Shocked, Monroe covered her mouth. Then she climbed into the ring to check on her seemingly injured friend.

"Just sellin' the move, kid," Kelly said to the Nawerssian. Then she squeezed Monroe's blue nose. The jokester made an obnoxious "Honk! Honk!" sound effect to assure the alien that it had all been part of the act.

Monroe laughed and admitted, "I feel like such a fool. I know we are in VR. And I know your style of wrestling is fake. Two layers of fiction, and it fooled me anyway!"

Fireball sprang into a standing position. He pointed a finger in the alien's face and reminded her, "Never say wrestling is *fake*. Where I'm from, that's the F-word that'll get you in hot water. Got it?"

Monroe nodded.

"Now let's see you try it. Your first belly-to-back suplex."

☠ ☠ ☠

ELEVEN MONTHS LATER
YEAR 2 + 118 DAYS (APRIL 28th)

Kelly Ka-Pow grabbed a handful of the auburn locks that had been surgically implanted into Monroe's scalp. "Watch the hair!" Fireball shouted as he played the role of referee for this match.

The clown complied, but not without voicing a couple of complaints towards the man who wore the striped shirt... and not before she gave one more tug to the Nawerssian's locks.

Monroe snarled. Then she retaliated by grabbing Kelly by her multicolored wig. Her revenge was complete once she yanked hard enough to drag the clown down to the mat.

"That's great!" Fireball shouted, momentarily leaving his current assignment and slipping back into the role of coach.

The alien didn't follow up the takedown. Instead, she looked off in the distance as a bearded young man approached. "Is that Brady?"

☠ ☠ ☠

The wrestling ring had been set up in the middle of a downtown plaza. Banners advertised a fictitious county fair, and even a concert by a popular country music artist from yesteryear.

Brady Emerson ignored those. He understood that those were frills intended to sell the reality of the virtual setting. But he wasn't there for sightseeing. He was there to be reunited with his friends.

His walk towards the squared circle was not without a delay or two. He paused on more than one occasion to stick his fingers in his ears or open his jaw as wide as possible. The actions were done in an effort to clear up his clouded hearing.

"You have fluid in your ears because you just entered the tanks," Monroe called to him.

Brady motioned that he couldn't understand a word she was saying.

The alien rolled out of the ring and jogged towards her dear friend.

"Start the count, ref!" Kelly Ka-Pow demanded. Despite the presence of the new arrival, she was unwilling to break character. She wanted Fireball to count Monroe out so the clown could earn a cheap victory.

Ignoring what was transpiring in the ring, Monroe wrapped her arms around Brady. She lifted her hands to the young man's face and made a flirtatious comment about his beard.

Brady, however, pulled away. He hadn't ventured into the tanks for any liplocks. He needed to tell the group— the entire group—that they were nearing the wormhole and that they were arriving significantly ahead of the projected schedule.

"Where's Jenn?"

☠ ☠ ☠

"Ye not be rasslin' with Monroe and Fireball today?"

"No," Jenn told Jagger as she joined him at the end of the pier. "Back on Earth, I worked out seven days a week, 365 days a year. Here? Every other day seems like enough. I told them I'd help out and train with them every other day. I figure that'll help keep my skills sharp enough... But today's a 'me' day. What about you? What are you doin'?"

The Captain looked out over the waters. "Methinks this virtual realm be missin' some wildlife. What be an ocean without fish? What be a pirate without a parrot to rest on her shoulder?"

"I'd like a parrot. Are there any on Oquezzi?"

Jagger laughed. "If there be, ye don't wanna step within fifty yards of the beasts. They'd be a hundred times nastier than Sareena... It's a rough and tumble moon where we be headed."

"I thought you said Oquezzi was 'safe haven.'"

"Safer than a black hole, I reckon. But it be home ta many a nasty animal... most of which walk on two legs. It be a good thing that Monroe be learning to fight and that ye be sharpenin' yer skills, too."

"Oh?"

Jagger finally looked away from the waters. Locking his one good eye in on Jenn, he explained. "Oquezzi be run by Hamurkan gangsters. They don't be all soft an' cuddly like ol' Poff and Mach. Hamurkans love ta fight. In fact, the most popular sport on Oquezzi also be the way they settle their scores... Tide Fighting."

10: LIGHT YEARS FROM HOME

"BORIS SPUTNIKOV! I have been to places you can only IMAGINE! I have survived battles FAR MORE TERRIFYING than your worst nightmare. When we meet in the ring, YOU WILL NOT SURVIVE... you will plummet into a nightmare THAT NEVER ENDS!"

-GALACTIC WARRIOR's promo given prior to his match with BORIS SPUTNIKOV filmed for "Wrestling's Greatest Matches: Volume V," a collection sold on VHS for three easy payments of $9.99.

NINETEEN YEARS EARLIER
ABOARD THE VALENTINE'S KISS
YEAR -17 + 38 DAYS (FEBRUARY 7th)

Cheating the Laws of Physics was no easy task. Fresh blood gushed down the front of Magellan's flight suit. Though his second trip through a wormhole was not as emotionally traumatic on the Skipper, the physical impact was every bit as extreme as his initial experience.

Four teeth fell out upon exiting the interstellar passage. He managed to get the bleeding from his mouth under control in a few minutes. The Skipper carefully placed the teeth in one of the hidden pockets of his flight suit. He hoped this latest voyage into an unknown solar system would lead to finding an intelligent being with the ability to implant them back in their proper place.

It took much longer to address the blood that flowed from his ear. He speculated that it was a ruptured eardrum. With most Nawerssians being born with two in each ear, his hearing would not be compromised significantly.

"That looks like *a lot* of blood," he worried.

Once the flow slowed to a trickle, Magellan changed into a fresh flight suit. Then he grabbed Jagger's clothing and hoisted the Captain's bulky prosthetic leg onto his shoulder. He hurried down Corridor 15 and gave the computer a series of commands. As expected, a mechanical arm extracted the General-turned-Captain from the life suspension tanks.

"Avast! Ye look like ye've returned from the depths o' Hell," Jagger declared as purple goo dripped from his nearly naked body.

A weary Magellan agreed. "Never again. As long as I live, I will never travel through another wormhole. Our Nawerssian bodies were not built to handle the strain. Where we stop is where I will stay!"

"Please don't be thinkin' of abandonin' ship before we find a habitable planet."

"You need not worry. We have arrived."

"Arrived, ye say? Tell me more, 'Gelly. Where exactly have ye dropped our anchor?"

☠   ☠   ☠

The two space travelers moved to the flight deck. From that vantagepoint, they soaked in the spectacular view from the port and starboard windows.

A massive, brown planet circled a nearby star. The world appeared scorched and barren. It was, however, orbited by a tiny moon that showed promise of sustaining life.

The moon shined a vibrant shade of scarlet. The ship's onboard computers reported that the ocean covering the moon contained potable drinking water. Because of the presence of many protein-dense, microscopic organisms, the appearance of those waters went from clear to crimson as they neared the moon's lone landmass.

"The onboard computer indicates that a full rotation of the moon takes approximately twenty-four hours. It takes exactly twice that long to make one revolution around its mother planet. The result is six hours of sunlight, followed by twelve hours of darkness, six more hours of sunlight, and then a twenty-four hour daily eclipse."

"That explains why she ain't burnt to a crisp," Jagger replied. "But adjusting to a normal sleep schedule on that floatin' red rock can't be easy."

"According to the computer, temperatures on the surface regularly exceed 130 degrees Fahrenheit (54.44 Celsius) during times of daylight. Temperatures drop to lows around 70 (21.11 Celsius) during the twenty-four hour eclipse... Additionally, the atmosphere contains sufficient levels of oxygen. The air contains no toxins of note and no significant pollutants. We should be able to breathe on the surface without any special equipment."

Jagger strained to hear Magellan's reports over non-stop chatter that came over the radio. "'Gelly, what be that infernal racket?"

"I am not certain. While passing through the wormhole, we were constantly picking up transmissions from all over the universe and throughout all of time. Since we emerged, I have not had the opportunity to run any diagnostics. Based on that awful noise we are hearing now, I suspect the onboard radio was damaged during the passage."

"Or could that 'awful noise' be communications from that red-hot moon down below? Do ye know anything 'bout her inhabitants?"

Following a quick verbal command from the Skipper, the shields that covered the stern windows lowered to give the pair a 360-degree view of their surroundings.

At least a dozen mighty spacecrafts hovered in the moon's upper atmosphere. Without enough room to set down on the solid land, the ships "docked" high in the sky with the occupants traveling down to the sandy surface in small shuttles.

The Nawerssians scanned the docked ships. They soon would learn that about half of the deep space cruisers belonged to a group of red-skinned gangsters known as Hamurkans. Nestled amongst those tremendous war machines was a single yacht. It wasn't designed for travel far from *terra firma*. Its primary purpose was to pamper the occupants with luxuries that were seldom included on crafts designed for battle.

Not far from the cluster of battleships was a pair of boomerang-shaped monoliths roughly the length of a football field. The craft were the property of feathered birdwomen that specialized in genetic engineering. They called themselves Davi-Loga.

Though much smaller than the others, three of the ships were smooth and sophisticated saucers. Those flying disks belonged to a collection of tiny grey aliens known as Valtayans, as well as the large array of robotic assistants that accompanied them.

"What is it they say on O.E.?" Magellan asked as he tried to recall a frequently recited movie quote. "'It feels as if there is a substantial likelihood that we are not in Kansas anymore.'"

Jagger laughed at Magellan's wooden delivery. "Don't be givin' up yer day job." A split second later, however, the Captain's weak eyes allowed him to recognize a hovering vessel docked near the end of the group of ships. "Well, 'Gelly, how do ye like that? Looks like our bastard brothers from the southern hemisphere beat us here."

The Skipper had no immediate response. Uncertain as to why Jagger seemed to consider the presence of their sworn enemies as good news, he waited for an explanation. When none followed, he finally suggested. "We could attempt to repair the radio, then put out a call… to see if the cyborgs will be hostile towards us." Knowing that Jagger wasn't going to like the next piece of news, Magellan hesitated before adding, "Of course, if the radio sustained serious damage, it may take a few hours to troubleshoot and fix the problem."

"Forget the radio. There be land below! Let's fill our packs and take a shuttle down right away. I, for one, would like to say

'Ahoy' to our new neighbors. Whether they be friend or foe, I wanna meet 'em... and plant me one good leg on solid ground for the first time in years.

☠ ☠ ☠

ON OQUEZZI

The temperatures dropped as the red moon's orbit took it towards the back side of the planet. "Let's get down there while there still be a bit o' light," Jagger suggested minutes before the pair of Nawerssians took a silver bullet shuttle to the surface.

Upon their arrival, they were instantly met by eight to ten blaster-toting giants with brick red skin. Each stood at a height just above seven feet and wore snow white hair woven in a single long braid.

Even though these aliens possessed enough muscle (or sufficient firepower) to separate his head from his shoulders, Jagger managed to joke, "Ye must be our welcomin' party!"

The security guards didn't understand.

Like all these red-skinned aliens, the guard closest to Jagger wore no shirt or other covering above the waist. The wardrobe choice allowed the huge being to display a collection of nasty scars that spanned from the middle of his chest up to his neck.

The scarred alien barked commands in an unfamiliar language. "Oquezzi gurlub vergoyush yurramopen!"

"Those don't exactly be words in me vocabulary. Do ye happen ta speak the Queen's English?"

The guard looked down to a small, computerized box on wheels. After a short delay, it provided a series of beeps before a mechanical voice "spoke" in the same alien language.

Jagger guessed that the purpose of the rolling machine was to provide some sort of interpretation. Sensing that it had not understood his request to speak English, the blue-skinned newcomer offered an alternative. "...Or how 'bout *Español*? *¡Yo no comprendo, señor!*"

Spanish had not worked any better than English. The guard again blurted out, "Oquezzi gurlub vergoyush yurramopen!" Then he pointed to the rolling robot and repeated, "Oquezzi gurlub vergoyush yurramopen!"

Magellan tried his luck. With his hands raised as a sign that he meant to impose no threat, he trembled as he said, "I am terribly sorry. We cannot understand what you are saying. It appears you cannot understand us, either."

The enormous alien glanced to the translator. Once it was clear the machine was not providing the output he was expecting, he grunted, jabbed his weapon into Magellan's ribs, and again repeated, "Oquezzi gurlub vergoyush yurramopen!"

Magellan wanted to shriek but didn't. He took a deep breath to help fight the urge to urinate. Then, he attempted one last effort to communicate. Mindful of the Cyborg Deep Space Traveler docked in the upper atmosphere, he spoke in the traditional language of his home world. "I apologize! Please! Is there anyone here that speaks Nawerssian!"

This time the translator bot recognized the language being spoken. A sequence of electronic noises chimed from the machine's speakers. A translation followed.

The leader then uttered his phrase for a fifth time. The bot followed with its translation in Traditional Nawerssian: "'Your armed transport is prohibited by Oquezzi Law.'"

Jagger leaned towards the translator bot and spoke in his native language, "We apologize. We will know better next time."

Though their conversation was constantly being delayed because of the need for translation, the armed hosts informed the new arrivals, "On Oquezzi, you call down first. Then we send a transport to fly you to the surface."

"Understood," Jagger replied, trying to keep his responses short and uncomplicated. "Now tell me this… who is in charge around here?"

☠ ☠ ☠

Half of the "welcoming party" remained behind to carefully inspect the Nawerssian transport. The others marched Jagger and Magellan towards town. At gunpoint.

The pirate aficionado tried to remain calm. He did, however, voice one concern to the Skipper. "Me worries there won't be much of a transport for the two of us to come back to. These red giants be lookin' for someone or some *thing*. They'll likely tear the vessel apart stem to stern."

The armed guard who had done most of the talking grunted and poked the end of his weapon into Jagger's back. The translator bot told them, "'No secrets! Speak in a language that the robot can understand.'"

"Under… stood," said Jagger. He hesitated mid-word as the end of the blaster was driven into his back once again.

"'Walk faster.'"

Jagger gritted his teeth together and did his best to keep his cool. Obediently omitting pirate jargon so the robot could perform its assigned task, he answered in Nawerssian, "My artificial leg was not made to walk on this sandy terrain."

The new arrivals did their best to march at a pace that was acceptable to their long-legged captors. Both Jagger and Magellan stopped in their tracks, however, when a pack of four-legged animals ran across their path. Each of the creatures was the size of a small dog, had facial features and a tail that resembled a fish, and blood-red fur that was severely tattered and tangled.

The beasts alarmed Magellan. "What are those things?"

"'Ocean mutts. Keep moving!'"

Jagger used the translation lag to scan and study everything in his vicinity. He watched the hairy animals scurry towards an incline that led to the nearby beach. Bright lights towered above and illuminated the area. They gave him the opportunity to observe some of the disgusting animals wiggling into crevices along the rocky walls that encircled the sands. Others nipped at workers wading in the shallow waters.

The Captain nudged Magellan and said, "Given those long, jagged teeth, I take it the mutts can do quite a number if they get ahold of ya with those chompers."

The workers were made up of several different alien species. There were several of the red-skinned giants that Jagger soon would learn called themselves "Hamurkans." Others were covered in green feathers and were said to hail from a cluster of watery planets called "Davi-Loga." A few short creatures covered in fur-lined, hooded coats were there; they were known as Valtayans. Many albino white beings (known as Flurroks) were present. They appeared quite jittery, constantly pushing wet, stringy hair away from bloodshot eyes.

The group also included a single Nawerssian girl. Based on the violet tone of her skin, Jagger surmised she had come from his home planet's southern hemisphere. She appeared to be between thirteen and sixteen years of age. This was somewhat confusing, however, because most females hailing from her part of Na-Werss would have undergone preliminary implantation procedures (the arms and legs she was born with would have been replaced by mechanical substitutes) by that point in their relatively young lives. Each of these workers had a collection of small mining tools attached to their belts. They used axes and handheld shovels to dig into the wet sand beneath the waves. Based on the presence of more armed guards standing along the stone walls, it was clear that the miners were not given an option to work somewhere else.

The head of security rammed his weapon into Jagger's back once again. "*Gravurpa!*"

"'Move!'" was the translation that followed.

"I got that one," Jagger replied. As he did so, he smiled in celebration of the fact that he'd already learned his first word from the language spoken by these scumbags.

"Do you mind if I ask you something? Do you have a name?"

Though the chit chat was delayed by the translation, the answer eventually came. "Of course, I have a name. Shut up and move."

"I know. I know. *Gravurpa!*" Then he reverted back to his pirate-ese. "Ye may not wanna tell ol' Jagger yer name. But mark me words… Learn it, I will. And then I'll cut out yer heart and feed yer scurvy carcass to these ocean mutts. That be a promise."

☠ ☠ ☠

The march through town continued as Jagger and Magellan were directed to turn inland. They walked past several clusters of makeshift huts. The structures looked as if they were thrown together with a little wood and many woven fronds from the large palms that towered all around them.

"This place did not look nearly as large from up above," Jagger commented (in Nawerssian so the robot assistant could understand). "My old body was not made for walks like this… but at least we got a tour of the low rent district."

The translation took so long that Jagger had nearly forgotten what he had said by the time he heard the scarred guard's response. "This is where gemstone miners live. If you are lucky, Zeal-O-Vay will put you in one of these instead of making you build your own."

"Keep tellin' yerself that," Jagger growled in his preferred swashbuckler's tongue.

The Hamurkan shouted an angry response. The translator reminded Jagger, "'No secrets! Speak in a language that the robot can understand.'"

Another turn took the group onto what appeared to be the main drag. Two rows of buildings faced one another. In between was a road of hard-packed sand, undoubtedly mashed down from millions of footsteps taken over many years. Some of the structures were crafted from stone. Others were made of the wood of the palm trees harvested from the miles of forest that stretched inland.

They came to a stop at the door of a large, wooden building. With music pumping on the inside, and a couple of drunken revelers hanging out of one of the windows, it was obvious this place was a tavern.

A grey alien greeted the newcomers in his native language. "Robba fobba bobba robba."

Jagger refused to waste a moment of his time. He used every second spent waiting for the translation to size up this seemingly friendly extraterrestrial. Only a tiny bit of grey skin was left exposed. The rest of his four and a half-foot frame was covered. Goggles were worn over his oversized, black eyes. A thick, blue cloth was wrapped over his mouth and nose. And a coat that was lined with fur went all the way down to his feet. (In the days and weeks to come, Jagger would come to learn that this was customary outdoor attire for those that called themselves Valtayans.)

"'Welcome to The Middle of Nowhere. Our humble establishment has exactly what you seek.'"

The pirate remained confident. "I could be wrong, but I think we are here to see Zeal-O-Vay."

The grey-skinned Valtayan did not need to wait for a translation. He understood Nawerssian but fired off a response in his native tongue. It sounded like "Fobba robba bobba fobba."

The security guards had no intention of permitting the conversation to continue. The scarred Hamurkan jabbed his weapon into Jagger's back once again. Not surprisingly, this action was accompanied with another command to move. "Gravurpa!"

The security goons paraded Jagger into The Middle of Nowhere. Though the patrons were still trickling in, it was obvious that this establishment was more than a simple watering hole. Aliens and androids performed striptease dances on raised platforms throughout the bar. Other robotic figures offered sexual favors for customers who paid extra to be seated at one of the tables.

The head of security gave a brief explanation. "Pleasure bots... Keep moving!"

They met another massive Hamurkan who stood outside an office door in the back of the establishment. He held up a hand, directing the group to stand still. He tapped his muscular red chest and introduced himself. "Nixx-O-Fee."

Jagger started to introduce himself and Magellan. "It be a pleasure, Nick Sophie…"

Not another syllable passed his thin, blue lips before Nixx-O-Fee silenced him. Then he took all the time he needed to carefully study the newcomers to the moon of Oquezzi.

"You are the ones that docked that big heap of garbage in the sky?"

Jagger took a moment before replying. He wanted to be certain that the gatekeeper was ready for a response. "Aye… yes."

"The two of you came down on an unauthorized shuttle. How many others are on your ship?"

There is no point in lying. He may possess the technology that would allow him to know the answer already. "None."

"Any robots, androids, cyborgs… that sort of thing?"

"None. Just us."

Nixx-O-Fee was skeptical. Still relying on the mobile translator, he warned the Nawerssians, "That is a very large ship for two passengers. It would be foolish to lie to me." He reached for the door. As he opened it, he added, "Let me be clear… If you lie to Zeal-O-Vay, it will be the last mistake you ever make."

☠   ☠   ☠

The man in charge was seated behind a large wooden desk. He mumbled something as he directed a green-feathered beauty to step away. She extended her wings, then wrapped them around her body as she exited the room.

With his office cleared of possible distractions, Zeal-O-Vay arose and stepped around his desk. This individual stood a full head taller than Nixx-O-Fee, the scarred security officer, and any of the other aliens Jagger and Magellan had encountered.

Zeal stepped forward, closing the gap between himself and the rest of the group. He looked to Nixx for a moment. Observing no signals from his righthand man, the gangster placed his meaty red hand on Jagger's face. He squeezed the Nawerssian's cheeks, forcing his mouth open. After he checked the blue man's teeth, he moved and did the same to Magellan.

Once the brief inspection was complete, he stepped back. Pointing to Magellan, he said something to his henchmen that would be translated "That one is the pilot."

He looked at Jagger once more. "You will work mining gemstones."

Though careful not to upset his boss, Nixx pointed out Jagger's prosthetic leg.

Even though he was confident he knew what the galactic gangster was saying, Jagger waited for the translator bot to perform its designed task. "Place him in shallow waters until the Cyborg Surgeon can give him a replacement."

Once he heard the full translation, the Nawerssian shook his head. "No."

Nixx whipped out a sharp blade and pressed it against Jagger's throat. "No one is to say 'no' to Zeal-O-Vay!"

Speaking Nawerssian so the robot could understand, Jagger replied, "That cannot be true. That would make Zeal-O-Vay a fool. And I do not believe he is a fool."

Nixx pressed his weapon until a trickle of crimson blood oozed from Jagger's neck. "Should I kill him in here? Or should I take him out back and make it hurt?"

"Neither..." The boss said. He was able to maintain his composure much better than his youthful, hot-tempered underling. "We do not know much about this creature and those from his world. I want to hear more from him before *I* decide if he lives or dies."

Jagger smiled. Once the translation was complete, he reached up and used two fingers to slowly push the blade a safe distance away from his throat. "As I was saying... Zeal-O-Vay should know that I am far more valuable than any of those wretches you have cast into the waters to mine... not particularly caring if they live or die."

This piqued the interest of the boss. "What makes you so valuable?"

"I am valuable because I am the only one on this hellhole of a moon that has ever set foot on Original Earth. I know that because your translator did not understand when I spoke English or Spanish, two of the most prominent languages on that lovely green planet... You see, I know the people of Earth. I speak and read their languages. I know all about their customs, their culture, their strengths, and their weaknesses. Something tells me that kind of information would be extremely valuable in a place like this."

"A place like this? This 'hellhole of a moon' is my home."

"I expect it will be my home, too. At least for a while." Jagger smiled again. This time he pushed Nixx's knife completely away from his throat. He didn't stop until the Hamurkan gangster held it at his side. "Those ships that are docked in the upper atmosphere... I am guessing that they did not come here to enjoy the beautiful weather on this moon. They did not come here to sample your wares, whether it is intoxicating liquors or robot lovers. These are stopping grounds. This is a place to wait until they journey towards Earth. Am I right?"

"I fear you may be far too bold and reckless, and your time here may be short... You are correct, however. Most of those who dock here are waiting for the appropriate time to travel to Earth. The time to slingshot through the belt of asteroids and meteors that surround the outer limits of Earth's solar system. We call that time

'The Slingshot Meteora.' And it is an occasion that does not often happen…" Zeal-O-Vay waited for his words to be translated. When Jagger offered no response, the Hamurkan gangster continued. "It sounds as if you have information that would be valuable to those who are docked here. If it is valuable to them, it is valuable to me… Especially if I can acquire that information first and can decide how it is disseminated."

Jagger resisted the urge to taunt the underling who had held a knife to his throat. "That is what I thought. That is why I said 'no' to working in the mines. Surely you have a job that is far more appropriate for someone in possession of a treasure trove of valuable information."

Zeal-O-Vay spoke a command directing the translator bot to momentarily shut itself down. Then he spoke to Nixx-O-Fee in Hamurkan.

☠ ☠ ☠

A FEW DAYS LATER
YEAR -17 + 44 DAYS (FEBRUARY 13th)

Magellan took unsteady steps. With a blindfold over his eyes and a pair of musclebound Hamurkans grasping each of his arms, the Skipper wasn't sure where he was being taken… or why.

The hard-packed sand beneath his feet signaled the nervous Nawerssian that he remained on the town's main path. He recoiled after hearing the red-skinned alien speak in English (albeit through a thick accent). "Step up."

After he climbed three wooden steps, the guards uncovered Magellan's eyes. He faced a well-weathered wooden door. "Inside," the Hamurkan on his left commanded.

Once through the doors, Magellan scanned the room. It looked as if he was standing in a saloon from Deadwood or Tombstone or some other gunslingers' oasis from America's Old West. Though his surroundings were unfamiliar, he was greeted by a voice he recognized. "'Gelly, get your rickety ol' bones in here!"

"What is this?" Magellan asked. "Are we in virtual reality?"

"Take a look around... I'm thinkin' of puttin' in a craps table, blackjack, maybe even a roulette wheel... We'll call the place 'Gelly's Saloon.'"

He couldn't hide his disbelief. "What? ...How?"

"Brokered a deal with Zeal-O-Vay, head honcho of all things important here on Oquezzi. He gave us this establishment that was once run by one of his rivals."

"He *gave* us this bar?"

"Ye wanna know the price? Simple. We keeps our eyes and ears open, and report back with anything that may be of interest," Jagger gestured to the pair of Hamurkans who escorted Magellan to the saloon. "I see ye've met Poff-O-Lan and his brother, Mach. They be one of the conditions of the bargain, as well. I wager they'll be keepin' their eyes and ears on us."

With a simple nod of his head, Jagger signaled for Poff to open the door. An instant later, the young, purple-skinned girl from the southern hemisphere of Na-Werss stepped through the door. She was a few inches shy of being six feet tall. Because this was a bit shorter than the height of a typical Nawerssian woman, Jagger estimated that this girl was sixteen years old. If she was still living on her home planet, Cyborg Surgeons already would have begun her transformation process.

She wore clothing made of a material similar to Spandex. Because the gangsters who ran the watery mines did not want their workers to conceal any valuable gemstones, the garment had no pockets and was made to cling tight to the body. Her forearms and the skin below her knees were covered by rubbery-tough, waterproof gloves and socks designed to protect the miners from the sharp teeth of the ocean mutts that frequented the shallow waters of Oquezzi.

"And this be Gal Lyxxidyr. 'Galixxy' if ye like… She was a stowaway on a ship hijacked by some cyborg students. The same ship we saw docked in the harbor a few miles above us." Jagger paused to gauge how Magellan would react to the introduction of someone who would have been seen as a mortal enemy back on their home planet. "Galixxy needs a place to stay, and a job that be better than mining in varmint-infested waters. Thankfully, Gelly's Saloon has both to offer."

☠ ☠ ☠

**NINETEEN YEARS LATER
ABOARD THE VALENTINE'S KISS
YEAR 2 + 130 DAYS (MAY 10th)**

Jagger had left instructions for his trio of cyborg crewmembers. They kept the shields raised over the section of windows that covered the back end of the bridge. The Captain hoped to recreate his own experience of seeing Oquezzi for the first time.

Those that had been pulled out of the life suspension tanks stood in awe as they viewed the reddish moon that orbited a lifeless planet.

Only after they had been given the particulars about life on the moon—including details concerning the strange pattern of daylight and darkness—did Jenn and her friends get a look at the twenty other spaceships that were docked in the lower atmosphere.

Expressions of amazement filled the room. "Unbelievable!" "Wow!" "Holy…!"

"Are those what I think they are?" Jenn asked.

"More alien vessels than ye can count? Aye!" Jagger responded. Then he added, "Oquezzi be covered with swabbies and scoundrels. Ye never know how welcomin' the welcomin' party may be. So yer Cap'n will be takin' a few down at a time. Me knows Poff 'n Mach be itchin' ta see their mates. They'll be on the first shuttle, along with me, and Long Jenn Silva."

Noting the chatter that came mostly from those that had not been selected, Jagger pulled Jenn aside. "There be room for one more on the shuttle. The choice be yer's. But be quick about it. We be leavin' soon as the sun goes down."

11: CUSTOMS

> "Customs. Costumes. I don't know if the words are related or not. But I do know this... When you see the face paint, the red nose, the crazy wig, the oversized shoes, and the squirting flower, there's little doubt... I'm dressed in a clown costume. I'm following all the clown customs."
>
> -Part of KELLY KA-POW'S rambling interview given after smoking a lot of marijuana at the Rock 'n Wrestling Festival near Denver, Colorado.

TWENTY MINUTES LATER
ABOARD THE VALENTINE'S KISS
YEAR 2 + 130 DAYS (MAY 10th)

Long Jenn Silva pulled Kelly to the side. "Go back to your sleeping quarters," she whispered. "Grab anything you might need, then meet us down by the launch tubes in fifteen minutes. We're heading to the surface as soon as the sun goes down."

Kelly shot an inquisitive look at Jenn. She ran her hands through her copper curls as she asked, "I thought Captain Jagger said it was just you and the 'A Team.' What gives?"

Jenn shushed the motormouth. "He said I could pick one more to go down on the first trip. And I picked you."

Kelly playfully batted her hand against Jenn's arm. "Aw, shucks! But why me? Seriously. What about Brady? I figured the two of you were about ready for a roll in the hay under normal gravity conditions."

Jenn looked past Kelly to see if anyone was listening to their conversation. Detecting no obvious eavesdroppers, she shrugged and said, "We've been apart for a few months. I don't know where his head's at after spending nearly a year with three sexy cyborgs. For all I know, he's moved on… Truth is, I picked you because you're my friend. I trust you one hundred percent. I've known you for a long time. I know you're good in a fight. I trust you've got my back… But I'm only taking you if you get a move on. You need to get your stuff and get to the launch tubes. And be quiet about it."

"I get it. I get it. Mum's the word," she replied at full volume. Before Jenn could make her exit, the joking jabroni grabbed her by the wrist and asked another question. "I see you're dressed in your ring gear. How 'bout me? Clown outfit or no?"

The luchadora smiled. Her pirate attire seemed to fit the occasion. *But Kelly's?* "I wouldn't. We don't know who we're dealing with. No offense, if I were you, I'd rather make my first impression in that Nawerssian flight suit than in rainbow-striped bellbottoms."

Kelly spoke much louder than Jenn would have preferred. "Point well taken. We'll save the clown getup for special occasions… I'll get goin'. See ya in a bit."

☠   ☠   ☠

ONE HOUR LATER
OQUEZZI

Once they reached the surface of Oquezzi, Jagger and his first batch of crew members followed a path very similar to the one he and Magellan took on their maiden expedition across the scorching hot moon. Their trek was delayed several times, however, when various Hamurkans stopped the group to greet Poff and Mach.

Jagger used each pause in the action to whisper various observations to Jenn. He pointed out an alien with skin that appeared to have been bleached white. "Flurroks… Most of 'em walk around stoned on a drug called 'Baynap.' They can't stand the heat here. Baynap brings their body temperature down, but fries their brains… You'll never see Flurroks out during daylight hours if they can help it. Like the rest of the inhabitants of this moon, they like ta venture out after the sun goes down. That especially be the case if there be a Tide Fight goin' down. And with as many Flurroks as be wanderin' about right now, it be a safe bet that a fight be about ta begin."

The Captain gestured to Poff and Mach. He wanted to take a detour towards the cliffs overlooking the beach. "That be where ye can get the best views of the Tide Fights at a safe distance. Hopefully there be room for us to see some o' the action."

Jagger led everyone to an opening large enough for the entire group to watch. "We'll look down from here. The fight will be below, near the edge of the water. During daylight hours, the waters be mined for gemstones by folks workin' under near-slavelike conditions. Then that same beach be the site of some o' the biggest parties on Oquezzi... once the sun disappears."

Besides pointing out the venue below, Jagger motioned for Jenn and Kelly to look at the clusters of aliens that had gathered nearby. To one side was a group of Flurrok males who came willing to bet on everything from the outcome of the fight to the direction the wind was blowing when the opening horn sounded.

A few Davi-Loga stood on the other side. Jagger leaned in and whispered to Jenn, "The birdwomen typically don't partake in watching the Tide Fights... not unless one o' their own be in the scrap."

Jenn had not enjoyed her encounters with Sareena, the one Davi-Loga she knew. "I guess I know which side I won't be pulling for."

"Not so loud, lassie," Jagger warned the post-apocalyptic pirate. "They were none too happy 'bout Sareena joinin' me crew. We'll need ta keep it under our hats that their fine feathered friend died at yer hands."

Jenn started to protest. She didn't get an opportunity to voice her objection. Instead, she was interrupted by a loud—almost deafening—humming sound that filled the air.

"What the hell was that?" she asked once the sound died down.

"Just watch," Jagger said. Then he pointed out a couple dozen animals that ran to escape the shallow waters. Most scurried about, seeking refuge inside the crevices in the rock walls. "Ocean mutts. They be filthy creatures. They like to hide in boxes. They squeeze themselves into cracks in the wall. And they be fond of coolin' off in the shallow water. Be careful. Their teeth be razor sharp… That sound ye heard was the Hamurkans getting' ready to shock the waters so the mutts don't interfere in the fight."

"Is the fight about to begin?" Jenn asked.

Poff stepped in between Jenn and Jagger. "Yes, it is. We cannot stay to watch. One of Nixx-O-Fee's men is here. Says we need to report in right away."

☠ ☠ ☠

"Welcome to The Middle of Nowhere. Our humble establishment has exactly what you seek."

For the first time since they had landed on the moon, Jagger determined that they had encountered someone who merited an introduction. Turning to the short, jovial alien dressed in dark, fur-lined robes, he said, "Ray Yandee, let me introduce ye to a pair o' lasses straight from Planet Earth… Kelly Powers and me First Mate, Long Jenn Silva."

"Robba robba."

Not waiting for a translation, Kelly fired back, "Back atcha, Hamburglar."

The jester's quick response caused the mechanical interpreter to blurt out an error message. Jagger explained, "It works best if ye wait for the bot to translate before ye reply. They need a bit o' time to work their magic… If ye talk before the thing be ready, the blasted machine can't keep the conversation straight in its tiny microchip brain."

The clown nodded. Then she raised her left hand and saluted the Captain. "Sure thing. I'll count to five before I open my mouth and start yappin'. That may even keep me from gettin' myself in trouble."

Jagger continued the introductions. "Yandee may look like he be nothin' but a doorman, but he crafts the finest androids and robots in this part o' the galaxy."

☠ ☠ ☠

FIVE YEARS EARLIER
TEXARKANA, ARKANSAS
YEAR -3 + 178 DAYS (JUNE 27th)

Other than their special events held annually on St. Patty's Day and Halloween, the Arkansas-Texas Wrestling Federation put on shows between April and September… always on the second and fourth Saturdays of each month. Their lone venue was an old drive-in movie theater just outside of Texarkana. Though they barely paid enough to justify showing up, Kelly Ka-Pow was good for at least one or two appearances a year.

Fans arrived early and placed their lawn chairs, coolers, and even small grills at ringside. Others chose to watch from the comfort of the cars parked in a row about fifty feet from the ring.

Jessi Quickdraw was a hometown hero with a cowgirl gimmick. The fan favorite had been the ATWF's Women's Champ for more than a year. She was gaining some buzz in the Internet Wrestling Community as a prospect likely to make the jump to a bigger promotion. They knew it was light's out when she locked in her cross-face chicken wing hold.

On this summer night, however, Kelly had managed to squirm over to the ropes both times Quickdraw attempted to apply her trademarked submission maneuver. It was a heated competition, and a chorus of "boos" rang out from the crowd. It frustrated them to think they'd paid their hard-earned money to see the challenger playing silly games instead of locking up with her opponent for a fair fight.

One angry fellow seated not far from the ring shouted out, "Quit screwin' around! Get in the ring and take the ass whippin' you deserve!"

The clown wasn't bashful about hurling insults right back at the paying audience. Eventually, though, she found herself on her heels again. Quickdraw was moving in for her big finish when the annoying blasts of a car alarm interrupted the match. The combatants paused and the fans jeered the offending vehicle. Both Jessi and Kelly leaned against the ropes. They momentarily united as they glared with disdain into the cluster of pickup trucks perched in the front row of the parked vehicles.

The alarm was coming from a heavily dented, old yellow Volkswagen nestled amongst the group of Fords and Chevys. Kelly placed her hand on her chest and offered an exaggerated apology. "Oh! I'm sorry! That's my little Slug Bug!"

She scooted out of the ring and walked past dozens of furious spectators. "I'm terribly sorry... This is so embarrassing... It'll never happen again." Once the joking jester made her way to her vehicle, she reached into her bra and pulled out a key fob. She repeatedly poked and jabbed at the tiny device. She pantomimed an exaggerated struggle to disable the flashing lights and blaring horn. After milking the joke for all it was worth, Kelly opened the door, reached inside, and silenced the alarm.

Finally!

The air filled with sarcastic applause. Kelly smiled, waved, bowed, and curtsied until the faux cheers turned to vulgarities and obscene gestures.

Jessi Quickdraw showed her displeasure with Kelly's antics, as well. She shouted, "Get your scrawny bee-hind back in between these ropes!"

"Okay! Okay… okay!" Kelly said. Before returning to the ring, she reached back into the vehicle and pulled out an oversized mallet. The foreign object looked like it was taken straight from the 'Test of Strength' game at the county fair.

She ran down to the ring, wildly swinging the weapon in her opponent's general direction. The defending champ had no choice but to flee the confines of the squared circle.

"Get back in here so I can clobber ya!"

Instead of awarding the match to Quickdraw via disqualification, the heel-leaning referee fired off the fastest ten-count in the history of the small wrestling promotion. "Here is your winner, as the result of a countout, Kelly Ka-Pow!"

The fans in attendance knew that their hometown favorite could only lose the title after a pinfall or submission. Jessi Quickdraw retained her status as Women's Champion. Even so, she was furious about picking up a nasty blemish to her won-loss record.

Water bottles and beer cans rained down on the ref, Kelly, and even the yellow VW. Once she was safely in the "backstage" area behind the towering outdoor movie screen, the clown remarked, "Thank the stars above that wasn't really my car! Otherwise, I'd be hoofin' it back to Memphis on foot... and I certainly wouldn't want to do that in clown shoes!"

☠ ☠ ☠

FIVE YEARS LATER
OQUEZZI
YEAR 2 + 130 DAYS (MAY 10th)

Without any further delay, Jagger marched the group to Nixx-O-Fee's office at the back of the club. The former henchman now occupied his boss's chair while Zeal-O-Vay spent most of his days lounging in his yacht docked several thousand feet above the moon.

Nixx spoke English without the need for a translator. "Jagger... Back from your excursion to Earth already? You weren't gone long enough for me to miss you."

"Aye. But long enough for ye to send a Davi-Loga ship to follow me."

"Guilty as charged. You slipped away before you had the chance to tell us how you got around the meteora."

"That back door be slammed shut now... Thanks ta yer trigger-happy friends."

Nixx held up his hands. He would never apologize. A gesture of truce was as good as Jagger could ever expect from the Hamurkan gangster. "But you are back... and it appears you brought friends. Are these lovely specimens from Earth?"

Jagger stepped forward and handed the new boss a tiny, holographic cube. "Here be an up-to-date manifest for the *Valentine's Kiss*."

Nixx posed a couple of the standard questions he asked all new arrivals. "Any robots, androids, cyborgs... that sort of thing?"

"Only three o' the cyborgs that left with me. Ye'll find the manifest be in order... Now let me introduce the first Earthlings ye have ever laid eyes on. Miss Kelly Powers and me First Mate, Long Jenn Silva."

Nixx stepped forward. He stood at a height more than eighteen inches greater than the women from Earth. The powerful gangster reached out and placed one of his hands atop each of their outer shoulders. After studying them for several seconds, he smiled. "I am very comfortable here on Oquezzi. But if all women on your planet look like you, I could be convinced to commandeer a ship and join the race to Earth."

Not wanting to draw the ire of this powerful man, Jenn nodded and politely replied, "Thank you."

Nixx noticed that the other woman remained silent. "Miss Kelly Powers, do you talk?"

Forgetting her promise to count to five before speaking, she opened the floodgates. "Usually, I use this piehole so much they can't shut me up. I guess I was just being quiet, soaking it in… and wondering what kind of monster profits by using slave labor in the mines, not to mention catering to customers who aren't bashful about bein' on the business end of pornographic acts with robots in here… Throw in the shitty weather conditions, and I'd say this place hits the trifecta for things I hate in a planet. No offense, but so far this lousy moon makes me wanna blow chunks."

Jagger attempted to step forward to diffuse the situation. "Me apologies. 'Tis been a long journey for all me crew."

Nixx tilted his head back and laughed. He looked at Jagger while pointing at Kelly. "I like this one." The red-skinned giant returned his gaze to Kelly, and said, "This is my home. I enjoy it here. I hope you, too, will come to appreciate Oquezzi. As far as the robots are concerned, I'm not really of fan of them, either. We *are* in business to make money, though. And we have many customers who prefer to seek satisfaction from Yandee's creations as opposed to real flesh and blood."

The Nawerssian stepped between Nixx and the women. He held his arms out and backed away from the Hamurkan. "We've takin' enough of yer time. We be headed to Gelly's if ye need me. Once the lasses be settled in, ol' Jagger 'ill take the shuttle back to the *Valentine's Kiss* to retrieve a few more members of me crew."

☠   ☠   ☠

THREE YEARS EARLIER
LOS ANGELES INTERNATIONAL AIRPORT
YEAR -1 + 267 DAYS (SEPTEMBER 24th)

It had been a long day and Kelly was in yet another long line. This one wrapped around with no end in sight. The Customs Agent rattled off questions like "How many people are in your traveling party?" and "You are the head of the household?" and "Are you traveling for business or pleasure?" and "How long will you be staying in the United States?" and "Would you mind taking off your glasses so I can take your photograph?" The inquiries seemed never-ending. Even so, the line continued to move at a steady pace.

As she approached the front, Kelly thought little of it when an agent nodded at one of his colleagues.

That same agent adjusted his reading glasses as he studied her CPB Forms. "Do you have anything else to declare?"

Kelly shrugged. She was returning from one of her two-week stints in Puerto Rico, followed by a weekend of drunken debauchery in Punta Cana. As far as she knew, the only things she brought back were her clothes, her wrestling gear, and the props she used to accent her gimmick. She shrugged and wondered if the agent was detecting the guilt she felt after having a one-night stand with a Portuguese expat on her last night in the Dominican.

The agent asked again. "Anything at all you may still need to declare?"

Never able to completely turn off her clown persona, Kelly misinterpreted the agent's suspicion as a cue that she should practice her improv. "Yeah. Here's my declaration… You can choke me till I'm blue in the face if I'm ever stupid enough to wear a thong on a twelve-hour flight again. That's gotta be one of the worst wardrobe choices of my entire life. I suppose you do dumb things after downing five or six Long Island Ice Teas the night before."

"Ma'am, this may seem like a laughing matter to you…"

Still oblivious to the potential gravity of her situation, Kelly continued, "No, not this in particular. Pretty much every aspect of my life is a joke. Sometimes if I listen real close, I swear I hear a laugh track in the background. You know, like on those cheesy sitcoms from the seventies and eighties?" Imitating a television announcer, she modified her voice to speak in a lower octave. "'*Kelly Ka-Pow* was taped before a live studio audience.'"

"Ma'am… please! This is a serious matter. Answer my question. Do you have anything else to declare?" It would have been obvious to all those in the vicinity that he did not want to detain her. "Perhaps Cuban cigars? You do understand that there are limitations to the amount of tobacco products that can be brought into the country?"

"Sorry, I know there's a line of people, and it's been a long day. It's just when I hear the word 'ma'am,' I turn around and start lookin' for my second grade teacher, Mrs. Oglethorpe…" It finally hit her. "Wait? Cigars? What are you talking about?"

Too little, too late.

"Please come with me, Miss Powers. You are being placed under arrest for suspicion of knowingly and willingly smuggling contraband into the United States of America, and illegally trading with an enemy of the United States Government."

"Wait... what? An enemy of the government?"

"Ma'am... Miss... Whatever you wish to be called... You have the right to remain silent. Anything you say may be used against you. Given that, if convicted, you could face a prison sentence of ten to twenty-three years, you may want to begin exercising your right to remain silent immediately."

☠ ☠ ☠

THREE DAYS LATER
IMMIGRATION & CUSTOMS DETENTION FACILITY
YEAR -1 + 270 DAYS (SEPTEMBER 27th)

The room was eight feet by eight feet. The cinderblock walls were painted beige and lined with a couple shelves of musty, old paperbacks. A metal table was positioned in the center of the room. Two metal benches were anchored to the floor on opposite sides of the table.

Dressed in a bright yellow jumpsuit, Kelly thumbed through a novel called *The Snowflake Killer*. She looked up from her suspense thriller when she heard the electronic locks begin to turn.

Her attorney, Carmen Chiu, was clad in a maroon skirt complimented by a black, silk blouse. Her hair was chopped short, with a few strands of gray intruding through the black. She looked down at her notepad. It contained the list of detainees she was scheduled to visit on this trip to the holding facility that also served as an immigration processing center.

"Kelly Powers?"

Though normally talkative to a fault, the wrestler could only muster a head nod.

Trying to put her client at ease, Ms. Chiu asked, "Did you find a good book in the 'library?'"

"It's mostly just trashy romances and Spanish Bibles... This one looks like it has potential. It's about a serial killer who never kills the same way twice."

"Why don't you leave it here for someone else to read? You can pick up a fresh copy on the outside."

Kelly's face lit up. "I'm gettin' outta this joint?"

Her attorney smiled and reported, "They are processing your paperwork right now. The case is being dismissed. You were fortunate that the resort in the Dominican located your wrestling gear... and an enormous hammer..."

"It's a mallet. A prop for when I'm in the ring."

"I was able to convince customs officials that you didn't knowingly bring those cigars into the country."

Interrupting once again, Kelly blurted out, "Hell no. Cigars are for pretentious old farts. What am I gonna do with five thousand dollars' worth of smelly cigars?"

"Sell them?" Chiu said, not allowing the impromptu comedy act to throw her off. "Thankfully, I was able to show them evidence of your discarded property and they agreed it was likely that someone at the resort planted them in your luggage when you weren't looking."

"Why would anyone do that?"

"My guess is it was someone who knew they were going to be on your flight," the attorney speculated. "It's possible that they planted them with the intention of stealing your bag once you passed through Customs. That way you assume the risk of getting caught bringing the goods into the country…"

"Or?"

"Or they'd seen you in action and knew you were a blabbermouth who couldn't control her tongue. They guessed correctly that you'd create a big enough distraction with the Customs Officers that they could walk right through with fifty thousand dollars' worth of cocaine strapped to their bodies… It's getting to be a fairly common trick employed by smugglers. Personally, that's the scenario I'd bet on in your case."

Kelly took a moment to let her attorney's words soak in. "Ms. Chiu, I think I'd be offended by that 'blabbermouth' comment if you hadn't just saved me from spending the next twenty years of my life in the federal pen… Thank you. I'll try to pick my spots better. I'll remember that stand-up is only appropriate in certain situations."

The lawyer laughed. "Good." It was as if she didn't entirely believe her client could live up to her promise of reformed behavior. "You should hold onto my business card… just in case."

☠ ☠ ☠

**THREE YEARS LATER
OQUEZZI
YEAR 2 + 130 DAYS (MAY 10th)**

Jagger did his best to hurry his entourage out of The Middle of Nowhere. He wanted to get everyone far away from Nixx-O-Fee before the gangster's curiosity and amusement changed to annoyance. If his mood swung, Oquezzi might not be the "safe haven" that the Nawerssian had hoped it would be.

As they made their exit, Ray Yandee offered a friendly farewell. "Robba robba fobba bobba robba."

"Keep walkin'," Jagger growled, making it clear that he was angry at Kelly for letting her uncontrollable urge to say what was on her mind get the best of her. His scowl also revealed that he was none too happy with Jenn for choosing the bodyslamming bozo as the fifth member of their party.

Everyone momentarily complied with his order. Then they heard Yandee's words translated into English: "I trust you ravishing creatures will return soon. Maybe next time you will be able to stay for a drink… and to show us a few of Earth's most popular dance moves."

Kelly stopped in her tracks. She spun on a heel and charged towards the Valtayan.

"Listen here, you goggle-wearing pervert. They might be mindless robots to you, but what's going on in there is NOT right! There are ethics and morals and values that we should all live by… no matter what godforsaken planet you flew in from! When you create machines like that, scumbags think they can do anything and everything they want… You know what that does?" She paused for a moment before realizing that it would take far too long for a translation. Somebody—Jenn or Jagger or perhaps someone from inside the tavern—was going to put a stop to this. She needed to unload as much of her righteous rant as possible. "It hardens their hearts! They become desensitized! It makes them think it's okay to treat real women and children the same way! You should be ashamed of yourself!"

Yandee stood speechless.

Help did come from inside the bar. One Davi-Loga dancer, then two more, stepped outside to investigate the commotion. Taleeya looked as if she could have been Sareena's clone.

The birdwoman's voice was melodic. "What is the problem out here?"

Yandee remained speechless. Though Jenn was tugging and pulling her in the opposite direction, Kelly felt the need to respond. "Don't you even dare stick your pointy nose in the middle of this, Tweety! It was your people that killed my friend's husband! It was your people who killed her best friend!"

Taleeya did not need to wait for a translation. She, like most of the Davi-Loga, had been learning English ever since Jagger and Magellan first arrived on Oquezzi. Still, she was confused by Kelly's outburst. She looked to familiar faces for an explanation. "There must be some sort of mistake... Yandee? Jagger?"

Kelly continued. "There's no mistake. You think you're the first Danny Lugo I ever saw? I bunked with Sareena for weeks..."

"Kelly, stop!" Jenn said as she tugged on her enraged friend's arm.

"Then one of your world's warships launched a blindside attack against our friends. Sent both ships and one more into a black hole. But Long Jenn Silva got her revenge! Drove a metal staff right through Sareena's chest! Feathers were everywhere! It was the coolest thing I ever saw in my life."

Taleeya glared at Jagger. "Sareena is dead?"

Jagger didn't know if the time was right to tell all of Oquezzi the particulars of the thwarted assassination... or even that there had been an attempt on his life, for that matter!

The birdwoman took the lack of a response as confirmation of Sareena's demise. The silence also fueled her suspicion that unsavory circumstances surrounded the incident.

Her soft, sweet tone changed to an evil hiss. Her black eyes fixated on Jenn. "You killed my sister?"

The pirate tried to walk away. Dragging Kelly alongside, Jenn replied, "We can talk about this later."

Taleeya coiled her body, then sprang into the air. Gliding, she quickly found herself standing directly in her foe's newly chosen path.

"My sister is dead. *I* will decide when we talk."

Jenn glanced towards Jagger. She hoped he would flash her a sign. The Captain was slow to decipher her reason for looking in his direction. This meant she was left to guess as to the most strategic answer.

She thought of the story Poff and Mach once told about the importance of fair fights. "We fought. I killed her. It was a fair fight... I stopped her from attacking a friend from behind."

Taleeya snarled. She whipped her head to the side and growled at Kelly, too. "It's obvious you do not choose your friends well..." Turning back to Jenn, she hissed, "You like to fight? I, Taleeya, challenge you two Earth women to a Tide Fight." She pointed towards one of her fellow Davi-Loga dancers as she said, "Areetha will be my second."

Jagger moved forward. He tried to separate the angry parties. "The tides be too high ta fight now. Ye will get yer fight. But fer now I'll be takin' these lasses outta the street and away from the angry mobs. Ye will see them again at the beginning of the Long Night."

The promise of a fight was enough the satisfy both the challenger and the collection of on-lookers who gathered in the vicinity. The group slowly disbursed. Some left only after they welcomed Poff and Mach back to Oquezzi.

When everyone else had left, Jagger pulled the Hamurkan brothers to the side. "Take the girls down to Gelly's. Don't ye stop for any reason. Get 'em inside and teach 'em everything ye can about Tide Fightin'. As fer me, I be headed back to the *Valentine's Kiss* to bring more of their friends down to the surface. I'm gonna need ta hurry if I'm ta get back before the sun comes up."

12: THE HARD WAY

> *"This ain't a game to me! While you and your sorority sisters were paintin' your nails at slumber parties, I was out there fightin' to stay alive. I served time in the pen. Steppin' in the ring with you ain't got me worried one bit."*
>
> -B.B. QUEEN *promo given prior to her match against* BRITTANI CHERRY *for the Everglades Impact League (aka EvIL Wrestling) Women's Championship.*

TEN YEARS EARLIER
SAN JUAN, PUERTO RICO
YEAR -8 + 114 DAYS (APRIL 24th)

Compared to most of those who trained and wrestled in Puerto Rico, Jenn was an angel. There was one young grappler, however, who had been tempting her to go astray more and more often.

"This is the Island of Enchantment! Sun, fun, and pleasure everywhere you go. Give in. Puerto Rico has a magnificent spell. Embrace your wild side. Have a little fun!"

Yaniel Víbora was a chiseled young man in his early twenties. He grew up in the streets of San Juan and chose the name "Víbora" because it was Spanish for "Viper." When in the ring, Yaniel typically wore a mask covered with green scales and matching wrestling tights. He was known for his arsenal of high flying moves and his ability to slither out of submission holds. His was a rising star in his homeland. Lately, he had been teamed with Jenn (aka "Lady Pirata") in several intergender tag team matches.

As had become their routine, Jenn and Yaniel spent the last few minutes of practice sparring with each other. Manny half-heartedly looked on. Though he was seated in the second row of steel chairs that faced the ring, their coach was distracted by frequent texts and calls coming from one of his former students.

Manny looked up and quickly decided that Yaniel had lingered too long in Jenn's side headlock. He may have been catching his breath. But it was much more likely that he was savoring the opportunity to rest his face against Jenn's chest. (Either way, it would have been a lousy display if such a hold would have been implemented in front of a paying audience.) The coach shouted, "Keep moving!"

The students complied without delay. Yaniel called out "Wrist lock!" Jenn grabbed the viper by his wrist and gave it a convincing twist.

The viper grimaced, selling the move to a non-existent audience. He followed this up by gingerly walking towards the corner. Then he hopped onto the second turnbuckle pad, sprang up from there and twisted his body until he was momentarily balancing across the top rope. A front flip back onto the canvas left him squatting at the feet of his opponent. The reversal turned into an offensive move when he tugged at Jenn with his now untwisted arm. The maneuver sent her sprawling onto the mat!

When the two locked up once again, Jenn whispered, "That was pretty cool."

"Now you try it."

Jenn hit a snag in each of her first two attempts. "That jump-twist move... It's hard to stick the landing and balance on the top rope!"

"Try it again. I know you can do it, *cariño*."

The third time was a charm. Jenn executed every step of the move with precision. She finished off by slinging Yaniel to the canvas. Pleased with her success, she looked to the row of chairs for Manny's reaction.

A frown crept across her face once Jenn discovered that her mentor had left the room.

"Great job, sweetheart," Yaniel told his sparring partner. Unlike Jenn, he didn't mind the fact that Manny had left the room. No overly protective coach around to voice his disapproval.

The young viper seized the opportunity. He coiled his arm around Jenn's waist and pulled her in for a quick kiss.

☠ ☠ ☠

FIVE DAYS LATER
ABOARD AN AIRPLANE
YEAR -8 + 119 DAYS (APRIL 29th)

Jenn puckered her lips and made her best efforts to flash seductive looks into the camera lens of her phone. A shirtless Yaniel was on the other end of the videochat.

"I'm so excited for you! Your first match on the mainland!" he said. "And you'll get to see your *mami*! That will be nice."

"Eh," Jenn shrugged, "She says she'll be there. I'll believe it when I see it... We'll see who and what she picks if Josh suddenly gets a craving for Cracker Barrel."

Manny glared from the next seat over. He didn't like hearing Jenn badmouth her mother.

"I wish I could go and watch," said an enthusiastic Yaniel.

"What? And see me job out in under five minutes?"

Ever the kayfabe proponent, Manny despised hearing the details of a future match being discussed in public. "Shush!" he snapped at the immature lovebirds. "Better yet... Hang up that phone! We're getting ready to take off any minute."

Jenn looked around. The teenager hadn't been on too many flights in her life. Even though it *did* look like the attendants were almost done with their pre-flight duties, she wasn't ready to say good-bye.

Manny cut her off mid-protest. He grabbed her phone and barked at Yaniel, *"¡Adios! ¡Te pones una camiseta... ahora!"* (Translated into English: "Good-bye! Put on a T-shirt... now!") He poked a red button before tossing the phone back to his protégé. "Now put this thing in airplane mode."

☠   ☠   ☠

THIRTY MINUTES LATER

The plane was cruising at fifteen thousand feet by the time Manny cooled down. He removed a headphone from his protégé's ear and said, "Let's talk about tomorrow night."

Jenn was mindful of her earlier admonishment not to talk in public about a future match. This left her uncertain of what was safe to say with others seated around her. "Okay… shoot."

"As you were so quick to announce to the world, you're going to put over B.B. Queen."

"Why is that, again?" Jenn interrupted. "I know she's your former student. But losing sucks. It especially sucks losing to someone I personally can't stand."

"That's precisely why you're doing it. The wrestling business is all about 'I scratch your back, you scratch mine.' You're doing a favor for one of *my* old students, which helps me. If B.B. makes it big, that will improve my reputation as a trainer. That will improve *your* reputation by being associated with me…"

Interrupting again, Jenn said, "That's a lot of 'ifs.' Besides, they're not paying us enough to cover our flights. I'm not even wrestling under my name. How exactly does that help?"

"You don't want to wrestle this match as 'Lady Pirata,'" he assured her. "Think about it. Taking a loss to a newcomer in an upstart promotion could tarnish your image. That's why tomorrow, there won't be any red and black in your costume. There won't be any skull 'n crossbones. You won't even be wearing a mask. Tomorrow you'll be in a green leotard with brown tights…"

"Ick! Brown tights?"

"You'll look a bit like a tree in a garden, *Genesis*." He smiled. He was proud of creating an alter ego that played off his pupil's actual name of Jennysis Quevedo.

With teen sarcasm dripping from her tone, Jenn rolled her eyes and said, "Clever."

The two sat in silence for a few moments. Manny continued to simmer, though, and eventually turned to Jenn to make a final point. "I need you to think about whether this is really what you want to do. Did you come to Puerto Rico so you could play kissy face with the first young punk that stumbled into my gym? Or did you come with me so you could rise to the top of the wrestling business? Immature kids only do what feels good at that very moment. They don't think about what might happen down the road. If you want to make it in this business, you've got to grow up and learn to play the long game. Sometimes that means jobbing out to someone you can't stand. It's the right move because that's ultimately what helps you out the most six, twelve, eighteen months into the future. You understand that, right?"

☠ ☠ ☠

TEN YEARS LATER
OQUEZZI
YEAR 2 + 130 DAYS (MAY 10th)

Poff and Mach slowed their hurried pace only once. When they encountered Galixxy in the street, they instructed the young Nawerssian girl to run back to Gelly's Tavern. "Tell barkeep to close up for the night. It is emergency. I will explain when we get there. Now go! Run!"

Kelly wasn't sure who Galixxy was or why her Hamurkan bodyguards had just told her to sprint down the street. "Jenn and I are professional athletes, you know. We could run if that would make things easier."

"No!" snapped the usually cordial Poff-O-Lan. "You must walk, not run. Others will think you run out of fear. Walk with confidence... but walk quickly."

Jenn had heard enough out of Kelly. "Don't you think maybe you should keep your stinkin' mouth shut for a few minutes?"

"Quiet! Both of you!" Poff demanded. "Don't say another word until I say it's okay!"

☠ ☠ ☠

The night's patrons had not fully vacated Gelly's Tavern by the time Poff and Mach were shuffling Jenn and Kelly through the front doors. Poff directed them to a table in the corner. "Sit here. Do not speak until I tell you."

A blue-skinned Nawerssian (Magellan) gathered glasses from the top of the bar. Based on the texture of his skin, he looked to be a bit younger than Jagger. Despite the fact that he carried no obvious war injuries, he moved slower than the Captain of the *Valentine's Kiss*.

"Wrap it up, people. We are closing early!" the tavern's proprietor called out. "We will open again at the start of the Long Night."

Poff and Mach stood shoulder to shoulder. Their intention was to shield the Earthlings from being gawked at by the handful of Hamurkans, Flurroks, and Valtayans who had lingered past Magellan's declaration of "Last Call."

"Can I at least get something to drink?" Kelly asked in a whisper designed to reach Poff's ears.

"Silence!"

"Something alcoholic? Something with a real kick."

Poff-O-Lan called to Galixxy, who had been waiting quietly in the opposite corner. "Two waters."

☠   ☠   ☠

Once the remaining stragglers had cleared out, Poff and Mach attempted to shower Jenn and Kelly with everything they needed to know to prepare for their upcoming Tide Fight. Both women had worked in "sports entertainment," fighting professionally for more than a decade on Earth. Still, it was a bit overwhelming to be hit with a rapid-fire wave of instructions.

"There will be loud buzzing sound, then a horn," Poff began in an accent that closely resembled those with origins in Eastern Europe. "When horn sounds, fight begins."

Mach jumped in. "Two fighters on each team." He pointed to Jenn. "Chief…" Then his finger jabbed the air towards Kelly, "And Second."

"Defeat or submission by the Chief ends fight immediately…"

"Beware of ocean mutts. Those dogs have razor-sharp teeth. They shock waters to run them off, but always some remain around beach area…"

"Tides will rise quickly. Some fighters will try to take fight into water. Others will try to stay away no matter what. Best strategy is to figure out how your opponent feels about waters. Use that to your advantage…"

The clown couldn't resist the urge to make a wisecrack that was certain to go over the heads of the aliens in the room. "If only we had Aaron Burr and some of the Founding Fathers to rap us the deets about Tide Fighting. I'm sure the rules would stick with us a lot better if that was the case."

Long Jenn Silva failed to see the humor in the situation. "Is everything a joke to you? Here we are… our first day on an alien moon, about to square off in a fight to the death!"

"Sorry, Chief."

Poff tried to set them straight, "Is not necessarily fight to the death. Some *do* die in Tide Fights, but usually is not the case."

Jenn pictured the deadly talons and the staff wielded by the last Davi-Loga she fought. Even if the Hamurkan brothers weren't overly concerned about the fight ending in a death or two, the luchadora couldn't get the thought out of her mind. "Are there weapons involved?"

Both Poff and Mach hesitated to answer. Finally, one of them offered, "Not usually. Is frowned upon, but they still show up in many Tide Fights…"

"Hidden in cliff walls or buried in the sand…"

"Like I said, is frowned upon. Probably will not be any weapons in your fight. But be on the lookout."

Jenn asked another question. "You said a submission by the Chief ends the fight immediately. How do I know Taleeya won't look to claw my eyes out after the fight is over?"

This time Poff was confident in his answer. "That, she will not do."

"Is frowned upon," Mach added. "Fighting after final horn sounds would bring great disgrace."

The post-apocalyptic pirate sat in silence for a moment. She looked down into the glass of water she'd been given. Her drink tasted a bit sweeter than she was accustomed to. It had a bit of a brown tinge throughout. Even so, it was palatable.

She sighed. "I can't help but worry that Kelly and I don't have much time to figure out which of these 'frowned upon' infractions are legit... and which ones are quickly forgotten in the heat of the moment. I worry that could get somebody killed."

☠ ☠ ☠

TEN YEARS EARLIER
FORT LAUDERDALE, FLORIDA
YEAR -8 + 120 DAYS (APRIL 30th)

The Everglades Impact League (aka EvIL Wrestling) held weekly matches in Fort Lauderdale. The promotion had been active for a couple of years. It catered to fans who preferred blood and gore. Most fans of EvIL Wrestling detested the PG-rated stuff that could regularly be seen on TV. Table matches and weapons wrapped in barbed wire were utilized quite frequently.

A building that had once housed one of Broward County's most successful EDM clubs served as EvIL's regular venue. With no locker rooms, there was little privacy backstage. Jenn was seated with Manny behind a flimsy screen when her mother finally located them.

"Knock knock!"

Jenn smiled for a moment. Then she caught herself and did her best to mask any excitement she may have been feeling about seeing her mother for the first time in months.

Her mother held up the gear that Manny had asked her to pick up. "I'm clueless about what type of gear you wear in the ring. I hope this is what you needed... It's not really all that different from the cute little outfits you wore for your tap and jazz dance competitions when you were little," she said.

Jenn held it up. The green leotard was covered with faux ivy leaves scattered across the fabric. Turning it around, she noticed that there was little coverage for her backside. Though it provided more coverage than what she typically wore to the beach, she couldn't resist criticizing the outfit her mother had brought with her. "It's pretty cheeky, isn't it? What is everyone going to think about me wrestling with half of each butt cheek hanging out?"

Manny was quick to speak up. "Don't you worry, *Genesis*. I asked your mother pick up these tights to go with the outfit. You'll look like the tree in the middle of the Garden of Eden."

Brown spandex tights. They look ridiculous!

Running with the concept, her mother added, "I even brought you a big, juicy apple for you to bite into when you get into the ring. A whole forbidden fruit theme!"

Manny seemed pleased. "Isn't it great that your mother is so excited about seeing her little girl wrestle?"

Cut the crap, Manny. Especially that 'little girl' B.S.

The luchadora snatched the apple out of her mom's hand. She measured its weight and feel by tossing it into the air and catching it. She made no attempt to take the brown tights. Whether she would be performing as "Lady Pirata" or "Genesis," Jenn was just a few months shy of her eighteenth birthday. She wasn't particularly interested in the sudden enthusiasm being shown by her absentee mother.

"It was *Eve* that ate the forbidden fruit, not the damn tree. And, if memory serves me right, Eve was naked in the Garden. I'm not wearing those ugly brown things. My fishnet tights will work just fine." She pivoted and marched towards the women's restroom to change into her gear… the outfit the way Jenn wanted to wear it.

Her mother muttered something about Jenn being immature, but those complaints drifted into the cosmos, forever ignored.

☠ ☠ ☠

Jenn stood at the bathroom mirror. She was applying the finishing touches to her eye makeup when her opponent for the night stepped out of one of the stalls.

The ex-con tilted her head and smirked. "It's a shame I've gotta kick that cute little ass of yours tonight."

"Good to see you, too, B.B."

From their months of training together, Jenn knew that B.B. wasn't much for discussing a match ahead of time. She preferred to make things up on the fly, communicating her next move with a head nod, a squeeze of the wrist, or even whispering the next sequence while locked up in the corner of the ring. She did have one area she wanted to clear up ahead of time, though.

Referencing the long-practiced trick of cutting oneself with a hidden razor, B.B. asked, "Manny says you're not blading tonight? You sure about that? EvIL fans are crazy about blood."

"No. No blading, I'm sure."

"Know this, Sweet Cheeks... I'm planning on makin' you bleed tonight. I guess we'll have to do it the hard way."

☠ ☠ ☠

ONE HOUR LATER

The EvIL Wrestling fans went gaga upon seeing Genesis's over-the-top entrance. The gorgeous newcomer's decision to seductively sink her teeth into the apple brought on a particularly large pop from the boisterous crowd.

Meanwhile, saliva ran down B.B. Queen's chin. She snarled from across the squared circle. It sounded like it came from a wild animal ready to sink its teeth into fresh meat for the first time in a week!

I guess not everyone is happy to see me.

A split second after the bell sounded to announce the start of the match, the "bad bitch" blasted Jenn with a running clothesline. She followed up her initial attack with a series of stomps that looked especially painful thanks to the bulky combat boots she wore into the ring.

Unabashedly playing the heel, B.B. screamed insults to the crowd as she pulled Jenn up by her hair. "You're nothin' but a bunch of buffoons! I'm gonna make this cute little sweetie pie beg for mercy!" She slammed Jenn to the mat and hit her with a hard, high knee before letting her get in any sort of offense of her own.

After blasting her foe with rapid fire kicks to each of her calves, Jenn grabbed her for a wrist lock. As she did so, she gave her an extra hard squeeze. (Doing this was a universal signal that she wanted B.B. to reverse the hold.)

Now on the wrong end of the wrist lock, Jenn gravitated towards the corner to attempt the new reversal she had added to her arsenal. It takes two to tango, though. And when the luchadora was balancing on the top rope, B.B. gave her a violent shove that sent Jenn crashing onto the unforgiving steel steps on the outside of the ring.

The referee was quick to spring out of the ring and check on the young wrestler. The top of her head had hit hard against the sharp corner. A river of blood gushed from her scalp. Even so, "Genesis" gave a firm squeeze to the fingers of the official, silently telling him she was okay to continue.

B.B. shoved the ref out of the way and moved in to continue her assault. She took a brief pause to make eye contact with Jenn.

This was the closest thing to an apology that she could offer mid-match.

Jenn nodded her head. In the next instant, she pounded B.B. with a closed fist to the gut followed by a hard elbow to the face. Neither blow was pulled one bit. The "receipt" had been given. Now crimson poured from her opponent's nostrils, as well.

☠   ☠   ☠

THIRTY MINUTES LATER

Jenn relaxed backstage while Manny dabbed her bloody scalp with a towel her mother had snagged from her hotel room. What had been white was now a definitive scarlet.

"You sure you don't need to go to the ER?" her mother asked.

"Na. It doesn't hurt."

Even though he himself may have suggested she get stitches, Manny supported his star pupil. "She should be fine, as long as the bleeding stops soon."

Their quiet celebration came to an abrupt end when B.B. barged into the room. The wrestler with a rap sheet lifted a six-pack of cheap beer into the air as she proclaimed, "Match of the night! Jenn, you've made a friend for life!"

Jenn's mother tried to intercept the twelve-ounce can before B.B. could pass it to her. "She's only seventeen."

She wagged a finger at the suddenly protective mother. "Listen, lady, you don't know me. She doesn't hafta drink it. But you're not gonna stop me from givin' my friend a well-deserved beer." Turning to Jenn and Manny, she reported, "EvIL signed me to a contract tonight! The money's small potatoes, but my foot's in the door and they're promising a big push. I may even get to challenge Brittani Cherry a few months down the road…" She popped the top on her can. After she licked off the foam that had oozed upwards, she tilted the can towards Jenn as if toasting her. "You made me look good tonight. I owe ya... Thanks for everything."

Jenn clanked her can against B.B.'s, then took a tiny sip of the watered-down lager. "You, too. Thanks for everything... Except for maybe that three-inch gash on my head."

☠   ☠   ☠

TEN YEARS LATER
OQUEZZI
YEAR 2 + 130 DAYS (MAY 10th)

The Tide Fight was about to begin. Long Jenn Silva and Poff-O-Lan stood in the circle drawn in the sand. Taleeya—the angry birdwoman who had issued the challenge to Jenn and Kelly—stood in a similar circle approximately thirty feet away. Between the two holding areas, Kelly and Areetha met with a Hamurkan who would serve as the bout's official. This pre-fight powwow was the most important of their assigned duties as "Seconds."

Poff spoke to Jenn. "I will have to leave soon. Do you have any more questions?"

Jenn fought the urge to roll her eyes at the inquiry. She was woefully unprepared for the fight that was about to go down. She had a million questions. "I wish I knew what to ask."

Poff momentarily stood on the tips of his toes as if gaining a couple of inches in height would allow him to hear the conversation between the "Seconds."

There was little hope of deciphering anything that was being said. Everything was being drowned out by the noise made by the dozens of Flurroks that were in attendance. The ghostly-pale aliens had endured the elements. They had made their wagers. They were ready to be entertained. In their eyes, the bloodier the fight, the better! True to form, they yelled insults and slurs and profanities designed to ignite the tempers of the combatants and send each fighter into a frenzy.

"How do you think negotiations are going?" Poff asked Jenn. The pirate didn't need to look. If she wanted someone to negotiate peace, Kelly Ka-Pow would have been her *last* choice among those on the crew of the *Valentine's Kiss*. Based on how the challenge went down, she didn't exactly get a choice in the matter.

The Hamurkan official removed a small pouch from the pocket of his pants.

"What are they doing?" Jenn asked as she watched her friend reach into the pouch and pull out a black cord.

"Drawing for first position," Poff explained as they watched the Davi-Loga representative remove a red cord from the pouch. "It is how participants know who is squaring off against who at the beginning of the Tide Fight."

Many of those atop the cliffs and surrounding the beach hooted and hollered. (This time the noise was not limited to the raucous Florroks.) Some were celebrating their first gambling victory of the Long Night. ("Flurroks will bet on anything... even the colors of the cords that are drawn at the start of the fight.") Others made noise to signify their pleasure when it became clear that the final efforts to diffuse the dispute had been unsuccessful.

The official directed Kelly to step towards Taleeya (who continued to stand in her circle). Next, he sent Areetha moving towards Jenn.

With the combatants moving into position, Poff wished Jenn "good luck" and explained that he had to move away from the fight area. Before he vacated his spot, however, he explained the use of the cords. "Random draw of opponents means you do not know exactly who to prepare for… Makes fight more fair."

Jenn shrugged. "'Makes the fight more fair,' huh?" she muttered to herself. "That might have been a nice detail to know ahead of time."

☠ ☠ ☠
TEN MINUTES EARLIER

Jagger and his next batch of crewmembers were delayed in making their return to the surface of Oquezzi. The mother planet already blocked the sun by the time he arrived with Armstrong, Monroe, Fireball, and Brady to the surface of Oquezzi. The Long Night had begun. Jenn and Kelly had already traveled to the beach for the Tide Fight.

As the newcomers neared the cliffs that overlooked the fight pit, the group got a quick look at "Galixxy."

Recognizing her to be a Nawerssian from the southern hemisphere, Armstrong asked, "Who is that?"

"Sorry, but there be no time for delays. The two o' ye 'ill have yer chances to say yer howdy-dos later. That be a promise," Jagger assured his fellow countryman. As he said these words, the Captain of the *Valentine's Kiss* never took his eyes off the pair that had drawn his attention.

Mach and Nixx-O-Fee stood alongside Orr Bo, a strung out Flurrok who had once tried to break into the safe of Gelly's Tavern. A last-minute pardon from Zeal-O-Vay was the only thing that kept the scumbag from being tied to the nearest palm tree and left there until his body was thoroughly baked in Oquezzi's extreme heat.

The trio stood among a group of aliens that were lined up to watch the much-anticipated fight. Jagger stopped long enough to ask, "Nixx-O-Fee, what be yer business here? And with one o' me Hamurkan bodyguards, no less??"

Zeal's top lieutenant answered in English. "It's bad for business if we say there's going to be a Tide Fight, but then the fighters lose their courage and magically disappear. I came to make sure the Earth girls showed up as scheduled."

"Aye! Ye need not 've worried that big rope o' hair into a knot. Ye will find neither o' me lasses be afraid ta mix it up."

"Girl fights are good for business. Yet another reason I think I'm going to like…"

The gangster stopped midsentence. An intense humming sound filled the air, overwhelming this and every other conversation in the vicinity of the beach. Goose pimples rose across the smoothly shaved portion of Nixx-O-Fee's head. It was a clear sign that the waters were being electrified to send the obnoxious ocean mutts swimming to deeper waters or scurrying for cover among the rocky cliffs.

"Fight time," Jagger explained to the newcomers that accompanied him. "Let's keep movin'. Mach, ya comin' with us?"

☠ ☠ ☠

TEN MINUTES LATER

Areetha spent the last few seconds before the opening horn snarling and trying to intimidate the luchadora. Jenn was not easily rattled. Plus, she had an advantage having fought a Davi-Loga once before. She knew she needed to get the jump on her opponent quickly, and to keep the birdwoman from doing any significant damage with her deadly talons.

Seconds after the horn sounded to signify the official start of the Tide Fight, Jenn sidestepped a wild kick attack from Areetha. Her artful dodge left the wrestler perfectly position to blast Areetha with a closed fist punch to the lower back.

No one said anything about closed fists being against the rules.

The Davi-Loga shrieked upon impact. The blow also caused her to spread her arms out to each side as she instinctively gulped in a massive breath.

Still facing Areetha's back, Long Jenn Silva stepped forward and pulled the birdwoman's right arm across her body until her palm rested on her left shoulder. Jenn clutched that arm while hopping onto her opponent's back. The cumulative effect was that Jenn had wrapped Areetha into a position that resulted in her choking herself.

With Jenn's legs wrapped around the Davi-Loga's waist, the positioning and the extra weight sent the combatants collapsing onto the ground.

Jenn attempted to smother Areetha face first in the sand. Unfortunately, her bird-like bone structure meant that the chokehold was not as lethal as it would have been against a being with a defined neck. Jenn was able to subdue her foe, but she failed to render her unconscious.

Kelly struck first in her matchup against Taleeya. The malicious mime wasn't afraid to dip into her bag of dirty tricks. She jabbed her thumb into the eye of her foe before the blast of the horn was complete. She followed this up with a personal favorite, her rendition of the crane kick seen at the end of *The Karate Kid*. This was followed with a taunt. "I'm gonna keep Miyagi-ing your ass until you scream 'I quit!'"

The cheap shot and the clown's insulting tone enraged Taleeya. Her talons were exposed and her blood was boiling. The birdwoman sprang up after being downed momentarily. Without hesitation, she charged directly at Kelly. Taleeya wrapped her winged arms around the Earthling, driving her backwards until their momentum was stopped by the rocky cliff wall on the edge of the beach. Grabbing a handful of Kelly's reddish curls, the Davi-Loga drove her opponent's head into the unforgiving rocks several times.

Kelly Ka-Pow dropped to her knees. With her eyes glazed over and a hollow expression on her face, it was clear that she had been knocked silly. She sank into the sand, unconscious.

☠ ☠ ☠

With her opponent subdued but nowhere near the point of being choked out, Jenn glanced across the sands to monitor how her partner was faring.

When she saw her friend topple into the sand, Jenn screamed, "Kelly!"

Taleeya responded with a slow and deliberate turn of her head. She locked eyes with Jenn, making no effort to hide her cold and evil smile as it spread across her lips.

Jenn felt a bit of panic. She feared she was about to face a two-on-one situation… normally discouraged on Oquezzi, but entirely legal in a Tide Fight when one combatant is rendered unable to continue.

To Jenn's surprise, Taleeya was in no hurry to advance towards her. Instead, the birdwoman wanted to make her watch as she repeatedly dug her massive talons deep into the flesh of Kelly's back. Chunks of skin and meat were yanked away from the clown's body, falling helplessly into the pool of blood collecting in the sands around them.

Seeing this merciless display made Jenn want to snap Areetha's neck, and then do the same to Taleeya. She knew that this wasn't an option, though. If she let the birdwoman drive her talons into her partner even one more time, it could be curtains for Kelly Ka-Pow!

Though the words tasted bitter as they flowed from her mouth, Jenn did what she had to do. "I yield! Enough! That's it! I yield!"

The horn sounded. Long Jenn Silva had lost the Tide Fight. She prayed she hadn't lost Kelly, too.

13: AVATAR

> *"It wasn't that long ago that I was the most searched women's wrestler on the internet. Injuries may have forced me to hang up my boots, but I still turn more than my share of heads."*
>
> *- Excerpt from COCOA FREEMAN shoot interview with the "Chatting with Champions" podcast.*

Brady hurried onto the beach as soon as the fight was over. He ignored the members of various alien species that were wandering across the coarse sands. There were plenty of things to discover on this strange new moon. Those would have to wait. His eyes locked onto one person.

"Jenn!" he called out as if it had been months, as opposed to hours, since he had last seen her. Knowing she was weary from her fight, Brady ran towards the post-apocalyptic pirate. She ran towards him, too… at least initially. Then she stopped short, opting not to complete what appeared to be a quest for a needed embrace. She downplayed any urge she may have felt to jump into the young man's arms. Nodding her head towards him, Jenn told Brady, "You're going to want to shave that thing off your face A.S.A.P. It's hotter than hell down here."

"Thanks," Brady replied, his tone betraying the fact that he was a little disappointed that their reunion had not led directly into an unforgettable, breathtaking liplock. The fact that she referred to his beard as "that thing on your face" added insult to injury. He managed to push through, though.

Always thinking of others, Brady reached into his back pocket and retrieved the luchadora's wrestling mask. "I heard you were scheduled to fight. I thought this might come in handy… Sorry we got here too late."

"You're one of a kind, Brady Emerson."

He's a good friend… and a welcome distraction.

Jenn needed a distraction at that very moment. Her oldest friend in the wrestling business had just been mangled by an alien monster looking to avenge a death that had come at Jenn's hands. For all she knew, Kelly was lying in the sand, bleeding out and dying just twenty feet away from her. But she couldn't look. It was too much. It was overwhelming.

Armstrong and Jagger are tending to Kelly. They can handle it. And Fireball's there, too. He's seen his share of injuries that happened as the result of botches inside and outside of the squared circle. She'll be fine... As long as they can get her back to the ship in time.

Long Jenn Silva refocused her attention back to Brady. He was more than a good friend. And he was far more than a welcome distraction.

She took the mask into her hand. When the young man with sandy blond hair and pearly white teeth did not immediately let go, she pulled it (and him) towards her.

What followed was the passionate kiss that Brady had been craving. Jenn wanted it, too. Her heart fluttered. She continued pulling him towards her until the two friends silently succumbed to their passion.

With the embrace came sentiments that were being spoken in their own private language. All were long overdue. The kiss continued until she couldn't see or hear or think about anyone or anything else around them. All her senses—sight, sound, smell, taste, and touch—were keyed in on Brady Emerson. She lifted her hands and let her fingers dance through the whiskers she'd just joked about. With the adrenaline from the fight still surging through her arteries, the pirate had no intention of bringing the exchange to an end at any point in the foreseeable future.

☠   ☠   ☠

Monroe stood perfectly still. She allowed herself to become paralyzed. She could hear her own heart thump as she watched Brady and Jenn lose themselves in their kiss. It was an embrace that seemed to taunt her by going on and on.

"Monroe!"

The kiss felt like an insult. It felt like a betrayal.

There was no denying that Brady had been bouncing back and forth between Monroe and Jenn and possibly Som Obostoo… and maybe even Sareena before she tried to murder Jagger. This kiss was altogether different. It felt like a public declaration that he had reached his decision. He'd chosen Jenn, not Monroe.

That thought brought an ache to the Nawerssian woman's heart. It didn't matter if his actions were the result of indecision or thoughtlessness. The pain felt the same either way.

Though she was in her mid-twenties, Monroe had experienced very few opportunities to pursue any sort of romance. It was an obvious consequence of being born in space. Her lack of intimacy was part of the collateral damage that came from being raised light years from the planet she was taught to consider home. Virtually every likely love interest that was out there for her resided on a planet she'd never even seen.

"Monroe!"

Activity buzzed all around her. Dozens of the filthy "ocean mutts" had retreated to deeper waters after the Hamurkans used electric charges to run them off. Now various alien creatures were hustling away from the beach before the quickly rising tides moved in and the mutts returned.

"Monroe! Get over here!"

Others, however, ran towards the water. Armed with tools that resembled a pickax on one end and a scoop shovel on the other, these desperate beings were willing to risk everything. They hoped to grab a precious gemstone before being bitten by the mutts or identified by Hamurkan security.

It was chaos all around her. Still, she couldn't take her eyes away from Brady and Jenn and their never-ending kiss.

"Monroe!"

She finally heard her name being called. The Nawerssian spun towards the source of the sound and spotted Poff-O-Lan carrying Kelly while Jagger did his best to drag himself across the beach.

As she got closer to her crewmates, Monroe got a better look at the gruesome injuries Kelly had sustained. Taleeya's talons had shredded the back of her flight suit. It was impossible to decipher how much of the clown's skin had been flayed. Her entire back was covered with blood and displaced chunks of flesh.

The Captain barked his orders to Monroe, "Go with Poff. Get her to the *Kiss* without delay!"

"The *Kiss*?"

"Aye! The *Valentine's Kiss*!" he repeated. "I trust our cyborg friends to patch her up. They be far more trustworthy than any doctor ye might find on Oquezzi!"

"Are you coming with us?"

"Go! Go! Ol' Jagger will just slow ye down! And there be not a moment ta spare!"

☠ ☠ ☠

TEN YEARS EARLIER
BLACK CANYON OF THE GUNNISON NATIONAL PARK
YEAR -8 + 172 DAYS (JUNE 21st)

Mylo Warner was set to enter his fifth and final year at Eastern Washington University. His longtime girlfriend was a free spirit named Shelly Shipley. Both were education majors who hoped to be nailing down teaching jobs in the not-too-distant future. With more and more school districts flirting with the idea of going to a year-round schedule, Mylo was dead set on giving Shelly the summer of her dreams before they graduated. They were going to explore all that this beautiful country had to offer.

The plan was to go backcountry camping in ten of the Western U.S.A.'s most beautiful national parks. They began in Wyoming with five nights in Yellowstone. Their grand adventure next took them to the Badlands of South Dakota. Rocky Mountain National Park was the first of two stops in Colorado. It was all building up to a surprise proposal—and hopefully an unforgettable wedding—in the shadows of Mount Rainier. Mylo planned to put the proverbial icing on the wedding cake by bringing their amazing summer to a close with an unforgettable honeymoon at Hawaii Volcanoes National Park on the "Big Island."

The young couple had slept under the stars, smoked a lot of grass, and gone skinny dipping in three states by the time they arrived at Black Canyon of the Gunnison.

"Longest day of the year…" Shelly reported as she momentarily stepped away from the campfire to admire the view of the Gunnison River below. Its waters had taken tens of thousands of years to cut a steep, spectacular gorge. "Down at the bottom, they get a little more than a half hour of sunlight a day!"

"That hit the spot," Mylo said as he patted his belly. The first night of each leg of their trip always included the same dinner: mac 'n cheese, a salad, and a grilled chicken breast. The plan for the next few days included a diet that consisted of easily packed and carried food… *food that wouldn't spoil*. That meant they would be chowing down on a lot of instant oatmeal, trail mix, beef jerky, tuna pouches, tortillas, and dehydrated fruit.

Shelly returned from marveling at her surroundings. She gathered Mylo's plate, utensils, and the pot used to cook the macaroni. "I'm going to go find a 'little girls' room,' then wash the dishes in the stream. Why don't you come looking for me in about ten minutes? Make it fifteen… we probably should digest first."

"I like the sound of that!"

The young lovers kissed before she headed towards the stream.

☠ ☠ ☠

ABOARD THE SILVER BULLET SHUTTLE

The scientists aboard the *Vilnagrom-II* were in need of a new batch of subjects to study. As always, a Pilot and Explorer would head to Earth's surface, then gas and grab one or two people who strayed into secluded places.

Avis and Armstrong had executed a great many abductions over their thirty-plus years orbiting the green planet. This would be the first time they were joined by their adopted daughter Monroe. It was her eighteenth birthday.

"The rock walls of this canyon are steep and rigid. There will not be many options for the hikers or campers to choose if they hope to run and hide," Armstrong explained as a highly detailed map of the area appeared on Monroe's display.

"Applying infrared overlay," Avis announced a second before pushing a button that would send a couple of red dots onto the map.

"Humans?" Monroe asked.

"Most likely," Armstrong replied. "Although those dots could represent bears. There are dangerous animals in this park. We need to be careful… Assuming those dots represent humans, we have two completely isolated. There is not another being within several miles."

☠ ☠ ☠

BLACK CANYON OF THE GUNNISON NATIONAL PARK

"Ready or not, here I come!" Mylo sprang to his feet. As he walked down the path Shelly had taken just a few minutes earlier, the college-aged adventurer unbuttoned his favorite shirt. He didn't need a repeat of their first night in the Badlands. There were still buttons somewhere on the ground in South Dakota after his passionate partner ripped the flannel away from his body.

"Shelly?" He could hear the trickling tributary where she had gone to rinse their dishes. "Shelly?" he called again, with worry now inching past excitement to color his tone.

Then he saw her. Standing right at the edge of the stream. With little moonlight bouncing off the smooth waters, she silhouetted. In an unexpected twist, there seemed to be a strange flickering of light coming from her torso.

"Hmm?" Mylo purred as he wondered what sort of trick Shelly had up her sleeve.

His pace quickened. He couldn't wait to see what the night would bring.

Then he *really* saw her. It wasn't Shelly at all. It was Monroe, doing as she had been instructed; blocking the young man's potential route of escape via the stream.

"Holy Hell!!!" he exclaimed. Turning and running in the opposite direction, the camper shouted a warning to his girlfriend. "Shelly! Run! It's a monster! An alien! She's hideous!"

Mylo ran directly into a cloud of gas that Armstrong had released a moment earlier. He crumbled to the ground. This made it easy for Armstrong and Monroe to load their newest abductees into the shuttle.

"Great job, Monroe!" Avis called from the pilot's seat.

Armstrong gave his adoptive daughter a traditional Nawerssian congratulation by rubbing his hand atop her smooth skull. "I will be recommending that you be promoted from Scout to Explorer in short order. Excellent work."

"Yeah… Thanks."

☠   ☠   ☠

TEN YEARS LATER
OQUEZZI
YEAR 2 + 130 DAYS (MAY 10th)

Transporting Kelly to the landing strip on the outskirts of town was no easy task. Monroe and Poff moved as quickly as they could. They were slowed, however, by the need to make frequent stops to check the wounded fighter's vital signs.

Kelly slipped in an out of consciousness. When she was awake, she screamed and writhed in agony. "She is much easier to move when sleeping!" Poff observed.

The trio was joined by Mach and Galixxy when they reached the shuttle. Kelly was awake again. And frantic. Galixxy responded by jabbing a needle into her arm, injecting a serum which immediately sedated the clown.

"Load her into the shuttle," Galixxy instructed Monroe and the Hamurkan brothers.

But Monroe didn't move. She was mesmerized by the sight of the stunning female from the southern hemisphere of her home world. It was her first time encountering someone of her kind. She couldn't help but ogle at the mulberry tint of the girl's pigment.

Galixxy kept a level head. "No time for delays!" She helped the Hamurkans load the wounded patient into the shuttle. Then she let out a deafening whistle, summoning a cyborg who was nearby.

"Tok Straconi, please fly my friends to the *Valentine's Kiss*. This one has been injured and needs immediate medical attention." Turning to Monroe, she took her by the hand and said, "You are covered in blood. Come with me."

Still overwhelmed by the situation, Monroe managed to spit out the words, "I am supposed to fly the shuttle."

"Tok Straconi is a good pilot and a medic. He is a good person. Your friend will be fine... Come with me."

☠ ☠ ☠

TEN MINUTES LATER

"Monroe! Monroe! My beautiful Monroe!"

She was a young child when she last saw Magellan aboard the *Vilnagrom-1*. Even after hearing his enthusiastic greeting, she barely said a word to him when Galixxy escorted her into the tavern.

The lavender-skinned Nawerssian apologized for her counterpart that she met just a few minutes earlier. "Monroe is overwhelmed. She needs to clean up and get into some fresh clothing."

The back door of the tavern was only a few steps from the shabby structure that Magellan, Galixxy, and Jagger (when he was on Oquezzi) called home. "Let us get you out of these bloody clothes before we go inside."

She lowered her head. Over the top of her glasses, Monroe's red eyes shot Galixxy a skeptical look.

"It looks a lot nicer on the inside," she assured her while simultaneously reaching up a pair of fingers to "unzip" the crimson-soaked flight suit. Monroe recoiled. After turning her back to Galixxy, she peeled out of her sticky, sweaty flight suit. Slowly turning back around, the blue-skinned Nawerssian used her long arms to obscure any view of her breasts and genitalia.

Her actions puzzled Galixxy. "Are you sure you are Nawerssian? I ask because every Nawerssian I have ever known had few, if any, qualms about being seen in the nude. And I have never seen a Nawerssian—from the north or the south—with hair like yours." Unable to resist, she reached to feel the texture of Monroe's orangish-red ponytail. "Is it synthetic? Or is it natural?"

Monroe pulled away. "Please…! Take me to the bath."

☠ ☠ ☠

Jagger and Magellan had taken great care in constructing a bathing facility that was nearly identical to that which was aboard the *Valentine's Kiss*. A pool of murky, orange liquid welcomed Monroe.

"So warm… pleasant… familiar…" Galixxy spoke in soothing tones. "A lot has happened. Relax and allow the bath to pull you out of the shock you are experiencing."

Monroe obediently followed Galixxy's gentle touch as she guided her downward until the bathing liquid covered the top of her head. She rose into a standing position and allowed the murky, orange liquid to slowly extract dirt and grime from every inch of her skin. Then she sank back into the waters to allow them to cover her once again.

"It is funny how a warm bath feels so comforting, even in a place as hot as Oquezzi," Galixxy remarked as she placed Monroe's bloody garments on a metal slab.

The pool was large enough for several Nawerssians to bathe at the same time. The substance used to clean them was designed to pull any grime down to the bottom and directly into a drain. Because of this, they believed sharing "bath water" was in no way unsanitary. And since the people of their home typically felt little shame about their naked form, a suggestion to bathe together normally would not be considered unexpected or inappropriate.

"It has been several days since I last bathed," Galixxy admitted. "And my clothes got bloody, as well. May I join you?"

Monroe was quiet for a moment. She smiled and locked her focus on the orange liquid directly in front of her. Finally, she managed to nod her head and whisper, "Yes."

☠ ☠ ☠

TEN YEARS EARLIER
ABOARD THE VILNAGROM-II
YEAR -8 + 173 DAYS (JUNE 22nd)

Avis, Armstrong, and Monroe sat together in the galley. The two men were relishing the opportunity to eat a breakfast prepared with some of the items contained within the packs of the recently abducted campers.

"It does not look much better than the synthetic protein we usually get for Firstmeal," Armstrong observed, "But this instant oatmeal is delicious... particularly if you try adding raisins or some of these dehydrated bananas and papayas."

"Eh," Monroe shrugged, sounding as much like an American teenager as any Nawerssian ever had.

Before her parents inquired about the reason for her emotional malaise, the group was greeted by the *V-II's* Cartographer (Polo) and Doctor (Clooney). "Great news!" an exuberant Polo began. "Our newest subjects entered into the virtual realm with very little difficulty. It may have been the smoothest transition into VR that I have observed on this mission."

Armstrong rubbed his hand atop his adoptive daughter's head. "That is a wonderful report. Your first abduction, a tremendous success!"

Monroe's reaction was much less enthusiastic. "Not bad for a 'hideous beast,' I suppose."

☠   ☠   ☠

ONE DAY LATER
YEAR -8 + 174 DAYS (JUNE 23rd)

Being assigned the role of "Scout" aboard the *Vilnagrom-II* brought several responsibilities. In addition to accompanying Avis and Armstrong on abduction missions, Monroe often assisted Polo in observing the subjects contained in virtual reality. Abnormal readings were often addressed by sending a crewmember into the tank to influence the actions of the test subjects. Oftentimes it was the Scout who was chosen to venture into VR.

That part of the job wore on her. One of the worst aspects was the fact that it was Polo who supervised the observation area. The Cartographer micromanaged every minute detail concerning how those in the VR tanks were to be watched, controlled, and influenced. He did so in a manner that made Monroe feel like he was somehow being aroused every time he "played God" and exercised control over the test subjects (and even the Nawerssians who worked under him).

Monroe dragged herself into the observation area. She made no effort to hide her displeasure. She hated the knot in her gut that she felt every time she had to check to see if she was going to be assigned any tasks for the day.

The tall scientist clapped his hands together upon spotting his helper. "Monroe! Good to see you!" When he recognized her depressed demeanor, he added a joke. "Why so blue today?"

He told that joke all the time.

"It is your job to observe…" she replied. "And yet you never have picked up on the fact that no one thinks that joke is even remotely funny."

"Perhaps you are not the intended audience. Perhaps I tell that joke for my own enjoyment, not yours."

"Perhaps that explains why you do not have a partner, and it is doubtful you ever will."

"Touché, young one. Touché."

After conceding victory in their brief verbal spar, Polo circled back around and attempted to express his concern in a more sincere manner. "In all seriousness… Monroe, you seem sad. Depressed. You are not still upset over what the male specimen said when you abducted him, are you?"

"You mean calling me a 'hideous beast?' Why would that upset me?"

"Sometimes beings are frightened by what they do not know. That remains true whether they are from Earth, Na-Werss, or somewhere in between. That does not mean they are correct. It means they are ignorant."

"Nice try, Polo, but I am a Scout. I want to be an Explorer. Both jobs require that I interact with human beings who think they are on Earth or actually are on Earth! Right or wrong, what they believe *does* matter. It matters a lot."

The Cartographer stopped and stood upright. He raised his left hand in the air and wiggled his long, blue fingers for a moment. This gesture customarily was given as an apology on their home planet. "I am sorry, Monroe. I am going about this all wrong. Please allow me to show you something that I have never shown anyone on this ship."

Polo went to his computer station. After poking his awkwardly long fingers against a few buttons on his device, the image of a young human girl appeared. "As you know, we all have avatars for when we enter virtual reality. I have programmed a separate set of avatars for when we enter an observation area that contains our human test subjects. Representations of ourselves as *Homo sapiens*, if you will."

Irritation radiated in Monroe's tone. "That little girl represents *me*?"

The image was of an awkward, prepubescent girl. Her most notable features included dozens of freckles smattered across an extremely pale face, a somewhat drastic overbite, and strawberry blond hair brushed into two long, braided pigtails.

"It was," Polo confessed. "Admittedly, that is not the most flattering of avatars. Before you get angry, you should see how our specimens see you now."

The new image depicted a beautiful young woman with clear skin, a radiant smile, and auburn hair that invited the wind to blow through it.

"Very pretty," Monroe admitted.

"When they see you in the virtual realm, you momentarily take their breath away!"

"I did like the first girl's braids," Monroe said as she flashed her first smile in two days. The smile instantly disappeared, though. She rubbed the top of her bald scalp. "But outside of VR, I have this big, bald, lumpy head that looks like a blue watermelon. And, no offense, but all I have to look forward to is gathering up a bunch of wrinkles across it like you."

Polo laughed and clapped his hands together once again. "That is where I believe you may be wrong."

☠ ☠ ☠

ONE WEEK LATER
YEAR -8 + 182 DAYS (JULY 1st)

Monroe awakened in a hospital bed in Sick Bay. She tried to sit up, but her body fought back hard. Her head throbbed.

"I can give you something for the pain you are experiencing. That will go away soon," the ship's Doctor (Clooney) told her. "You will want to remain as still as possible for the next couple of days… while the dermis recovers and the implanted hair follicles become locked in place."

Clooney and Polo stood over their patient. Both were smiling, radiant in response to their medical triumph.

"Can I see it?" Monroe asked.

"Of course!" Responding to the request, Clooney swung a bedside monitor over until it was positioned for Monroe's use. With the press of a button, the screen became reflective like a mirror.

"You look spectacular," Polo told Monroe as his hand momentarily rested atop hers. "No one will ever call you 'hideous' again."

The Doctor agreed. "It looks very good. Polo has been trying to convince Hazel to get hair implants for years. Once she sees you, we may have a brunette to go along with our redhead."

Monroe tilted her head to admire herself from different angles. She was pleased with the addition of hair to her once-naked scalp. However, her smiled vanished a moment later.

"Is something wrong?"

"No, not at all," Monroe assured the Doctor. "I was simply wondering… Is there anything you could do with my nose? It is so flat. Could you give it a bit of a bridge… like a human on Earth?"

☠ ☠ ☠

TEN YEARS LATER
OQUEZZI
YEAR 2 + 130 DAYS (MAY 10th)

Galixxy lowered herself into the bath. With the bathing liquid only coming up to her midsection, she slowly and deliberately sank to her knees. She eased her body downward until even the top of her purple, hairless scalp disappeared beneath the gritty, orange fluid. As she rose back to a standing position the solution glided down her body.

Monroe's eyes were glued to Galixxy the entire time.

The Nawerssian from the southern hemisphere smiled as their red eyes met. "You do not say much. Why is that?"

Monroe looked away as quickly as possible. She whipped her head to one side, forcing herself to dwell upon the concern she was feeling for her friend Kelly. It was difficult to remained focused, however. She was frustrated about seeing Brady kissing Jenn. But that pain was softening surprisingly fast. Now she was starting to recognize a new variety of confusion.

Strange feelings. What is it about this young woman that calls herself "Galixxy?" Do I have to deal with all this at once?

"You don't have to answer me," the purple-skinned woman said as she wiped away a bit of the orange bathing fluid. "Take all the time you need."

Monroe had been told that all Nawerssian adolescents from the southern hemisphere were conscripted into "service" by their mid-teens. That began with surgeries in which their arms and legs were replaced with mechanical upgrades. Soon thereafter, the males received additional transformations until they had fully cyborg bodies. The final procedures for the females were delayed until they had "done their duty" and given birth to at least two healthy children, thus allowing their kind to survive for another generation.

Galixxy's body appeared fully organic. Either the models had advanced significantly since Som Obostoo and the other cyborgs aboard the *Valentine's Kiss* underwent their surgeries, or Galixxy somehow avoided the process.

"How old are you?" Monroe finally asked.

"Old enough," she responded while slowly drifting towards her curious counterpart. "Old enough that if I had not been a stowaway on a military ship that left Na-Werss years ago, I would have had this smooth, beautiful skin replaced with artificial, unnatural synthetics. Old enough to know that I have met beings from ten different planets, and I have never seen one…" Galixxy reached up, then ran her hands through Monroe's wet hair.

"...nearly as beautiful as you. You fascinate me... And I think *I* fascinate you. Am I right?"

With her fingers still entwined among Monroe's transplanted strands, Galixxy gently tugged on the hair as she closed the remaining gap between the two of them.

They were virtual strangers. That did not stop them from enjoying a kiss. Then another. Then one kiss melted into the next without a clear beginning or end. The exchange was every bit as passionate and intimate as the one Brady and Jenn had shared on the beach a few hours earlier.

Monroe wasn't sure about Brady and Jenn. She wasn't sure she even cared. She did believe, however, that the kisses she shared with Galixxy were the type that would change her life forever.

14: TWO COMETS AND A BAYNAP TREE

"Ace Cutler? That guy loved to gamble. Horses, cards, slots… you name it. But he *hated* to lose. I dreaded going to Vegas when we were both wrestling in the IWO. If he lost at the craps tables on Friday night, he'd take it out on you in the ring on Saturday!"

-GRIZZLY JACK GRISSOM shoot interview given for "Wrestling with Demons," a documentary series filmed for the short-lived "666 Sports" streaming service.

ONE MONTH LATER
OQUEZZI
YEAR 2 + 168 DAYS (JUNE 17th)

Developing a routine on Oquezzi was no simple task. One twenty-four-hour period began with six hours of light, followed by twelve hours of darkness, and then six more hours of light. An eclipse followed. The next twenty-four hours were spent with the light of the sun being blocked out by the massive, barren planet the moon orbited. Those forty-eight hours constituted one of the red moon's journeys around its mother planet. And they made counting the days far more confusing than on Earth.

Following Jagger's suggestion, Long Jenn Silva and her fellow crew members quickly established some daily rituals. Perhaps the most important of these was their regular rendezvous at Gelly's Tavern. The entire crew of the *Valentine's Kiss* met in the final hour of sunlight before the beginning of the Long Night. (Those that were aboard the massive spacecraft docked in the atmosphere above called to check in, too.)

It wasn't a social gathering. Evil took many forms and lurked around every corner on the red moon. That made it essential to keep track of where everyone was and what they would be doing once the twenty-four hours of darkness began.

Long Jenn Silva descended the sixteen steps that led from her apartment above to the tavern below. Because they were originally constructed for much taller Hamurkans, it took some time to get accustomed to navigating the stairs. After several weeks of going up and down the staircase, the luchadora handled them like a pro… regardless of how much alcohol was flowing through her veins.

On this particular day, she handled the short trip with a high degree of caution. Unfamiliar sounds were coming from the lower level. The noise resembled a conversation, but the words sounded like a mixture of gargling and gibberish.

She peeked down. Armstrong was seated at his favorite table in the tavern. He was joined by a Valtayan. Though it was impossible to tell them apart beneath their many layers of fur-lined clothing, Jenn noticed that pieces of blue material highlighted much of this alien's attire.

Just like the robot tinkerer who works the door at The Middle of Nowhere.

Armstrong called out, "We can see you." The Nawerssian wasn't trying to embarrass her. He did not see any need for her to skulk in the shadows, either. "Please join us... Jenn, I believe you know Ray Yandee."

Why would I want to sit at the table with him? This guy works for the enemy. Buried beneath all those blankets and robes is nothing but a little creep who makes robots designed to fulfill the darkest desires of galactic criminals.

"I'd rather kiss a wookiee."

Let your stupid translator bot have fun with that one.

Yandee arose from his seat. He wasn't much taller than the chair he'd occupied. *"Bobba fobba bo robba fobba."*

Translation: "All is fine. I must be leaving. It is almost time for me to check in with my employers."

The tiny grey alien spun around and bowed towards Jenn. *"Robba fo robba."*

Translation: "Good day, Long Jenn Silva. I hope we will have the opportunity to get to know one another better. If given enough time, I am confident I will be able to convince you to join the crew of my ship."

Jenn laughed. "All that from 'robba robba?' That must be one strange language they speak on your planet."

Yandee did not need his machine to provide an interpretation. The Valtayan understood everything Jenn had said. He spoke once more in his native tongue. Translated, he said, "It is a strange language, indeed. Much less nuanced than the one you speak. Even with all of its complexities, I notice your response was not a rejection to my request. I will hold out hope that you and I may soon join forces as members of the same crew."

Jenn shook her head from side to side. "Here's an English expression that you may not know... You and me on the same crew? That'll happen when pigs fly."

☠ ☠ ☠

After the Valtayan completed his departure, Armstrong looked at Jenn. "Please... have a seat."

"I feel a lecture coming on. Odd that the alien who abducted me thinks he has a right to..."

"Please!" Armstrong repeated. There was more than a tinge of anger and frustration in his tone. "Have a seat. I would like for you to explain why you were so abrasive to Ray Yandee."

"Why don't you start by explaining why you were so nice to him?"

"If you will recall, I am an Explorer," the blue-skinned alien explained. "That was my role while living and working on the *Vilnagrom-1*, the ship we now call the *Valentine's Kiss*. It is in my nature to ask questions and to study those I encounter. That remains the same whether those that I choose to learn about come from another side of the world or another world entirely."

Jenn patted the front of her wrestling tights, then moved her hands around the back as if searching imaginary pockets. "Gimme a second..." she said. "I'm sure I've got some sort of blue ribbon tucked away in here somewhere. You sound like you need a prize."

The Nawerssian did nothing to mask his disappointment. "You have changed, Jennysis Quevedo."

"Good thing, too. Someone needs to use their friggin' brain to keep us alive here. I'm not sure what's going on in that enormous blue noggin on the top of your shoulders. Our crew meets here every day about this time. We check in. We tell everyone what we're going to be doing during the Long Night. We act like a family... and it keeps us alive. You... you invite a guy that works the front door of The Middle of Nowhere, the front door of that seedy little cantina that serves as Checkpoint One for every evil act that goes down on this moon. Yeah, I've changed. And you need to change, too, before it isn't just Ray Yandee crashing the party, but Nixx-O-Fee and a whole bunch of armed Hamurkans!"

Armstrong gestured to every other table in the tavern. Each one was empty. "There is no one else here. Ray Yandee did not crash any party. His being here did not put anyone in danger."

"Whatever."

"More importantly," he continued, "He is *not* our enemy!"

Jenn stopped her offensive. Recognizing that he was acting much more aggressively than was typical for most Nawerssians, she silently invited him to continue.

"Learning about Yandee and the Valtayans is a good thing. It is strategic to learn as much as possible about those we interact with. It helps us discover who can be trusted, who can be bribed, and those with whom we should never turn our backs."

"Which is Yandee?"

"I do not know... yet. Perhaps Jagger already does. He and I still do not speak that often."

Jenn laughed. "I know you think he's one we should never turn our back on. If you ask me…"

Armstrong held up his hand and cut her off. "That is a conversation for another time. For now, let us continue talking about Yandee and the Valtayans. You might find this useful."

"Fair enough."

"For instance, did you know that the Valtayans and Flurroks were from the same solar system?"

"The Flurroks are the pasty, white addicts with long, stringy hair?" Jenn asked. "Makes sense."

"According to Ray Yandee, his people had a far superior military. They had enough android soldiers to obliterate the Florroks. Instead of destroying them, the Valtayans chose peace and sacrifice. They relocated to a planet further from their sun. Over time, they were able to manipulate their genetics in a way that left them impervious to extreme temperatures. They can survive and thrive in extreme heat or extreme cold. That is why they do not mind dressing in layers on this sweltering moon. And that is why they can drink liquids that are nearly boiling."

"What about ice cream headaches?"

"What?"

Jenn reworded her sarcastic question. "The real test would be to see how quickly Yandee can down a pint of Chunky Monkey without getting an ice cream headache."

Armstrong frowned. "I am sure there are those that think it is humorous when Kelly Ka-Pow cracks her jokes. Even when she does so with little regard if the timing is appropriate given the audience and venue. When you respond in the same manner, it feels like you have not listened to anything I have said. You are simply looking for the next opportunity to offer your own insult or sarcastic remark. I understand that each of us deal with loss and grieve differently. I fear, however, that your growing edge is going to lead to trouble. If I can give you one piece of advice..."

"Shoot."

"Be a peacemaker whenever possible. Do not go looking for quarrels. Plenty of fights will find each of us in our lifetimes... particularly on this troubled moon."

Their one-on-one conversation ended when Monroe entered the room with Poff and Mach. Jagger and Fireball Freeman were not far behind them.

Jenn arose and looked towards the table that she typically shared with Brady. Before she changed spots, she smiled at Armstrong. "I'm glad we had this talk, cue ball."

☠ ☠ ☠

THREE MONTHS LATER – OQUEZZI
YEAR 2 + 233 DAYS (AUGUST 21st)

More times than not, Jenn and Armstrong were the first two crew members to assemble in Gelly's Tavern. Sometimes they enjoyed heartfelt conversations in which the Nawerssian was able to impart some fatherly advice. At other times, the luchadora was able to tell a story that allowed the Explorer to better understand the ways of Earth from the unique perspective of a young Latina who was born and raised in Central Florida, and then lived in the Caribbean and Mexico in her years of adulthood.

On most occasions, Jenn was busy regretting her decision to return to a life in space. Meanwhile, Armstrong was consumed with worry that he might be allowing Monroe to steer herself in the wrong direction as she spent more and more time with Galixxy. It was those times that the two said very little to one another.

Jenn's footsteps took her straight from the stairway to behind the bar. She craved some of the tequila or rum that Jagger had brought from Earth... *but that's saved for special occasions.* Since it was "Just another lousy day on Oquezzi," she opted for a mug of Meezuh. The fermented tea from Na-Werss was not in short supply. "There's always plenty of this crap available," she said to Armstrong while pouring mugs for the two of them.

The Nawerssian Explorer sat at his customary table. He positioned himself close to the window so he could observe those that were walking down the street.

He spoke to Jenn as she joined him. "I recommend restraint when drinking Meezuh. The intoxicating effects strike quickly. I personally have observed citizens of my home world engage in highly destructive behaviors after consuming too much."

The pirate smiled. Her eyes met the reflection in Armstrong's dark glasses. "Is that your Nawerssian way of saying it packs a punch?" She laughed. "No offense, but the way you say things makes you seem like such a dweeb."

"Beginning your insult with no offense does not..."

Jenn interrupted the blue-skinned alien. "I'm sorry. Jeez! I wasn't trying to insult you..." She held her hands in the air and wiggled her fingers. It was a half-hearted attempt to mimic the gesture Nawerssians made while apologizing. "And you can relax. I don't plan on drinking too much of this stuff, even if I have grown to like the taste. It kinda reminds me of the *sake* I had when Fireball took a bunch of us to Japan."

A bell signaled that their one-on-one time was over. Brady and Som Obostoo walked through the front door.

Jenn was unconcerned with the fact that Brady had been spending time with the beautiful cyborg. She chalked it up to the fact that they were following Jagger's stern suggestion that no one from the *Valentine's Kiss* venture out alone.

Noting his drenched hair and his clothing saturated in sweat, she asked, "Where have you been? Did you run a 10-K in a sauna? You better get a glass of 'water' so you don't get dehydrated." (Jenn used air quotes to highlight the fact that the substance that passed as "water" on the red moon wasn't exactly like the H_2O they drank back on Earth.)

"I went with Som Obostoo to meet with a Cyborg Surgeon. He believes he can repurpose the parts from one of Ray Yandee's robots to construct a new arm for her. The new arm should be ready in a few days."

Som Obostoo returned from the bar with a tall glass of the sweet, brown solution that passed for water. Before handing it to Brady, the cyborg stuck her left index finger into the liquid. After submerging her mechanical fingertip, a bright light pulsed from the end. A series of rapid-fire flashes followed. At the end of the process, the water in the glass was crystal clear.

Brady happily accepted the glass and chugged the water.

"I don't know if I am grossed out or absolutely amazed," Jenn remarked. "Maybe a little of both."

Monroe and Galixxy were the next to enter the tavern. They announced they were taking Armstrong to the Tide Fights that were scheduled to begin within the next few hours. The young couple directed their collective attention away from one another just long enough to issue an invitation for others to join them. They quickly retreated to a table in a secluded corner before they could be subjected to any bothersome follow-up questions.

Jenn looked at Monroe's adoptive father. "You don't seem like the type that enjoys a night at the fights, Armstrong. Are you going as a fan? Or are you babysitting your not-so-little girl?"

He shook his head. "Monroe needs no chaperone. She has reached a sufficient age to make her own decisions. As an Explorer, it is in my nature to study the ways of the people who occupy a planet... or, in this case, moon. If Tide Fights are an essential part of the culture here on Oquezzi, I want to learn as much as possible about the fights. I am not as interested in the gruesome bouts as I am in the fanfare that surrounds them."

"Thanks for that answer, Professor."

"Will you be joining us?"

"Not a chance," Jenn replied without hesitation. Though she didn't want to admit it, she continued to be haunted by the damage that had been inflicted upon Kelly Ka-Pow during their fight that took place on their first night on Oquezzi.

Galixxy jumped in from her seat in the shadows. "Not all Tide Fights are gruesome. Long Jenn Silva, you should go."

Brady recognized the luchadora's continued hesitation. Realizing that she was dealing with difficult emotions that came with seeing her friend sustain such brutal injuries, he made his own suggestion. "Why don't we hop on the next shuttle up to the *Valentine's Kiss*? Som Obostoo is flying Poff up to make some repairs. Fireball is going with them so he can visit Kelly. There's room in the shuttle for two more. We should join them."

Jenn nodded. "I'd like that."

☠ ☠ ☠

The tides were coming in. The sun prepared to go into hiding. As the Long Night began, no sunlight would shine on Oquezzi for the equivalent of an entire day on Earth. The streets could be expected to remain active for the first half of the Long Night. After that, most of the spaceport's residents would need to wind down.

"When do the fights begin?" Armstrong asked Mach as they—along with Monroe and Galixxy—walked towards the bluffs that overlooked the bay.

The Hamurkan was no tour guide. His primary job was to protect the crew. He didn't reply to Armstrong's question. Instead, he mumbled something about wishing that his brother had accompanied the group. Then he elaborated. "There is strange energy in the air on this night." With a heightened level of concern, Mach's head was on a swivel as he constantly surveyed their surroundings for potential threats.

Galixxy made it no secret that she wanted their fight night adventure to remain a joyful occasion. Since she had lived on Oquezzi for quite some time, she confidently answered the question posed by the Explorer. "Gemstone mining continues until every bit of daylight is gone. Once the eclipse has begun, the waters rise quickly. Soon they will be too deep. The Hamurkans clear everyone out, turn on the lights, and shock the water to scare away the ocean mutts. Once that's done, the fights will begin. No more than two hours from now… a little less."

"Two hours seems like a long time to wait," Armstrong said, eager to learn as much as he could about an important part of the culture on Oquezzi. "Why does everyone come so early?"

"Time means very little on this moon. Besides, that is when everyone in attendance places their bets. It also gives everyone a chance to find a good seat… You will not be bored. There will be plenty of music and dancing to keep you entertained. If we are fortunate, the Valtayans will send out robots selling bags of something called 'popped corn.' It's delicious."

"Popcorn!" Monroe beamed. She had enjoyed the treat during excursions to Earth. "This must be our lucky day!"

☠ ☠ ☠

TWO HOURS LATER
YEAR 2 + 233 DAYS (AUGUST 21st)

With ghostly white skin and virtually no pigmentation, Flurroks made few exceptions to their avoidance of being exposed to natural light. They detested standing out in the scorching sun that shown on Oquezzi.

One major exception came in their efforts to seek out Baynap. It was a pink, powdery substance found in abundance on the planet they called home. When mixed with a few drops of water, Baynap became a gummy ball of goo that could be smoked for hours. The intoxicating effects ranged from absolute euphoria to horrific hallucinations. Virtually every Flurrok who lived on Oquezzi possessed an insatiable addiction to the drug (or a synthetic knockoff called Bazznazz).

The Tide Fights were another occasion that brought on Flurrok sightings. They loved to gamble. They'd bet on anything. And they braved the sun's relentless rays to obtain the best spots for watching the weekly battles.

Galixxy approached a strung out Flurrok who occupied a bench positioned near the edge of the cliff. Blisters gathered across the alien's pale face. His eyes bulged outward, as if they were trying to escape their sockets. Ignoring his hideous appearance, she said, "This gentleman is the father of my gal pal. Armstrong is his name. This is his first time attending the Tide Fights from start to finish… and I would like for him to enjoy the opportunity with an unobstructed view of the action. Care to make a bet?"

It took a moment for the bot to take Galixxy's message (spoken in English) and repeat it in Flurri. Once the translation was complete, the Flurrok answered. "Urr Bo is always up for a game of Marzova. Do you have anything worth wagering?"

Because most Flurroks couldn't resist the urge to gamble, they typically considered most items an acceptable ante. Galixxy was taking no chances. She reached into a hidden pocket in the lining of her glove. "One game of Marzova. You put up the four seats on that bench. I'll wager 40 glugs of Baynap."

(Forty glugs of Baynap would be enough to satisfy his perpetual need for a fix for five or six days… if he could keep from gambling some or all of it away for that long.)

"What are you doing with that?" an alarmed Monroe asked.

"I have been holding onto it for this very occasion."

Urr Bo provided a bag of small tiles. Each was marked with an image from his home world.

The Game of Marzova worked much like five card stud. Players took turns removing tiles from the bag. Each tile had a specific point value. Some were positive, some were negative. Others magnified or diminished the value of other tiles. The game pieces were to be placed face up, with frequent opportunities to increase the wagers based on the tiles that had been revealed up to that point in the game.

When the drawing was complete, Galixxy was holding two comets, a Baynap tree, a hammer, and a snowbear tile. With two comets and a Baynap tree, she'd been dealt an unbeatable hand! She passed on the opportunity to modify her wager. The purple-skinned alien was content with taking the premium seats for viewing the upcoming fights.

Angered in defeat, the Flurrok snatched the tiles out of her hand. He jammed them back into his satchel while growling something in his native language.

A humming sound filled the air. The Tide Fight officials were preparing to shock the waters to send the ocean mutts away from the action.

The sound seemed to trigger something in the Flurrok. As if his anger was amplified by the nearby surge of electricity, Urr Bo repeated his insult as he charged towards an unsuspecting Armstrong. The Flurrok clutched onto the Nawerssian's silver flight suit. With a violent tug, he sent him flying over the cliff into the ocean below.

If the fall didn't kill him, the electrification of the waters certainly would. Armstrong had been murdered by a raging Flurrok angry over his gambling loss.

Monroe shrieked before collapsing to the ground.

Even though an unprovoked attack from a Flurrok was extremely rare, Mach appeared unphased. He had sensed danger a bit earlier. Now it was his duty to apprehend the murderer and take him to be tried by Nixx-O-Fee.

Mach raised his blaster. "Do not move!" he shouted.

As the Hamurkan stepped towards the culprit, two of Urr Bo's friends ambushed Mach from behind. Both Flurroks pulled out a pair of sharp stones and drove them into Mach's muscular back. The original murderer charged forward with his own pair of jagged rocks. All three repeatedly stabbed the Hamurkan bodyguard until blood oozed from dozens of puncture wounds.

The trio of Flurroks dropped their weapons. It didn't take them long to disappear by blending in with the countless panicked spectators that were fleeing the area.

15: MONTERREY SCREWJOB

> *"Jenn's going to tear her head off when they fight in San Antonio. She and Beautiful Star have legitimate heat. It all goes back to an incident that happened six or seven years ago… It might take a few weeks or it might take a few years, but if you cross Long Jenn Silva, she IS going to get her revenge."*
>
> *- Excerpt from LASZLO BARBA shoot interview on the "Repeat the Heat" podcast.*

ONE DAY LATER
YEAR 2 + 234 DAYS (AUGUST 22nd)

A tattered sheet served as a curtain. It was successful in keeping most of the blazing sun's obnoxious rays from invading the room. It provided sufficient darkness to momentarily obscure the fact that she been sprawled across the bed, crying until her body could produce no more tears.

There was a soft knock at her door. Though her hearing was enhanced well beyond that with which she had been born, Som Obostoo politely waited and acted as if she had not heard Jenn's sobs. "Are you in there?" the cyborg called, pretending to be unsure as to whether the luchadora was on the other side of the door. Using as delicate of a tone as her manufactured vocalizer would allow, she said, "There are people downstairs. Friends. Everyone needs to be with friends at times like these."

"Go away!" Jenn's voice sounded raw.

"As you wish."

Jenn counted the steps as the cyborg's footsteps settled atop each of the sixteen boards that comprised the wooden staircase. Once she was confident there were no eavesdroppers on the other side of the door, she got up and walked across the room. Leaning against a dresser that Magellan had fashioned out of a large shipping crate, she looked into a reflective glass that served as a mirror. "Armstrong? What the hell did he ever do to anyone on this damn moon? Why would the Flurroks attack Mach? It doesn't make any sense." She glared into the glass, angrily waiting for an answer that wasn't coming.

Jenn returned to the side of her bed long enough to retrieve a tumbler filled with some sort of distilled liquor made by the Valtayans. She dipped the tip of her dagger inside, stirring the stagnant liquid until it seemed fresh again. "Tastes like sake… except with a chalky aftertaste. Oh well, the alcohol does the trick," she said to herself immediately before swallowing the alien concoction.

A loud thumping followed.

Is the liquor making my head do that? Or is someone else pounding on the door?

"Jenn…" Brady called through the locked door. "Will you please come down and join us? Me, Fireball, Jagger, Som Obostoo… We're all downstairs. Galixxy was with us a little earlier, but now she's checking on Monroe."

"I'm glad they had the teacher's pet there to take attendance."

Brady did not respond to the insult. (For some reason, comments like that were coming from the mouth of Long Jenn Silva much more frequently as of late.)

"People are going to keep knocking on my door until I come down, aren't they?"

"That's probably a safe bet."

☠ ☠ ☠

It took much longer for Jenn to take the sixteen steps down to the main floor of Gelly's Tavern than it had for Som Ombostoo to descend the same staircase a few minutes earlier. That could have had something to do with the Valtayan hooch she had pounded. Or maybe it was because hadn't gotten any quality sleep in about thirty-six hours. *Most likely, it was some combination of both of those factors.*

Brady offered his seat. Jenn gladly accepted, even though she didn't thank him or acknowledge his sacrifice. Instead, she spun the chair around so she could straddle the sides and lean forward into the chair's back. "What did I miss?"

"Look like Hell, ye do," Jagger blurted out.

Fireball echoed him. "You sure you're alright?"

"I'm fine. Armstrong's death just hit me hard for some reason... I don't exactly know why. He's the S.O.B. that abducted me from my happy life on Earth. I should've hated him, but I didn't. I really liked the guy. And his death..." She searched for the right words to express what she was feeling. "After losing Lazz and Cocoa and so many others... knowing Kelly's probably never going to be the same after getting torn to shreds in a Tide Fight... there was something about losing Armstrong that caused me to snap... What is it they say? 'That was the straw that broke the camel's back.'"

The group was silent. Some nodded in agreement. Most were experiencing the same emotions as Jenn, but it took her to express those feelings. She spoke for all of them.

The luchadora continued, "What did I miss? What was so important that you had to keep sending errand boys to drag me down here?"

Brady didn't like the increasing frequency with which she was willing to call him insulting names. "Errand boy?"

If anyone else took umbrage to Jenn's comments or attitude, they didn't speak up. Instead, Jagger jumped back into the previous point in their conversation.

"I've spent a great deal o' time on this moon. These killings reek o' the scent o' Nixx-O-Fee. Feels like a declaration of war 'gainst the crew of the *Valentine's Kiss*."

Fireball displayed his fiery temper. "Then I say we take out the trash! Tit for tat! An eye for an eye! Let's put our heads together and figure out the best way to kill that scumbag."

Jagger cautioned them against taking a direct approach. "No one starts a war on Oquezzi without the approval of the man who pulls all the strings from the comfort of his yacht in the sky... High above the surface o' the moon."

"What are you saying? We take out Zeal-O-Vay?" Jenn asked.

Jagger shook his head. "The feat would be near impossible, says I. And a suicide mission any way ya look at it."

"We're hardly equipped to fight a war!" Brady said with a degree of panic in his voice. "Step outside and look around. The Hamurkans outnumber us 20-to-1!"

Som Obostoo was quick to correct Brady's math with an exact breakdown of the population. "More accurately, they outnumber us 43.9090-repeating to one. There currently are nine able-bodied crewmembers on the Manifest of the *Valentine's Kiss*. If we were to count Magellan and Galixxy, that would give us eleven... There are at least 483 Hamurkans on Oquezzi. That number does not take into account the number of Davi-Loga, Flurroks, and Valtayans living on the moon. Most, if not all, members of those factions are aligned with the Hamurkans. Those that are not loyal to Zeal-O-Vay certainly fear him and what he can do."

Jenn was getting irritated. "What do we do? Tuck our tails and run? Wait to be picked off one-by-one? I don't like the sound of either of those options."

Jagger was tapping into his military experience. There appeared to be some ideas already simmering inside his mind. "We be needin' to buy some time. Get the Hamurkans on their heels. And we needs to send a message that has 'em thinkin' twice about messing with this crew... If we be smart and if we be lucky, methinks we can come up with a plan that accomplishes all those goals in one fell swoop."

Brady shook his head. "I generally consider myself a pretty lucky guy, but I don't know of anyone in the world—this one or back on Earth—that has that much good fortune."

"Don't be so sure. Ya see, there's two good things about luck," Fireball said. He repositioned himself in his seat as he looked to make sure he had the full attention of those around the table. "Luck don't cost a thing. And you can make your own." The veteran wrestler paused and made eye contact with Jenn. He smirked and pointed at the luchadora before continuing. "Cocoa told me a story about you… back when she was tryin' to convince me to sign you to a contract. You've got a little bit of history when it comes to makin' people regret tryin' to screw with you, don't you, Long Jenn Silva?"

☠ ☠ ☠

NINE YEARS EARLIER
MEXICO CITY
YEAR -7 + 88 DAYS (MARCH 29th)

The tiny studio apartment appeared to have been ransacked. The couch had been pushed so close to the entryway that the door could not be opened completely. The mattress hidden inside the couch was partially pulled out. Cushions had been tossed aside with little regard for where they landed.

A clock was positioned on an end table. It repeatedly flashed "12:00" in bright red digital numbers. For the moment, it's most valuable contribution to the apartment's occupants was the fact that it precariously kept upright the bong that was tilted against it.

Empty beer bottles were scattered across the floor. (Upon a closer inspection, they would look as if they'd been set up as bowling pins and later taken down by a seven-ten split.)

Manny Vargas announced his presence by bellowing, "It smells like my sweaty armpit's ass in here!"

Jenn was sprawled across the floor. Her legs were draped over a bulky couch cushion. Hearing Manny's booming voice startled her. Her head jerked upwards, stopping abruptly when her forehead slammed against the underside of a glass coffee table.

"Good thing you wear a mask any time you go out in public," Manny said, his voice purposely elevated in hopes that the volume would cause the teenage luchadora to regret her excessive partying. "You're gonna have quite a bruise where you just conked your melon!"

"*¡Ay, cállate!*"

The exclamation (the Spanish equivalent of *"Ugh, shut up!"*) came from beneath another discarded couch cushion. The young wrestler who called herself "Relámpaga" pulled her head out from beneath her smelly, makeshift pillow and groaned, *"¿Que hora es?"*

"What time is it? I don't know. Time for me to kick you so hard in the ass that my toes come out your mouth?" Manny wanted to leave little doubt that he was upset. "You're corrupting my protégé!"

"Oh, yes," the sassy young woman answered in English since that was Manny's preferred tongue. "Lady Pirata… Just a poor, sweet, innocent angel until she spent a couple of nights in Mexico City with Relámpaga!"

Jenn tried to ignore the spat going on between her new friend and her old coach (or *"maestro"* as he was called in Lucha Libre circles). She tossed a green and gold mask to Relámpaga, then pulled a crimson and black mask over her own face.

Manny looked at his budding star and winked. "Good girl." Looking back to Relámpaga, he barked out, "You... get your clothes on and get to the gym. Sanguinario's waiting for you. He's been trying to call for at least an hour."

"¿*Verdad? ¿Que hora es?*"

"*Once y media.*" ("11:30 a.m.")

Jenn smiled. Holding her malfunctioning alarm clock by its cord, she pointed to the "12:00" displayed in red. "See? It was almost right."

Though his tone was somewhat playful, Manny meant to whip his pupil into shape. "Oh, I see... now you're not only a wrestler, but also a comedian? Hardy har har. Is that what you want?" Knowing that he had Jenn's full attention, he told her, "We've got a long drive ahead of us. You need to pack a bag so we can hit the road. Before we can do that, you need to clean up this garbage. And do a good job if you don't want this place infested with rats by the time we get back."

Relámpaga stuck her head out of the bathroom. "A road trip? Where are we going?"

"You're not going anywhere. Lady Pirata and I are going to Monterrey. I've booked one match for her there and another the next night in Acuña. From there we might try going to San Antonio... But we're still workin' on that."

As she obediently shoved empty beer bottles into a trash bag, Jenn inquired, "This is the first I'm hearing of it. Who am I fighting?" Quickly correcting herself, she reworded her question as a declaration of her growing confidence. "Who am I *beating*?"

"You're *fighting* Estrella Bella."

Relámpaga emerged from the bathroom fully dressed. "Estrella Bella! Now I *really* want to go!"

Literally translated, the wrestler's moniker meant "Beautiful Star." Estrella Bella was a household name among fans of Lucha Libre. She had held championships in each of the country's major promotions, and even had a prominent role in a popular soap opera! Getting an opportunity to wrestle someone with such notoriety would go a long way towards establishing Lady Pirata as a force to be reckoned with throughout Mexican wrestling.

Manny looked at Relámpaga. "You're not going." Turning his attention to Jenn, he snapped his fingers and instructed her, "You, keep it moving. My truck will only go so far before it needs to cool down. Luckily, San Luis Potosí is about the halfway point between here and Monterrey. I reserved a room for us tonight just outside the city. I'd like to get there while there's still some daylight."

☠ ☠ ☠

ONE DAY LATER
MONTERREY, MEXICO
YEAR -7 + 89 DAYS (MARCH 30th)

They were weary after consecutive days of at least six hours on the road. Much of that time was spent with the windows rolled down to combat the lack of air conditioning in Manny's beat up old pickup.

Jenn wiped several beads of sweat from her forehead. "It's not even April yet. Riding in this truck of yours is already getting to be unbearable. By the time summer rolls around, taking long road trips in this thing is going to be awful! If we're going to start spending a lot of time traveling from city to city, I think you should spring for a new vehicle."

"Do you know what it costs to buy a new truck?"

"It doesn't have to be new. Just something with working air."

Manny shook his head. "Don't turn into a 'diva' on me... I'll have someone look at the A/C. For now, let's talk about Chuleta Castilla."

"Who's that?"

"He's the booker that set up your matches with Estrella Bella."

Castilla was a former wrestler who enjoyed only a few sporadic victories during his days between the ropes. His fortunes changed, however, when he moved on to playing the roles of referee, talent scout, and promoter. Some would describe him as possessing a sharp mind and a habit for sniffing out financial opportunities.

Her maestro described him differently. "Chuleta knows how to make money. In the wrestling business, turning a profit isn't as easy as it looks. That's why we try to stay on his good side, even if he's a snake in the grass who cannot be trusted."

Manny's assessment of his fellow wrestler-turned-promoter sparked a bit of curiosity. "If he's such a scumbag, why does a legend like Estrella Bella allow herself to be associated with him?"

"Good question."

ONE HOUR LATER

"We're almost there," Manny told his passenger.

Without needing to be told, Jenn put on her mask and began to get into character.

The venue was once used as a school gymnasium. It had been abandoned for almost a decade when a local businessman bought the building and turned it into a community center.

"They call this place *'La Catedral,'*" explained Manny. "All the windows had been busted out when they went to fix the place up. The businessman replaced them with stained glass windows that he salvaged from an abandoned church. Sometimes the light shines through, with rays of red, blue, and purple light graffitied across the center of the ring. Some people love it. Some people hate it. They can't get accustomed to watching wrestling in a cathedral… especially when the sunbeams hit the stained glass depiction of the Ascension of Jesus."

Harkening back to comments made by Relámpaga a day earlier, Jenn replied, "Shouldn't bother me. I'm an 'angel,' remember?"

☠ ☠ ☠

Chuleta Castilla was short and stocky, almost as round as he was tall. He pounced on Manny and Jenn while they were still in the parking lot. "Welcome to Monterrey!" he said as he held his arms outstretched, inviting an embrace.

Manny opted for a fist bump.

"Welcome to *'La Catedral,'* home of my syndicated Lucha Libre television program. Every other Friday we tape two one-hour shows… And you must be Lady Pirata. I've watched several of your matches on the Youtube. Very impressive," he beamed as Jenn accepted his bearhug squeeze. While still holding Jenn in his clutches, Chuleta looked at Manny and said, "I hear some are already referring to your young pupil as 'The Future of Lucha Libre.' Exciting stuff!"

Once Chuleta released her from the hug, he offered a quick wink as he said to her, "*Señorita,* please don't forget your friends when you're rich and famous."

"Speaking of 'rich and famous,' when do we get to meet Estrella Bella? Lady Pirata is eager to talk to her about tonight's match."

"*¡Absolutamente!* My Beautiful Star! One day you may both be fighting for Lucha Libre championships!"

Manny and Jenn looked to one another. They shared the same concern. Chuleta's comment seemed strange. Estrella Bella was in the waning stages of a fantastic wrestling career. Over the past fifteen years, she had possessed every women's title in Lucha Libre.

The trio was not waiting long before two black SUVs turned into the parking lot. The lead vehicle's heavily-tinted passenger side window lowered. Chuleta stepped towards the SUV, nodded his head, then uttered a few indecipherable words. Once he moved away from the vehicle, a teenaged Mexican girl opened the back door and stepped onto the pavement.

"Bye bye, *papi!* See you tonight!"

Once the SUVs had roared back onto the roadway, Chuleta introduced the young woman. "Manny Vargas, Lady Pirata... I'd like for you to meet *my* protégé... I call her 'Beautiful Star.'"

☠   ☠   ☠

Jenn and Manny had been duped. Chuleta had been talking up a match against "Beautiful Star." Perhaps confused by the chubby promoter's habit of jumping back and forth between Spanish and English, Manny assumed he was talking about "Estrella Bella" instead of an unknown.

"I would have never agreed to drive up here for you to lose a pair of matches to someone who got her first pair of wrestling boots at last month's *quinceañera.*"

Despite Manny's apology, Jenn knew that she was on the hook to drop that night's contest to an unknown newcomer. Given the fact that the match would air on television stations throughout Nuevo Leon, Coahuila, and Chihuahua, the reputation of "Lady Pirata" would be tarnished for years to come!

"Why don't we just explain the confusion? I'll job out to her, but as 'Genesis.'"

Manny shook his head. "Chuleta's sold tickets, printed posters, and paid for ads on the radio. He wanted 'Lady Pirata: The Future of Lucha Libre' for a reason.' Go… Go spar with your opponent. I'll try to work something out."

☠   ☠   ☠

TWENTY MINUTES LATER

Jenn wore gray sweatpants with a dropped armhole tank top over a sports bra. Her practice session began with her seated in the center of the ring. She reached towards her toes as she stretched her hamstrings. She was fully loosened up by the time Beautiful Star returned from her private dressing area.

As her opponent approached, Jenn remembered that the young woman had spoken to her father in English. She called out, "Good, you're here. Why don't you set your stuff down? You can stretch or do whatever you need to warm up. Then we can start working out some of the details of tonight's match."

The local hot shot left little to the imagination. She wore a cleavage-revealing halter top that looked like it was designed for club hopping instead of any sort of contact sport. And her highrising spandex shorts were certain to make her a favorite among the young—and not-so-young—male members of the audience. Beautiful Star let her bag drop to the ground with a thud. "I don't need to warm up. I'm ready."

Jenn chose not to acknowledge her opponent's wardrobe choice (except for one missing item). "You don't wear a mask?"

When no immediate answer followed, the luchadora looked to begin the sparring session. She lifted her hands skyward. She expected Beautiful Star to recognize the signal for a "test of strength," a common way for professional wrestlers to lock up at the beginning of a fight.

Taking a disinterested posture with her hands at her side, Star finally replied to the inquiry about her lack of a key piece of her wardrobe, "My mask makes me sweaty. I'll wear it tonight... but not for practice."

"Is it the mask that makes us sweaty? Or the fact that we live in Mexico?"

Without warning, the spoiled brat was ready to get down to business. "What's your name again? 'Pirate Girl?' I like to start each match by attacking my opponent when they turn their back. You bend over to adjust your boot or something, and I'll hit you from behind."

Jenn was confused. *Surely they're booking this hometown girl as a fan favorite.* "Do you wrestle as a *technico* or a *rudo*?"

As if insulted by the silly question, Star dismissively answered, "I'm the good guy."

"It's getting harder to tell these days."

The younger of the two stood in silence.

Jenn did little to hide her growing frustration as she asked, "Then what? Does your sneak attack send me to the mat... to the floor? You could knock me out of the ring, then hit me with a suicide dive. That would bring a pop from the crowd right at the very beginning."

"Suicide dive? Are you crazy? I'm not about to risk breaking my neck for a silly wrestling match."

Why exactly did this girl want to be part of Lucha Libre?

Beautiful Star finally suggested a little choreography. "I'll kick you in the butt, and you'll somersault into the turnbuckle. You can do a somersault, can't you?"

"I think I can manage."

"The crowd will get a big kick out of that... Then you stand up, rubbing your head. While you're not paying attention, I'll roll you up and get a quick two-count... You complain to the referee that he's counting too fast. While you're doing that, I'll drop kick you in the back and you can flop out of the ring."

"When do I get to stop getting hit from behind? Better yet, when do I get to mount some sort of offense of my own?" Jenn asked.

"You don't like my suggestions?"

"We should probably bounce some of these ideas off of Manny and Chuleta," Jenn said. *I'm trying to be polite here, but if we use her ideas, it's going to be the worst match in Lucha Libre history.*

Star stood with her arms folded across her chest as she repeated her question. "You *don't* like my suggestions, do you?"

"No offense, but I didn't drive for two days to look like some idiot who never stepped foot in a ring before. Some of your ideas are okay, but I'd say the plan needs some work," Jenn said as diplomatically as possible. "If you don't want to do a suicide dive, maybe I could hit you with one myself... We've got to give the audience something."

"We are." The moody wrestler pointed her hands towards herself and slowly moved them downward. She wanted Jenn to know that she would impress the spectators with *her voluptuous curves*... even if she may be a bit inexperienced inside the squared circle. "The fans like to look, even if they can't touch. *Papi* would have them killed if they tried to touch."

☠ ☠ ☠

THIRTY MINUTES LATER

Though it took some time, Jenn was able to convince Beautiful Star that she needed to be able to mount at least a little bit of offense if the wrestling match was going to be entertaining. By the time their coaches returned to the ringside area, Jenn had taught the newcomer a few basics like how to be on the receiving end of an arm drag takedown and how to safely get hit with a double ax handle attack.

Chuleta had a huge smile on his face. He was quick to brag about how amazing his Beautiful Star looked. His outward joy turned to a bit of concern when he noticed that the wrestlers were working on selling a Lady Pirata sleeper hold.

"Careful not to mess up your hair, my Beautiful Star."

Unlike his counterpart, Manny felt no need to be such a kiss-ass. He clapped his hands together, making a thunderous noise. "Break the hold, ladies, and come here. We've got some things we need to discuss."

The maestros moved to separate areas so they could have private conversations with their respective students. Jenn didn't bother speaking in hushed tones. She cared very little about how private her remarks would remain.

"That girl goes stiff every time I try to make a move! She's gonna get someone seriously injured. I just hope it's not me... This *pendeja* is more obsessed with how she looks than how she wrestles. She's probably just using Lucha Libre to break into a spot on reality TV... 'Beautiful Star!?' She should shorten her name to 'B.S!'"

"Enough," Manny said while holding his hands upward and directing the luchadora to calm down. "You weren't too hard on her, were you?

"Na."

"Good girl. Because think about this... Think back to your first match: B.B. Queen vs. Genesis. A very headstrong Genesis, if memory serves me right... Would you have been that much different if Chuleta Castilla was your coach and mentor instead of me?"

Jenn knew he was right. She pursed her lips together and shook her head.

"'*Pero por la gracia de Dios, voy allí.*'" Manny said, referencing the verse from 1 Corinthians. Then he repeated it in English. "'There, but by the grace of God, go I.' Promise me you'll remember that... Do that and I'll keep working on a solution. I'll get you out of this predicament I've gotten you into."

☠ ☠ ☠

FIVE HOURS LATER

The popular trio known as Circo Loco did their job of electrifying the audience in the *Primera Lucha* (the first contest of the night). The bout between Lady Pirata and Beautiful Star was scheduled to be the second match on the card.

Lady Pirata was booked as the *rudo* (or "villain"). Obedient to the role, she snarled at those in the audience and even reared back as if she might slug one obnoxious fan. Eventually she climbed into the ring and gave the referee a kiss on the cheek and a friendly swat on the backside. It was all designed to make the fans fear that the fix was in.

The crowd initially met Beautiful Star with a lukewarm greeting. They soon got louder, following a few airhorn blasts from plants in the audience. It also didn't hurt that the young wrestler's father, the rich local businessman who had been instrumental in transforming *La Catedral* into a community complex, stood and gestured for those in attendance to make some noise.

☠ ☠ ☠

The early stages of the match were best described as "awkward," if not plain "boring." Beautiful Star levied a bit of offense in the form of sneak attacks when Lady Pirata had her back turned. Any time Lady Pirata went to strike back, the *prima donna* made an unscripted exit by slipping out of the ring. If the post-apocalyptic pirate tried to lock up with her opponent, Beautiful Star would force a break by sticking her torso between the middle and top ropes.

The Monterrey crowd seemed to enjoy Beautiful Star's antics... as if she was employing some sort of advanced strategic gamesmanship. Lady Pirata barked insults to the crowd as her frustration continued to grow.

As she was jawing with those in the ringside seats, the luchadora was subjected to another surprise attack. Beautiful Star grabbed Lady Pirata by her tights, flipped her over the top rope and out of the ring.

Everyone in *La Catedral* could see that Lady Pirata was livid! Jenn moved towards the timekeeper's table and pulled the poor old man out of his seat. Unable to control her anger, she flipped his steel chair up into the air, over the ropes, and onto the wrestling canvas.

Before returning to the ring, she screamed, *"¡Viene el dolor!"* (meaning "The pain is coming!")

Beautiful Star wisely tried to flee. But she wasn't fast enough. Jenn grabbed her by the hair and yanked her into the center of the ring.

"You're doing great," Jenn whispered to her kayfabe enemy a second before slinging her to the canvas with an arm drag takedown.

While Beautiful Star remained on the mat, Lady Pirata bounced onto to the second turnbuckle. With her arms held over her head, she leapt. She nailed her with the double ax handle maneuver that they had rehearsed hours earlier.

Beautiful Star flopped around as if she'd walked into the path of a speeding motorcycle.

She may have a future in the ring, after all. That is, if Chuleta Castilla doesn't ruin her.

The next move in the pre-planned sequence was an ankle lock. Jenn and Beautiful Star had opted for that particular rest hold over a sleeper because they didn't want to draw the ire of Chuleta. *Why ruffle his feathers if we don't have to? We don't want anybody pissed off because Beautiful Star's precious hair got mussed... not when an equally effective hold was available.*

With Beautiful Star still on her back, Jenn zoomed in and grabbed her left foot. Tucking the foot under her armpit, Jenn twisted the appendage. The move was designed for the two

wrestlers to catch their breath, all while making it look like Lady Pirata was contorting Beautiful Star into an agonizing position. Much to the surprise of both wrestlers, the referee waved his hands wildly. The timekeeper—who now occupied a new chair—rang the bell. And the ring announcer declared to the world, "Here is your winner, by submission, Lady Pirata!"
"What!" shrieked Beautiful Star.
"What?" Jenn whispered to herself.
"What the hell!" Chuleta screamed from his spot in his protégé's corner.
The luchadora looked to Manny. "Jenn, let's get out of here... Now!"
Boos filled *La Catedral*. Food, cups, bottles, and even a couple of chairs were flung into the air and towards the ring. Something wasn't right. It was clear to all in attendance.
A screwjob had just gone down... A Monterrey Screwjob.

☠   ☠   ☠

Chuleta Castilla caught up with Jenn and Manny near the back exit of *La Catedral*. The portly promoter was furious with the unexpected result of the match.
"Beautiful Star was supposed to beat Lady Pirata!"
Spit flew from Chuleta's mouth as he pointed and screamed at Manny. He'd wisely brought a couple of beefy wrestlers to "hold him back." If he'd dared get in Manny's face without reinforcements at the ready, the Puerto Rican badass would have knocked him out cold.
"I don't know what the hell just happened in there but you can forget about tomorrow night's show in Acuña!" Chuleta screamed, "And know this... It'll be a cold day in hell before Lady Pirata

wrestles in Monterrey again! Thanks to that little stunt you pulled, she's got no future here!"

Scars climbed atop scars as Manny furrowed his brow. After taking a deep breath to collect himself, he offered a response. "You're obviously upset. I'm not going to say anything to escalate the situation. Neither is Lady Pirata. Instead, we're going to take a taxi to the airport and catch the next flight back to Mexico City."

"Good! Run like the coward you are!"

Manny laughed and shook his head. "When you step back and think about it, you'll realize that you harbor much of the blame. You tricked us into thinking Lady Pirata was going to be fighting Estrella Bella, not some spoiled little rich girl. You'll realize that I didn't have any choice but to do what I did tonight."

Chuleta snarled once or twice as he played up his efforts to regain his composure. Glancing back towards the inside of the arena, he remarked, "You're lucky I have to get back in there for the other matches."

"Or you'd knock me out?" Manny interrupted, practically begging him to take a swing. "Whatever. We're leaving. But, Chuleta… Jenn, I mean Lady Pirata, didn't have anything to do with this. That screwjob was all me. Don't hold it against her. She's the Future of Lucha Libre. And you'd be a damn fool to keep her from wrestling here—*and making lots of money for you*—in the future."

Manny waved for the nearby taxi driver to pull up to the back door.

"¿Tienes aire acondicionado?"

"Sí."

"Aeropuerto."

Once he tossed his bag and Jenn's travel suitcase into the trunk, Manny joined Jenn in the back seat of the taxi.

Still wearing her mask and dressed in her in-ring attire, Jenn asked her coach, "I get that we're getting out of town as quickly as possible. And I appreciate the fact that we've got some A/C. But what about your truck?"

Manny laughed before answering. "It's not my truck anymore. I sold it. Got three thousand dollars cash. Just enough to pay off the referee, the timekeeper, and the ring announcer."

☠ ☠ ☠

NINE YEARS LATER
OQUEZZI
YEAR 2 + 234 DAYS (AUGUST 22nd)

"How 'bout it, Long Jenn Silva…?" Fireball asked. "Do you have any ideas about what we can do to even the score?"

Jenn laughed. She was glad to have been given a little reminder of a couple of important things. She's a survivor. And, if you cross her, she will get her revenge.

"I think Jagger and I can put our heads together and come up with something. We won't take this lying down."

16: SACRIFICES

"Who do you think you are, little man? Stick your finger in my face again and I'll rip your entire arm away from your body! Then I'll knock you over the head with that arm. You'll be my personal little piñata."
   - SANTA SAWS, moments after his interview was interrupted by HIJO DEL SANGUINARIO. The two would fight later that night as part of the AWWA's "One Night in Tijuana" pay-per-view.

ACADEMY 1120 – SOUTHERN HEMISPHER OF NA-WERSS
YEAR -25 + 266 DAYS (SEPTEMBER 23rd)

Pollution was terrible in the southern hemisphere of Na-Werss. Much of it occurred naturally. The toxic levels of silver had led to some strange mutations of their species over the two thousand plus years since they colonized the planet. Two thousand years of technological innovations had not brought about adequate means to dispose of the advances of industry or the consequences of war.

Poor blood circulation was one of the first symptoms the Nawerssians noticed once the poisons began overwhelming their bodies. It came early in life. Even little children felt a constant tingle in their extremities.

"Sit like this, so most of your weight rests on the top of your feet." Som Obostoo (then thirteen years of age) demonstrated the correct position to the younger girls at Academy 1120. Those that had not yet lost their arms and legs in their first round of transplants often passed the time with sleepy feet races. "About ten minutes is all it takes. Then you feel the needles in your feet... if you feel anything at all!"

Most of the children laughed. Some tried to cheat. All of them kept an eye on the clock, waiting for the time to come when they rose to their feet and sprinted towards a chalk line drawn on the ground about fifty meters in the distance.

"It is not as easy as it sounds when your feet are tingling," Som Obostoo reminded the little ones. "If you fall, you are out. No crawling. You can walk or you can run. But you must cross the finish line on your feet."

The Academy Mother caused a loud, whistling sound to blare from her cyborg mouth. With that, the children rushed to their feet.

Some toppled over immediately. Others were able to hobble or walk towards the finish line.

Though her numbed feet forced her to move like she was marching through deep snow, Som Obostoo was ahead of the pack. *Of those who still possessed their organic appendages, she had the longest legs in the Academy.*

Som Obostoo glanced over her shoulder. Only one other girl was close. Knowing that a victory would mean more to a seven-year-old than it would to her, Som Obostoo flopped to the ground as she allowed her legs to give out beneath her.

"Great job, Gal Lyxxidyr!" the woman Som Obostoo knew as "Mother" declared as she scooped up and celebrated with the winner of the race. "You did it!"

Som Obostoo remained on the ground for several moments. She smiled. With her first transplants scheduled in the very near future, she knew that she'd most likely participated in her last sleepy feet race. Womanhood was fast approaching... but she already was learning how to make sacrifices and other adult decisions.

☠ ☠ ☠

SIX YEARS LATER
YEAR -19 + 266 DAYS (SEPTEMBER 23rd)

Screams and alarms. That's all Som Obostoo could hear. These sounds signifying the terror around them weren't filling the air because of war with their enemies from the north. These were coming because her people recognized that their own leaders were tyrants and oppressors.

"After what we just witnessed, can you say there is anyone or anything worthy of trust on this poisoned planet? I know of a group that intends to hijack a military spacecraft and fly far, far away from this awful world. They need Navigators. Come with me... Now... Before this escalates any further... before the order is given to shoot anyone who is not confined to their room." Viv Mystova clutched her friend's arms while making a desperate plea for her to join those fleeing Na-Werss.

Som Obostoo felt her organic heart thumping within her mostly mechanical body. She'd heard of cyborgs passing out on rare occasion. As her mind raced back to the emotions she felt while watching the Academy Mother drag her students away from the chaos on campus, she worried her knees might buckle.

"Som Obostoo... Please!"

She nodded. "We must make one stop before we go."

☠ ☠ ☠

TWENTY MINUTES LATER

Som Obostoo's hurried pace slowed. She halted in the street to look at the building and adjoining playground in front of her.

"Is this it?" Viv Mystova asked. There was a high degree of urgency in her voice. Every second they delayed increased the likelihood that they'd be arrested in the street... or the hijacked ship would leave without them.

Academy 1120. It was the place she—along with nineteen other girls—had been raised. She called Academy 1120 "home" from infancy until the moment her final surgical procedures transformed the young woman from mostly organic to a cyborg with an almost entirely mechanical body. "Yes. This is it."

Som Obostoo felt some trepidation at the idea of going inside. Though she believed her Academy Mother was a good person, the entire system was constructed around fear and neglect. "Mother" was an active participant in molding that fear in the hearts and minds of the children under her watch. "I will not be long."

There was no chaperone guarding the door. That made it easy for the cyborg to disable the lock and gain access.

Once inside, she called out, "Hello?"

There was no response.

Som Obostoo moved immediately to the "safety room" in the basement. It was there that, as a child, she had spent entire nights in the arms of "Mother" while bombs shelled the city above.

As she expected, "Mother" and a pair of chaperones (Academy Mothers in training) were doing their best to comfort twenty panicked children.

"Som Obostoo! Why are you here?"

The Model 12 showed no surprised upon being recognized. A low whistle and the words "Som Obostoo" would have buzzed in the ears of each of the cyborgs in the room. Such radio transmissions not only alerted each cyborg that another was nearby, but also announced the identity of the individual that was approaching.

"I am leaving this planet. I am here to take them with me."

"Who?"

Som Obostoo replied, "The children... All of them."

"No. It is not safe," protested one of the young chaperones.

"Staying on this planet is not safe!" insisted Som Obostoo. "If you do not let them go, my friend and I will..."

"Mother" did not want the children to hear any threats or witness any violence. "Stop!" She shook her head very slowly. She handed an infant to one of the older children. "Let us speak in the hallway."

Som Obostoo agreed. Viv Mystova reminded them that they were in a hurry.

"Mother" shut the door so her charges could not eavesdrop on her discussion. Then she moved towards Som Obostoo and wrapped her arms around her in a powerful embrace. "Thank the Original Creator you are here! I fear for each and every one of these girls… But you cannot take all of them."

"Do you not understand what is going on just outside? We may be on the brink of a revolution."

"Mother" corrected her, "We may be on the brink of a bloodbath if those in power decide to quash this latest uprising…"

Viv Mystova interrupted. She was getting impatient. "That ship might leave without us! We need to leave… now!"

"Mother" rested her soft palm across a spot just below Som Obostoo's throat. It was the same expression of love that she had performed every night of Som Obostoo's childhood, as she was putting her to bed. "Take one… Knock me out and take one child with you. If you take any more than that, the authorities will assume I permitted you to do so. They will have me executed."

With her mechanical eyelids fluttering, Som Obostoo nodded her head. "We will take one. Thank you, Mother."

☠   ☠   ☠

Som Obostoo's eyes continued to flutter. She blinked rapidly while gazing upon the group of terrified children who clung to one another for protection.

One girl caught her attention. Other than the pair of infants that were being held by the chaperones, this child was one of the smallest in the room. No older than four years of age. It was four years ago that Som Obostoo had given birth to two children—one male, one female—only to have government authorities snatch her babies away before she ever had the chance to hold them.

"That girl could be mine," she whispered.

"Take her and let us go!" Viv Mystova said anxiously.

Then she looked at another girl. Gal Lyxxidyr was the young one that had won the sleeping feet race years earlier. Now, fast approaching womanhood, she looked as if she'd be taken to receive her first transplants within a matter of days.

"This world might change over the next ten years. The one that could be my daughter may have a chance. Gal Lyxxidyr has no chance if we do not take her."

"Fine! Take *her*!" Viv Mystova said without hiding the panic she was feeling.

"Gal Lyxxidyr… come with us. We are taking you away from this awful place."

☠ ☠ ☠

TWENTY-ONE YEARS LATER
OQUEZZI
YEAR 2 + 238 DAYS (AUGUST 26th)

Things were extremely quiet two-thirds of the way through The Long Night. With many of Oquezzi's residents passed out following hours and hours of debauchery, and others resting up before a lengthy shift of grueling work in the shallow waters of the mines, Gelly's Saloon had closed its doors to outside customers. Long Jenn Silva, Fireball Freeman, and Captain Jagger huddled around a single table. A dimly lit lantern provided the room's only illumination. Two cyborgs remained in the nearby shadows as they changed out of their usual attire.

Fireball leaned in towards Jenn and whispered. "You're sure you're up for this?"

Jenn was unwavering. "We've got to do something. We've got to strike back hard. Otherwise, Nixx is going to take each of us out, one by one until there's no one left."

"Then listen up… Payin' particular attention to detail will be what keeps ye alive when ye walk into the belly o' the beast," said Jagger as he went over his meticulously detailed plan for a final time. "Nixx's bodyguards will be drunk on Villetra and damn near comatose sixteen hours into The Long Night. If the path to his door be clear of obstacles, Ray Yandee 'ill greet ya."

Long Jenn Silva wanted to leave nothing to chance. She'd rehearsed the lines again and again until they were memorized. "Are you here for a drink and a dance? Or are you finally going to take me up on the offer to come work for my crew?"

Jagger clapped his hands together. "If the li'l gray man says anything but those very words, ye are to abort. Ye hear me?" The Captain continued laying out the carefully crafted script. "As an extra layer of protection, the Cyborg DJ will switch the music from syntho-beats to 'Oquezzi Disco.' Ye do know how to tell the difference?"

Fireball jumped in. He didn't care for either variety. "One feels like you're gettin' tortured. The other makes you want to torture yourself."

Jenn laughed and confirmed that she knew the difference.

"Nixx won't be alone," Jagger continued while welcoming Som Obostoo and Vix Mystova into the room.

The cyborgs had changed out of their customary attire. Their androgynous tuxedo uniforms had been replaced with short, shiny dresses that offered very little covering. The dazzling material flowed across their soft—but mechanical—frames in a way that left one to guess the exact moment that every glorious detail of their cyborg bodies would be on display.

Regardless of their planets of origin, each of the men in the room were momentarily frozen while they stared at the ravishing cyborgs.

Jenn broke the silence, "You look spectacular. But how do we know Nixx will pick our girls instead of the androids and aliens in the brothel?"

"The bastard 'ill happily tell ye that he's been there and done that with all the Davi-Loga and Hamurkan women that work there. And the pleasure bots be of li'l interest ta Nixx-O-Fee. The man prefers ta leave a lasting memory. He don't particularly care if it be euphoria or shame or guilt or disgust… as long as he's left his imprint on another soul, he be satisfied for the night."

Jenn sucked in a deep breath. It was almost time to go.

Jagger found another point worth emphasizing. "Now don't ye forget, Nixx 'ill be wantin' to leave his imprint on ye, as well."

"Ugh. What does that mean… exactly?"

"Of that, we can't be sure. It's at that point ye will need to be ready to improvise. Now look me in me one good eye and tell me… Can ye handle that, Long Jenn Silva?"

Jenn exhaled. She thought long and hard about the dangers she was facing by "stepping into the belly of the beast" (as Jagger had put it). A single tear trickled down her cheek as she thought of all of those that she'd lost over the last few months. "This isn't just for Armstrong. It's not just for Mach. It's for Lazz, Cocoa, and Avis, and everyone we've lost… This is what we have to do to bring an end to this long journey down a path surrounded with death and despair. Hell yeah, I can handle it."

Fireball spoke for her before Jenn could the words out. "She's got this. Jenn's not just a champion. She's a survivor."

Jagger clapped his hands together once again. "Alrighty then! Som Obostoo, radio Ray Yandee and tell him that ye will be walkin' through the door in ten minutes. Then Long Jenn Silva will follow as soon as the music changes."

Som Obostoo's response was short. "Right away, sir."

No one bothered to ask the cyborgs if *they* had any qualms about risking everything by being part of this dangerous mission. She refused to let it bother her.

☠ ☠ ☠

FIFTEEN MINUTES LATER

The door swung open. Nixx-O-Fee laughed aloud as he greeted the pair of sultry cyborgs. "My lucky night!" The Hamurkan stepped forward and rotated his body 180 degrees. He moved between the two cyborgs and wrapped one arm around each of them. "Please come in," he said while reaching each hand down to palm their backsides.

Both Som Obostoo (a Model 12) and Viv Mystova (a Model 10) were given mechanical shells that did not fail to honor the feminine form. Though they were no longer equipped to give birth, they were designed with wide hips that often triggered animal impulses in male suitors who might subconsciously desire to increase their progeny. A generous curvature of the butt did not go unnoticed, either.

"I am grateful to those cyborg craftsmen who designed you," he laughed while helping himself to firm squeezes.

Once the door was shut behind him, Nixx-O-Fee slid behind his desk. He gestured for Viv Mystova to take the seat across from him and for Som Obostoo to stand at her side.

"First off, introductions… What are your names?"

Raising her fully functional arm, Som Obostoo pointed to her chest and announced, "I am Som Obostoo. This is my best friend in the universe, Viv Mystova."

Nixx nodded. He'd heard their names before. "From the *Valentine's Kiss*." Given the recent deaths at the Tide Fights, the Hamurkan gangster was somewhat suspicious of their timing. "What brings you *here… to me…* tonight?"

"We celebrate this night every year," Som Obostoo said, continuing her part of their well-rehearsed story. "It is the date we have chosen to remember when we left the polluted environment and poisoned thinking of our home planet."

Viv Mystova jumped in. "We put on beautiful clothes, then go out and do sexy things."

Nixx remained cautious. "That explains tonight… Why here? Why me?"

"My replacement was late to relieve me on the deck of the *Valentine's Kiss*. We took a shuttle down as soon as we got dressed for our night on the town. All of Oquezzi was fast asleep by the time we got here."

"Except you," Som Obostoo said with a smile. "Like you said, it is your lucky night."

"This has nothing to do with the dead Nawerssian? The one they called Armstrong?"

Som Obostoo shook her head. It was a question they had anticipated. The cyborg provided the answer she had rehearsed. "The one called 'Armstrong' was from the northern hemisphere of our planet. We cyborgs come from the south. Our people are constantly at war with his. Captain Jagger is the only blue-skinned Nawerssian with whom we are on friendly terms… and he does not seem too concerned about the death of Armstrong."

That satisfied him.

"What are we going to do now?"

Viv Mystova smiled. "On Original Earth they play a game called Show and Tell."

"How does that work?"

Som Obostoo stepped forward and begin to move her fingers along the straps of her gold, glittery dress. "We dance. We show you what we look like when our dresses hit the floor. Then you tell us what to do next."

"Good thing there are two of you," Nixx said with a twinkle in his eye. Pointing to Som Obostoo first, then Viv Mystova, he directed them, "Why don't you have a seat and keep working on that dress? Slow. Take your time… As for you, why don't you come over here?" He grimaced as he twisted his neck to one side. "I'm telling you to show me what kind of tender massage you can give me with those cyborg hands."

Som Obostoo obediently sat across the table from the Hamurkan. Her jacket was already on the floor. As instructed, she slowly worked her way out of the tiny garment that glided along the curvature of her chest. The cyborg craftsmen had given her functionally pointless breasts plenty of volume. As she stared at Nixx from across the table, she finally began to appreciate how effective her cyborg shell could be at mesmerizing members of the opposite sex. (This remained true regardless of the individual male's planet of origin.)

"Very nice," purred Nixx-O-Fee, completely absorbed in the show up to this point.

Viv Mystova was positioned behind Nixx. She remained fully clothed. She began kneading his massive trapezius muscles. She knew how to maneuver her mechanical hands in a manner that was much more satisfying than a backrub from an android.

It was at that point that Long Jenn Silva entered the room. Little was said about how she'd made it to the office in the back of the establishment.

Nixx did his best to keep his cool. He spoke to Jenn in English. "I want to apologize for what transpired a few days ago... I understand you and he were extremely close."

"I'm not happy, but I get it. Business is business."

Nixx-O-Fee let out a low groan signifying his pleasure. Smiling, he glanced upwards towards Viv Mystova. He kissed her fingers and thanked her for the wonderful job she had been doing while massaging his pronounced shoulder muscles. Next, the mighty Hamurkan brushed his thick braid to one side, then repositioned the cyborg's hands so they rested at the base of his neck. "Right here, princess... That's it. Rub right there."

Jenn began to seethe. "Are we done?"

"Sadly, no... You said it yourself: 'Business is business.' From my perspective, you and your comrades are loose ends. Unless we can figure something out, each one of you is going to meet the same fate as that chump you called a friend."

"That's why I'm standing here. I didn't come to get some phony apology. I came to tell you that the rest of my gang and I are going to join Ray Yandee. We'll be making some repairs to his ship. After that, we plan to stay aboard until it's time for The Slingshot. Oquezzi will be a distant memory. And we'll be outta your hair for good."

The luchadora's use of the word "hair" triggered something within the Hamurkan. Nixx stroked the braided rope attached to his scalp. His smile grew even wider. While grasping Viv Mystova's arm, he pulled her down until their lips met.

Som Obostoo momentarily halted her striptease. It was a welcome pause considering she had almost finished removing any remaining—and completely unnecessary—undergarments that had covered her mechanical frame.

Turning his attention to Long Jenn Silva, Nixx said, "You should know, the Hamurkans have a tradition. When a man and woman enter into an agreement, they seal the deal with a kiss."

The wrestler with a post-apocalyptic pirate gimmick saw that the lines were blurring between her fictitious persona and her new reality. She peeled away the glove that had been covering her left hand. A split second later, she extracted the dagger she had sheathed along her hip. "Back on Earth, pirates are known to seal a covenant in blood."

She glided the edge across the top of her exposed hand, causing crimson to flow to the surface. Revealing the murky liquid that ran along her brown skin, she instructed the gangster, "Now we blade *your* hand. We smear our blood together... Then our covenant cannot be broken."

Nixx gestured for Som Obostoo to step aside to allow his uninvited guest to move closer.

Finally.

Having very little use of her arm (which had been intended to be a "temporary replacement"), the cyborg momentarily struggled to gather her discarded clothing. She finally managed to do so, and Jenn took the seat that the cyborg previously occupied.

Nixx-O-Fee planted his palm atop the table. Looking at Jenn, he said, "I like the way you conduct business."

The pirate's frown vanished. A smirk appeared a split second before she drove the dagger through the back of Nixx's meaty hand. The steel point lodged deep into the table, anchoring the Hamurkan's palm to the spot in which he had confidently planted it a moment earlier.

Turning to Som Obostoo, Jenn spoke over the scream of her foe. "Get dressed."

The screaming stopped. It was replaced by the sound of crunching bones. Viv Mystova clamped her cyborg hands around his throat like a vice. She would continue tightening her grip until she had squeezed the life out of him.

17: ONE OH SIX

"I've been places most people can't even imagine in their wildest dreams. One thing I've learned is there's no place in this universe that I'd rather be than the United States of America. From sea to shining sea, it's the greatest patch of real estate that God ever made... on this planet or any other!"

    -Promo given by THE LAST AMERICAN in advance of his match against European Champion ALEKSANDAR BENZ at All-World Wrestling's Triple B:33 VirtualView^{TM} event.

OQUEZZI
YEAR 2 + 233 DAYS (AUGUST 21st)

"Som Obostoo, what happened to your arm?"

The question was posed by Cax Bodnusup, head nurse to Oquezzi's only Cyborg Surgeon. A Model 16, the nurse had left Na-Werss on the same hijacked ship that brought Som Obostoo to the red moon many years earlier.

When the question went unanswered, Cax Bodnusup gave Brady a disapproving glance. Not surprisingly, her look of disdain went unnoticed. (Most fleshy species could not recognize the subtle nuances of cyborg facial inflections.) Prior to exiting the room, the nurse offered, "Such are the consequences when you align with pirates. Perhaps it would be safer if you returned to living among your own kind."

Once they were alone, Brady asked, "She doesn't like me, does she?"

"Ignore her. She is a poor judge of character with an icy cold heart. She is not to be trusted."

"The longer I'm on this moon, the more I realize it's not safe to ignore those that can't be trusted."

The discussion was cut short when the Cyborg Surgeon entered the room. "Som Obostoo!" He greeted her with an embrace that went from warm to awkward in a matter of seconds.

The surgeon turned towards Brady. Speaking in his native Nawerssian tongue, he asked, "Is he from Earth?"

Without requesting permission to do so, he reached up and pressed his hands against Brady's jaw and cheekbones. He applied the minimum amount of pressure needed to pry the young man's mouth open. He spoke in English while examining his teeth. "Do all people from your planet have perfect dental structure?"

Brady's response was muffled by the presence of cyborg fingers exploring the inside of his mouth. "Noooowwrr... norrrt reeeely."

"Fascinating. With your permission, I would be honored to have the opportunity to study your anatomy much more closely... Both you and a female from your planet, if it could be arranged. It could be most beneficial in providing a greater understanding of how your bodies evolved into ours. It excites me to think that we may be approaching the first step in curing the diseases that ravage each of our planets! The possibilities are endless."

Though he was glad to have the mechanical fingers removed from his mouth, he didn't know how to respond to the cyborg's forward request. "Okay?"

The Cyborg Surgeon turned to Som Obostoo. "I cannot fathom how you have been functioning with this piece of garbage hanging at your side." He paused to study the makeshift prosthetic, paying particular attention to the point where the rickety black metal attached to her original cyborg shell. "I am happy to report that I believe I can fashion a much more suitable replacement using the parts from Ray Yandee's discarded androids."

After removing Som Obostoo's arm, he took a series of measurements and made note of the few original cables that remained intact. "Good. Many of these connections can be repaired. It will take approximately five days for me to construct and program the implant. We can schedule your procedure soon thereafter. When we are done, you will have a fully functioning arm once more... The procedure, of course, would take place on our Nawerssian warship. The conditions are much cleaner there. Here on Oquezzi we get so little rain. The result is that everything is covered by a fine layer of dust. As I am sure you can imagine, dust is an unwelcome intruder in the operating room of a Cyborg Surgeon."

The cyborg turned to exit. "Please talk to Cax Bodnusup about scheduling a shuttle to our ship. And please bring…" he paused because he had not been formally introduced to the Earthling.

"Brady. Brady Emerson."

"Please bring Mr. Emerson with you. I could take some fluid samples and administer some tests while you are recovering from the procedure." Once he observed the Earthing's nervous reaction to his request, the Cyborg Surgeon added, "My tests will be one hundred percent safe and non-invasive. I promise. There will be nothing about which you should worry."

☠ ☠ ☠

SEVEN DAYS LATER
YEAR 2 + 240 DAYS (AUGUST 28th)

A lot had transpired in the week following Som Obostoo's first appointment with the Cyborg Surgeon. Most notably, of course, Long Jenn Silva had assassinated Nixx-O-Fee. (It was a hit job in which Som Obostoo was an accomplice). In the wake of that development, Jagger admonished the entire crew of the *Valentine's Kiss* to avoid going into the streets of Oquezzi alone.

The buzz on the red moon was constant. It never let up, even during the scorching daylight hours when the streets usually were empty. Because of the escalating tension, Brady and Som Obostoo knew it was imperative to follow the Captain's advice. Even if the Cyborg Surgeon had not invited Brady to accompany Som Obostoo for her procedure, the duo would have insisted that he be allowed to join her.

Unnerving silence fell over the streets outside Gelly's Tavern. Brady tried focusing on the sound of the hard-packed sand crunching beneath his feet. No matter what he tried, he couldn't shake the fact that there were plenty of Hamurkan and Davi-Loga in the vicinity. And all had their eyes fixated on the Earthling and his cyborg companion.

"My arm," Som Obostoo worried. "Every creature on this moon can recognize me by my arm. They know I was there when Nixx-O-Fee was killed... It was selfish of me to bring you."

"Don't be silly," Brady said. "We'll be at the launch pad soon enough. Their dirty looks won't bother us once we're aboard the shuttle and traveling up to your old ship."

Cax Bodnusup, the Cyborg Surgeon's head nurse, met them at the launch pad. "I am terribly sorry," she said as they approached. "The Cyborg Surgeon is going to be unable to conduct your procedure today. There will be no shuttle to the Nawerssian warship."

"Why not?" Brady demanded.

Perhaps misunderstanding the Earthling's question, the nurse answered, "There is no need for a shuttle because there will be no procedure."

Som Obostoo asked the question in a manner that Cax Bodnusup could better understand. "Why will there be no procedure? Does the Cyborg Surgeon need a few more days?"

"There will be no procedure. He no longer has the available materials to construct a suitable replacement." Without waiting to see if Som Obostoo had any follow-up questions, the nurse pivoted and walked away.

Brady started to pursue the nurse. His path was inhibited, however, by a growling Hamurkan.

"You are from the crew of *Valentine's Kiss*?"

To Brady's untrained ear, the Hamurkan's deep voice rumbled like a freight train passing in the distance.

"I am Brav-O-Dee... Zeal-O-Vay's top lieutenant." The Hamurkan gangster promoted to replace Nixx-O-Fee looked every bit as imposing as his predecessor. "Zeal-O-Vay challenges your crew to an *O-Cim-Atta*. A Tide Fight between four members of your crew and four fighters of his choosing. Tomorrow at beginning of The Long Night."

Brav-O-Dee handed Brady a parchment covered in alien scrawls. As he did so, he snarled a reminder. "Tomorrow's Long Night."

☠ ☠ ☠

THIRTY MINUTES LATER

Most of the crew of the *Valentine's Kiss* gathered in Gelly's Tavern. The rest appeared via a holographic transmission from the *Valentine's Kiss*. Poff-O-Lan read the parchment that Brady had been given. A bot provided the translation:

"Tide Fight... Tomorrow's Long Night... *O-Cim-Atta*... Four against four... Fair fight... Brav-O-Dee, the Davi-Loga known as Taleeya, the coward known as Orr Bo, and the mighty Zeal-O-Vay challenge the vengeful murderer Long Jenn Silva and any three crew members of the *Valentine's Kiss*... appear or bring perpetual shame on yourself and your crew."

Several crew members blurted out their reactions at once. The translator bot struggled to key in on one speaker.

"Shut that thing down!" Jagger demanded. "And ask yer questions one at a time."

"Who is 'the coward, Orr Bo?'"

Monroe knew the answer. With little inflection in her voice, she said, "That's the Flurrok who killed my father."

"Aye. Hamurkan justice. If the Flurrok survives the Tide Fight, the gods be on his side. Zeal will see no reason to punish him further fer killin' Armstrong," Jagger explained as he momentarily presumed to know the mindset of the Hamurkan boss.

"Zeal-O-Vay is going to be one of the fighters?"

"Aye. He stands a head taller than any other Hamurkan I ever laid me eyes upon. Takin' part in a Tide Fight will serve as a good reminder to all as to why he calls the shots on Oquezzi."

"Who will be fighting for us?"

Poff-O-Lan needed very few words to make it clear that he wanted one of the spots. "They killed my brother."

Kelly Ka-Pow was participating in this meeting from aboard the ship. Though she had not set foot on the surface of Oquezzi since she'd obtained her gruesome injuries in her previous Tide Fight, she wanted in on the action. "That sheet of paper said Taleeya was one of the fighters? She and I have a score to settle. Count me in!"

Some inside the tavern—Poff being the most vehement—tried to protest. Fireball Freeman cut them off. He'd visited her dozens of times as she was nursed back to health. There was not a shred of doubt in his voice when he told them, "She's ready."

Monroe stepped forward to volunteer for the final slot.

"No!" Galixxy tugged on the sleeve of her lover's flight suit as she pleaded. "It is too dangerous! Jagger is right. Zeal-O-Vay is the biggest Hamurkan and best fighter on the entire moon. Brav-O-Dee and Taleeya? They are tremendous fighters, too. Please, Monroe! Please! Do not do it!"

Monroe argued with the lavender-skinned alien in hushed tones. She wanted to avenge the death of her father. However, the arguments made by the only one she'd ever loved romantically were impacting her decision.

Everyone in the room could see that Monroe was torn.

"I'll be our fourth!" Brady announced.

Several of his fellow crew members were skeptical.

"Have you ever been in a fight in your life?" Fireball asked.

Brady nodded his head and confidently puffed his chest out. "I can hold my own... I was a regional champ on my high school wrestling team."

☠ ☠ ☠

TEN YEARS EARLIER
KING CITY HIGH SCHOOL – CENTRAL ILLINOIS
YEAR -8 + 309 DAYS (NOVEMBER 5th)

Brady Emerson. Marshall O'Neill. Greg Puckett. Perhaps it was a coincidence. Or maybe their first grade teacher thought she was being clever when she stuck Greg, Marshall, and Brady together at the same learning table. Either way, the boys quickly became best friends and the group known as "The Brady Bunch" was born.

Fast forward to ninth grade, and the inseparable trio of Freshman boys decided to try out for the high school wrestling team. Dressed in tennis shoes, tube socks, and their King City High School P.E. uniforms, they looked like green rookies.

Brady, in particular, stood out... if you could spot him at all. Puberty had begun, but it was a slow process. He began his first year of high school standing just above five feet in height and weighing in at a whopping 98 pounds. After binging on a couple of bags of leftover Halloween candy, he'd finally eclipsed the one hundred pound mark just in time for the first day of tryouts.

"Hamilton... Brad Hamilton!" Coach Augie Forsett shouted while looking at the signup sheet he had attached to a clipboard. "Brad Hamilton!"

Brady sheepishly raised his hand. "Could that be Brady Emerson, sir?"

Forsett raised the clipboard. Holding it directly in front of his face, he squinted and flipped his glasses onto his forehead. "Yeah, that's it... You need to work on your handwriting."

Never wanting to pass up the chance to make his buddies chuckle, Brady replied to the coach, "I would've thought you would be more concerned with my pinfalls than my penmanship."

Coach Forsett stared blankly at the scrawny Freshman.

"...Sir."

"So? Brad's a comedian? Stay in school, kid."

The coach started to walk away. After another glimpse at his clipboard, he stepped back in Brady's direction. "By the way, congratulations. You made the team."

That was quite a surprise. Tryouts only started five minutes earlier. The newcomers had been reminded repeatedly that there were only a limited number of spots on the junior varsity squad.

Seeing that it was now Brady who wore a blank stare across his face, the coach explained. "We've only got two people on this team small enough to wrestle at One Oh Six: you and Casey Graziano. Find Graziano and get to work..." He turned his body to speak to the remaining young hopefuls. "As for the rest of you, let's see what you've got. We'll start by running laps. Gimme ten around this gym." He blasted his whistle. "Now!"

Brady was elated to learn that he'd made his first high school sports squad. Now he could switch to the next two objectives. First, figure out a way to keep Coach Forsett from calling him "Brad." He knew that every instance in which he did so would amount to Greg and Marshall jokingly using the wrong name for an extra week!

The second objective was more important. Find Casey Graziano. Graziano—or any other Italian name, for that matter—wasn't all that common of a name in rural King City, Illinois. Brady guessed this guy's parents were in some way employed by Central Illinois University. It was either that or perhaps they owned the new authentic pizzeria that was being built near campus.

He approached a long-haired upperclassman who clearly weighed more than 106 pounds. "Casey Graziano?"

The late-arriving wrestler didn't look up from tying his shoe. Instead, he pointed over his left shoulder and said, "Somewhere over there." As soon as he was done with his double-knot, he sprinted to join the pack now on their second lap around the gym.

"Don't think I didn't see that, Grant!" Coach Forsett shouted to the late-arriving wrestler.

Casey Graziano. The name rang a bell. Sort of. Brady was fairly certain there was a Graziano who had been selected to the Homecoming Court. She may even have been runner-up to Carissa Tanner, the younger sister of a former Miss Teen USA contestant who hailed from King City. *Maybe Casey's her brother.*

"Hey, Freshman! Are you lost?"

The words came from the only female in the gym. *Was she the equipment manager? Maybe the coach's daughter?*

Once he looked past her long brown ponytail and unexpectedly bright blue eyes, Brady noticed that this young woman was wearing a purple and gold singlet. *Purple and gold. The colors of the King City Knights.*

"I'm Casey Graziano," she said as she extended her hand.

Yep, there it is. Purple knight from a chessboard. Golden lightning bolt in the background. The logo for his high school team... magnificently plastered atop the most form-fitting wrestling uniform he'd ever imagined.

"Brady... Brady Emerson."

The knockout looked at Brady's scrawny, hairless legs and his knobby knees. "One oh six weight class?"

Brady nodded nervously.

"You ever wrestle before?"

"No... not really."

"Lemme guess, you and your buddies watch some on TV? Grizzly Jack Grissom, Rocket Rodriguez, and Ace Cutler?"

"Something like that."

"I can't decide if rolling with you is going to be fun or like a trip to the dentist," she said while flashing a fantastic smile. "You ready to hit the mat so I can show you a thing or two? We'll start with the basics. Once you get those figured out, I'll share a few tricks of the trade."

☠ ☠ ☠

TWO WEEKS LATER
YEAR -8 + 323 DAYS (NOVEMBER 19th)

With two weeks of practice behind them, the King City Knights starting varsity and JV squads stood in a line. Brady and Casey Graziano occupied the far end, with the squad members getting progressively larger in size as one traveled towards the opposite end of the gym.

Casey's uniform was shiny, multicolored, and featured the school's logo prominently displayed on her left hip and again atop her right breast.

Gotta stop looking at that thing. I don't want to get punched in the mouth!

This was the Senior's fourth year wrestling varsity. Those in the know said she was a lock to take home the conference title in the 106-lb Division. And since each of the six teams at regionals were part of King City High's Power 10 Conference, she had every expectation of waltzing into the State Sectionals.

Brady's singlet was not nearly as flashy. The material was dull and worn from years of use by other JV grapplers. There were no logos or secondary colors. Instead, the passed-down purple one-piece was plain except for the letters "K.C." stitched in white across the stomach.

"Our first meet is on Saturday!" Coach Forsett bellowed to his team. "The Turkey Day Tourney in Teutopolis."

"Try saying that five times fast!" Greg joked to those around him.

Brady laughed aloud. Casey was quick to shush him.

"The bus leaves at six o'clock in the morning. If you show up at 6:05... too damn bad. The bus will already be barreling down the highway towards Teutopolis. If you're varsity, your JV counterpart will be wrestling in your place. If you're JV and you miss the bus, don't expect to have a spot on this team when you show up to practice on Monday. Am I clear?"

A few wrestlers—Casey included—answered, "Yes, sir."

The volume of the group's response wasn't nearly loud enough for the coach's liking. "AM I CLEAR?"

This time everyone got the message. The entire team shouted in unison, "Sir! Yes, sir!"

"And I don't want any of you wimps using the excuse 'But it was the first match of the season,'" he told them, using an insultingly whiny voice to imitate any excuse-makers. "Hit the mats. Work out any last-minute bugs. I wanna win this tournament on Saturday!"

☠ ☠ ☠

While Brady and Casey stood waiting for their turn to spar in one of the available circles, they watched Greg tussle with fellow Freshman D'Angelo Jenkins. Jenkins was an incredible athlete. He'd be wrestling varsity during his first year. It took very little time for him to secure a pinfall.

Brady shouted a word of encouragement to his longtime pal. "Get 'em next time, Greg."

Casey shook her head. "Your buddy's never going to crack varsity as long as he's in the same weight class as D.J."

"You're probably right."

"I know I'm right," she said while moving towards the mat. "Let's work on escapes."

Casey dropped to her hands and knees. It was a starting posture often referred to as "referee's position" in amateur wrestling. After a slight hesitation, Brady moved in behind her. He wrapped one hand around her waist, while locking the other against her elbow.

It took the seasoned veteran less than five seconds to complete a "low level escape" (worth one point). The move was simple. She got her feet beneath her, then moved like she was slithering under a limbo stick until she was free to rise into a standing position.

Brady was unable to hide his discouragement. He softly said, "That was quick."

"Now you try."

Brady obediently positioned himself in the referee's position. On Casey's "Go," he tried to mimic her limbo maneuver. A second later, however, he'd let out a loud shriek and was flat on his back.

"What the heck was that?" he demanded, raising his voice at his partner for the first time in his life.

"Brady? Are you okay?" asked a concerned Greg.

D'Angelo knew what had transpired. Amidst uncontrollable laughter, he managed to spit out the words, "Bro! She just checked your oil!"

Lowering his voice to a whisper, he asked Casey once again. "What the heck was that?"

"You were about to escape. I couldn't let you score a point." She smiled and held up her index and middle fingers... digits that unexpectedly pushed the fabric of his wrestling attire deep towards where the sun don't shine! "Poking these up your butt put a stop to it, didn't it? Little tricks like that are the difference between winning and losing. Just don't get caught." Casey moved back to the mat and dropped into the referee's position once more. "Now you try."

Brady sheepishly moved behind her. With his voice just above a whisper, he asked, "You want me to put my fingers...?"

"If you want to learn how to wrestle and how to win, you need to learn how to bend the rules and get away with it... This is your one and only chance. And don't keep 'em there all day long. In and out real quick. You do anything weird and I'll tell my boyfriend. He *will* kill you. Got it?"

"Got it."

☠ ☠ ☠

THREE MONTHS LATER
YEAR -7 + 56 DAYS (FEBRUARY 25th)

5:15 a.m... *What time is it? 5:15 a.m.! Who keeps calling my cell phone at 5:15 a.m.?*
"Brad?"
The voice was almost instantly recognizable. Brady's Saturday morning slumber was being violated by an unexpected call from Coach Augie Forsett.
"Brady, sir. Brady Emerson."
"That's what I said," the coach insisted. "I hope you haven't been loading up on tacos and pizza over the last week."
"No more than usual, sir." *What's this about?*
"How fast can you get down to the high school? Bus for regionals leaves in thirty minutes. I'm worried Graziano isn't going to make it. I need you here so you can wrestle one oh six if she's a no show."
"Why would she be a no show?"
"No time to explain. How quickly can you get over here?"
"I can be there in fifteen minutes... sir."

☠ ☠ ☠

There were plenty of empty seats on the yellow school bus. Even so, Brady and Greg decided to share one near the front.
"Thanks for coming, boys," Coach Forsett said as he scooted into the green bench seat across from them. With his body twisted towards them and his knees hanging into the aisle, he explained, "You've heard of this bad flu goin' around? Basically, all around the country?"

Brady and Greg nodded.

"Most of our varsity squad…" he paused to cough into his hand, "Most of our varsity wrestlers got it. Headache, fever, fatigue, cough, runny nose. For some, it includes an awful case of diarrhea, too."

Forsett stopped again. This time it wasn't just one cough. An uncontrollable hacking fit delayed him for at least twenty seconds. "Now you ready for the good news?"

Brady couldn't imagine what the "good news" could be. Many of his teammates had come down with this superflu that was freaking out all the talking heads from Fox News, CNN, and even ESPN! Casey's chances at making State were spiraling down the drain! And Brady—a clueless Freshman with an unimpressive junior varsity record of five wins and eight losses—was going to be representing the King City Knights at Regionals?

"The good news is that they think they came down with it at the Conference Championships," the coach said as he laughed at the irony. "Every other coach from our region is having to do the same as me this morning… They're scrambling to put together a lineup made up of scrubs and rejects who have no business wrestling varsity."

☠   ☠   ☠

NINE HOURS LATER
YEAR -7 + 152 DAYS (JUNE 1st)

Brady took his turn climbing to the top of the champion's platform. It was a structure built to hold the top three finishers in the competition. On this particular Saturday, however, he was the only 106-pounder to show up and make weight.

The public address announcer never mentioned the fact that each of his three victories on the day had come via forfeit. Some of his scheduled opponents were struck down by the dreaded virus. For others, it was an inability to lay off corn chips and Twinkies that meant that they were unable to make weight. Glossing over the fact that Brady never broke a sweat at Regionals, the public address announcer enthusiastically declared to the world, "Representing the 106-lb division, in first place and advancing on to Sectionals, a Freshman from King City High School, Brady Emerson!"

Several photographers snapped pictures for their local newspapers. Others— including Brady's mom, dad, and buddy Greg— used their smartphones to commemorate the occasion. Brady smiled and whispered a silent prayer in which he thanked God that he didn't quit the team the moment Casey Graziano checked his oil.

"And please help her get well soon… Everyone from the team, but especially Casey."

There would be no Sectional Tournament for Brady to attend. By the middle of the next week, the State Athletic Board had suspended all sports in response to the mysterious illness that was wreaking havoc across the country and across the world.

(By the time tryouts rolled around in the following year, Brady had grown six inches and added sixty pounds of solid muscle to his frame. D'Angelo Jenkins had filled out a bit, too. With both landing in the same weight class, it became easy for Brady to decide that his amateur wrestling days were behind him. He'd "retire" from the sport with eight wins and eight losses on his record, a varsity "KC" for his letterman's jacket, and the title of "Regional Champion.")

☠ ☠ ☠

THE BEACH - OQUEZZI
YEAR 2 + 242 DAYS (AUGUST 30th)

Even though it took almost forty-eight hours for the red moon of Oquezzi to make one trip around its mother planet, "Tomorrow's Long Night" came very quickly. Brady used most of the time between the issuance of the challenge and the night of the fight to work out and make sure he was back in peak physical condition. He also took advantage of the opportunity to get some pointers from Fireball Freeman. The wrestling pioneer could only teach him a few basic holds and escapes. In the end, the legend worried, "Son, I'm not sure you're anywhere close to being ready for this."

"You nervous?" Jenn asked.

Brady looked in her eyes. There they were, standing on the same beach where they once shared a glorious kiss. Though the two of them had been drifting apart since that magical moment, he knew he couldn't lie to her. "Am I nervous? Yeah... I'm petrified."

"Why did you do it? Why volunteer to be part of this fight?"

A memory from happier times flashed into Brady's consciousness. He laughed, then realized that he needed to share another story from his childhood.

"I thought about going to baseball tryouts when I was eight... Things can get downright cold in my part of Illinois in early April. On the day of tryouts, I don't think the temperature ever got over forty degrees. It had rained the night before. The ground was completely saturated. Soaked to the point that even a scrawny little kid would sink into the mud with every step he took... The wind was swirling and whipping around in different directions. It was blowing so much much so that there was no blocking it. Arctic blasts in your face no matter which way you stood… Needless to say, there weren't many eight-year-olds who were able to field a groundball, catch a popup, or make any solid contact with the four or five pitches the coach threw to you. By the time we were done, I was frozen stiff and practically in tears. My dad told me that we were going to my favorite fast food restaurant to celebrate making it through those awful tryouts."

"I could go for a greasy burger and fries right about now," Jenn interjected.

"Well, as soon as I walked in the door at Rocco's, I saw a sign for cookies 'n cream ice cream with gummy worms. They covered it in whipped cream and called it a dirt and worms sundae…"

Jenn laughed, "I like ice cream and I like gummy worms. Putting them together? That sounds disgusting!"

"Forgetting that I was freezing my butt off, I asked my dad if I could get it. Without blinking an eye, he said 'yes.' I'm sure he knew it was a total waste of five dollars and that I wouldn't want another bite after the first one. So what did he do? He didn't order any food for himself. He loved their burgers. But he sat there smiling and waiting. Then he ate the rest of the sundae himself after I decided it was too cold and I didn't want it."

The luchadora smiled. "I've missed you. I wish I hadn't let all the bullshit that comes with living on this moon get in the way of my relationship with you."

Brady nodded. "Just all the more reason we need to make it out of here alive."

"True… But I still don't get why baseball tryouts and ice cream led you to volunteer for the fight."

"I don't like to see people I care about making decisions for all the wrong reasons. We should make our choices based on who and what we love, not who and what we hate… It broke my dad's heart to think that I might decide that I didn't like baseball simply because my crummy day got made worse when he wouldn't let me get ice cream. He'd do whatever it took to salvage the day and make it a good one... Here it was the same thing. I looked at Monroe. She'd suffered enough heartbreak lately. She'd already lost Avis, then Armstrong. Now she's got Galixxy and it's obvious they're crazy about each other. I didn't want that getting messed up. I didn't want her to join a fight she didn't really want to be in if she based that decision on reasons like anger or revenge."

Jenn took a deep breath and scanned the ever-growing group of spectators that had gathered around the beach. After exhaling, she turned and said, "I'm fascinated to know the things that motivate you, Brady Emerson." She pulled him close and pressed her lips against his. She lingered for a moment, welcoming him to explore and enjoy. When they were done, she whispered, "Hopefully that'll be enough motivation for both of us to push through and survive this."

☠ ☠ ☠

Poff-O-Lan joined the Earthlings on the beach. "Are you ready for fight of your lives?" he asked.

"You Hamurkans aren't the only ones who get a kick out of fighting," Long Jenn Silva told him with a surprising degree of confidence. "Back on Earth, boxing and wrestling and mixed martial arts are some of our most popular sports. We won't back down. We'll be ready."

"I believe you are ready," said Poff. "Kelly the Clown... she is one I worry about."

Jenn adjusted her Lucha Libre mask while she listened to the Hamurkan continue to bicker about why it was unwise to include

Kelly on the team. "She did terrible in first Tide Fight. Almost got killed. She's been on ship nursing injuries for weeks. What makes you think she'll be ready?"

"She'll be ready," the luchadora said. This time her confidence wasn't feigned. She *knew* Kelly Ka-Pow would answer the call when the battle began.

Brady remained silent. He listened to their back and forth without offering his own opinion. Instead, he silently prayed that the topic of their debate didn't switch to whether *he* was prepared for what lay ahead.

He scanned the area around the beach. The spots near the cliffs had filled up long ago. It wasn't just Flurroks willing to brave the sunlight so they could have the best vantagepoints to follow their wagers. It was Hamurkans, Davi-Loga, cyborgs, and even a few Valtayans that occupied the prime seating.

Others gathered in clusters on the beach. The snow-white braids of the Hamurkan men whipped through the air as a bullet shuttle flew disturbingly close. The aircraft made little noise but generated a tiny whirlwind against the towering cliffs.

Like most of the longtime residents of Oquezzi, Poff was alarmed by the break in protocol. (The shuttles were required to touchdown at the strip on the outskirts of town.) "What is that?"

Jenn was unphased. "It's Kelly Ka-Pow… making her entrance."

Though Zek Evrazda objected to the deliberate violation of the rules established by the Hamurkans in charge, the chaotic clown convinced the cyborg to fly the shuttle down to the beach. Kelly winked and said, "Thanks for the ride, Toots!" Then she hopped over the side of the stealthy transport.

With Kelly now standing on the beach, she sought to make it clear that she wasn't shirking away from the clown persona.

However, there were quite a few modifications from the jovial jester outfit that her crew members had seen. There were no more sunburst yellows, cardinal reds, and royal blues. She ditched the kitschy bellbottoms and oversized props. Gone were the squirting flower and rainbow-colored afro wig. Those were replaced with a look that was much more macabre.

    This version of Kelly was dark. She wore a purple tuxedo vest taken from some of the garments worn by the cyborgs aboard the *Valentine's Kiss*. Her wrestling tights were shiny and green, constructed from scraps of an old Nawerssian flight suit. Most of her orangish-red hair had been hacked off. What remained was slicked back. Her makeup was all white, except for purple lipstick and black eye shadow… both of which were smeared across her face in a manner that made it look like they were applied while she was on a moving roller coaster.

    Kelly didn't want anyone interfering with her grand entrance. She brushed past Brady and the others. Instead of greeting her partners, she stepped to the front of the group, and bowed towards the crowd. Ignoring the fact that there were far more jeers than cheers, she belted out the most primordial scream any of them had ever heard. Paying homage to Heath Ledger's Joker, she offered an exaggerated smile before yelling out, "Wanna hear how I got these scars?"

A bit of fanfare followed. Then came announcements (in several languages) that the spectators should make their wagers and find their seats. Once those details were out of the way, the opposition arrived.

Leading the pack was Taleeya. The Davi-Loga birdwoman had challenged Jenn and Kelly to a Tide Fight in their very first hours on Oquezzi. She'd done quite a number on Kelly during that brawl… and now she looked to take down Jenn for killing her sister while aboard the *Valentine's Kiss*.

Next came Orr Bo and Brav-O-Dee. The Hamurkan henchman had to drag the strung out Flurrok onto the beach. Orr Bo wanted nothing to do with this Tide Fight. However, it wasn't his choice. He had been conscripted to be the fourth member of Zeal's team. That was the gangster's way of pronouncing justice on the scumbag who murdered Armstrong in a fit of rage that was uncharacteristic for his alien species.

Finally, Zeal-O-Vay emerged from the shadows. As the last light of the day shown upon him, the powerful gangster proudly displayed his new, cyborg enhancement. The arm that had been intended for Som Obostoo had been implanted onto the Hamurkan. Because he stood at a height more than twelve inches taller than the cyborgs, he had opted for the appendage to be attached *below* his elbow. This made his arm freakishly long…

"…and dangerous," Poff-O-Lan cautioned Brady and the rest of his team, "…if he's figured out how to use it."

Brady burned with anger upon seeing that the Hamurkan gangster had taken the arm meant for Som Obostoo. "That belongs to someone else, you lousy piece of…"

Poff covered Brady's mouth before he crossed a line and said something that might draw Zeal's notorious ire.

"That's right. You would be wise to say nothing," Zeal-O-Vay said as he affixed the stare from his cold, black eyes on Brady. "This may have been meant for your cyborg friend. But I took it. That Number 12 was an accomplice to the murder of my top lieutenant. Yet she did not answer my challenge. She does not deserve this arm. She does not deserve to live."

Brady nodded in acknowledgement of Zeal's motivation. A slight smile slid onto his face as he realized that the anger he felt was replacing that ache of dread and despair that had been burrowed deep within his gut.

"Zeal-O-Vay hacked off his own arm and got cyborg transplant installed for this…" Poff said. *Was that a bit of fear in the Hamurkan's voice?* "This Tide Fight is serious in Zeal's eyes. Be careful. He will stop at nothing."

Brady wished he hadn't heard that. The bitter taste of rage and anger had calmed his nervous stomach. Now he was worried he might puke.

18: LONG TERM BOOKING

"I never liked you. I didn't like you when I watched you on TV ten years ago. I didn't like you when you treated me like garbage when I first joined All World. And I can't stand you now that you think you deserve a shot at MY championship belt!"

-ZOË RYDER promo cut prior to her match against B.B. QUEEN for the AWW WOMEN'S CHAMPIONSHIP.

THE BEACH ON OQUEZZI
YEAR 2 + 242 DAYS (AUGUST 30th)

One by one, the combatants reached into the leather pouch. Once they had done so, they were instructed to keep their hands clasped closed. This heightened the drama for the simultaneous revelations of the colors each had drawn. The random process purportedly was approved by those mythical "Hamurkan gods" who were said to have decreed exactly how fair fights were to be conducted. And it was used to determine who was to be matched up against whom when the blast of the mighty horn proclaimed the Tide Fight had begun.

RED. Poff-O-Lan stood across from Zeal-O-Vay. To many atop the cliffs and aligning the beach, it seemed odd to see any Hamurkan daring to square off against the top dog on the red moon. Poff, however, was pleased with the opportunity to face the tyrant who called the shots on Oquezzi. He was convinced that Zeal had a hand in the death of his brother. Even if it had not been part of the gangster's master plan, Mach's death would have been foreseeable based on his proximity to Armstrong on the night he was killed.

Poff glared at Zeal. He'd never dared say a word to the powerful leader. With a confident snarl, he declared, "I fight to avenge my brother, Mach-O-Man."

GREEN. Kelly Ka-Pow and Taleeya. When they fought several weeks earlier, the birdwoman from Davi 4 had left the skin on the crazed clown's back looking as if it had gone through a cheese grater. They had a score to settle. And the fact that they both drew green cords gave credence to the notion that the "Hamurkan gods" played a role in the outcome of Tide Fights.

Taleeya hissed at Kelly. "Coming back was a terrible mistake. My sister is dead. Davi-Loga custom demands blood for blood. Soon you will be joining her… no matter the cost."

WHITE. Brady looked across the sands at Orr Bo. Taking on the murderous Flurrok looked like a favorable matchup. This was especially the case given how frantic the strung out alien was in his efforts to talk himself off of Zeal-O-Vay's team.

"Be careful," Poff warned Brady. "He is desperate man. And he has killed before. Do not take him lightly."

☠ ☠ ☠

Long Jenn Silva and Brav-O-Dee each held black cords.

"Good!" Brav declared. "You walked right past me on the night you killed Nixx-O-Fee. Now I get my chance to redeem myself and tear you to pieces. When I get done with you, no one will recognize your pretty face. They will see bloody mess and think you were eaten alive by pack of ocean mutts."

The luchadora nodded but felt no inclination to return fire in the exchange of pregame smack talk. Instead, she glanced over to a crevice in the nearby rocks. She had a plan. Now she needed the horn to announce the beginning of the Tide Fight.

The blast from the horn filled the air around Oquezzi. The battle had begun.

Jenn turned her back on Brav-O-Dee. She sprinted towards the cliffs and reached into a long, narrow crack in the stone wall.

NOTHING!

Jenn felt around the crevice. She looked around to double-check that she'd reached her arm into the right one.

NOTHING! Her weapon was not where she had stashed it.

"Long Jenn Silva… Perhaps you are looking for this?"

Zeal called to her from a distance that seemed like a half a football field away. He held one of Jenn's daggers high in the sky for her to see. It was the same blade that she'd driven deep into Nixx's hand on the night she killed him. Now it was being jabbed directly into Poff's muscular chest.

The Hamurkan gangster had landed a swift, fatal blow. Directly into Poff's heart.

"Hear this before you die, friend… I did not kill your brother."

☠ ☠ ☠

NINETEEN YEARS EARLIER
YEAR -17 + 40 DAYS (FEBRUARY 9th)

Jagger braved the extreme heat as he walked down the streets of Oquezzi. Other than those conscripted to the tortuous activity of mining the shallow waters, things were silent on the red moon during daylight hours.

The Captain of the *Valentine's Kiss* ducked into the brothel in which he'd met Zeal-O-Vay only a couple days earlier.

Ray Yandee was inside. He was tinkering with one of his android creations. Other than the friendly Valtayan and the robots waiting to be serviced, the place was empty.

"I see why this place is called 'The Middle of Nowhere,'" Jagger said in Traditional Nawerssian so that the translator bot could understand him and perform its assigned task without a lot of error messages. "There's nothing around here, is there?"

"Robba fobba rob ro bobba."

Once translated, Yandee's words were: "You are wrong, my friend. While everyone sleeps, this moon may seem desolate. That is true. But we are near so many wormholes! This is not the middle of nowhere. This place is a crossroads to everywhere!"

Jagger sat down across from the Valtayan. He marveled at the fact that the tiny alien was covered in fur-lined clothing. In the heat of Oquezzi, a weathered flight suit, overcoat, and tricorn hat was way too much for the Nawerssian. And it didn't feel like he'd escaped the heat by coming inside the bar.

"Back on Original Earth they have this thing called air conditioning. Cools things down right away. I would think you would want something like that here."

"Bobba fobba... Bo ro bo fobba."

Translation: "I do not require such a luxury. Sit down. Sit still. You will feel a cool breeze come through as soon as you do."

Jagger scanned the area. He saw little advantage in continuing to talk with the low man on the totem pole... the one stuck calibrating pleasure bots while the powerful slept.

"Actually, I was hoping to meet with Zeal-O-Vay."

"Ro bobba. Fobba bo robba robba." ("He is not here. He stays on his yacht most of the time.")

The Nawerssian finally settled into a chair. "In that case, can you relay a message to him? Tell him that Captain Jagger would like to meet with him."

Yandee momentarily lifted his goggles to study the next android to step forward. He pulled out a tiny, handheld light and shined it on the hip joint of the lifelike machine. He returned his eyewear to its place covering his gray orbs. Then he motioned for the android to move to the opposite side of the room.

Uncertain of whether he was being ignored, Jagger pushed the issue. "What can you tell me about the boss man? Zeal-O-Vay?"

The Valtayan spun around slowly. He tapped then lenses of his goggles, then patted the sides of his head where his ears were presumably hidden under layers of furry material. *"Fobba... Fobba bo robba fobba."* ("Always... Always wait for him to summon you.")

Jagger nodded. He took special note of Yandee's choice to point to his eyes and ears before repeating his language's word for "always."

So... Zeal-O-Vay always be watchin' and always be listenin'? I'll be keepin' that piece of intel in mind.

☠ ☠ ☠

TWO DAYS LATER
ZEAL-O-VAY'S YACHT
YEAR -17 + 42 DAYS (FEBRUARY 11th)

Zeal-O-Vay's yacht hovered in the skies above Oquezzi. It stayed positioned at a much lower altitude than the *Vilnagrom-I* and the collection of ships that were docked high above the moon. The preferred parking spot was given to the man who called the shots on the surface below.

Zeal spent most of his time on the lower deck. He was joined by a pair of Davi-Loga women, lounging beside a spacious pool of water. A filtration system sucked liquid from the bottom, cleaned it, and returned it to the pool via a spectacular waterfall.

If the sights aboard the ship could not command his full attention, the Hamurkan had the option of gazing out an enormous window that offered a panoramic view of the moon below. If the broad-brush view was insufficient, he could look to the wall behind him. It was covered by at least twenty monitors that cycled through hundreds of different feeds, candidly watching the people that occupied the land below.

"Quite a setup," Jagger said as he was escorted onto the deck by one of Zeal's bodyguards.

Zeal whispered something to his escorts on either side of him. They responded by taking turns kissing him before departing.

The second one lingered for just a moment. She was unable to escape because he had playfully sunk a sharp incisor into her lip. This was a sign that she should kiss him more deeply… a request that she seemed happy to accommodate. Finally, the Hamurkan whispered something in the birdwoman's language, and she left the room without daring to look in Jagger's direction.

Zeal turned to Jagger and spoke as if there had been no delay from the Nawerssian's initial comment. "I am glad you like it… Come, sit down. Get comfortable."

CLANG! CLANG! CLANG!

There was no hiding the sound that his archaic prosthetic leg made as it dropped onto the metal floor beneath him. Jagger stepped with his right leg, then swung his hip to whip the left leg around to move forward.

Through the assistance of a translator bot, Zeal said, "I could have the Cyborg Surgeon come aboard. He could fit you with a much more modern, much more functional replacement for that leg."

"That is something I would not consider," Jagger replied, mindful that he needed to speak Traditional Nawerssian so the translator could understand. "My people and the cyborgs from the southern part of my planet are sworn enemies."

"You may grow to see them in a more favorable light now that you are away from your home planet. While you are here, you are not fighting over the same pieces of land and same limited resources. With those obstacles out of the way, I suspect you may begin to see that your peoples have much in common."

Jagger offered only a half-nod. He wasn't ready to concede that he might soon befriend some of his sworn enemies. Still, he had to admit that he had given a great deal of thought to the lavender-skinned miner that he had observed on his first day on Oquezzi. It was at that moment that she appeared on one of the many monitors on the wall.

Zeal was quick to pick up on what occupied his visitor's attention. He called out, "Computer, hold on Monitor Eight."

The other screens continued to cycle through images of the beings on the surface. They showed painfully candid views, including a Hamurkan couple engaged in an act of vigorous sexual intercourse, and another that showed a trio of Florruks passing a pipe filled with Bazznazz. Monitor Eight, however, remained locked on the young woman from the southern hemisphere of Na-Werss.

Zeal took a moment to explain the cameras. "Knowledge is power. And when there are no secrets on the ground below, I can run things on that moon amidst all of the comforts of this floating paradise in the sky."

Jagger stepped towards the monitors. He reached out and tapped the screen of Monitor Eight.

The Nawerssian was knee-deep in the waters near the cliffs. As she walked, she shuffled her feet and felt in the sands below. Occasionally, she would pull a mining tool from her belt, reach downward, and begin chopping with the ax or digging with the shovel she'd been provided.

"What is she doing?"

"Dangerous work," the gangster replied before removing a large violet gemstone from atop a nearby desk. "Mining for these."

Taking the stone into his hand, Jagger studied every centimeter of the dazzling gem. He had never seen a stone nearly so beautiful... not on Na-Werss and not on Earth. "Amazing!"

Zeal-O-Vay snatched the stone from Jagger's hand. Without hesitating, he spiked it onto the metal floor. It fractured and scattered across the floor in a hundred pieces. The Hamurkan knelt. He ran his finger across the deck, collecting a fine, bluish powder on the tip. Then he stood and showed his guest the remnants of the once breathtaking gem.

"This! This is beautiful. It is the power source our ships run on when they travel into deep space. It will propel your ugly spacecraft twice as fast as it has ever flown before. But use it sparingly. It does not come cheap."

"Because it's rare?"

"Because I am a shrewd businessman!"

Jagger remained unflappable, even when the red-skinned giant who towered over him raised his voice. Instead of flinching, the Captain of the *Valentine's Kiss* pointed to another monitor. This screen depicted the scarred security guard who seemed to relish digging his blaster into Jagger's back.

"Tell me about this one... How did he get those scars across his chest and neck."

"Computer. Hold on Monitor Twenty-Four." Zeal laughed. It was a low rumble. "Neek-O-Lye... His scars came from swimming with the ocean mutts when he was much younger. It was not by choice. His father was a bad man. He tried to kill his own son for spilling a cauldron of Villetra... a popular, but expensive, green liquor that you can sample at any of the taverns I run on Oquezzi."

"Are there any taverns on Oquezzi that you do not run?"

Zeal laughed again. This time the Hamurkan did nothing to suppress the rumble. "You are a smart man. There are many on this moon that possess physical strength. The Hamurkans have the muscle to win in hand-to-hand combat. The Davi-Loga can glide through the air and inflict a tremendous amount of damage with their talons. The cyborgs from your planet have very few weaknesses. Those traits cannot best superior knowledge. Knowledge is power. You and I both know this. That is why I believe we will be friends… You have acquired some specific intelligence that I do not possess. Therefore, I'd like to propose a mutually beneficial arrangement."

☠ ☠ ☠

TWO MONTHS LATER
YEAR -17 + 101 DAYS (APRIL 11th)

Poff-O-Lan and his brother, Mach, wore scowls across their faces as they delivered a very heavy crate. It took every bit of the muscle each could offer to lug it to the back of Gelly's Tavern.

"Place 'em up against the wall, if ye don't mind."

With a nod, the Hamurkans slid the huge box against the wall. Poff used a metal bar to pry away one side. A burlap sack tumbled out and flopped onto the floor with a thud.

"I know it weren't an easy task. For this, I thank ye, boys. Go get some rest." As they departed, Jagger made a final request, "But first, watch the door fer a bit, would ya?"

Once the Hamurkans brothers had exited the kitchen, Jagger grabbed a knife to cut into the burlap material. He struggled to tear through the fabric with the dull instrument in his hand. "Damn this sorry excuse for a blade!"

He stopped and stared at the weapon. It was significantly inferior to his two beautiful daggers that Armstrong confiscated while the pair lived aboard the *Vilnagrom-I*. "Damn that sorry excuse for a man!"

Turning his attention to his recent delivery, Jagger returned to the task of puncturing the burlap. Once he'd cut a tiny opening in the fabric, he stuck his hands into the hole and yanked. Soon he'd ripped a gash in the bag that let him inspect the prize inside.

He reached inside and ran his hands across smooth skin. His smile returned when his fingers met a series of course ridges along the corpse's chest and neck. With great enthusiasm, Jagger tugged against the fabric. The opening expanded all the way to the end.

The scarred Hamurkan security guard lay inside.

"Neek-O-Lye… ye jabbed yer blaster in me back one too many times. I told ye I'd learn yer name. I did. And I told ye I'd cut out yer heart and feed yer lousy carcass to the ocean mutts." Jagger held his dull knife in the air. It shimmered as it momentarily caught a ray of light the peeked through the doorway. "Now be the time fer extractin' yer heart."

☠ ☠ ☠

THREE HOURS LATER

The brick red heart was roughly the same size as two of Jagger's fists. It was so large, in fact, that the Nawerssian had difficulty squeezing his trophy into the jar he'd selected to preserve his prize.

The rest of the body? That was systematically run through the meat grinder.

"Ya know, 'Gelly, this job wouldn't take nearly as long if ye would get off yer lazy arse and take a turn."

The former Skipper of the *Vilnagrom-I* fought the urge to vomit. "I cannot believe I am even able to be in the same room as you! What were you thinking!"

"Made a promise, I did. This... this be my way o' keepin' that promise."

"You are going to get us killed!" said the worrisome Magellan. "What happens when Zeal-O-Vay finds out? This tavern he gave you... the Nawerssian girl... *OUR LIVES!* You have put it all in jeopardy!"

"Be quiet and listen!" Jagger demanded. "Zeal already knows. I wouldn't have done the deed without his blessing."

"But how?"

"There be two things you ought ta know about me by now," said the Captain. "I be a tough man to keep down. And there ain't a creature in this universe that's better at makin' deals than ol' Jagger."

Though he was starting to come around, Magellan was slow to convince. He let out a half shriek when the door swung open.

"Relax, 'Gelly!" Jagger said while shoving another chunk of the dead Hamurkan's flesh into the meat grinder. "It just be our friend Galixxy, here to take away another bag of this spoiled meat."

Clueless about the actual source of the "spoiled meat," the lavender-skinned alien asked, "Am I to dump it in the ocean like the last two?"

"Yes, me lass. That'll do just fine. Feed this garbage to the disgusting creatures that frequent those waters. Methinks even they deserve a treat from time to time."

"We had a saying in the mines... 'Keep the mutts on your good side. It could pay off in the long run.'"

☠ ☠ ☠

NINETEEN YEARS LATER
OQUEZZI
YEAR 2 + 233 DAYS (AUGUST 21st)

The scorching sun was still high in the sky when the Flurrok nearly collapsed upon entering Gelly's Tavern. He was on the verge of hyperventilation, gasping as he tried to suck in air.

A voice came from a shadowy corner of the otherwise empty watering hole. "Did ye run here?"

"Yossa yes!" was the response as the Flurrok struggled to return to a standing position. The expression would have been considered an explicative on the pasty white alien's home planet.

"Hold it down, will ya?" Jagger insisted. "I can't have ya wakin' up me friends."

"My people call me Urr Bo. Nixx-O-Fee told me…"

"Yer name means nothin' ta me!" Jagger cut him off, making obvious the agitation in his voice. "T'would be much better if ye didn't say it and I didn't know it. Do ye get me drift?"

Urr Bo nodded. Following a brief hesitation, he picked up from where he'd been interrupted. "I was… I was told you have some Bazznazz you were looking to unload?" With his skin covered in blisters because he'd ventured out during the daylight hours, the desperate Flurrok could do little to hide his eagerness to acquire the synthetic drug.

"I got two hundred glogs o' the stuff. Enough to get ye and yer friends spinnin' in the cosmos for a long, long time indeed… It'll come at a hefty price. And yer gonna need ta follow me instructions to the letter."

☠ ☠ ☠

TWELVE HOURS LATER
YEAR 2 + 233 DAYS (AUGUST 21st)

Silence filled Gelly's Tavern in the hours after Armstrong and Mach had been murdered. In the wake of that night's violence, not even the saloon's regulars dared to venture away from their homes. It was a rare occasion in which even the poorly constructed beachside huts and shanties seemed preferable to exposure on the streets of Oquezzi.

Jagger reached beneath the bar. He dug into his stash of liquor he'd brought from Original Earth. *The good stuff.* The old pirate used his teeth to extract the cork from the bottle, then downed several gulps of a rich crimson Malbec from Argentina.

He was nearing the bottom of the bottle when a figure stepped through the door. Before realizing who had interrupted his solitary state, Jagger called out, "We be closed!"

It was Galixxy. "Pour me a glass of whatever you're drinking, old timer."

"Come a long way, have ye…" he replied as he pulled out a glass from behind the bar. "'Twas not that long ago that ye would've been happy to drink from the same bottle as me."

"After a night like tonight, I figure everyone could use a little space."

"How's Monroe?"

"Crying her eyes out… as can be expected," Galixxy replied. "She said she wanted to be alone. Once I was sure she was not entertaining thoughts of going out to look for some vigilante justice, I decided to give her the space she wanted."

Jagger lowered his dark glasses and studied the purple-skinned young woman from his planet's southern hemisphere. "Ye've got somethin' on yer mind? Out wit' it."

Galixxy spoke up. "You saved me from the mines. I will follow you to the end... You know that?"

"Aye."

"But Mach...? Why did Mach have to die, too?"

"Mach was not to be trusted. Hamurkans be hired guns, loyal to the highest bidder. And I've been fearin' fer some time that Nixx-O-Fee had a mind to make a play against this tavern, against me, and the *Valentine's Kiss*. Methinks Mach woulda been willin' to do the dirty work, if that meant he never had to leave his friends on Oquezzi e'er again."

The two drank in silence for several minutes. When it came time for Jagger to refill Galixxy's glass, she asked, "May I ask you another question? What happens next? Should I be worried about what you might do to Monroe? Or Jenn? ...Or even me? Help me understand why you did what you did today."

"Every single day of life be precious. There was a time when Ol' Jagger was locked in the brig of me own ship... for five... long... years. Five wasted years that coulda been spent in the hibernation tanks to delay the aging process on me war-torn body. But neither the sacrifices I made for me people, nor those aches 'n pains 'n lost years mattered one bit to me biggest enemy. Pronounced a death sentence, did he. Well, Cap'n Jagger made a vow of me own that day. A promise that there'd be no rest 'til that man who signed me death warrant was no more. Today it was checkmate for Armstrong... and if that meant sacrificin' a couple knights ta keep the king 'n his queens on the board, so be it."

19: FALLS COUNT ANYWHERE

"You tell me when and where! Do you want to fight in a steel cage? Maybe a lumberjack match? No disqualifications? It doesn't matter to me. You name the time. You name the place. You name the conditions. I'll be there. And I'll beat you... Again."

-LONG JENN SILVA promo cut prior to her rematch against SAVANNAH LYONS.

THE TIDE FIGHTS
OQUEZZI
YEAR 2 + 242 DAYS (AUGUST 30th)

Jenn stood frozen. Losing Poff caused her soul to ache. The manner in which he'd been so quickly discarded horrified her. This was not the beginning she had envisioned.

With his foe distracted, Brav-O-Dee charged towards the luchadora. Once he'd closed the gap between them, he grabbed Jenn and effortlessly slammed her into the cliff wall.

The Hamurkan gave no indication that he would be letting up. He marched towards his downed opponent and lifted a massive boot to stomp on her head.

Long Jenn Silva rolled out of the way at the last possible second. Desperate to mount some sort of offense, she flung a handful of coarse sand into the Hamurkan's eyes.

☠ ☠ ☠

Brady already had balled his fists when the horn sounded. He had drawn the cord that pitted him against Orr Bo, the Flurrok who killed Armstrong.

Sweat covered the alien who'd much rather be puffing on a gummy ball of Baynap. The combination of grief, fear, and intense drug addiction meant that Orr Bo hadn't slept in days. He was willing to try anything to get out of taking a beating in his first Tide Fight.

He dropped to his knees and held his hands in the air. "Please! I beg of you…!"

Brady stood over him, still ready to strike. But he waited. He wanted to hear what desperation would drive this murderer to say.

No words followed. Orr Bo bowed his head and wept.

"Yes?" Brady's was growing impatient with the groveling Flurrok.

Without any warning, Orr Bo took a wild swing. His sweaty fist slammed into Brady's groin. With the low blow dropping the athletic Earthling to one knee, the Flurrok jumped to his feet and sprinted away.

☠ ☠ ☠

Kelly Ka-Pow had replayed her previous tangle with Taleeya in her mind dozens of times over the last few months. That fight resulted in the chaotic clown being confined to a bed in sick bay. Making matters worse, she'd been branded with hideous scars across her back. Those scars covered painful wounds that would be with her for life.

"Don't let her spread her wings. Keep her close, but not too close. You've gotta disable those talons or she'll tear you to shreds!" Fireball had told her in the hours leading up to their second confrontation.

Kelly knew there was no time for trash talk. No time to try working her way inside the head of the Davi-Loga birdwoman. If she was going to walk away from this Tide Fight, she needed to strike at the first possible opportunity. And she needed to stay on top of Taleeya until there was nothing left of her but a pile of green feathers.

The horn sounded to signify the beginning of the Tide Fight. A split-second later, Kelly left her feet and lunged towards Taleeya. The birdwoman was caught off guard by such a quick attack… and the fact that the clown's elbow crashed against the long, narrow bridge of her nose.

Kelly followed up her initial strike with an unscripted bit of insanity. She pressed her hands and forearms against Taleeya's upper torso, then leaned in to sink her teeth deep beneath the feathers that covered her neck. With the taste of blood enveloping her lips and tongue, and with crimson streams running down her chin, Kelly continued to chomp and gnaw into the flesh below with an unhealthy enthusiasm.

It came as little surprise to anyone when Taleeya's response to Kelly's vampire routine included the exposure of the birdwoman's talons. She could even the score in a hurry if those sliced into the clown's flesh.

Kelly was ready for them. She had positioned herself to bite the Davi-Loga from behind. This made it easy for her to slip back, wrap her hands underneath Taleeya's wings, and lift upwards in a full nelson. The classic wrestling move left the birdwoman with no ability to control of her arms. And it opened the door for Kelly to reach up and begin breaking off the talons one-by-one.

☠ ☠ ☠

From his perch atop the cliffs, Jagger displayed a degree of urgency in his tone when he shouted down to Jenn, "Get away from those damn rocks. There be plenty o' ocean mutts hidin' in the cracks!"

The luchadora didn't have to be reminded twice. Jenn had observed those walking barracudas up close. She didn't want to be anywhere near the teeth of one of those beasts. Heeding Jagger's advice, she scrambled towards the center of the beach. This position put her far from the perils that lurked within the rocky cliffs, and far from the dangers that came with fighting near the rising tides of blood red water.

Once Brav-O-Dee scraped most of the sand out of his eyes, he trudged towards Jenn. He cursed in his own language before shifting to English and shouting insults at his new enemy. "You're gonna run, little girl? I expected more from one who killed Nixx-O-Fee. Oh, that's right… you don't have cyborg friends to help you tonight. You never would have beaten Nixx in fair fight. Now I will give you beating you deserve."

Jenn had no intention of backing down or running away. She charged towards the Hamurkan, launching herself in the air when she got close. Though she drilled him with a kick to the midsection, the blow bounced off with little effect.

Brav swung his powerful fists at Jenn. She succeeded in ducking out of the way of the first two punches. Unfortunately, she moved directly into the path of the next one.

A mixture of blood and saliva sprayed from Jenn's mouth. The punch dropped her to the ground. She was fortunate not to have lost a tooth or two.

The impact of the punch also resulted in much of the material from Jenn's Lucha Libre mask being torn away. With a large black and red strip now flopping in the wind, Jenn had no choice but to remove the mask before it became a visual impediment that worked to her disadvantage.

Brav-O-Dee made another attempt to stop on her head. Jenn rolled out of the way, then swung her foot back to blast him with a kick to the shin of his planted leg. He lost his balance and crashed to the ground like a felled oak.

With her much larger opponent knocked down to her level, Jenn pushed forward. She hopped onto his back and hit him with a series of rapid-fire blows to the back of his rock-hard skull. Brav reached back and tried to pull her off, but Jenn held on tight.

The Hamurkan's next move was to try rising to a standing position. His efforts were working even with the thrashing pirate still on his back. He had risen to his knees when Jenn altered her attack. She nailed him with a furious flurry of strikes to his kidneys and lower back.

"Finish him!" Fireball screamed from his position next to Jagger.

The post-apocalyptic pirate knew that her old boss and occasional mentor was right. Brav-O-Dee was a mighty powerhouse… and now he was enraged. If she didn't put him away quickly, he'd land another power-packed punch, and she would be the one who was ripe for the picking.

The repeated blows to his lower back caused Brav-O-Dee to gasp for air. He stretched his arms outward. With his full wingspan still on display, he unleashed a deafening roar. It was designed to intimidate his much smaller foe. Instead, it signaled that her next move was one of pure brilliance.

"Rrrrraaaagggh!" The sound was, at first, quite intimidating. It soon turned into a panicked gurgle. "Aggg… emll… ell… eh…"

Long Jenn Silva had grabbed the Hamurkan's long, white rope of hair and wrapped it around his throat. She planted her right boot against his back. A forceful kick thrusted Brav-O-Dee facedown into the sand (a move that others had called a "wicked stepsister" back on Earth).

The luchadora pulled on the braid with every bit of strength she could muster. She wasn't sure if strangling a man with his own hair was a maneuver that would upset the Hamurkan "gods" that Poff and Mach had once told her about. She didn't care. Cutting off the flow of oxygen to Brav's thick head was highly effective. Unconscious, his body lay unmoving in the warm sands of Oquezzi.

☠ ☠ ☠

Orr Bo ran towards a mass of spectators that had gathered on the beach. He found little help from the mixture of Hamurkans and Flurroks in the group. Instead, they showered him with insults like "craven" and "yellow-bellied" and "wimp" (and far worse). With several translator bots aligning the beach, it sounded as if there were a hundred different words to describe his act of cowardice.

The group ignored his pleas. They impeded his escape and pushed him back towards the fight.

It didn't take long for Brady to recover from the cheap shot that turned out to be no more than a glancing blow. He closed the distance between himself and his fleeing foe. Once he was within range, he left his feet and launched his body towards the cowardly Flurrok.

Brady felt like a blitzing middle linebacker spearing an unprotected quarterback. He drove his shoulder into Orr Bo's midsection. Once on top of his opponent, he pelted him with a barrage of closed-fist punches. Right, left, right, left.

Four right-left combos rendered the Flurrok bloodied and incapacitated. Many in the crowd cheered. Others groaned as they handed over glugs of Baynap, gems, and other currencies that were wagered at the fights.

While straddling his foe, Brady watched as Orr Bo's bloodshot eyes rolled back in his head. It wasn't enough to know that he'd bested his opponent. He needed to enact a bit of revenge. He blasted the murderer with one last punch, a bullseye to the center of Orr Bo's already broken nose.

As he did so, Brady declared, "That's for Armstrong, you lousy scumbag!"

☠ ☠ ☠

Though Kelly had snapped off most of Taleeya's deadly talons, the jagged shards that remained still had the capacity to do a lot of damage. This became apparent when the birdwoman jabbed the remnant of one of her claws into Kelly's side. Pain shot through the clown's body and she broke the hold.

Hoping to regroup, the winged woman looked to use her ability to glide through the air to her advantage. With a running start, Taleeya sprang up onto a ledge along the walls of the cliffs.

Kelly foolishly pursued her foe, racing to the side of the wall of rocks. After hurling a couple of stones towards the obnoxious Earthling, Taleeya dove off the ledge. A booted foot nearly knocked the clown silly as it slammed into the side of her face.

With her opponent dazed, Taleeya scurried to her feet and leapt towards the ledge once more. This time, Kelly grabbed on. Because she was being pulled down from the ground, the birdwoman smacked into the wall.

Seeing that it was now Taleeya that was dazed, Kelly smirked and quipped, "I'd do that again. But I won't because it made your ugly face look better."

Taleeya started to banter back, but her words stopped abruptly when the tip of a Davi-Loga staff ripped through her chest. Unconcerned with the traditions of Tide Fighting, Areetha had come up from behind and driven the staff through her own sister's back.

Kelly stood speechless. She wanted Taleeya dead, but something didn't seem right about what had just transpired. Still confused, she took a step towards her freshly murdered opponent to verify that her eyes were not deceiving her.

That single step was all that was needed. Areetha pushed against the end of her staff once more. The staff moved deeper... almost completely through Taleeya. It only stopped surging forward when it was firmly lodged into Kelly's chest.

It was a kill shot. The metal weapon entered at an angle and skewered through more than one of her vital organs.

"Davi-Loga customs demand that I avenge Sareena's death... even if I had to kill Taleeya to do so," Areetha explained to the puzzled clown as she breathed her final breaths.

"How do you like that? Kabobbed by an oversized canary?" Kelly muttered. "Aliens and their customs... damn."

☠ ☠ ☠

Zeal-O-Vay waited patiently for the field to narrow. After he completed his swift slaughter of Poff-O-Lan, the Hamurkan head honcho stood savoring the feeling of the gentle waves washing over his unsandaled feet. It was an extreme contrast to the acts of carnage he observed from his peaceful vantage point.

Once most of the combatants from both sides of the Tide Fight became incapacitated, he reached down and adjusted his cyborg arm.

Because the appendage was designed for a much smaller individual, Zeal chose to have it attached below his elbow. It took some time to get accustomed to a doubly jointed arm that was approximately ten inches longer than the other. This small handicap was worth the sacrifice, however, because of the deadly weapons and other gadgets that were tucked beneath the rubbery, synthetic skin.

He called out, "It's down to you and me, Long Jenn Silva... as it should be!"

☠ ☠ ☠

Though he was nursing sore knuckles—and possibly a broken bone or two in his hands—Brady considered himself to be an active member of the Tide Fight. Once he heard Zeal declare that it was down to a duel between himself and Long Jenn Silva, the athletic Earthling hoped he could surprise the powerful giant.

The young man moved towards the gangster with skin that held both the color and texture of bricks. His advance quickly became impeded. Several Hamurkans tugged at Brady's shirt and grabbed him by the arms. "Is fair fight! One on one!"

He had heard this before. He also knew that Jenn didn't particularly care about Hamurkan traditions or superstitions. If he could help, his instructions were to help.

As Brady broke away from the interfering spectators, Zeal-O-Vay spotted him in his peripheral vision. Without bothering to turn his head, the Hamurkan lifted his right arm and pointed it towards the charging Earthling. He made a fist and three darts shot out from the top of his newly attached cyborg hand. Two embedded in Brady's torso. The first hit him in his chest, the second in his stomach. The third dart anchored deep into the bare forearm of one of the Hamurkan audience members that had been holding Brady back.

The tranquilizers took effect immediately. Brady tried to lift his arm to extract the dart stuck in his stomach. He couldn't do it. Instead, he and the audience member who had been struck toppled onto one another.

With the remaining obstacle sleeping soundly and out of the way, Zeal-O-Vay repeated his recent declaration. This time, with the inflection on different words, he said, "*Now* it's fair fight... One on one..."

☠ ☠ ☠

Jenn had no intention of running away from Zeal-O-Vay. If the leader of these Hamurkan gangsters wanted a fight, she was ready to give it to him. She'd already proven that when she killed his top lieutenant a few days earlier. She showed that wasn't a fluke when she choked out the new chief underling just a few seconds ago.

Having chosen to go barefoot for the Tide Fight, Zeal had very little difficulty moving atop the sandy beach. He closed the distance between himself and the luchadora in surprisingly little time.

Zeal was in the middle of barking out an insult when Jenn rushed towards him. She grabbed his new cyborg arm by the wrist and tried to yank it away from the rest of his body.

It worked for Santa Saws back when Kelly and Fireball were abducted.

The Hamurkan was unphased by the poorly planned attack. Instead, he reached over with his other hand and gave the mechanical arm a quarter twist. This sent an electrical surge up and down the cyborg appendage… and the shock was severe enough to send Jenn flailing backwards.

"Don't give me an excuse to use my recent upgrade, little girl."

What was with this "little girl" garbage? Apparently, the Hamurkans think this is a major insult.

Jenn and Zeal faced one another, never daring to blink, much less glance in another direction. Each calculated their next move as they padded around in a small circle.

The pirate decided to do a little trash talking of her own. "For someone that uses the phrase 'fair fight' a lot… I don't think you even know what those words mean."

Zeal refused to take the bait. Instead, he grabbed Jenn by the arm. He squeezed so hard that Jenn worried he was about to break her wrist.

"I want your bones to snap and crumble like Nixx-O-Fee's did."

The luchadora didn't panic. Instead, she thought back to the move Víbora taught her in Puerto Rico many years earlier. She'd run towards the rocks, hoping to hop onto them and turn Zeal's vice grip on her wrist into the arm drag reversal that once dazzled fans of Lucha Libre.

Jenn could not run far, though. Instead, Zeal lifted her into the air. He held her upright as if she was a pennant and his cyborg arm was a flagstick. After allowing her to dangle in the air for a bit, he spiked her face first into the rocky sand.

She collected herself, taking just a second to look at the sand. It was not a soft cushion. Every time she was slammed onto the beach below, it knocked the wind out of her and further exhausted her.

Throwing sand in the eyes of her opponent worked in her battle with Brav-O-Dee. *Maybe it'll work again. Then I'll strangle him with his own braid.*

Zeal saw the attack coming from a mile away. He turned and ducked out of the path of the sand that Jenn slung towards his face. When she charged towards him, the gangster stood his ground.

What he did not see coming was the fact that his opponent now wielded a weapon. Jenn had located a mining tool buried deep beneath the sands. On one end of the handheld implement was a six-inch pickax designed to dig below the wet sand in the shallow waters. On the other end, there was a scoop designed to spoon through those same sands once a submerged gemstone had been located.

Jenn jumped into the air, hoping to whack him with a flying knee. He swatted her away with little difficulty. As he was doing so, Jenn swiped across with the mining tool. The pickax dug through several layers of flesh, muscle, and bone.

Zeal-O-Vay unleased an unholy scream! He was intent on putting an end to this game.

Make him come to me.

He didn't hesitate to do so. As he moved in, he took advantage of his abnormally long arm and extra elbow joint. He was able to reach down a grasp at Jenn's feet without moving close enough for her to have a chance of hitting him. It took three attempts to do so, but on the third pass, Zeal got a good grip on her leg.

Painfully clamping down on her leg, Zeal-O-Vay slid and spun around Jenn. He squeezed on her calf like Popeye the Sailor might open a can of spinach.

"Arrggh!" Jenn yelled.

"I love making you scream, little girl!"

Zeal's taunt momentarily opened the door for Jenn to get in a bit of offense of her own. As he tried to intimidate her, she came back with an elbow across his throat. If Hamurkans had Adam's apples, Zeal's would have gone shooting out of the back of his neck. The impact forced him to release his grip on Jenn's leg.

Now *he* was gasping for air!

Grab the braid. Grab the braid!

Jenn charged towards her stunned opponent. Instead of striking, she ducked and rolled past him. Her plan was to grab Zeal's hair and choke him out.

He was not surprised.

With a smirk, Zeal-O-Vay whipped his mechanical arm towards Jenn. The backhand blow from a mechanical arm moving at such velocity was like an uppercut swing with an aluminum baseball bat. It knocked Jenn out of her own boots and sent her flying in the air for several feet.

☠ ☠ ☠

The backhand blow from Zeal-O-Vay lifted Long Jenn Silva off the ground. Her head hit hard against the saturated sands along the shoreline. She lay there motionless. Sweet, salty waves of red water came rushing over her.

She needed to catch her breath. She needed a moment to negotiate with her body… to find a source of energy to push her through this fight long after she'd used up all the adrenaline she had in reserve.

Tide's rising. Can't lay here long.

The salt in the water stung her eyes and filled her nostrils. The tide was rising quickly. She couldn't deal with the consequences of one wave before the next crashed down and covered her face.

Gotta get up.

Zeal-O-Vay planted his bare foot atop the luchadora's chest. "I liked you from the moment I met you," he snarled. "There was room in my organization for you. You could have been part of my crew. Part of my family."

Another wave rushed over Jenn's face. This one filled her mouth with water. She turned her head and spat out the disgusting liquid before turning back to face Zeal. "But now?"

She'd NEVER join forces with that piece of filth. The conditions he forced his miners to live in were horrific. The things that went on in his brothel were unspeakable. And it all happened while he watched from above, safely hidden away aboard a cushy space yacht high in the sky.

"What's that?" he asked.

"Is there room… in your organization… now?"
She had to keep him talking a little longer.
"Why would there be?" he asked. Then he dropped down. He straddled her with one knee implanted in the sand on either side of her much smaller body. "Why would I want to hire a dead girl?"

Zeal reached up and pulled the mining tool out of his shoulder. Brown, syrupy blood that looked like it belonged in a spittoon oozed out of his wound. That same substance dripped off the edge of the dull pickax that he held inches from Jenn's face.

Jenn reached up with both hands. She was desperate to pry the weapon from the gangster's grasp.

"You like trophies?" Zeal asked. It was an obvious reference to the long rope of hair the former wrestling champ had taken with her after she killed Nixx-O-Fee. "So do I!"

Another wave crashed over Jenn's face. She tried to shake her head and keep the water from flooding into her nose and mouth. She opened her eyes but could only see a blur. Zeal-O-Vay moved the tool towards her.

The pain was excruciating! He made no effort to make the extraction quick and painless. Instead, he took all the time he needed to dig his instrument in deep and scoop the orb from its socket!

Zeal celebrated by holding his prize above his head. He shouted something to the crowd. However, Jenn's cries momentarily drowned out his words.

She let out a deafening shriek, then a low groan. The pirate clenched her fists and fought her body's instinct to pass out in response to the all-out assault on the nerves that surrounded her eyes. She stretched each arm outward. Clawing into the sand, she hoped to grab a rock or gemstone or some other item that she could use to whack the side of Zeal's gigantic head.

I've got to get him off me! Now! Now... or I'm dead!
There were no rocks or gemstones buried in her vicinity. It appeared all was lost when she felt a series of jagged cuts tearing into her gloved hand. She knew the pain had to be intense to distract her from the agony she'd just experienced from having her eye extracted.
The pain reminded her of...
Hillbilly hand fishing in Alabama... Noodling for catfish on her honeymoon with Lazz. "*I'll be joining you soon,*" she whispered to her husband who'd been swallowed into the blackness of the wormhole at Jupiter's Red Spot. *The Eye of Jupiter.*
That pain isn't coming from a catfish!
With her last bit of available energy, Long Jenn Silva squeezed her right hand into a fist. It hurt to do so. The ocean mutt's razor-sharp teeth pierced through her hand now! As she let out another carnal scream, she yanked her arm upward to lift the forty-pound monster that was attached to her hand. She raised the beast towards the bastard who'd just taken her eye.

The ocean mutt biting her hand was thought to be half-dog, half-shark. Like its brothers and sisters that often terrorized those who mined the waters of Oquezzi, it was always hungry. And when given an opportunity to latch onto something meaty, it jumped from Jenn's bony hand to Zeal's thick neck.

"Urrr-aggghh... gaaah!"
Jenn rolled out of the way. She made it to her knees and crawled until she was comfortably positioned on dry sand. Only then did she allow herself to collapse.

Zeal-O-Vay's body wiggled and jerked violently in the shallow waters. But he didn't move far. He couldn't escaped the ferocious jaws of the ocean mutt. The "Urrr-aggghh... gaaah!" he had bellowed would be the last sound he ever made. The flesh along the neck and shoulder made a satisfying dinner for one ravenous creature. The side of his face was going to be its dessert before a couple of Hamurkans rushed in and stopped it from defiling the corpse of their fallen leader.

Long Jenn Silva had paid a heavy price. She'd lost two more members of her crew. She'd lost an eye. But she had been declared the victor of the Tide Fight.

20: UNDER THE MILKY WAY

> *"People think they're being so clever when they say that wrestling's fake. I've got two knee replacements and a titanium hip that say otherwise... Fifteen surgeries during my twenty-one years in the business, then another eight after I hung up my boots. Maybe 'fake' isn't quite the right term."*
>
> *-Excerpt from "Stars and Scars," the best-selling autobiography of wrestling legend MANNY VARGAS.*

FOUR WEEKS LATER
OQUEZZI
YEAR 2 + 265 DAYS (SEPTEMBER 22nd)

Light penetrated the holes and tears in the tattered fabric that passed for curtains. Stray beams of annoying brightness poked at the sleeping pirate. Soon another of Oquezzi's daily eclipses was a piece of history. The massive mother planet no longer shielded the small moon from an invasion of intense heat and light from the nearby sun.

Long Jenn Silva stretched her arm towards the empty barrel that served as a nightstand. She felt around until she located an eyepatch. Then she positioned the swatch of black leather over her right socket. Only after that task was complete did the weary wrestler feel comfortable letting her feet hit the floor. She did not require a stitch of clothing... *Not in this ridiculous heat!* But Jenn remained sensitive about her appearance. She wasn't leaving the bed unless she covered that hideous wound.

The luchadora moved across the room, stopping to study her face in the cracked, reflective glass that served as a mirror. It helped to stare. Studying her scowling face had become part of her routine. A long look served as a reminder of *all* that she had lost over the last two years. Those reminders helped drag her back into the personal darkness she had come to prefer to the blinding light.

My eye wasn't the only thing that's been taken from me.

Kelly Ka-Pow. The "joking jabroni" was her oldest friend in the business. She had shown Jenn the importance of storytelling, as well as how to sell a chokehold so well that the audience would worry that she was no more than a few seconds away from certain death. She always knew exactly what to say to cheer someone up. She was cute, too. Kelly could have made a ton of money working for Griffin Conrad and the IWO... *if* she would have been willing to trade in her obnoxiously bright costume for something a bit sexier. She believed in the character she played so much that she refused to do so. *That silly clown gave me crap for being a "kayfabe devotee." Deep down inside, she was one, too!*

Poff and Mach. Jenn didn't know them nearly as well as she knew Kelly. She had to admit they were good people, though, *especially for aliens.* They stuck to their principles and sided with their friends. That meant the brothers had occasions in which they clashed with their fellow Hamurkans. Unfortunately, it also meant they died long before their time.

Armstrong and Avis. *Apparently "A" stands for Alien Abductors.* Jenn should have been angry at this old couple. They played key roles in snatching her away from her cozy life on Earth. After fighting side by side with that Nawerssian odd couple, though, Jenn came to see the good in each of those blue bastards. Armstrong, in particular, occupied a special place in the pirate's heart. He convinced her to return to a life of space adventure and had taken the time to provide a good deal of fatherly advice along the journey. *I should hate them, but I loved those guys.*

Cleo and Ptolemy. They were a pair of Nawerssian children on the *V-II*. Jenn never got the opportunity to know them that well, but they did interact some. *And dammit! They were just sweet little kids when they got pulled into the Eye of Jupiter.*

Cocoa Freeman. At times Cocoa was Jenn's best friend and biggest advocate. Even when she was making decisions like telling Jenn she was going to have to drop the AWWA title, she did so with respect. *You always were a straight shooter, Cocoa. You deserved better.*

Laszlo Barba. There was so much unfinished business when it came to her relationship with her husband. Jenn and Lazz were infatuated with one another when they rushed into their marriage. Unfortunately, they let their busy careers in competing promotions keep them separated for weeks at a time. When their relationship was starting to get a little momentum, Jenn was snatched up by aliens and taken to outer space. Things weren't the same when she returned. Not even close. And now he was gone. Forever. In Jenn's mind, her relationship with her husband was the very definition of unfinished business.

The sounds of Brady's footsteps were partially obscured by the rumbling of a low flying spacecraft. Ignoring the noise (and the rattling of her rickety furniture), he crept up from behind and draped the bedsheet over her shoulders.

Given the scorching heat on Oquezzi, the cover was hardly necessary. Jenn accepted it, nonetheless. Even though it was inviting a reminder that her body was covered with a film of dirt and sweat, she adjusted the sheet, wearing it like she'd been given a floor-length toga.

Brady leaned down and whispered a request. "Come back to bed." He followed this up with a kiss on the back of her neck.

The whiskers from his beard did far more than simply tickling her. Jenn felt herself melting. She grew eager for him to carry her back to her lumpy mattress. She yearned for a repeat performance of the previous night's vigorous marathon. Then she caught herself.

She squirmed out of his arms. "You're still here?"

The young man stood in silence. Disbelief turned to fear of a broken heart. After a moment of allowing Jenn's words to sink in, Brady answered with a sad nod of his head. His retreat led him to drift towards the pile of clothes on the floor. As he began to dress, he said, "I wish I knew what you were looking for."

"Same as you, I suppose… Thanks for last night."

Disappointed and insulted by the words of the pirate, Brady was dangerously close to the predicted heartbreak. He refused to let Jenn go without a fight. Even though he risked amplifying the tension that had arisen between the two of them, he shot back, "Are you kidding me? Do you honestly think I was looking for some sort of one-night stand? I'd do anything for you! Don't you realize that?"

"Anything?" Her response was cold. Indifference was the best weapon at Jenn's disposal if she wanted to drive a wedge between herself and another person she couldn't bear to lose. "Then leave. You'll be doing yourself a favor."

"Oh, come on!"

"Jagger once said something very interesting about this place... It leads you here, despite your destination." Finally turning around so she could look directly at the man who might be her one remaining friend, she explained, "That describes me... perfectly. I've got a track record, Brady. Whether we're talking about family, friends, or lovers. *I'm* the Bermuda Triangle! *I'm* the black hole! Everyone who gets close to me suffers. It's the same fate for each and every one of them... Death."

"That's ridiculous."

It didn't sound ridiculous to someone who had just run through the list in her mind. "Is it? Kelly Ka-Pow, Poff and Mach, Avis and Armstrong, Cleo and Ptolemy... Tavia Patton, Arnold Grayson, Cocoa Freeman..." Jenn paused. She had a brief inward debate as to whether she should include the next name on her list. She hated to verbally acknowledge that her husband had perished. "Laszlo Barba... Think about the time that's passed since the aliens snatched us from that commuter train in St. Louis. Now that seems so long ago, so far away. But be honest with yourself. Think about all those names I rattled off. They represent a lifetime of death and despair. A lifetime? Try two years! All of them died at some point since they took us off that train."

"Jenn, everybody you just named..."

The pirate wasn't done. "Do you really have that much of a death wish that you want to be with me? Even after all of that?"

"Jenn..."

The luchadora cut him off once more. "Don't even try. There's not a nugget of 'Brady Wisdom' that can solve this problem. You know why?" She pounded her chest. "*I am the problem!* I care too much about you. I can't let you get close to me, because I don't want your name added to that list. I'm serious, Brady... Pick up your clothes, get dressed, and leave."

☠ ☠ ☠

The rejected lover was down the stairs before he finished pulling his tank top over his head. Paired with khaki cargo shorts and brown sandals, he was dressed for the unrelenting heat of Oquezzi.

Brady paused for a moment, noting that Magellan wasn't in his customary spot behind the bar. He shrugged it off. "It's early," he said aloud, though he was the only one in the room.

Once he stepped out the door, Brady was immediately flattened by Som Ombostoo.

"I am terribly sorry, Brady Emerson," the cyborg apologized. After rising to her feet, she extended her android arm to help pull the young man into a standing position. "It is fortunate I found you. Pack your things without delay. Jagger wants the entire crew ready to board the *Valentine's Kiss* within the next quarter hour."

"What's going on?"

"No time to explain. We will be preparing to depart at once. Do you know if Long Jenn Silva is in her room?"

☠ ☠ ☠

TEN MINUTES EARLIER

Fireball Freeman and Jagger walked down the sandy street in front of Gelly's Tavern. Though the wrestling icon's body suffered from decades of taking hard bumps inside the squared circle, he frequently had to pause to give the Nawerssian war veteran a chance to catch up.

He watched as Jagger swung his prosthetic right leg ahead of his body, then dragged his left behind him. He repeated this painstaking process, made even more difficult by the fact that, with each step, the metallic peg sunk into the sand.

"I've known quite a few amputees and plenty of dudes with bad knees," said Fireball, "But you're the only one I've ever seen walk like that... leadin' with your bad leg."

Jagger laughed. "That's where ye be mistaken. Me right leg be me good leg, even if I only got a metal rod beginnin' from where me knee once was." He stopped long enough to pound his fist against his left thigh. "These muscles be dead. The hip? Altogether useless. But I be a stubborn ol' cuss. And I weren't about to let 'em give me cyborg legs. That meant me only options were ta hobble 'round like this, or ta let 'em chop off both me legs and stick me in a Nawerssian version of a wheelchair... This be the only option that ever made any sense."

Fireball nodded and held out his hand for a fist bump. "I hear ya loud and clear."

Their conversation was interrupted by a rumbling in the sky. A Davi-Loga fighter entered the red moon's atmosphere. Shaking violently, it plunged towards the surface.

Jagger and Fireball (and everyone else out in the street) looked up at the noisy flying machine. Though the fighter was in distress, it still troubled the masses who were accustomed to seeing only unarmed transports traveling towards the surface of Oquezzi.

Seeing that others had begun to scatter, Fireball looked to Jagger and asked, "Should we be worried?"

"A fighter like that weren't designed for long distance voyages through deep space… From the looks of this one, I'd say she's been from one end o' the Milky Way to the other," the cool Captain observed. "This don't have the looks of an attack. I say they be desperate to touch down and didn't bother ta take the time to learn our local protocols."

While others in the street scrambled to take cover, Jagger and Fireball stood their ground. They watched as the fighter thudded onto the nearest landing pad. The Davi-Loga ship crushed two unoccupied transports as it came to a stop.

☠ ☠ ☠

Monroe raced over to join Fireball and Jagger. Since the recent tide fights, she made it no secret that she felt much more solidarity towards her fellow crewmembers. *Plus, there is safety in numbers.*

As the trio observed the new arrival from a safe distance, Monroe asked, "Do we need to be ready for a fight?"

"I know I've only spent a limited amount of time here," Fireball responded, "but, for as long as we're on this rock, I think we should *always* be ready for a fight."

Jagger wasn't worried. "Relax." He pointed out that at least a dozen armed Hamurkan Guards had moved between their vantage point and Oquezzi's newest uninvited guests. "Let's see how this plays out."

There was a substantial delay between the ship's crash landing and any attempts by the pilot and/or passengers to exit the fighter.

Safety devices extinguished a few small blazes that had ignited upon the vessel's fiery impact. Onboard cameras scanned the crowd and assessed the Hamurkans that had filled the area around the hanger. Finally, the covering over the top of the cockpit began to raise.

The pilot stood upright and waited for a ladder to extend from the side of the craft. He raised his hands. The gesture appeared to be either a sign of surrender or an indication of a temporary truce.

One thing was clear to Jagger, though. "That pilot's no Davi-Loga. The pilot's got no wings. And he be a bit taller than any Davi-Loga I ever laid eyes on. From the looks of that flight suit, I'd render a guess that he be Nawerssian."

He was dressed in a well-weathered flight suit. The gray, synthetic fabric was engineered to be skin-tight and waterproof. Several areas of the suit shimmered thanks to amber strips of reinforced material covering the wearer's forearms, crotch, and around the knees. Jagger and company were too far away to read the sequence of dots, dashes, squiggles, and hooks etched onto a patch that ran across the left side of his chest. The amber accents, however, communicated that the wearer was a pilot.

Years of wear and tear resulted in a reduction of the suit's elasticity and breathability. Now it simply hung on the pilot's body. "Even me threadbare old suit has held together better than that," remarked Jagger.

The pilot removed his helmet, confirming that the mysterious newcomer was a Nawerssian male. To Monroe, however, this newcomer had a familiar face. The blue-skinned pilot resembled the cocksure flyboy she once knew as "Quetzal." She last saw him a couple of years earlier, fleeing the *Vilnagrom-II* while carrying an urgent message for the *V-III*.

After studying the cluster of deep wrinkles on his forehead, Monroe concluded that this man could not possibly be Quetzal. *He looks far too old.*

Two more figures followed the pilot out of the ship. The first was another Nawerssian male. His features revealed that he was much younger than the pilot. In fact, he appeared to be close to Monroe in age.

The final figure to exit the ship stood a few inches shorter than the Nawerssians. He was a middle-aged human male with bright blond hair. He held his hands above his eyes. It was a desperate attempt to adjust to the blinding sunlight on the red moon. Though the Hamurkan Guards inched towards them, he looked past them. He turned, speaking to the younger Nawerssian and then the pilot.

The pilot returned to the cockpit and retrieved a collection of photographs and other documents for inspection by the Hamurkans. Soon those in the crowd grew bold enough to inch forward. *What was happening? What did the arrival of this spacecraft mean to the many crews that had been waiting on Oquezzi?*

Monroe leaned in towards Jagger and asked, "Can a small fighter like that even make it through a wormhole?"

"Not bloody likely."

If these weary travelers had journeyed from Earth's solar system, they would have had to successfully pass through the dense layer of rock, ice, and asteroids that was commonly referred to as 'the Meteora.' If the newcomers survived the passage, it was a sign that the narrow window was open. Those on Oquezzi could slide through the passageway into Earth's solar system.

Various alien species and many translator bots now encircled the landing pad. Their voices began to ring out with the same

phrases, uttered in different languages from distant worlds. "It is time. The Slingshot Meteora… It is time. The Slingshot Meteora." "Slingshot Meteora… Slingshot Meteora… Slingshot Meteora…"
These words sent travelers and mercenaries double-timing back to their ships. The long-awaited race for Earth's solar system—and, ultimately, to Earth itself—had begun.

☠ ☠ ☠

Monroe knew there was no time to waste. "Someone needs to get Jenn and Brady… I need to get Galixxy."

Jagger held out his arm. It was a signal that they should show a bit of patience before joining the mad dashers headed towards the ships docked in Oquezzi's upper atmosphere. "Those be *our* people that just stepped off that fighter. Let's find out who they be, exactly where they came from, and what they've got ta say."

They did not have to wait long. Though the pilot remained near the Davi-Loga fighter, the younger Nawerssian and the blond-haired human made their way towards Jagger, Monroe, and Fireball.

The younger Nawerssian broke into a run. He stopped just a few feet shy of the trio. "Monroe? Is that you? You look exactly the same!"

Puzzled, she shook her head. She did not recognize him.

"It is me… Toly. Ptolemy."

The human pulled up alongside the Nawerssian who claimed to be Ptolemy. "It can't be!" he declared. "Fireball Freeman?"

Back on Earth, Fireball occasionally enjoyed a bit of the perks of being a celebrity. However, the old wrestler never expected to be recognized in another solar system.

Pointing to his tattered letterman's jacket, he attempted to remind Fireball of their connection. "Charlie Patton... Years ago my sister and I tried out for you and the AWWA. I even fought a dark match against your son."

He shook his head in disbelief. "Well, I'll be damned."

As the group made their surprising introductions, the translator bots began to overload. The announcement of the "Slingshot Meteora" was being made in many languages at once. Their programming caused the devices to link together and join in unison:

"Slingshot Meteora... Slingshot Meteora... Slingshot Meteora..."

Everyone on the red moon would hear the news within the next few minutes.

Jagger turned to Monroe. "*Now* ye need to gather the others. Tell 'em to get to our ship without delay!"

☠   ☠   ☠

ABOARD THE VALENTINE'S KISS

The *Valentine's Kiss* was one of almost twenty ships that had been docked above Oquezzi. The arrival of the Davi-Loga fighter signaled that there was a perfectly positioned gap in the cluster of asteroids that surrounded the Earth's solar system. The time was right to slingshot around the massive planet they orbited, propelling them towards the wormhole that would expel travelers just outside the Earth's solar system. Once they passed safely through "The Meteora," the crews would race towards Earth.

Jenn was stepping onto the flight deck when Som Obostoo approached Jagger. "Progress Report: We have completed charting the path of our orbit for the slingshot around the planet. Based on our calculations, we believe we will be able to pass most of the ships that left port ahead of the *Valentine's Kiss*."

"Excellent. Bein' first in open space be nice... but it not be as good as takin' the time to chart the course that gets ye to yer destination the quickest!" he responded as he sank into his Captain's chair. "I want ye cyborgs ta give me and Long Jenn Silva the room for a minute. Gather the crew. Tell 'em 'Cap'n Jagger wants everyone on the bridge as we begin our voyage.'"

Once the cyborgs left, Jenn asked, "You wanted to see me?"

This was the first opportunity for Jenn and Jagger to talk since Charlie Patton, Ptolemy, and Quetzal arrived. They were on the brink of the long-promised moment the Nawerssians called "the Vilnagrom*"* (literally translated "the return home"). It also would be a return for Jenn... but with so much having happened, the world likely would look and feel quite different to her.

"Yer Cap'n needs ta make it official." His expression revealed that he regretted sitting down a moment earlier. He struggled to rise to a standing position. "I be a bit of a scoundrel, I know... But I recognize that ye've endured a tremendous amount of loss and suffering. Yer a survivor, Long Jenn Silva. Just like me. Ye have become the pirate ye once pretended to be. Am I right?"

Jenn nodded her head.

Jagger continued. "As I look into yer eye, I see it... Ye now know that ye don't hafta be everyone's friend ta be a hero. Sometimes the world needs a scoundrel and a pirate ta save the day. That's why I be promotin' ye to First Mate, Long Jenn Silva. Ye answer to no one but me."

TWENTY MINUTES LATER

Jagger issued an order for the entire crew to assemble on the flight deck. The Captain was going to discuss their roles and responsibilities as they began a two-year voyage back to Earth (or, as many of them referred to it, "O.E.").

He began by introducing himself and his newly appointed First Mate. "She answers only ta me," he declared. "Perhaps more important, unless yer name be 'Jagger,' ye will be expected ta follow any orders Long Jenn Silva may give ye."

He went down the list, naming Monroe as the *VK's* Chief Scout and Senior Explorer. He explained, "'Tis true that me and her old man didn't always see eye to eye. But mighty good at his job, Armstrong was. I be confident she'll be every bit as good."

Jagger continued. Though he had just met the three newcomers, he was glad to have Quetzal aboard. "The *Valentine's Kiss* finally has a bona fide Pilot amongst her ranks."

Or did they? Monroe leaned in towards Galixxy, "I am not such a bad pilot myself. Besides, look at Quetzal. How has he grown so old, so quickly? What the hell happened?"

Quetzal once had a reputation of being an arrogant bigmouth who loved to go on and on about his accomplishments during the wars on Na-Werss. Since his unexpected arrival on Oquezzi, however, the blowhard hadn't said much at all. He just sat around looking old and defeated.

Then Monroe looked at Toly. Now her questions weren't just whispered to her lover; they were vocalized for the entire crew to hear. "I understand a considerable amount of time has passed, but how long has it really been? Toly was just a boy when I last saw him. Now he is a fully-grown man. How does that happen in two years?" After a brief pause, it hit her. "Perhaps I should not be asking 'how did that happen' at all. Perhaps the better question is *When* did that happen?' How long has it really been?"

Though no one aboard the ship knew Quetzal and Toly as well as Monroe did, her questions immediately amplified the concerns of the others.

"If there be a scientific explanation, I don't have it," Jagger told the group as he removed his tricorn hat to show off his groove-free scalp. "But 'tis true ol' Jagger's barely aged a day since first settin' foot on Oquezzi. While Armstrong—rest his weary soul—continued to orbit the Earth, more and more wrinkles appeared atop his bald head. Mine, as ye can see, remains quite smooth fer me age." He placed the hat back atop his head and boasted, "And I don't mind tellin' ye that this dirty dog still be surprisingly youthful and prolific below the belt, as well!"

Though she was repulsed by the thought of Jagger's sexual prowess, Monroe wanted to know more about Oquezzi's strange effects on the aging process. She wasn't the only one. "*Why* has this happened?" asked many among them.

"It appears time passes more slowly on Oquezzi. I have me suspicions it has somethin' to do with the moon's proximity to so many wormholes. We all know that the laws of space, time, and physics go askew 'round those curious portals... I've heard others reckon that maybe that little moon's red waters be like the purple goo in our life suspension tanks... Whate'er the actual reason be, what seemed like a few months to us on Oquezzi may have been fifteen or twenty years on Earth... and apparently around the Eye of Jupiter, too."

Toly stepped to the front. "Perhaps I can provide some of the answers you seek... The equivalent of twenty-four years on Earth. That is how much time has passed since the Battle of Jupiter. Those aboard the *Vilnagrom-II* were ambushed by the Davi-Loga.

At the climax of the battle, the *V-III* suddenly emerged from the wormhole. It was terrible timing. The ships collided and all three spacecraft were pulled into the mouth of the wormhole."

Silence engulfed the bridge.

Toly continued, "We were forced to work together to survive. We remained trapped inside the Eye of Jupiter for the equivalent of eighteen years. During that time, we intercepted signals from across time and across the galaxy. These signals were drawn into the wormhole. They allowed us to accumulate a tremendous amount of knowledge."

He paused to consider how much he wanted to disclose at once. "For a time, we forged an alliance: Nawerssians, cyborgs, the Davi-Loga, and even the few Earthly humans that survived…" He paused again, this time to peer at the cyborgs on the deck. The blue man's expression changed. His fists clenched.

If looks could kill cyborgs.

"Then our people were betrayed. One Nawerssian aligned with the cyborgs that had been aboard the *V-III*. Several good people were executed. Quetzel, Charlie Patton, and I managed to escape. We are not certain what happened to the others."

Toly stopped and allowed his audience to absorb this information.

Charlie jumped in with a conclusion of his own. "We are not certain what happened to the others… but it can't be good."

These revelations sparked many questions, many concerns. All were blurted out at once. Some wanted to know who had survived and who had perished. Others wanted to accuse the trio of being cowards for running away.

Fireball jumped into the fray. He had grown close to Jagger during their time on Oquezzi. This latest bit of news caused him to reassess that relationship. "Ladies, Gents… Don't be so hard on these fellows…" He took a couple of steps towards Jagger to avoid being accused of hurling an insult from far away. "The way I see it, tuckin' your tails and runnin' comes natural to all you Nawerssians. We were there when those ships got sucked into the wormhole. We saw the whole thing. But did our Captain even take a moment to consider goin' to help? If he did, it'd be news to me… That chicken shit didn't care about my daughter, or Jenn's husband, or even his own people. First chance he got, he made the decision to run. Run and never look back. Wait it out on Oquezzi for God knows how long."

The name-calling and accusations continued to escalate. Toly raised his voice to finish his tale. "It is our suspicion that the Alliance intends to invade Earth. Given the time it took us to travel to Oquezzi, it is likely they already have arrived."

"Darn right they are there!" Quetzal interjected. "We would be fools to go back. I realize I am new here, but if I get a vote, I say we turn this ship around. We could go back to your little moon and spend our days wallowing in the Fountain of Youth. It sounds like paradise compared to traveling to Earth to meet certain death."

"Enough!" Long Jenn Silva shouted. She was going to put a stop to this debate. "Death is certain no matter where you go. And if you think Oquezzi sounds like 'paradise,' you don't know anything about Heaven *or* Hell." The luchadora held up her dagger. She used it to point to her eye patch. Then she snarled, "I paid a heavy price for the privilege of living on that moon. We all did. This is our chance to go home. Hear me loud and clear. There's not going to be a vote. We *are* going to Earth."

21: GO HOME SHOW

> *"We always try to book something special for the last broadcast before a big pay-per-view event. Hopefully, the 'Go Home Show' gets the fans pumped up about the upcoming matches. And what's more exciting than a blindside attack or an unexpected return?"*
>
> *- KaPHONSO FREEMAN quote from the "Behind the Curtain" holographic chat-cast in which fans from around the world can question their favorite wrestling personalities in a Town Hall setting.*

NATIONAL NEWS BROADCAST
YEAR 23 + 365 DAYS (DECEMBER 31st)

The video feed showed four primitive androids. Each exited a large vehicle designed for all-terrain travel across the rocky surface of Mars. The manlike machines walked on two feet while removing building materials from the back of the vehicle.

A reporter named Cassandra read the copy in a sing-songy voice. "The Multi-National Alliance has released some amazing footage from the surface of Mars. While billions here on Earth celebrated Christmas, Hanukkah, or Kwanza, the astronauts from the Alliance's Mars Mission were busy observing a team of androids placing communication towers across the area known as the Aldrin Valley."

The on-screen graphic switched to a colorized satellite image depicting the surface of Mars. When the director zoomed in, the viewer could see an "X" not far away. The superimposed image was added to show where the DAVINCI 3 had landed.

"Roughly the size of Connecticut, the valley is believed to have been carved out by an ancient Martian river. Its terrain is much flatter and smoother than the surrounding area. The Multi-National Alliance hopes to construct five dome-like structures within the valley. The structures will be connected by a series of tunnels, with each of the domes capable of housing a community of as many as one hundred people. Inside these structures, the first permanent Mars dwellers will grow their own hydroponic food, conduct scientific experiments, and live day-to-day life as similar to that on Earth as possible.

"The towers being constructed by the team of androids will be used to help future DAVINCI teams communicate from one domed community to another. Perhaps even more remarkably, it is believed that the structures can be converted and used for moisture collection as scientists progress in their efforts to terraform the Aldrin Valley."

The attractive news anchor looked to her co-host before turning and smiling directly into the camera. "As we prepare to flip the page on the calendar to close out another year, there is one statement that has never been truer than it is today… We live in fascinating times."

The toothy co-host smiled to the camera, throwing in a slight nod of his head. With a deep and silky smooth voice, he delivered his well-rehearsed response. "Fascinating times, Cassandra. Fascinating times indeed."

☠ ☠ ☠

SEVEN MONTHS LATER
SCHRIEVER SPACE FORCE BASE - COLORADO
YEAR 24 + 196 DAYS (JULY 15th)

Dr. Yaron Harazi didn't make it a habit of watching the live feed from Mission Control. Dressed in jeans, a cream-colored dress shirt, and a tweed jacket, he was the only one in civilian clothing seated at the conference room table. His credentials revealed that the UAPTF (Unidentified Arial Phenomenon Task Force) had become part of the Space Force and rebranded SF:ETC ("Space Force: Extraterrestrial Contact"). Still, many of his colleagues treated him like an outsider.

"Any updates?" several asked Lieutenant Colonel Wiggins as she entered the room. The DAVINCI 3 Mars Transport was experiencing an unexpected period of radio silence. By the time the loss of contact reached the six-hour mark, most within the Space Force were experiencing a certain degree of dread.

"Nothing's certain," Wiggins reminded them as she pressed a button on the frames of her glasses. A second later, a holographic image of the DAVINCI's flight path floated in the air in front of her. The officer used a stylus to draw in the air. Those etchings appeared atop the projected display. Once she was done, the revised image would be uploaded to the whiteboard against the wall. "For the time being, those in Houston are blaming it on 'celestial interference.'"

"What's that?" several asked at once.

"Over the last few hours, the Earth, the Mars Transport, Mars itself, *and* the anomaly in Jupiter's orbit have been aligned within a few degrees of one another…"

"What are the odds of that?" someone asked.

Taking the interruption in stride, Wiggins replied, "No one knows. The anomaly has been disrupting Jupiter's orbit for more than two decades now. Sometimes it moves like normal. Other times, it just hangs in the sky… Whatever the reason, they think its current position maybe to blame for our loss of radio contact with DAVINCI. That's why someone more clever than any of us coined this phenomenon 'celestial interference.'"

Another officer had an alternative theory. "I still think it's either the Russians or the Chinese to blame… maybe both working in cahoots." It made sense. Astronauts from six countries (the United States, Peru, Latvia, Egypt, India, and Australia) representing six continents had been chosen to travel to Mars. Neither of the superpowers had been bashful about voicing their displeasure over their exclusion from the Multi-National Alliance's 21-month mission.

A third officer hoped to lighten the mood. Pointing to Harazi, he threw out another suggestion. "We all know what this guy is thinking… 'Aliens.'"

Here I am working for the SPACE FORCE. *Even here people think I'm a crackpot for believing in extraterrestrial life. If they only knew what I know!*

☠   ☠   ☠

THREE WEEKS EARLIER
TOP SECRET GOVERNMENT FACILITY - NEVADA
YEAR 24 + 175 DAYS (JUNE 24th)

Twenty-nine years had passed since Dr. Harazi made his first trip to the Top Secret government facility. Since then, he'd made dozens of visits to the prison located in curious proximity to what many referred to as "Area 51."

At the time of his first visit, the alien expert preferred to wear T-shirts that featured silkscreened images from classic video games. Asteroids and Space Invaders were among his favorites. Back then, his hair was completely black and his career was just beginning.

When the visits began, most Americans were quite leery of driverless cars. That was twenty-nine years ago. Now only a few stubborn holdouts—mostly radical conspiracy theorists—ever sat behind the steering wheel of an automobile.

On this occasion, the self-driving vehicle stopped a half mile away from the facility. Its programming would not permit it to take passengers any closer to the front gate. Harazi looked down at the bag of Chinese food that he held in his hands. "It would be nice if my security clearance could override the half-mile protective bubble," he had complained to his Space Force superiors. With no one around to hear his grumblings, he added, "In this heat, I'm going to be soaked to the bone in sweat. Yet somehow the food is going to get cold."

In the end, the opportunity to meet with the blue-skinned extraterrestrial known as Hazel far outweighed the hassles of a half-mile walk in the heat of the Nevada desert. Harazi had come to interview her no fewer than two times per year for the last twenty-nine years! There was no other place he could acquire the insight and information that she provided.

Over the years, the doctor and the extraterrestrial went over the details of the crash landing in which her silver bullet shuttle obliterated a large portion of a golf course near the Maryland-Pennsylvania border. As she became more comfortable with him, she revealed more about her home world, her people, and life in space.

"You'll need to wear gloves and a mask if you're going to be in the same room as the subject," a baby-faced guard informed Harazi upon his arrival.

The doctor flashed his Space Force credentials. "Surely there's been a mistake. No one has ever made me do that before."

The guard shook his head. "She's not well, sir."

Harazi was led to a different room within the facility. "Sick bay?"

The young man took notice of the bag of Chinese food in the visitor's hands. "You're not going to be able to take that in there. I can hold onto it until you're ready to leave."

"It's never been a problem before."

This time the guard nodded. "Like I said, she's not well... She's dying."

Harazi stepped into the medical offices within the facility. He was astonished to see his alien friend placed in a clear, plastic bubble. Sweat covered her blue skin, even though she wore next to nothing. Electrodes had been affixed at numerous points along her disturbingly lean body.

Hazel's voice had weakened to the point that it faded in and out. She trembled as she spoke, "What is it they say here on Earth? You look like you have seen a ghost."

Harazi's busy schedule meant he hadn't visited her in more than six months. There was also a tinge of guilt over that fact in his voice. More so, however, he was angered that he had not been informed of the decline in the condition of his alien friend. "They say you're dying. How long have you been like this!"

Choosing to save her strength, the extraterrestrial responded with a feeble shake of her head.

"I thought the beings from your planet had a much longer life expectancy than humans."

There was a long pause. She would have to work up the strength to speak. Hazel carefully chose her words. She needed to make every syllable count. "On my planet, absolutely... Even with all the pollution, an ordinary Nawerssian would be expected to live for the equivalent of 120 years on Earth..." She held up a finger, signaling that she had more to say. Before she could do so, she needed to breathe in plenty of oxygen. "My body has experienced and endured many variables: long distance space travel... years of eating nothing but synthetic food... living in a zero gravity environment... three decades of captivity... I guess whether you are from Earth or Na-Werss or anywhere in between, living in captivity takes a toll on the mind and body. To be honest, I am surprised I have lived this long."

Tears ran down Harazi's face. He did nothing to impede their flow. "You looked just fine the last time I saw you."

"I know you care for me. I have been putting on an act. I hoped to spare you the pain of seeing me... Of seeing me as I was deteriorating."

Harazi had a list of questions he'd hoped to ask his alien friend as they enjoyed their customary helpings of General Tso's. He scrapped that list. Instead, he sat quietly by her side for about an hour as she faded in and out of sleep.

Once she appeared to be sleeping soundly, he stood up and whispered his good-byes. "I was privileged to have known you, Hazel."

☠ ☠ ☠

It seemed to take forever until the driverless car that Harazi had summoned finally appeared. The vehicle was clear and spherical, spacious enough to comfortably seat two in the front and three in the back. Two metal bars rested at the bottom of the globe. The push the vehicle received from the magnetically-charged roadway below caused it to hover about two to three feet above the ground.

Once he was comfortably seated, Harazi stated clearly, "Ready. Please transport me to Creech Air Force Base."

A feminine computerized voice responded, "Destination confirmed. Is English your preferred language?" The network-controlled vehicle could have communicated with its passengers in English, Spanish, Portuguese, French, Arabic, Hindi-Urdu, Russian, Chinese, or Japanese.

"Yes. English."

A scanner detected the bag of food in Harazi's hands. "You may be assessed a cleanup fee in addition to the cost of transportation. Do you acknowledge?"

"Yes." The alien expert wondered why he hadn't pitched his lunch before leaving the government facility. *I don't think my stomach would be able to handle lukewarm Chinese food.*

Disclaimers like "Neither this transport company nor the operators of the magnetic roadway are responsible for any injuries sustained by a passenger who attempts to exit the transport while it is in motion" were being played when a notification flashed from Harazi's glasses. An automated voice interrupted with a message. "Incoming call. Unknown number."

"Answer."

A moment later, an image of the young guard was displayed across the inner front panel of the self-driving vehicle. "Dr. Harazi? It's Sergeant Frye. We met earlier... I wanted to let you know that Inmate H4281-NF died just a few minutes after you left. She was a good person, or... um..." The officer hesitated, clearly confused about whether the alien could be classified as a "person" and how much he should say over an unsecure communication link.

"I appreciate the call. Thank you, Sergeant."

Harazi wiped a single tear away from his cheek.

After sitting in silence for a few minutes, he pulled a fortune cookie out of his bag of food. He cracked it open and read what was written on the tiny sliver of paper: "Very soon you will meet someone from a distant land."

☠ ☠ ☠

THREE WEEKS LATER
MISSION CONTROL – HOUSTON
YEAR 24 + 196 DAYS (JULY 15th)

Following almost nine hours of radio silence, Mission Control was filled with a chorus of cheers.

The unexpected breakdown in communication concluded with Commander Darrion Holt (USA) responding to one of the many desperate calls from Earth. "Holt here. All systems normal aboard the DAVINCI 3. Houston, do you copy?"

The CAPCOM (Spacecraft Communicator)—a seasoned American astronaut named Simon Tanaka—spoke for everyone within the facility. "You gave us quite a scare, Commander. Please don't give us the silent treatment ever again."

Though the astronaut had conveyed a message of "Business as Usual," the computers aboard the Mars transport sent out a different message. Those computers were programmed to routinely broadcast their own updates on the systems operating aboard the DAVINCI 3. The data most recently received contradicted Holt's report.

The EECOM (Electrical, Environmental, and Consumables Manager) yanked a paper away from his station's printer. Alarmed, he raced across the room to show it directly to the Flight Director. At the Flight Director's request, they were joined by both Tanaka and the Flight Surgeon.

Tanaka kept his cool as he spoke an urgent message that would take twenty minutes to reach its recipient. "Commander Holt, we are concerned about some readings sent to us by the onboard computers. It appears that the temperatures have risen throughout the manned areas of the ship. Oxygen use and water consumption have spiked drastically. Humidity is on the rise. Please conduct manual checks and report back ASAP."

It would take twenty minutes for the message to travel the considerable distance between Mission Control and the DAVINCI 3. It would take an additional twenty for a reply to return. Throw in the time it took to perform the manual checks of the ship's life support systems, and Houston would be waiting for answers for at least another hour.

☠ ☠ ☠

The response from Commander Holt took almost twice as long as expected. So much time passed that many began to speculate that the 'celestial interference' had caused another period of radio silence.

"Holt here. All systems normal aboard the DAVINCI 3. Manual tests confirm. All systems appear to be in the optimum range. Houston, do you copy?"

Minutes later, updated reports generated by the onboard computers reached Mission Control. That data confirmed Holt's analysis.

Mission Control, NASA engineers, and a team of scientists from the Multi-National Alliance would agree that the alarming reports had been broadcast in error. They concluded that the prior reports most likely came from data that had been used months earlier, during a pre-launch drill.

☠ ☠ ☠

FIVE MONTHS LATER
EDWARDS AIR FORCE BASE - CALIFORNIA
YEAR 24 + 365 DAYS (DECEMBER 31st)

Firetrucks, ambulances, and military vehicles gathered towards the far end of the massive landing area in Rogers Dry Lake. Various emergency personnel—along with a busload of dignitaries and another busload of reporters from around the globe—gathered to observe the scheduled touchdown of the DAVINCI 3 transport on its historic return from Mars.

The returning spacecraft made a deafening sound as it tore through the Earth's upper atmosphere. The DAVINCI 3 glowed fiery orange and rattled through the sky for hundreds of miles before it leveled off and made its planned descent. Hats, papers, banners, and umbrellas scattered around the landing zone as the spectators hadn't been properly made aware of how the landing procedures for the mighty ship would create enough rocketdraft to simulate the winds of a small tornado.

Soon the unexpected chaos surrounding the noisy, windy landing was forgotten. It was replaced with thunderous applause.

To the eager spectators, the post-landing safety checks occurring on the inside of the ship seemed to take an eternity. They were there to witness the return of six international heroes. They were ready to welcome them back to Earth after a wildly successful mission. History was being made. The world was watching. And everyone in the vicinity of the returning ship was ready to celebrate.

A blast of steam surged into the air as the crew prepared to swing open the pressure-locked doors. As expected, six astronauts smiled and waved as they stepped onto a mobile scaffolding that surrounded the DAVINCI 3.

"They all look significantly thinner than when they left," Harazi remarked to one of his colleagues from SF:ETC.

The diverse batch of space travelers included representatives from six different continents. The mission's leader, Commander Darrion Holt, was a decorated pilot from the U.S. Navy. His wife, Daphne, greeted him with a kiss as she was the first to join the heroes on the platform that had been moved next to the ship.

After another kiss—much longer than the first—and a few private words for his spouse, Commander Holt stepped up to a microphone to introduce the astronauts who had joined him on their journey to and from Mars that began twenty-one months earlier.

Before introducing the members of his crew, Holt offered a prepared statement:

"I am one of the select few that has been afforded the privilege of traveling to and from Mars. I've dragged my feet in the rocky sand of our sister planet. I've observed glorious sunsets over her spectacular red horizon. But... like Dorothy from *The Wizard of Oz*, I can honestly say 'There's no place like home.' It truly is a place that is welcoming like no other under the Milky Way.

"I'm elated to be back on Earth with my beautiful bride at my side. I'm thrilled to have been the Commander on what has been—up to now—the greatest flight in our world's history. I am confident you soon will discover that the DAVINCI 3 brings back to Earth more than a few hundred pounds of rocks from Mars. We bring more than the photo opps and stories that will ring throughout the airwaves over the next few weeks and months.

"Without further adieux, please let me take advantage of one other opportunity that comes with being the Commander of this historic flight. That is the privilege of introducing my fellow crew members... five international heroes."

Over the course of the next several minutes, the Commander Holt was joined on the platform by Flight Engineer Aziz Sobhi from Egypt, Robotics Specialist Valērijs Lasmanas from Latvia, Doctor Siddharth Sahu from India, Module Pilot Morgan Davies from Australia, and Mission Specialist Fabiola Solis from Peru.

Reporters from across the globe had been assigned a predetermined order to ask their questions. The first of those was ringing out when Commander Holt indicated that he was not done with his prepared remarks.

He held up his hands before offering a slight shake of his head. "I mentioned that we brought back more than rocks from the surface of Mars..." Holt paused. Then he, followed by his fellow crewmembers, turned and looked towards the craft they had just exited.

A white-haired male stepped through the door. His silver and violet flight suit shined beneath the cloudless skies of the California desert. The attire fit snugly, showing the world that this man—a human—possessed a physique with massive muscles stacked atop one another. He turned back towards the transport, yelled something undecipherable, and waited until he was joined by a second person.

She, too, was human. She was much smaller than the muscular man, and young enough to be his daughter. Her skin tone was several shades darker. Her shoulder-length, brown dreadlocks became a burnt orange as the hair grew further from her scalp.

The young woman wore no shoes. A cottony white skirt traveled to just above her ankles. Her chest was wrapped in a silky material. The single strip of fabric began over the right breast, slid back behind and around her neck, then over the left breast, then stretched back around.

With the exception of the astronauts and an unflinching Harazi, there was utter confusion in the shadow of the DAVINCI 3.

Military officials barked out conflicting orders over the radio. Some of the soldiers responded by raising their weapons. Others hesitated or sought clarification from their superiors.

The collection of reporters ignored their government-issued directions for covering the landing of the Mars transport. There was nothing in those scripts that dealt with the appearance of these unexpected guests. Dozens of questions were shouted out at once. Words like "stowaways" and "aliens" could be heard above the noisy mishmash from the media.

Things went from chaotic to uncontrollable when a trio of additional figures emerged from the Mars Transport:

The first through the door was a cyborg. She resembled a Model 10 from Na-Werss's southern hemisphere. However, though her outer shell maintained a metallic sheen, it was white instead of silver. She also did not wear garments that resembled those once worn on Earth. Instead, a metallic cuirass—violet in color—covered her shoulders and chest, leaving her upper arms exposed. Synthetic straps resembling leather protected her wrists and forearms. Bands of this material also hung from a belt, protecting her waist and thighs. A final detail would have gone unnoticed to those unfamiliar with the cyborgs from Na-Werss. Her eyes did not glow bright red. Instead, they were a soft and mesmerizing shade of Nordic blue.

A tall Nawerssian followed the cyborg out the door. The passage of time had taken its toll on the Cartographer who called himself "Polo." It was not just his forehead that was covered in deep groves. His jowls had grown extremely saggy in the years since the *Vilnagrom-II* hovered in an orbit between Earth and its moon.

The third extraterrestrial being to emerge from the ship was a birdwoman. She walked upright. Her vibrant green feathers were a stark contrast to Polo's dull blue and the cyborg's metallic white.

Commander Holt tried to quell the chaotic response. He raised his hands once more. "Please listen to me!" he bellowed, hoping to be heard above the shouting reporters, the humming of military machinery, and the hurried shuffling of rifles. "Stand down!" he shouted to those troopers who had raised their weapons. "Stand down!"

Dozens of raised weapons were pointed at the unexpected arrivals. Few of the troops that aligned the runway responded to

Holt's request. "Lower your weapons!" he repeated. "Please! Give them an opportunity to speak!"

His words were met with continued hesitation. This collection of troopers was compiled from among the best the Army, Navy, Marines, Air Force, and Space Force had to offer. Still, they were uncertain as to whether they were supposed to follow the orders given by the astronaut… particularly one that may have been in a compromised position.

Harazi had moved to the front of the group of dignitaries and military officials. He stepped forward. Though he was dressed in civilian clothes, everyone on the platform knew who he was. Beyond that, they knew that if he requested it, the authority would be granted from the highest-ranking officers in the U.S. Military.

Upon seeing Harazi nod his head, a booming voice repeated Holt's direction, "Lower your weapons!"

Compliance was followed by silence.

Then a final individual emerged from the Mars transport.

Tall. Slender. Beautiful. Radiant. Her skin looked like smooth caramel. She was dressed in a long white cloak that featured sparkly flecks of amethyst that glimmered when caught by the light. She wore a white belt around her waist, with shiny leggings in the same shade of amethyst. The attire left her midsection exposed, revealing a chiseled stomach highlighted with well-defined abdominal muscles. Her chest was covered by a silky material, a single strip wrapped around her (much like it had the younger woman) until it circled her waist and was covered by the belt.

She walked with a confidence that announced to the world that she was their leader. The woman stood with her arms outstretched, inviting the breeze to rush against her skin. She tilted her head backwards to suck in a massive gulp of fresh air. After taking another step forward, she squeezed the hand of her husband before addressing those attending the landing… as well as the billions of people watching around the world.

"Greetings…" she began before pausing to soak in the sensation of her curly, silver hair blowing in the desert wind. "My name is Cocoa Freeman. First, let me say that, after many years away, it feels good to be home… With me is my husband, Laszlo Barba; our daughter, Beatrix; and representatives from three distant civilizations, each light years away, but with their origins here on Planet Earth… We come united. We come devoted to peace. We come with advanced knowledge gathered from the opportunity to look thousands of years into the past and thousands of years into the future. We come with the ability to assist the people of this world in making drastic technological, medical, agricultural, and societal advancements… The improvements we can offer will elevate the Earth beyond the wildest of imaginations. I urge you to trust us. Do not panic. We bring with us the ability to *transform* this world into the most wonderful paradise in the entire galaxy."

END OF BOOK TWO

PARTS UNKNOWN

COMING IN 2023

FUTURE ENDEAVORS
LONG JENN SILVA SERIES: BOOK 3

PARTS UNKNOWN

GALLERY OF CHARACTERS:

Jennysis Quevedo & Brady Emerson
Home Planet: Earth

Galixxy & Monroe
Home Planet: Na-Werss

*Som Obostoo
Home Planet Na-Werss
(Southern Hemisphere)*

Sareena
Home Planet: Davi 4

Nixx-O-Fee
Home Planet: Hamurka

Jagger
Captain: Valentine's Kiss

Long Jenn Silva
First Mate: Valentine's Kiss

BONUS MATERIAL:

The following is a collection of deleted scenes from **PARTS UNKNOWN.**

XX: *LOSER LEAVES TOWN*

> *"Before that night, Karl Freeman was nothing more than an ordinary jobber. After he ran through that wall and saved all those lives, we knew he his days of playin' second fiddle were behind him. Only one question remained... Were we gonna call him 'Wrecking Ball Karl' or 'Fireball Freeman?'"*
>
> -DENNY NASHVILLE *shoot interview on the "Chatting with Champions" podcast.*

THIRTY-SIX YEARS AGO
YEAR -36 + 269 DAYS (SEPTEMBER 25th)

"I can't move... It's out of the question. I've got a daughter on the way. Her mother lives here. If I move across the country, I'll never see my kid."

Though he wasn't yet known as "Fireball," Karl Freeman was a steadily rising star in the world of professional wrestling. He'd bounced around, jerking the curtain in Memphis and New Orleans. After some time learning from legends in Calgary and then Portland, he returned to the Midwest and worked his way up the mid-card in hot spots like Kansas City, St. Louis, and Indianapolis. Lately, however, he had grown comfortable working as a heel in TKO Wrestling.

TKO was a regional promotion that operated in a territory that stretched across Eastern Tennessee, most of Kentucky, and the southern third of Ohio. (The "T" stood for "Tennessee," the "K" for "Kentucky," and the "O" for "Ohio.") In the late-1980s and early-1990s, a penny pincher named JoJo Dalton was in charge of the promotion.

"That's the nature of the business, Karl," JoJo replied. "Babyfaces stay put. Heels stick around for a little while, then move on to another territory. That way they can generate fresh heat in front of a new set of fans."

The solution seemed simple to the man who would soon be known as "Fireball Freeman." Trying to conceal his desperation, he raised his feet and rested his brand new Air Jordans atop Dalton's desk. "Then let's do a face turn."

Dalton stopped him. "Karl, let's get two things straight... First off, never put your big, smelly feet on my desk again. Particularly if you're wearin' those Gawd-awful basketball shoes. You're a grown man. Try investing in a nice pair of cowboy boots instead."

"What's the second thing?"

"Second?" JoJo took a moment to recollect exactly what it was—apart from footwear—that they had been discussing. "Second... There's not going to be a face turn."

Freeman persisted. "I could run in and stop the Galactic Warrior from gettin' his tail kicked by this new hardcore Texan that you were tellin' me about... Needles Nelson or whatever he's called."

Dalton wasn't buying Freeman's pitch. "Charlie Cactus. And he's from New Mexico, not Texas."

"That's the one. Exactly."

Dalton shook his head. "*Not* exactly... I'm sorry, Karl, there's no future in you as a babyface. You're a solid wrestler. Strong as an ox, stubborn as a mule. But I don't see you ever developing that quality that I need from a top babyface."

"What quality is that?"

"A top babyface has the ability to sell merch! Stuff like T-shirts, posters, and autographed pictures. He's also got the ability to attract paying spectators. You're not over with the fans that way. And as much as this may sound cruel and insensitive, I can't envision a scenario in which you ever will be... at least not in this part of the country."

Freeman stood. As he did so, he pushed on the arms of his chair to aid his sore knees in the process. "These shoes cost me sixty-five dollars. Money well spent, if you ask me." Then he leaned in to make his point. "They say you make your own luck. Give me two weeks. I'll prove you wrong. You'll see who can put fannies in the seats."

☠ ☠ ☠

TWO WEEKS LATER
YEAR -36 + 280 DAYS (OCTOBER 7th)

JoJo Dalton's introduction to his promotion's weekly syndicated wrestling show was always the same. The only variation was the name of the town from which that week's episode was being broadcast. "Welcome to 'TKO Tonight!' We're here in Bardstown, Kentucky, showcasing some of the finest wrestling talent from sea to shining sea! With me, as always, is my partner at the announcer's table, Mister Denny Nashville."

"That's right, JoJo! Tonight we've got an outstanding hour of wrestling action! First off, a tag team match featuring the Cold-Blooded Cowboys versus the oddball pairing of Renegade Mike and the American Ninja… a 30-Minute Iron Man Match between bitter rivals Corporal Chambers and Boris Sputnikov… and, in the Main Event, a 'Loser Leaves Town' match between the wildly popular Galactic Warrior and that wrecking ball of a man, Karl Freeman! Let's get to the action!"

☠ ☠ ☠

FORTY-FIVE MINUTES LATER

As was the case with many bouts that featured the Cold-Blooded Cowboys, their tag match against Renegade Mike and the American Ninja quickly broke down into a schmozz. The villainous duo known as The Samurai and The Sultan interfered almost immediately after the match began. With his partner handcuffed to the ring post, the fight turned into a four-on-one beatdown of the Ninja. Though the disqualification meant that they were considered the victors, poor Mike and the battered Ninja didn't feel like winners.

Next came the Iron Man Match between the stars 'n stripes waving Corporal Chambers and the Soviet snake Boris Sputnikov. This contest was originally slated to be the Main Event of the night, but Dalton decided to bump Freeman up from the mid-card to the premiere slot for his final match.

The clash between enemies on opposite sides of the Cold War electrified the Bardstown crowd. It was a match that featured brutal slams, steel chair shots, and blood gushing from the foreheads of both competitors. They had electrified the audience.

"This crowd has been worked into a frenzy," JoJo told his partner as the ring was being cleared of paper cups that had been thrown at the nasty Russian. After making sure he was not talking into a hot mic, he added, "It'll be a nice send off for Karl."

Moments later, the lights dimmed and the bell rang. The ring announcer stated the particulars of the night's final combatants. "This match is scheduled for one fall… Introducing first, from Parts Unknown… weighing in at 235 pounds… the Galactic Warrior!"

Keyboard-laden, big hair band, heavy metal music began playing over the loudspeakers. A spotlight hit the Warrior. That was his cue to begin aggressively flexing his steroid-enhanced muscles. Standing at the far end of the gym, the Warrior was flanked by Roman candles on each side. The pyrotechnics weren't exactly in the same league as some of the bigger promotions from nearby territories, but the fans loved TKO's efforts towards putting on an indoor fireworks show, nonetheless.

"The Galactic Warrior always thrills the fans with his spectacular entrance!" Denny Nashville said as part of his color commentary.

The fireworks screeched and shot fiery balls towards the ceiling. Some were still smoldering when they landed among some oily rags that appeared to have been recklessly discarded and long forgotten in a dark corner of the gymnasium.

Oblivious to the looming inferno, the Warrior violently shook the ropes as he made his way inside the ring. He continued to delight the fans by pounding his fists across his steroid-enhanced chest muscles.

Those inside the gym were enraptured by the high-adrenaline pre-match routine. None of the five hundred plus people inside noticed the blaze until the flames climbed the walls of the old building.

Unsure of how to proceed, the ring announcer flashed a questioning glance in JoJo Dalton's direction. When no immediate response came from his awe-struck boss, the announcer continued his introductions. "And his opponent… hailing from West Memphis, Arkansas… weighing in at 261 pounds…"

A noisy fire alarm drowned out the sounds coming from the PA system. The crowd became restless as more and more of them realized that the raging flames were not part of the act.

Denny Nashville tried to bring some organization to the chaos. He left his position at the announcers' table and shouted to the fans, "Please move towards the exits in an orderly fashion!"

A pair of off-duty sheriff's deputies served as local security for the event. They made their best efforts to direct the panicked fans towards the lobby, even though doing so would mean they would have to move dangerously close to the blaze. Still, that was preferable to trying the doors on the west side of the gym. They'd already tried that exit and determined that the doors were blocked by mountains of TKO Wrestling equipment and a pair of illegally parked television trucks!

Thankfully, Karl Freeman came to the rescue. Armed with two fire extinguishers, he began dousing the blaze. His heroic actions didn't completely quell the threat, but they significantly slowed its progress. Soon Deputies Adams and Mays swooped in with blankets that they used to smother the remaining flames.

The crowd roared with approval.

Covering his microphone, Dalton rolled his eyes as Denny Nashville returned to his seat. "I think that crazy son of a gun started that fire... I think that's what he meant when he said 'you make your own luck.' Too bad for Karl, he needed to do a whole lot more than that to go over and stay over as a babyface in this territory."

Once the chaos died down and everyone had returned to their seats, they resumed the match and the taping of "TKO Tonight."

Denny Nashville made a couple of observations as Freeman trotted down towards the squared circle. "Karl Freeman's receiving quite a few more cheers than he's accustomed to hearing. More interesting than that, in my opinion, is his choice of footwear for tonight's match."

Dalton jumped in. "He's not wearing wrestling boots. Instead, he's got on those ridiculous basketball shoes. He must be mixed up and confusing slam dunks with body slams!"

"I have it on good authority that those shoes aren't cheap," Denny Nashville reported before making another observation. "Or maybe he got dressed in a hurry. He's also wearing a wristwatch... Either way, that's an interesting fashion statement that Freeman's making for what could be his final match in TKO Wrestling."

The bell rang again. Freeman locked horns with the Galactic Warrior. They traded headlocks and armbars for a couple of minutes. Then the crowd began to stir again.

The fire alarms blasted once more. This time smoke poured into the gym from the locker room area. Raging flames quickly followed. Jolene Dalton came running in from the lobby and screamed, "Daddy, the doors are locked! I can't get 'em open! We're trapped inside!"

☠ ☠ ☠

FORTY MINUTES EARLIER

The venue was an old high school gymnasium in Bardstown, Kentucky. When the fans arrived, each happily shelled out five bucks for a general admission ticket. Many spent ten or twenty more on a programs, posters, or T-shirts depicting images of their favorite wrestler's face, logo, or catch phrase. Once they found their seats, they tended to stay put until a second rush to the merch tables and autograph booths at the conclusion of the show.

JoJo Dalton's promotion was a family affair. Jolene, Josiah, and JoJo Junior manned the ticket counter and sale of merchandise in the gym's front lobby. With the 30-Minute Iron Man Match between Corporal Chambers and Boris Sputnikov just beginning, having all three siblings hocking shirts and posters was overkill.

As good fortune would have it, Karl Freeman stepped into the lobby with a bikini-clad beauty on each arm. "Josiah and Junior… just the two strappin' bucks I was hopin' to see. You boys have always been good to me. Since this is my last night with this promotion, I figured I'd drive over to Lexington. Found me a couple of *Kentucky wild cats*. Boys, let me introduce you to Ginger and Corvette. They're dancers at a club called Big Stevie's... located just on the outskirts of town. It's all very legitimate."

On cue, Ginger unlatched herself from Freeman's right arm and moved to cling onto Josiah's. Corvette did the same with Junior.

"I've paid these ladies handsomely. They're here to give you boys a private show. Thirty minutes in paradise. That is, if you can find your way towards some sort of cozy corner. Or maybe it'd be best if you accompanied them to the parking lot."

The young men didn't have to be asked twice. And no amount of protests from their sister could slow them down.

"Man the fort, Jolene," Junior instructed his sister a split second before he bolted for the door. "We'll be back before the end of the show."

Josiah's exit took only a few seconds longer. The young man delayed long enough to show his gratitude. "Thanks a lot, Karl. I really appreciate this! My brother does too!"

"No problem, boys. No problem."

With them out of the way, it would be much easier to block the gym's front exit. With them out of the way, it would be much more likely that the fire the wrestler was about to start in the men's locker room would grow into a raging inferno before it was discovered.

And then it would be up to Fireball Freeman to save the good people of Bardstown from certain doom.

"There's not a babyface wrestler on the planet with a better backstory than that," he said to himself as he realized that every step of his plan was falling into place.

FORTY MINUTES LATER

Pandemonium. From his perch inside the ring, Karl Freeman scanned his surroundings and watched as five or six hundred wrestling fans scrambled to escape the second blaze of the night. They were trapped in a rickety, old gym with one set of doors blocked by a pair of semis and the other set mysteriously locked. He whispered a silent prayer that no one would be hurt, and that his stunt would go exactly as he'd planned.

Freeman had wrestled in this gym at least a half dozen times during his tenure with TKO Wrestling. He knew there was another door beneath the bleachers. Right by an annex where there was a janitorial closet and a nook where they stored retired sporting equipment and dusty trophies.

The beefy wrestler hopped out of the ring with surprising speed. He grabbed the microphone that had been left by the panicked ring announcer. "Everyone, remain calm. Follow me!"

He had to repeat his announcement several times before he gathered the collective attention of the hysterical fans. Then he calmly marched towards the wooden door beneath the bleachers. "Locked from the outside," he reported to those around him. "Don't worry. I got this."

Karl Freeman—strong as an ox, stubborn as a mule—took four steps back. "I got this," he repeated. Then he ran towards the door, lowered his shoulder, and crashed through the old wooden barricade as if he was the Kool-Aid Man delivering a sweet, sugary beverage on a hot summer day!

He'd saved the day! Wrestling fans would be talking about his act of heroism—and his turn from heel to beloved babyface—for years to come.

ABOUT THE AUTHOR

Scott Quinn wears many hats atop his bald head: defense attorney, husband, father of five, baseball coach, award-winning home cook, and author. With so many life experiences, it should come as no surprise that he has hundreds of story ideas swimming around in his head. For the time being, he's going to continue writing about pro wrestling champs and time-traveling aliens... with the idea that Long Jenn Silva is going to lead him (and his readers) on an incredible adventure across the galaxy!

ALSO BY SCOTT QUINN
OUTSIDE INTERFERENCE
(Long Jenn Silva Series: Book 1)

COMING IN 2023
FUTURE ENDEAVORS
(Long Jenn Silva Series: Book 3)

Made in the USA
Columbia, SC
28 May 2022